# Private Dancer

... Nothing is Rarely What it Seems

Conzuelus "Zayin Love" Strozier

# DEDICATION

This book is dedicated to my surrogate mother, Mary Frances Bonner, my son, Ali Strozier and my daughter, Kendra Strozier, who always believed in me and urged me to finish this work. My only regret is that Mary and my son are no longer here to witness the fruits. I honor them today and I thank God for the gift that He vested in me.

# CONTENTS

# CONTENTS

# ACKNOWLEDGMENTS

This book is a mixture of personal testimony and fictitious accounts. All the characters are figments of my imagination, however, having witnessed many events at the strip club there is a lot of reality represented in Private Dancer. I would like to thank several people for their hard work, encouragement and dedication to friendship. God has used so many but these were there from the start.

Pastor and First Lady: Bishop Barry D. Walker, thank you for always encouraging me to be about business and achievement. I will never forget that in the beginning you would stop me and ask me have I still been writing. That meant more to me than you will ever know. First Lady Kathy, thank you for being an example of what a true woman of God should be. I pattern myself after you and hope never to let you down.

Mentor and Book Cover Photographer: Regina "Gena-Mae" Wells, of Gena-Mae Productions, thank you for pushing me to be the best version of me. And also for schooling me, giving me a pattern to follow in the writing business. Your book, Tangled Web, was amazing and I can't wait for the sequel.

Content Editor: Kendra Strozier, thank you for keeping it real with me. As my oldest child, you never pulled any punches and I appreciate that every single day. Because of you, there are no gaps in this story. Our readers will get the full experience of Private Dancer.

Co-Editor: Tinisha McKay, thank you for your careful attention to detail helping to make the flow of the book a huge success.

Book Cover Designer: Syreeta Leaks of LMP Plus LLC, thank you for the skill you use in creating beautiful designs. You always have a way of bringing my vision to life.

Best Friend and Personal Photographer: Sherryl Wilson, for being a rock and a model for me. God sent you to me in one of my darkest hours and you helped me bring to life so many gifts. I cherish you as my friend.

# Chapter 1: Falling Apart

Walter was in his office for well over twelve hours reading, studying and calculating. His eyes hurt, head was aching and his legs were extremely sore. *You're getting old Wally Old Boy!* He thought, rubbing his left knee. Why did the voice in his head always sound like his father, taunting him? He needed a break from his study, to stretch and to find peace in Kindness. He probably should take a nap but the sound of her sweet voice was more appealing than the fluff a pillow. Besides, she always knew exactly what to do to ease his mental strain. However, when he opened the door, the house was mouse quiet. He walked its length in search of his little princess. Although, Kindness was 20 years old and far from little, to Walter she would always be daddy's little girl.

"Kindness!" Walter bellowed. "Kindness where are you?!"

There was no answer. He walked around the staircase, stood at the bottom and yelled for her again.

"Princess?!!" Not a sound.

Jay dragged in a few hours before Kindness left but he dared not answer for her. There was nothing he wanted to hear least than another lecture from the world's most perfect father. He rolled his eyes at the thought of facing him, then plopped back down on the bed.

"I wonder where that girl done run off to," he muttered under his breath. "I know she done run off cause she usually comes dashing right away when I call."

It was 4:30 in the evening and she had not told him of a change in her plans. They usually watched a movie, eating popcorn and other snack foods, winding down after a long day of laboring before the Lord, which was a pleasure in itself. But all the studying and researching and praying took a lot of strength. It always felt good to take a little break. He didn't mind the challenge because being able to cool it with his princess made it like having his cake and eating it too! This week in particular was incredibly grueling. Walter had to put in a lot of overtime since Pastor and First Lady Trinton were out of town. The great task and blessed burden was now on his shoulders. Being the senior elder, he was often left in charge of bringing forth the revealed Word of God when the Pastor was called away on business.

It seemed as if since the day he was told he would be needed this week, his whole family began falling apart. That was only eight short months ago. He and Angela didn't have the perfect marriage, but he prided himself for being an understanding, caring husband and father, instead of the dictator, male chauvinistic pig his father had been to his mother. People always told them they had the perfect marriage and the perfect family, but everyone in their house knew better. Elder often interjected saying they simply worked together to become a more cohesive unit, but in actuality the unit wasn't anything more than a facade. It was never an easy feat to fulfill other people's image of them, but these past few weeks there seemed to be extra strain on family life. And that was just the beginning. Walter Jr. was acting a fool every day and somehow Kindness had become more and more distant. Wednesday he called a family meeting, where everyone was in attendance except "the boy". Jay didn't feel like a meeting was necessary to work on their family unit, but he was so wrong. It was very evident that he missed the prayer meeting because instead of being a help, he was becoming more a part of the problem, than a participant striving towards a solid resolution. *Maybe Jay was the originator, who knows.* The thought made him even more irritated as he struggled to cast down negative emotions, not to mention Kindness was nowhere to be found.

"Oh well," he sighed, "I know where I can find one member of my family.  And hopefully she has some idea where my Kindness done run off to."

Angela was a woman who stood by her man at all times and she always told him the truth rationally, in private. She never put him on blast in public, not even at home in front of the kids. *Who can find a virtuous wife? I did, with the help of the Lord of course!* When they met, neither one was saved. But Angela's background in the church led her back to God and Walter followed.

He walked through the kitchen, out onto the patio, taking a deep, relaxing breath before scouring the yard for the love of his life.  He knew she would be out in the garden watering plants, picking weeds and singing praises.  It was her mid-evening Saturday ritual, when the sun set low but there was still plenty of natural light. He stood there for a moment listening to his song bird sing with the voice of an angel.  He smiled at the sight of her bending down, tending the flowers.  It had been over twenty five years and she still looked just as divine as she did the first day he laid eyes on her. Angela looked up and caught him watching.

"What are you doing out here eyeballing me?"

"Admiring, that's all."

"Why don't you make yourself useful and come and help pull up these chickweeds and dandelions."

Walter grinned at her command, replying, "Nah, I'll pass.  Gardening is not my cup of tea, or don't you remember. I have a brown thumb! You'll mess around and have to replant everything 'cause I'll kill 'em all."

Angela laughed heartily remembering how he managed to kill almost all of her house plants while she was away on the Women's Retreat last year, in one week's time!

"Now that I think about it, you're probably right.  Go back in the house and let me finish up then.  I am enjoying quiet time with my Jesus anyway!" She started back humming her favorite tune.

"Fine with me! Just do me one favor and tell me where *my* Kindness is and I'll sho' nuff get out of your hair?"

"Well if that's all it takes to get rid of you, I'll oblige. She had dance practice this evening, but she told me to tell you that she loves you and she will be back as soon as possible."

Walter pouted, "Why didn't she come and tell me herself?"

Angela rolled her eyes in exaggerated disgust, "Princess knows her daddy all too well.  She knew you would wonder why she left without saying goodbye, but she did not want to bother you while you were working.  So she let me be the messenger before rushing out to pick up one of her dance members for an emergency practice.  Is that okay with you?"

"Yeah, I guess it has to be.  She's gone now and it *is* ministry."

Angela grunted, "Mm, mm, mm... that's sad.  A grown man acting like *that*!"

"Like what?" Walter still pouting.

"You know like what. Like a little boy in love for the very first time. Like puppy love! It's sickening! She has had you wrapped around her little pinky finger since the day we brought her home from the hospital. And the grip keeps getting tighter and tighter."

"Whatever!" He brushed her off.  "You're just jealous." She laughed at the ridiculousness of their relationship like she always did. Walter, still struggling with negative emotions, changed the subject.

"Where is that son of yours?" he half teased.

He and Walter Jr. hadn't had a meaningful conversation in months. And in the past few weeks things had gotten considerably worse. No matter what he did or said, the relationship continued to disintegrate. Jay was like a ticking time bomb! You couldn't reason with him. You could barely talk to him.

"**Our** son came in about two and a half hours ago and raided the refrigerator.  He's probably upstairs napping," Angela replied, ignoring the words, 'son of yours', because she knew he was more for real than playing.  That was a can of worms best left shut tight. If it was going to be opened, she wasn't going to be the one to do it.

"**He** needs to be down here helping you with these weeds.  Humph, he needs to be doing something constructive.  That boy is turning into a bum!"  The frown on his face warned of his impending actions and Angela prepared herself for the inevitable.

"Walter, come on now. Check yourself. Don't go looking for trouble! You'll find it."

"I'm not going looking for any trouble. I just wanna have a chat with the boy and see where his head is. You can't deny he got issues. It's high time we stop brushing them under the rug, especially when the issues continue to grow worse." *I knew it, I knew it!* Angela thought, interjecting.

"Now W.D., don't you go starting no fight. Yea, something serious is going on with that boy but we have yet to know what that something is, and if you go too hard you're going to push him away before we find out what's wrong. And you know my mama used to always tell me something and I believe I've heard it slip past your lips."

"What's that?" He was getting tired of the lecture but decided it wouldn't be a good idea to tick off his best ally, aside from Jesus.

"You go looking for trouble you always find it."

Walter exhaled noisily and said through clinched teeth and a fake smile, "Didn't I tell you I'm not look for any trouble. I'm just going to talk to the boy, that's all Angel." Angela looked at him intently from the yard for a short time, and then loosed her stare.

"Alright, just make sure that is *all* you do!"

Walter went back into the house with a calm demeanor that is until he was out of her sight. As soon as he turned the corner, the truth came out in his almost trot. Walter hurried straight to the bottom of the stairs. The previous façade displayed for Angela was gone. He rested impatiently in his favorite spot at the bottom of the stair well trying to gather his emotions. These days his son had the total opposite effect on him than Kindness, and, though W.D. thought things couldn't get any worse, Jay's attitude had deteriorated over the past several months. No one had a clue what was going on with him or how to reach him. It was frustrating trying to find balance between discipline and concern, especially with such a recently disruptive child.

"Jay, get down these stairs this instant! I need to talk to you boy!"

There was no answer, but W alter could hear his son moving around in his room, deliberately ignoring his father. He made sure his dad knew he heard him, intentionally giving no response. Total disrespect! One minute passed, then two, three, four, five. Walter was growing more and more agitated but still tried to remain cool.

"Jay, I know you hear me up there! Come here now!" Finally, he yelled back with extreme loathing,

"Man, you still down there waiting. Haven't you got the picture yet!? I don't wanna hear nuttin' you gotta say!"

That's all it took to turn hot to boiling. As a matter of fact, Walter was steaming. *Who does this boy think he is? Does he think he wears the pants in this house or something?* Walter stood with pent up anxiety seriously considering his sons words. *What happened to our relationship? We've never been extremely close, but the past few months had been disturbing. Jay must have gotten mixed up with the wrong person or persons, but who?* The questions clouding his mind made him demand Jay's immediate attention. He needed answers and he would not rest until he got them. Things had gone on far too long and it was time to deal with the issues that were being ignored. Walter regrouped and hollered for his son again.
"Boy I didn't ask for your back talk! I said get here and I mean right now!"

The boy did not reply though Walter could hear him mumbling indistinctly. His patience was running thin and fury was building up inside. He knew he needed to calm down but emotions were already raging, and with Kindness gone and Angela outside in the garden, there was bound to be an argument. Walter had had enough of this madness. He started up the stairs with wrath on his agenda. It was at that very moment Jay appeared at the top of the staircase.

"Heeey, don't get your panties in a wad old man."

He was leaning against the railing with a sheepish grin on his face. Lately he seemed to know exactly what buttons to push to get his father to acting out of holy character. Delighting in his success, he pushed off the rail and sauntered nonchalantly down the stairs. That approach was enough to push Walter over the edge.

"Panties? Old man?" Walter bellowed through clinched teeth.

It was all he could do to keep his hands by his sides. Easily he could have choked the boy until he passed out, but what good would that do? Besides, He left all of that hood behavior in the streets when he found salvation, or rather when salvation found him. After all Walter was the one who was lost, not Jesus. No way was he going to let this boy make him lash out when such a great task was being laid before him. He had to preach in the morning. That knowledge helped him to calm down a little, though it was short lived. The look in his sons eyes said, 'Try me!" Jay stood with a bold smirk, waiting patiently. *Okay, if this is how you wanna play boy, I'm game!* He took a step up the stairs and Jay stepped down one. They were eye to eye.

"You call me out of my name or make one more negative reference to my character, just one more time lil boy and I'll show you how much pep I still got in my step! I left the streets a long time ago, but I still know where to find them! They right outside that door!" Jay rolled his eyes and brushed his father off with a wave of the hand, taking the last step down onto the floor.

He walked past Walter saying, "Man you ain't gone do nuttin'!

Walter clinched his teeth and growled, "Try me!!!"

Jay looked back as if someone had tapped him on the shoulder. *I know this old man don't want a piece of me after what he's done,* he thought. Well if he wanted a piece he was surely about to get it! Matter of fact, he was about to get a few pieces if he wasn't careful. Lil Walt turned full circle to stand directly in front of his dad. They were just about the same height. Walter hadn't really noticed how much alike they had become until that very moment. Jay reminded him of himself before Jesus. It scared him a little and the pit of his stomach started lurching. He felt like he would have to hurt his own son just to make his point and he really didn't want to do that. Jay spoke first, snapping his father back to reality.

Looking Walter dead in the eyes he said without blinking, "You aint nuttin' but a broke down, no good, half-steppin Christian who lets his wife run the house! You a **punk**! Why should I eva listen to you or do anything you say. You're a liar! You don't do nuttin you say you're gonna do anyway!" Fury turned to confusion. *What in the world is this boy talking about?*

"Wait? What do you mean? What is really going on with you? Please just tell me! We can work this out Jay. I know we can, if you would just talk to me."

"Oh forget it! Talk don't do nobody no good anyhow! I'm outta here bruh!"

Walter sensed the hurt in his son's voice and wanted desperately to try and rectify the situation. It was really taking a toll on his mind. Walter was still dazed from the lack of continuity in his son's words. He had no idea what the boy was talking about, but obviously he felt strongly about what he was saying. Jay knew full well what he was talking about, he just wasn't in the mood to share! *That would spoil the surprise!*

Walter shook his head in amazement half conscious and half in thought, he said lackadaisically, "Wait boy. I'm not through talking to you. We both need to calm down and sort this thing out."

Walter grabbed his son by the shoulder to turn him back around but his attempt to reconcile was met with a hard left to the jaw instead. He had forgotten one of the most important rules of confrontation. *Never let your guard down!* Losing his balance, Walter's head hit the wall hard and he fell to the ground. Jay jumped right on top of him beating him with fierce aversion and talking with every swing.

"Man – don't – you – ever – put – your – hands – on – me – again! I'm – sick – of – you – and – all – of – your – lectures-and rules! I – don't – need – your – opinions – or – your advice – you – Mutha—!"

Angela ran into the house full speed, her hip barely missing the dining room table as she slid across the floor.

"Jay!" She screamed. "Jay, what are you doing to your father? Get off of him!!!" she screamed

8

frantically as she tried to pull her son off of her husband."

Walt Jr. got up and stumbled back a couple of steps realizing what he had done. He looked at his mother, tears streaming down her face, holding her unconscious man. It was hard to see clearly through the rage. But he couldn't miss the look on his mother's face. The question 'Why' filled her eyes, through the tears. In his heart was nothing but mixed emotion and breathing was becoming a chore. He was about to start hyperventilating, observing her crying, and the sight of his dad lying in a pool of blood. *What have I done?!!* Panic set in and he bolted out of the house with his mother calling after him.

"Jay! Please don't leave! What's going on? Please come back!" He was running full speed and never looked back.

# Chapter 2: Picking Up The Pieces

Angela still kneeled on the floor with Walter's head in her lap. She was crying and praying for both her husband and her son, not caring that her new flowered print house dress was now covered in blood, sweat and tears. In the midst of prayer, Angie's mind couldn't help but wonder what had happened between the two of them that could have landed them in the middle of this nonsense.

She was strolling in the back yard talking to the Lord when she first heard the yelling. By the time she reached the back door, the windows were shaking. They argued many times before and she was always the designated mediator. Calming down the men in her life was no easy task. They both were stubborn as mules, and strong as a yoke of oxen. When Walter left her in the garden earlier she expected a verbal onslaught would follow, it always did. However, she never encountered a scene like this. *It's amazing how the devil will attack even when you are doing right. It's to be expected though, since that is his purpose. We are counted as sheep for the slaughter. Every day he seeks to steal, kill and destroy something in the lives of God's children. We have to stay sober, vigilant and be instant in prayer, and still the enemy is coming.*

No one in her family knew that better than she did. But she never thought the devil would use her own child to bring confusion into their household. She knew something was up when he started skipping church. Then he started skipping school. They took away his car and allowance, and made him get a job, but he didn't keep that up long. He was still going somewhere every day. And he wasn't worried about money. He had new things every week. Kindness always took up for him saying she bought them, but her daughter wasn't a very good liar. Nevertheless, Angie didn't push because someone had to talk to the boy and the only person he still opened up to was his sister. That is until recently. Now he was shutting down on every one. *What love is taking the place of God in his life? Is he selling drugs? Is he in a gang?* So many questions.

She looked up to the sky and asked vehemently through sobs, "Lord! Whoever has bewitched my son, please rebuke them! And if you don't remove them, give all of us the strength to endure the trial that you have allowed to befall us."

Walter opened his eyes and tried to get up, grunting all the while. "Oh sweetheart! Please be still! Are you okay?" Angela was kissing his head.

"Sure. Sure I'm okay," he lied.

He was a proud man. No way was he going to let his wife know he had been blindsided by his own son. Despite verbal efforts on his part, she knew he wasn't okay, but she didn't make any reference to the fact.

"I'm so glad you woke up. I didn't want to call the police or the ambulance cause I know that is not what you want. So I prayed for you to open your eyes and talk to me again. And for the safe return of our son." He squinted his eyes trying to defy the pain in his head, pushing to get up again.

"Honey please just lay still for a minute while I go get the First Aid kit and a pillow. Okay."

She kissed his cheek, not caring about the smell of blood, before softly letting his head rest on the floor. He groaned. The pain from nodding made him think twice before moving again. Tears were filling his eyes, not from the pain of the cuts and bruises left by his son's rage, but from the pain in his heart. He cried because of the broken relationship that he had no idea how to mend. He had been praying incessantly for an answer but none came, not directly. He would just have to keep praying until God decides to answer openly. Then he remembered something Pastor Trinton often preached. *'God always answers prayers, it's just that sometimes the answer is 'No' or 'Not yet' or it will come by actions.' Maybe all of this is leading up to the answers I am searching for, hoping for, praying for.* As he rested on the floor, reflection of the events leading to this point flooded his mind. Not just of today but when he was just a boy himself, wanting the love of his father. But he never received that fatherly love.

*Walter remembered back when he was fourteen years old. There was this kid who bullied him every day. The bully was twice his size and his goal was to kill his desire to play football. Walter knew he was good, but would not step up to the plate when his oppressor was in the room, which was all the time. He had gotten tired of it and needed some advice. Walter's dad was not the best dad in the world, but he was the only one he had, so he decided to muster up some courage and ask his dad for counsel, even knowing the outcome could be tragic.*

*When Walter got home from practice one day, he went looking for his father. He found him in his favorite spot, the den. He was "chillin'" as he called it and looked as if he did not want to be bothered. Walter swallowed hard thinking whether he really wanted to take a step into his father's sanctuary. His legs would not move. So he just stood in the doorway.*

*"What do you want boy?" His father said without even looking up at him, making it obvious he really didn't care to hear. He just wanted Walt to get out of his peripheral.*

*"WHAT DO YOU WANT!!? He asked again, raising up out of his recliner this time looking at the boy, hatred mixed with liquor filled his eyes. Hoping to scare him away so he could get back to relaxing.*

*"Um, um, um," Walt stammered nervously.*

*"Spit it out sissy! What do you want?"*

*"Um, nothing, never mind," he turned to walk away, hoping to escape his father's belligerent anger.*

*"No. No never mind now. You have disturbed my peace for something. Now you better tell me what-it-is!"*

*His dad stood up and took off his belt. Walter knew he had better get to talking fast or he would never get the chance, but he couldn't think clearly to even remember the whole story so he just stammered through it.*

*"Um, well I-I play football for the school b-but I don't st-step up a-and there's th-this kid who always telling me n-not, not to and so I don't and I was thinking about quitting but I-I really don't want to cause I like playing ball- and I'm good b-but when I do good and coach tells me so that kid follows me home with three of his friends so I was wondering..."*

*"You was wondering what? If I would go to the school and talk to the principal or the coach? Or*

*maybe you want **me** to handle those boys who you scared of? Huh? You was wondering what?"*

*"Um, I-I just wanted to know what you thought about the matter. Y-you know like what do you think I should do?"*

*Otis began weaving his belt back into the loops and walked back to his easy chair. He sat down with his buckle still unfastened, popped a fresh beer before responding to the boy. Walter sat waiting patiently, thinking his dad was finally going to give him some advice. Maybe they could even have a normal relationship one day. Maybe.*

*"So you want to know what I think, huh? Well I'll tell you what I think. I think that handling situations like this is a woman's job. You know, a wife, a mother. And since you killed yours, you got two choices. You can either find a teacher who cares or you can handle it yourself. I mean you the closest thing to a woman without the real thing anyway. As a matter of fact, get in that bedroom and get ready for daddy to give you another lesson in your female duties! You aint good for nothing else!" He gave a sinister laugh that would haunt the boy well into his adult years.*

*Walter remembered running out of the back door crying. He never intended on going back but three days later he did. He had grown tired of eating out of back alleys and dumpsters. His return was only to grab a few cans of food, a can opener, some cereal and a few personal items. When he broke the lock on the door, he was hoping his dad was already at work or too drunk to notice he was in the house. He tiptoed through the kitchen to check the den. His dad was not there. He crept up the hallway checking each room as he past, but thankfully Otis was nowhere to be found. Walter rushed to grab his knapsack from boy scouts. He packed his sleeping bag, underwear and clothes for a week, canned goods, a can opener, matches and... Where is my mom's picture? He changed hiding places often because his dad would find it and use it to torture him. His room was a mess so he knew his dad had found "the secret weapon to pleasure" he called it.*

*Even though the man was not home, Walter was still reluctant to go in his bedroom. There were too many bad memories, however he was not leaving without his mom. Still tiptoeing through the house, he came to stand at his dad's bedroom door. He took one step into the bedroom. It was cold. Somehow it always felt colder than the rest of the house, even in the summertime. He* took another step, then another. Without touching anything, he scoured the room hoping to find the picture laying around. No luck. He was going to have to move some things, touch some things. Just as he got started, he heard the lock from the front door click. He was home! Walter knew he had to get out of there, but was still adamant about finding the only memory left of his mom. Frantically, he opened the closet, opening shoe box after shoe box. Then he heard him speak.

"Hey who's back there? Who's in my house? Is it my little sweet lips? I hope so, cause I missed you last night. I had to go to bed without being satisfied!" He laughed that sinister laugh again. The boy was hoping he would never have the chance to hear it again, at least not in real time. Walter could hear him stumbling down the hallway so he grabbed the gun he had found in one of the boxes. As he turned towards the window, he thought again about his mom. He was terrified, but he was not leaving without her. On an impulse, he lifted the mattress and there she was, beautiful, special. He grabbed the picture and dropped the mattress. And there he was. Standing against the doorjamb. Instinctively, Walter raised the gun and pointed it straight at his dad. His hands were shaking but he didn't let go of the picture or the gun.

"What you got there boy?" He smirked. "Is that 'the secret weapon to pleasure'?"

Walter looked down at it then back to his father. From somewhere he got the courage to speak. He wasn't sure if it was the power of having a gun or if he was just sick and tired of being pushed around.

"No! It's not 'the secret weapon to pleasure'! It's the secret to my freedom!"

Walter wasn't talking about the picture anymore. He was speaking in reference to the piece of iron he was holding that was filled with lead just waiting to shoot hot right into his dad's cold heart. Thoughts of the many times he practiced aiming the gun, shooting cans when his dad was so drunk he didn't notice he was gone. Now it was time to put practice into action. He raised and aimed the gun.

"Now what are you gonna do with that, huh?"

*"I'm gonna kill you!" He frightened himself with the cold-hearted voice in which he spoke.*

*His dad laughed so hard, he fell back into the wall. "You little punk! You aint gone do squat!" He managed to push off of the wall, walking towards the boy.*

*"Give me the gun," he said calmly, not knowing he was in real danger. Walter cocked the gun.*

*"Boy, give me that gun before someone gets hurt."*

*"No! I'm gone use this gun so someone doesn't get hurt, ever again. And that someone is me!"*

*"But what about me? If you shoot me, I'm gone get hurt. And I know you don't want that. Right? I mean, I know I don't want that!" he said smiling, jokingly.*

*Walter noticed for some reason his dad's smile oozed of nervousness. It was as if he thought his son might actually do it. It was almost as if he knew what was about to happen, in some sinister way connected to his death appointment.*

*"You know what dad, that's the funny thing. I used to care. I used to want us to be close, you know without all the funny stuff, 'the secret weapon of pleasure', the torture stories about how I killed my mom. But now, I don't care!" he cried. "I used to want us to be able to live like normal people. I wanted us to be a family! I wanted you to stay alive because you are the only parent I have left! But now I don't care! Now I want to live and I don't care if you have to die so I can do it! I don't care if I have to go to jail for killing you! I WILL LIVE!"*

*His dad burst into a drunken laughter. "Boy give me that gun! You blowing my high!" he said, laughter ladled with anger. The man took two steps closer to Walter and that was two steps too many. "Pow!"*

*Walter watched with uncanny excitement as his father stumbled a few steps forward, then backwards against the wall, before sliding down in a seated position, legs sprawled out awkwardly before him. The boy sat on the floor in front of his dad and watched as his breathing became slower and slower. Finally, his dad slumped over to the side. His chest was no longer rising and falling. Those were the last steps he would ever take. Target practice had paid off. Walter was finally free.*

"Sorry it took so long," Angela said, re-entering the living room. "I couldn't for the life of me find the first aid kit. I guess since the kids got older we haven't had much need for these things." Walter was lying on the floor, his eyes closed. A single tear rolled from the corner of his eye.

"Honey? Honey, are you okay?"

"Yeah, I'm okay."

His head didn't hurt so much anymore but he had no desire to move. Angela knew what he was thinking. They had an unspoken understanding of each other's feelings. From the day they met the connection was surreal, neither explanation nor understanding escaped the power of God. It had to be God who brought them together. How else could they have this great bond? He wanted to be a great father, better than his father was to him. She knew he couldn't bear things to continue this way.

"You know, it's still okay to feel sad about the relationship you had or didn't have with your father. But when you ran away from home, you made up in your mind that you would have a wonderful family. And you do. Sure, we got some kinks to work out, but every family has issues. Some are worse than others but God can fix them all. And we have to just be thankful that our situation is not as bad as someone else's. Some other family has it worse than we do."

"I killed him Ang." It was not the response she was expecting.

"No you didn't. He'll be back home and we will get this thing under control soon enough. Just let your faith in God work baby. You know He is able to do exceedingly abundantly above all we could..."

"No, no! Not Jay, my dad! I killed my dad Ang!"

"What? No. No you didn't. You left home and he was drunk in an easy chair. He may be dead now, but you didn't kill him Walter! Whatever happened to that man, he did it to himself! Probably deserves it, after everything he put you through."

Walter took a deep breath. There were so many secrets not even their God given connection could reveal. So many things he had not told his wife, but he had a feeling before this was all over, no secret would be left unrevealed.

"I never told you the whole truth about my father Angel." Walter paused. "He was a horrible man. He accused me of killing my mom almost every day and abused me in every way. Physically, mentally, emotionally and..." There was a longer pause. Angela thought he must have been caught up in a memory because he fell dead silent.

"And what sweetheart?"

Concern was in her eyes. She could tell how hard this was for him to say. He couldn't even face her. He closed his eyes again and turned his head to feel more comfortable and she busied herself with cleaning up his cuts and bruises. It was like old times when there was a bar brawl and he had to man handle some men. He would come home and tell her all about it while she cleaned him up. He never went to the hospital. He said she was his doctor, his nurse, his angel sent from heaven to finally show him that people are capable of real love. *It was scary to think that after all these years he might lose her.*

"And what?" she said again, a little quieter than before, hoping to ease him back into the conversation.

"Sexually," he almost whispered.

"Oh honey, I'm sorry, I don't think I heard you right. Did you say sexually?"

"Yes," he whispered again.

"Oh Walter! Honey! Why didn't you tell me before?"

She hugged him knowing full well why he didn't tell her, but she had to keep the conversation moving forward somehow or he would shut down.

"I didn't know how. I didn't want you to know. I wanted to just forget that it ever happened but I can't. I see it. Every day, I face it. I would like to no longer be bound by it, but I can't shake it. I've been wishing it away, hoping it away, praying it away for years, but the memories never fade. I need help! I need your help to get rid of this!"

His voice was frantic and quivering but there were no tears this time. The pain was almost too great to speak. Angie didn't say anything to the fact, but he was really scaring her. She suddenly got the feeling that the process to their complete deliverance wasn't going to be easy. Walt called out to her as if she had not heard him the first time.

Now sobbing he jerked with tears, "Ang, I need your help to get rid of this pain! Can you help me? Will you help me?!"

"Of course," she said without hesitation, holding him close to her body.

*Lord what in the world is going on!? How much do I not know about this man I've been married to for 22 years!?*

---

Walter heard Kindness pull up in the driveway. But it took her at least thirty minutes to come into the house. He was thankful for the gap. It gave him time to compose himself. What he had just revealed to Angela, his princess never needed to know, but she was sure to have a lot of questions. He was still laying on the couch when she entered. It looked like she had already been crying, but immediately a fresh flow emerged. The conversation with Jay. The demands from Money. Nothing prepared her for what she walked into. They both sat in tears and silence. It was a sad moment. There was nothing to be asked or said. Every answer would come in it's own time. Right now there were other things to worry about. Kindness didn't know how to tell her parents what she had to do. Now was definitely not the time, but soon enough it would be. She was going to have to move out. She had never been without her parents. But maybe this wouldn't be all bad. Finally she would have the opportunity to see how the rest of the world lives. *Non-Christians. Sinners.* Her parents never let her and Jay associate with them outside of school and other events where they couldn't be avoided, but some of them didn't seem half bad. It was high time she made decisions for herself. *May as well look on the bright side.*

# Chapter 3: New Identity

For the home she had grown to hate, suddenly she had a deep longing. Yesterday a prison, today a sanctuary. It was getting harder and harder to face her parents. And without Jay there, nothing was the same. All of them walked around the house on eggshells, afraid to speak on the subject. The police came by frequently asking questions, and church folks were parading in and out all day long. Some came to check on her parents and pray with them. Others were only there to be nosey and see how the "perfect family" would fare now that everything was falling apart.

It had only been a week since Jay was taken and this was her first night at the club. How could she do this? How was she supposed to go from being a leader in her church to... this!? Her dance team would be so disappointed if they knew where she was and what she was about to do. As a leader, she was their example and chastised them from time to time about dancing for the wrong master. And now look at where she was and what she was about to do! This was worse than being at home without Jay.

Thinking back Kindness noticed that as they grew older, she and her brother grew apart but there was still comfort in knowing someone you've known most of your life was right there through thick and thin. Now that he was gone, she felt so alone there. Her parents couldn't possibly understand and there was no way she could explain the changes in her life. *Jay I miss you man. This I do for you. I will find you my brother and we both will be saved!* She started to walk towards the door when a group of young ladies scantily dressed stopped her in her tracks. They emerged from the back of the building and entered, laughing and talking loudly.

"No. No! I can't do this! I won't!!" She screamed outside of the club, walking back to her car. "What are you thinking? Kindness? There has to be another way to save Jay. There just has to be!!"

Finally reaching her car, she got in and started it up. But a booming, eerie voice commanded her to stay. She could hear the words clearly, fear striking her heart.

*"If you miss one day! Just one!! You can say goodbye to little brother. Have you ever wondered what it feels like to be an only child?"*

*"No."*

*"Well if you ever want to find out, miss a day, miss a payment, miss a phone call!!!"*

*"I won't! I promise!! Just please, don't hurt my brother." He hung up.*

Tears were flowing and she laid her head on the steering wheel.

" I don't have a choice. I've got to do it. Kindness you have got to muster up all the strength you have left and do this! Do it for Jay!"

"Tap, tap, tap."

She ignored the noise thinking if she didn't look up whoever it was would disappear. Besides, it could be Money. There was no way she could face him in person right now. No way!

Tap, tap, tap!"

"Uuurgh! What?!" Her head snapped up, face severely stained with mascara and dried tears.

"Chill girl! I was checking on ya! You know, making sure you were **alive**!" Kindness rolled down the window so the young lady wouldn't have to yell anymore.

"Yea, I'm okay," she said, calming her emotions.

"You sure? You don't look okay to me."

"That's because you walk by sight," she whispered.

"Huh?!"

"Nothing."

She couldn't explain to a sinner what the words meant when she would be nothing more than that once this night was over with. Repentance was always a daily practice but after tonight, the word would take on a whole new meaning.

"Girl, come on. Get out of the car. It'll be aiight!" She pulled the door handle and gave Kindness her hand, never missing a beat. " I remember my first night. I was petrified!!" She laughed a little. "But after your first run, you'll be fine, as long as you don't bomb out!"

"That's the part I'm most worried about." Kindness lied.

"Don't worry, you'll do fine as long as you can dance. You **can** dance can't you?"

"Yes."

She spoke definitely. It was a God given talent she vowed to use only for Him. She shook her head and tears welled up once again.

"Don't cry girl," the young lady said, finding a napkin in her bag to wipe Kindness's tears.

"Thank you for being so kind to me. You don't even know me."

"No problem." The girl shrugged. "You seem to be a pretty cool chick. What's your name?"

"Kindness."

"Kindness, huh?! That's different. I like it. But you can't use that name on stage. The clients and members would never take you seriously!! Not to mention these hoodrats!"

"I haven't thought about that. Why do I have to change my name?"

"Girl, you are going to be performing for money. You got to make the audience believe in you before they'll pay up and a name says a lot. Like Kindness, for example. You are a kind person, from the heart. I can tell. And where you come from that may be okay, but in here, you will get eaten alive!"

"I'm sure." She said sarcastically.

"So we got to come up with something that's you but with an edge."

"Okay. Any ideas?"

"Let me think about it for a minute. Come on. I'll introduce you to the other girls and **we** will come up with something awesome and amazing for you."

"Okay," she said hesitantly.

"Oh come on, you'll be aiight. Now I ain't gone sugar coat nothin'. It's a shark tank in here. All of these girls want to make money just like you. It's a competition! You have to be fierce and confident, or the night could end with a cat fight. Stand your ground. Mean what you say and follow me."

"Okay." Kindness sighed heavily, while taking baby steps, shuffling her feet. The young lady watched in awe.

"Umm... And you can't walk like that!" The girl laughed. "Look. Watch me. You see how I take long confident strides with my head held high?"

"Yes."

"Now you try."

Kindness stuck her head and her nose in the air and walked with confidence like she'd been taught to for years.

"Not bad. Not bad. But lower your nose a little bit. If you come off snooty, the cat fight will be definite tonight!" She laughed again. "Try again." Kindness lowered her nose like the girl said and felt better already.

"Nailed it!" They both smiled. "Okay, now let's wash your face and gloss you up."

The girl pulled a kit from her bag, walking back across the parking lot. Kindness followed. She sat the kit on Kindness's car, then pulled out a mirror and sat it beside the kit. Taking a makeup remover wipe, she cleaned the mascara and tears from Kindness's face and started to apply lip gloss. After her face dried, the girl powdered her and applied concealer, liner, and mascara.

"Now, take a look."

"Wow, I like the shimmer in that powder. You're good at this."

"Thanks. Comes from a lot of practice." She paused and gestured her head towards the club "You ready to go in?"

"As ready as I'll ever be."

"You got that right! Let's go."

"Wait?"

"Kindness, you can't let jitters stop you. Let's get this money!!"

"No, not that. I mean, I do have the jitters but I'm going in regardless. I was just wondering... What's **your** name?"

"Oh, right. Girrrl, in the hustle and bustle I forgot to introduce myself. My name is Channing Traylor, but up in here, I'm Chance."

"Nice to meet you Chance." She shook her hand and thanked God for a kind heart and a new friend. In this place, she was going to need one.

"Nice to meet you too. Come on."

As soon as they walked inside, they were greeted by the smell of fried chicken and hot sauce. It was Big Boi and his favorite snack, hot wings, extra crispy, as he always said.

"Chance! You late!!"

"No I'm not. I've been in the parking lot helping the new girl get her dancing legs together!"

"Well you weren't in the building, so that makes you late!!"

"Whatever Big Boi! I don't dance for another hour and a half. I'm good!"

"You know what happens when you're late! You have to clean the bathrooms all night long!!" He smirked.

"I ain't cleanin nothing! I come to dance and stack checks!! That is it!"

"You do what I tell you!"

"Wrong!!"

"I'm the Boss around here, got it!!"

"Wrong again!!"

"Chance, you pushin ya luck!"

"Whatever Big Boi!"

"I got yo whatever!!"

"You know I know what's up! So, What-e-ver!!!"

Kindness's eyes volleyed back and forth, watching them go at it. Is this how she was expected to act in order to survive?

"And who are you?!" Big Boi bellowed.

"Oh, um, my name is Kindness." He gave her a blank stare, so she continued. "Money sent me." Immediately the man's disposition changed, and he shared a short but definite look with Chance.

"Oh, okay cool," he looked around, dropping his plate, as if he expected someone to jump out and beat him up. "Okay, um, Chance, why don't you show her to the dressing room and find her a locker. I gotta make a phone call and then she'll need to do a practice run before I can put her on stage. Have her ready in thirty minutes."

"You got it Big Boi." Chance snickered, muttering under her breath. "That's probably the only thing that makes him lose his appetite."

"I heard that! And get that cross eyed girl to come clean this mess up and the toilets need to be scrubbed too!"

"Okay, okay!" She laughed as Kindness stifled a few herself.

"Wow! He sure did get upset fast!!"

"That's Big Boi! Anytime you mention Money's name, he go to actin all kindsa stupid!!"

"You know him too?"

"Who? Money?"

"Yes."

"Yea. Who doesn't know Money?"

"What is he like?"

"You don't know?"

"Kind of, but we have only talked on the phone."

Chance pulled her close. "Well consider yourself lucky."

"My mother would say 'blessed'."

"Kindness, blessed or lucky, Money is nobody to play with. Whatever he tells you to do, just do it okay. I don't know why he sent you here and I don't need to know, but you gotta be careful. He's ruthless. He don't care about nobody, especially women."

"Have you ever seen him face to face?"

"Not in a while and I hope never again."

"What does he look like?"

"Hey, don't you mind that! Just pray you never have to find out!!"

"Okay. I get it. Touchy subject for everyone, I see!"

"Yea, cause we walk by sight up in here," she said sarcastically, remembering Kindness's words earlier.

"About that..." The girl put her hand up.

"Later. Right now, we got work to do."

Chance walked ahead, and Kindness slowly followed. She could tell that the girl's feelings were hurt and wanted to explain. Friends are not easy to find, not real ones, and Chance seemed realer than any she had ever met. Kindness felt that together they could get through anything. True kindred spirits.

"Kindness, come on girl!"

"Coming," she hustled to catch the door before it closed.

Inside the room were more than twenty girls and somewhere around forty stations. Kindness had the tourism look going on, and Chance moved quickly to kill it before anyone else noticed and started asking questions. She grabbed Kindness's arm

"Ow, that hurts..."

"Don't be in here lookin like a tourist," she whispered, ignoring the girls cries. "Shark tank, remember. Cat fights can break out up in here like wild fire in California. Combustible and hard to put out!"

"Got it."

"And work on your language."

"My language? What does that have to do with anything?"

"A lot! Nothing says 'green and naive' better than proper English!"

"So, how should I talk?"

"You gotta learn to mix in some slang. You know, shorten some words and replace others with street terms."

"But I don't know any street terms."

"Then I suggest you Google it!"

"What is this? Urban Living 101?" She laughed.

"Naw fool, it's called Chance 101, aka 'Staying Alive!" They both laughed, then Chance turned her attention back to the room.

"Hey everybody, listen up. We got a new girl here who doesn't have a stage name."

All the ladies got quiet, some applying makeup, some watching with envy, some not really caring, but they all listened. When Chance noticed that she had the floor, she swayed and danced towards Kindness seductively.

"So, we gone let her give us a little preview. Her name should fit her dance." She walked around Kindness, touching her body. "Come on girl, let's see what you got!"

Kindness started dancing the only way she knew how. She was a little stiff at first but quickly loosened up and settled into the movements. The girls were staring and snickering, but Chance noticed something. She was graceful. Her balance was excellent, elegant like a swan. She had strength control out of this world. Her eyes were beautiful and so was her smile. But the way she danced needed some work if she was ever going to make money.

"Okay stop." Kindness came to a halt and looked around.

"What did you think?"

"I think we got a lot of work to do in fifteen minutes!!"

"You didn't like it?"

"I did. You move sublime! But there's too much of some things and then something is missing."

"Okay, give it to me straight."

"Aiight, I will. This is not a ballet. You can't be twirling and tip toeing in here. You liable to get booed off the stage!" All the girls laughed.

"So what do I need to do?" Kindness looked around giving the girls some ugly stares. Some backed down and some did not. *I see we got some guppies in this Shark Tank!*

"Watch me. You got to move slowly, seductively. Use your hands, those pouty lips and bedroom eyes to beckon the men and women into the dance. Make them wish they were on stage with you. Like this."

Chance popped her butt into the air, slowly dropping and lifting, making it bounce. Then she walked around the room like it was her stage, touching the women and getting close enough to kiss some of them. Many of the girls enjoyed the show immensely, awakening Kindness to be on guard for the women just as much as the men when she danced. That was a territory she absolutely refused to tread. Chance made it back around to Kindness and bowed.

"Any questions?"

"Yea. How do you handle when a woman wants you to dance for her but you're not a lesbian?" They all laughed again.

"You handle it just like you would a man. At the end of the day, it's all money. Pop that butt and strut yo stuff just like you would for a man and..." She raised her hands in the air, directing the ladies to scream.

"MAKE THAT MONEY!!!" She turned back to Kindness.

"Now you try."

Reluctantly at first, Kindness moved around the room, utilizing people, tables, poles and every inch of her body. She was a natural, slowly moving into a comfort zone. The flexibility of her twenty years of dance training was about to pay off in a way she never dreamed of. Not every stripper could do the things she could do. And some of the moves she had, none of them had ever seen or performed. Jealousy began to emerge from the group. Kindness made her way back to Chance, raised her leg up past her head and slowly placed it on Chance's shoulder leaning in almost kissing her.

"How's that?" Chance had never been so turned on before and she was not a lesbian.

"If you knew how hot you just made me, you wouldn't have to ask that question. Your muscle control and body strength are off the chain. You about to get pi-zaid!!" They laughed as Kindness removed her leg and sat at the station she thought to soon call her on.

"Come on. Let's get you made up and dressed. We got five minutes to be on that stage."

"Where are we going?"

"Oh, the best dancers got a special area. I'm the only one in there right now." She looked around with a little arrogance. "But hopefully after tonight, I'll have some company."

Some of the girls rolled their eyes and muttered nasty comments under their breath.

"Aww ladies. Don't be jelly! Get yo game up!!! Ha, ha, ha!" She grabbed Kindness's hand. "Come on girl."

"Wait."

"Not this again. We not going backwards now hunni!"

"Oh no. Never. I was just wondering... What about my stage name?"

"How about Grace?" Peaches shouted, always ear hustling.

"Nah, this aint church!" Chance snickered.

"Oooh I got it. Elegance!!" Cotton Candy shouted from the back.

"Nah, that's too soft. Ooh, perfect."

"My stage name is Perfect?"

"No, but I got the perfect name for you. Ka-ri-sma!"

"Oh, that is perfect."

"Aiight, let's get you dressed!"

"Yea, okay." She could feel the confidence moving through her mental and hoped it lasted. This was only a test. But the true test was yet to come.

A few minutes later, Big Boi came strolling into the ladies dressing room.

"I hope ain't none of yall decent, cause I wanna see evrey thang!"

"Big Boi, you so nasty!"

"Nasty as I wanna be!!!" His laugh sounded almost like a cough, and he always seemed to be hard of breathing. "Where's Chance and that new gal?"

"Oh, they're in Chance's dressing room."

"What she doin back der? She ain't earned that privelege!" He bagan stomping towards the back, but Cotton Candy stopped him with her words.

"Well, wait to you see her dance!" Peaches answered the unspoken question.

He leaned towards her and whispered, "Is she any good?"

"Yea, she is." He walked towards the girl, still whispering.

"Is she as good as Chance?"

"Oh yea. Chance said so herself. She got all aroused and everythang!"

"What do you think? Who's better?"

"Karisma!"

"That's her name?"

"It's her stage name. Chance gave it to her after seeing her dance."

"Mmmmm, Karisma. I need me some of dat!"

"Big Boi, that girl wouldn't have you!!"

"Why not? What's wrong with me?"

"Too much to name!"

"Whatever! You shut up anyway!! I'm fine and paid!"

"Yea, whatever is right. She way out of your 'fine and paid' league!!"

"Shut up!! Chance!!! Get that girl on stage right now!!!" He yelled, leaving the dressing room.

"Coming!!!"

Chance grabbed Kindness's hand and raced up the ramp towards the stage.

"You ready?"

"As ready as I'll ever be!"

"I know that's right!" They laughed. "Okay, go."

Kindness stepped out onto the stage and immediately there were several whistles and cattle calls. She had no idea that anyone would be in the club this early. Big Boi made it seem like she would have to practice with just him before he allowed her to make any money. Someone was throwing twenties on the stage before the DJ could introduce her.

"I present to you all coming to Queen City's stage for the first time, Ka-rismaaaa!"

The lights were shining so bright, she couldn't see the men if she wanted to. At this point, that was a blessing in disguise. She didn't know who they were and she didn't care. Thankful that the drink Chance made for her and the hit off the bong was kicking in. Haziness quickly took the place of deeply instilled morals. *"It's time to work yo jelly," Chance told her before leaving the dressing room.* She took a short, deep breath and copied what she did earlier with the girls, making note that she would have to learn diversity and not pull all her tricks every time. When she was done, the stage was full of money and the men cheered. Big Boi met her at the stage and helped her down.

"How did I do?"

"It was aiight."

"That's it?"

"That's all you get from me," he walked away muttering. "Needy women looking for validation get on my dang nerves."

"You need to stop watching Dr. Phil and Steve Harvey Big Boi! You just mad that the lovely lady did an excellent job!" Big Boi waved off the gentleman in the audience.

Kindness searched to see who spoke, while gathering her money. *Never get too close to the patrons. Keep it professional. Provide the fantasy but never mix it with reality.* Chance was a good teacher. Then she heard the smooth, deep voice of the stranger in the audience, closer this time.

"So how much did you make?"

He was sitting right behind her and her cheeks were directly in his face. She moved nervously.

"I'm not sure. But it looks like I've almost met my goal for the week."

"A stripper with goals? I like that."

"Yea."

She wanted to say she wasn't really a stripper, but only a young woman trying to save her brother. However, remembering what Chance said she declined the thought.

"Where are you from?"

"Not far from here. Just outside of Atlanta."

"Me too. What do you know? We have something in common." He smiled.

"My name is Marcus. What's yours?"

"Um, my friend told me it's not good to become too casual with the patrons. It's bad for business."

"What is she? Your mama?"

"Nah. Just a friend, showing the new girl the ropes."

"I understand that. Well next time I see you, maybe it will be outside the club. Then we can have a nice conversation."

"Yea, maybe."

"Karisma, get yo tail back in there. You ain't no bar girl!!" Big Boi bellowed from the bar.

"Okay, okay!" She yelled back. "Well, I'd better get going. I don't want to mess up on my first day of work."

"You did great by the way."

"You think so?"

"Absolutely! Don't listen to that old greasy negro. He just want you that's all, but it's against the rules." She looked at Big Boi and shuttered at the thought.

"I wouldn't have him."

"I don't know what woman would, unless she was taking his money." Marcus leaned in, "And I hear he pays very well."

"I'll never know!" He laughed.

"I'm just saying."

"Me too, indefinitely!"

"Okay, Ms. Karisma. Whatever you say." She started to walk away. "It was a pleasure meeting you."

"You too, Marcus."

Kindness hurried to the back. Chance met her right before she disappeared behind the curtain, startling the already jittery new girl.

"Not bad! Not bad at all!"

"Oh, you scared me girl. I didn't see you out there."

"I wasn't there long. But I did catch the enda yo dance, and the heavy flirting from the gentleman who threw all that cash on stage."

"Oh, yea. Well, he was flirting a little I guess. But me, I was too nervous to do anything except get out of there."

"Don't worry. You'll relax more after a few dances."

"I hope so. I don't need the extra stress."

"Tell me about it." Chance pulled a brand new money bag from her Louis Vouitton. "Here, put yo money in this bag. If you go in there like that, one of the girl is sure to catch you slippin!"

"And she might slip off into a butt whoopin too!"

"Oh, you tough now! I see you learn fast."

"Yea, I've always been ahead of the learnin curve."

"And that language is gettin betta." Chance mocked a tear and wiped it's imaginary trail. "Mama baby growin up so fast."

"Shut up!" They laughed.

"Come on. You got to get ready for your next dance."

"Wait. I just danced."

"That was practice. The next one will be for real."

"How much realer can it get?"

"Come see for yourself!"

Chance gave her a knowing look that told Kindness the real is something she would have to experience on her own. No one could explain all the tricks the girls do. Reality kicked in when they entered the dressing room. There was glitter and gadgets everywhere. It looked like a circus.

"Oh my goodness. Do I got to do that?"

Peaches was lying on the glass table with caramel apples in her hand to feed the patrons, which she placed on her private and let them eat. Cotton Candy was playing the patron. Kindness watched as she unwrapped one and held it in position. Cotton Candy eagerly devoured the tasty treat. Chance couldn't help but to laugh. The look on Kindness's face let her know the girl had never seen lesbian play.

"What's funny?! I don't see nothin funny!"

"Yo face!! Girrrl, if I had a camera. You'd be an internet celeb in thirty minutes! Ha, ha, ha!"

"I imagine that my face must look funny to you, but I can't laugh right now. You didn't answer my question."

"What's that?"

"DO I GOT TO DO DAT!!" She pointed at the ladies and Chance still laughing shook her head no. Queen B walked up as Kindness was pointing.

"Naw, you ain't got to do no tricks, but they bring in da money doe."

"Well, what do **you** do?"

"Nothing fancy. I just let em lick honey off of a part of my body. The mo private, the mo money!!"

"Oh wow! I couldn't do anything like that!"

"Uh-oh," Chance said.

"Uh-oh, what?"

"You done went proper on us again."

"Sorry, that threw me a little off character."

"I see. Look, just about every girl in here has a little trick that they do. We switch it up every now and then cause the regulars won't keep paying for the same old thang. It has to be fresh and exciting. Since you new, you got the upper hand."

"Upper hand? How?"

"You new! Which means you fresh meat and that excites them dogs up in there!"

"Dogs?!"

"Yea, dogs! Like, men!! They'll bark too."

"And some of them will bite!" Queen B chimed in.

"Not unless they pay me!" Kindness shouted.

"Dat's what I'm talkin bout! My girl. You sho'll do learn fast!"

"So, what's **your** trick?"

"I use the pole. A lot of the girls do, but it helps to have something extra that's all yours. I do Burlesque sometimes. The girls think I'm crazy, but the guys like it. You have to have something that makes you memorable and keeps you relevant."

"Cause once you're irrelevant, GOODBYE!!" Cotton Candy joined the class.

"Dang right!"

Kindness continued to watch some of the girls practice their tricks on each other, and wondered why. Why do they need to practice? These were freaky tricks but cut and dry. Then it dawned on her that they were getting freaky with each other for their own pleasure.

"Um, I need to go in your dressing room and think for a minute."

"Fine with me. Besides, after tonight, it looks like you will be the first to join me." Kindness looked around once more before leaving.

"Thank God for that." She muttered so that only she and Chance could hear.

"Cotton Candy, you up in 5! So get yo monkey behind up that ramp in 3!!" It was Big Boi over the loud speaker.

"And so the night begins," the girl shook her head and started up the ramp. Chance followed Kindness to help her get ready.

"It's gone be a looong night," she whispered.

# Chapter 4: Emergency Room

"Carla Chivers."

"Yea, that's me."

"We have an exam room ready for you."

"Well, it's about time."

The nurse ignored the comment, leading the way while looking at the girl's chart. Cotton Candy had been in the ER for two hours waiting for a room. She almost left several times, but the words of Crazy Legs kept coming back to haunt her.

*"If you don't get yourself checked now, you won't have proof later if you need it."*

*"Why would I need proof?"*

*"You just never know."*

*"I don't know if anything happened. I passed out, remember."*

*"Yea, I remember. The same thing happened to me not too long ago."*

*"Did you get checked out?"*

*"Yep."*

*"And?"*

*"And what?"*

*"And what happened? What was the result?"*

*"See now you bein nosey. Just get yoself checked fo yoself and let me worry about me."*

*"Fine. I'll go. I guess I do owe it to myself to make sure nothing is wrong."*

*"Yea, you do."*

It wasn't what she said so much as the look in her eyes when she said it. Something happened to her the night she passed out. She doesn't remember, but her test results must've revealed something bad. A lot of nights she looked sad, but like many of the girls, she did what she had to do to survive. It was hard to live the life they lived with only a welfare check or working a nine to five job. Most of them came right out of high school into Queen City. They always joked that it was their college. But since some of the girls never graduated, they felt that this was the only way to make the kind of money they needed to live hood rich.

"Room No. 3, Ms. Chivers. Just get undressed, put on this gown and lay down on the table. The doctor will be in here shortly."

"Okay. Thank you."

The girl pulled out her phone and scrolled social media to pass the time. Pictures of her colleagues flooded her home page. She loved those girls. They were always good for a laugh or two. Selfies, new tattoos, baby pics and baby daddy drama for the most part. Then she saw it. Crazy Legs posted a pic of the two of them wishing her well. There were a lot of comments. Mostly the girls wanted to know if she was hurt in a car accident or if she had the stomach flu. Even Big Boi commented that she'd better get well before work or she'd work doubles for a week. Leave it to Big Boi Shane to mess up a good thing. The post brought tears to her eyes.

She was feeling so alone since her son's father abandoned them. It was understandable that he left her. They hadn't gotten along for months, but how could he leave his own son. The boy asked about him every day and she was running out of excuses. How do you tell a five year old his daddy left because he no longer loved his mommy? He wouldn't understand that. All he knows is that daddy is gone. He asked her the night before when she was dropping him off at the baby sitters if his dad was coming back.

*"Mom, is my daddy ever coming back home?"*

*"I don't know baby. He hasn't answered my calls."*

*"Call him now. Maybe if I talk to him, he'll come back."*

*"If I had more time, we would call together. But I don't think he'll answer. Every time I call it goes straight to voicemail."*

The boy sat in the passenger seat silent for a few minutes. She knew what he was thinking. Then he asked it.

*"Why doesn't my daddy love me anymore?"*

She grabbed him from the seat and sat him in her lap. Both of them were crying. She didn't know how to answer the question honestly, but she didn't want to spoil the boy's image of his father. So she told him what he needed to hear.

*"He still loves you baby. Daddy just needs time to get his thoughts together and find a new place. I'm sure he will come for you when he has his own."*

*"Maybe grandma knows." He said sobbing.*

*"I'm sure she does. We'll go see her tomorrow okay."*

*"Okay." He wiped his tears. "Mom?"*

*"What baby?"*

*"I love you even if daddy doesn't."*

*"I love you too sweetheart."*

It was what kept her going. The only reason she had not tried to end it all. *Suicide.* She fought so hard not to want to die. Her son was her only reason to live. She hoped that the results after tonight were all good. There was no room for anymore bad news in her life. What she couldn't bare to tell her son was that his father found another woman that he loved more than them. And he didn't want to ruin their relationship. It was the reason he blocked her calls. He told her when he was ready to introduce his new girl to his son, he'd call her back. Six years. Six years they had been together and then he found this new girl and she whisked him away. *Was it really that easy to take him? What happened? They were once so in love. No one could separate them. How did that side piece catch his attention? It had to be because I was working all the time, trying to save money to move and get a fresh start.* He wanted her to quit dancing and move to Buckhead with him. And even though she refused, she was definitely thinking about it, that is until he left.

"Ms. Chivers?"

"Yes."

"Hi. I'm Dr. Reid. How are you feeling?"

"A little woozy."

"Understandably. It is an after effect of Roofies."

"The date rape drug?"

"You've heard of it huh?"

"Yea, on the news. But I've never seen what one looks like."

"So you didn't take the pill?"

"No sir."

"Then someone put it in your drink."

"What? Who?"

"I was hoping you could tell me."

"Honestly, it could have been anybody at the club."

"Were you out partying?"

"No. I'm a dancer, a stripper." His eyes lit up. She was sure he must be a fan of strip clubs. Most men were.

"What club do you work at Ms. Chivers?"

"Queen City."

"Mhmm. And have you ever passed out before and woke up feeling the way you do now?"

"Once or twice I remember feeling this way."

"Why didn't you get yourself checked out before?"

"I didn't really know I should. I mean, I get high and drunk all the time. I thought it was a hangover or something."

"Oh, it's a hangover alright. But not from weed or alcohol."

"That's what my friend said."

"And who is your friend?"

"She told me not to mention her name, but she has been here about the same thing."

"Mhmm. Okay." Dr. Reid took some time to write down a few notes. "Ms. Chivers, I would like to perform a rape kit on you. Do I have your permission?"

"Rape kit? Why would I need one of those?"

Private Dancer

"It's just a safety precaution. You don't know what happened during the time you were out. If evidence is not collected right away it will be lost forever."

"Okay. Um, but I hope **that** didn't happen to me."

"Me too."

"Is there something I need to sign before you do it? I have to pick up my son from the babysitter in an hour."

"Just sign right here. And we can go ahead and get started." But he didn't hand her the clipboard.

"Ms. Chivers, before I do the kit, can I ask you something about last night?"

"Go ahead."

"Where were you when you passed out?"

"I think I was at the bar. Queen B was dancing and I was cheering her on as usual. But then things got hazy. After that, I don't remember anything."

"Mhmm. And when you woke up, where were you?"

"In the dressing room."

"How did you get there?"

"I dunno. I assumed some of the girls moved me. We help each other out like that. Well some of us do. But, now I'm not so sure how I got there."

"The fact that you passed out in one place and woke up in another does throw up red flags."

He wrote more notes. Carla realized he had been writing in a personal memo pad, not her hospital file. *What is he, a doctor or a detective?* Finally he handed her the form. Carla signed the affidavit and proceeded to follow the doctor's instructions for the exam. She was so ready for it to be over, and then it was. She gathered her things, got dressed, signed the release papers and left the hospital.

Her son was still asleep when she picked him up. She decided to keep him out of school. It was Friday and she was tired. Maybe she would even call out of work tonight and take him on a date. *Yea.* They hadn't had mother son time in a long time. Without his father there, she had to change her focus. *We can make it without him. Ending my life is not a solution. My son needs*

40

*me!* She had thought about suicide on several occasions and if it wasn't for her child, she may have went through with it. At the moment the only thing she could think of was getting home and taking a long, hot shower before climbing into bed.

Then there was a surprise. Her son's father was on her steps when they got home. He didn't say a word. He simply looked at her and grabbed his son so that she could unlock the door. Anger burned inside, but she didn't want to wake the boy. And since he had been crying for his daddy, what a nice surprise it would be to wake up and he was right beside him. He laid the boy in his bed and came back into the living room.

"Can we talk?"

"About?" She said sarcastically, closing but not locking the door.

"About us."

"There is no us. You left."

She walked into the kitchen to unpack her son's snack bag. He followed.

"Okay. That's not how I should have started."

"Rewind and start again." *Why wasn't she yelling? She didn't even look angry. Is this some 'Thin Line Between Love and Hate' stuff?*

"That's fair of you." He gave her the side eye. "Okay, here goes. I'm sorry."

"You're sorry for what?"

"For leaving you and my son."

"That would be an okay apology if you only left. But since you chose some hoe over me and your son, I'd say you got a lot more beggin to do!" *Ahh there it is. She is angry. Good, that means she cares.*

"That's fair."

"Get to it then. No time like the present."

"Let's go into our room and I'll show you better than I can tell you."

"Nice try, but that would be a No."

"It was worth a shot." He walked to the refrigerator, opened it and shut it. There was nothing in there for him. She had wiped him out. He turned back to her.

"Look, you know I am a man of few words."

"It doesn't take an autobiography to tell the truth."

"You're right. And I know you have questions, so what first?"

"What happened to your girlfriend? Did she die?"

"No, not quite."

"Dang." She joked slightly. "So what happened?"

He looked guilty and hurt, but he had no choice but to be completely honest if he was ever going to win her trust again.

"She... She had a husband."

"Oh, a husband. Glad someone feels like someone is worth a ring. I mean, she had two men. I can't even get one to be faithful to me."

"Okay, now **that is not** fair."

"Really? So what's your definition of faithful?"

He didn't respond. There was no easy answer. If he gave a good one, she would want to know why he didn't live up to it. But he had to give account.

"Look, I know I screwed up. I knew it the day I left. But I thought I had travelled too far to turn back."

"No, you thought you had a gold mine when all you had was shimmer dust!"

"You right. She was nothing that she seemed to be."

"And how did you not know she had a husband?"

"He works out of town a lot. She tried to explain that he wasn't supposed to be back for three months."

"But he paid a surprise visit and found you in his bed?"

"Something like that."

"So what happened?"

"She said she was going to get a divorce and have him served before he returned. But I didn't believe her. I didn't know she was married to begin with."

"You thought she was single?"

"Yes. But I should have known. She didn't have a job, but she lived well. She told me her parents left her a chunk of change when they died in a car accident five years ago."

"She lied?"

"Yes and no."

"Explain."

"They did leave her a wad, but she spent it all. She was living off of the money her husband sent her every week."

"But she was going to get a divorce?" She asked sarcastically.

"I know. It all seems so stupid now."

"It was stupid then!! And even more stupid now!"

He sat at the kitchen table with his head in his hands. She resisted the urge to stroke his head and let him know everything would work out. But he deserved to feel whatever she had felt times ten. She was good to him. And never even looked at another man to be an option. Why did he?

"What made you think it was okay to look for another option? What did I do so wrong that all of a sudden you didn't want me no more?" She was crying again and it was the last thing she wanted him to see her doing. It was his turn to cry. She looked up and he was crying too.

"I don't know Carla. I'm stupid, that's all I can think. You gave me no reason to cheat and yet, like an idiot, I still found a way to screw up the best thing I ever had!!"

"Why? Why Steven?!"

"Because I was scared!"

"Scared of what!!! Am I all of a sudden scary to you?"

"No, not of you. Of commitment. I was debating whether to ask you to marry me. I got in my own head and talked myself out of my wife. And for that, I'm sorry."

"So instead of the ring, you gave me your butt to kiss!" She walked over and slapped him. "Do you know what you put me through? Huh?! I spent night after night at this very table contemplating whether I should end my own life because after six years I'm still not good enough!!! And you think it's going to be easy to get a second chance?!! Well think again nig..."

"Mommy are you okay?" The little boy was rubbing his eyes.

"Yes baby. Mommy is just talking to..."

"Daddy!!"

"Hey. How's my boy?!"

"Good. Are you staying with us again?"

He looked at Carla. "That's up to mama." He knew he didn't deserve it but his eyes pleaded for a second chance.

"We will see baby."

"Yeeey!! Daddy, I made you something." The boy got up and started down the hallway, then turned back and added. "Don't leave, okay."

"I'm not going nowhere."

The boy ran and reappeared with an ashtray. "Ta da!"

"It's an ashtray."

"Yep!"

"But I don't smoke buddy."

"That's what I told my teacher, but she said you can keep it as a souvenir of my kindergarten days. But she uses hers as a holder for her earrings."

"She's absolutely right. I'm sure I can find something to use it for. As a matter of fact, I have the perfect idea for it."

"What is it?"

"It's a surprise. But I'll talk to you about it later."

Carla butted into their conversation. "I'm tired. I haven't been to sleep all night. Can you watch him for a few hours while I take a nap."

"Of course. I'm not going nowhere."

"Yea, I can see that." Her voice lacked the enthusiasm of a five year old boy who missed his father. It was going to take a whole lot more to put a smile on her face again. He knew it and so did she.

"Go to bed. We'll finish our... talk, when you get up."

"Okay."

Carla slept for five hours and woke up with both her men in the bed with her. Steven had his arm around her waist and SJ's head was right under her chin. She was in a sandwich and there wasn't anywhere else she'd rather be. Steven heard her rustling and held her tighter.

"Did you sleep well?"

"Better than I have in a long time."

"I hope you can forgive me."

"That's going to be a work in progress."

"I know. But a man can hope for the best can't he?"

"He'd better!"

"Mommy?"

"Yes baby."

"Can daddy stay? He said it was up to you." She turned her head towards Steven.

"I'm sorry Candy. He kept asking. I had to tell him the truth."

She thought about it and nodded. It would be nice to not have to come up with excuses for why he wasn't there.

"Sure. But he will be sleeping with you most nights."

Steven pulled her tight. "That's fine with me. You work most nights anyway." She fought the urge to laugh. He was right. She was working so much they rarely saw one another. It was time for her to take some time off. Her savings account had over $50,000 in it that he didn't know about. She would work a few more weeks, but after that she was quitting. It was time to build her family. Working so much had to play it's hand in the deterioration of their relationship. She would never let that happen again. He loved her despite her occupation. That had to count for something.

"Hey, I got to tell you something."

"What is it?"

"I'll tell you but you've got to promise not to get mad."

"What happened?"

"Promise me."

"Okay. I promise. Now what happened?"

"I passed out at the club."

"Are you okay?"

"Yea, I'm okay. But the doctor at the ER says someone put roofies in my drink."

"What?! Who?!!"

"I dunno. Maybe they are gonna do some kind of investigation or something because he did a rape kit on me."

"Rape kit! Somebody raped you?!! I'll kill em!"

"Calm down Steve. You promised you wouldn't get mad."

"That was before you told me somebody tried to rape you." He was up out of the bed. Then remembering their son was still in the room, he calmed down.

"SJ? Go get you a snack out of the refrigerator and watch cartoons in the living room okay. Daddy will be in there to join you in a minute."

"Yes daddy."

The boy jumped out of bed and did exactly what his father said. When he was out of earshot, the man struggled to keep his composure.

"Now tell me again why I shouldn't be mad!"

"Because you promised."

"I did. But how can you expect me not to be mad when you tell me somebody basically drugged you?!"

"I know it's hard. But you have to be patient. I believe the ER doctor is going to have the club investigated."

"What makes you think that?"

"He asked a lot of questions. The name of the club. Who owned it. He even asked if I knew of anyone else this has happened to." She didn't tell him that it was highly likely that she had been drugged before.

"Has it happened to someone else?"

"I think so. This girl they call Crazy Legs was the one who told me to get myself checked out. I believe it happened to her, but she didn't say for sure."

"I'm going down there."

"No baby, please. Let the doctor and the authorities handle it. I don't need you gettin into no more trouble, alright. Your son needs you."

"And what about you?"

"That is another subject."

"Please, just forgive me."

"I do. Forgiving is as easy as making the decision. But you hurt me. And **that** is going to take time to heal."

"I understand. Just let me know if there is hope. That's all I ask."

"There is always hope." She smiled. He smiled back.

"Are you going back to that club?"

"Not tonight. But next week I am."

"I don't want you going back there."

"I already said I was taking SJ to the movies tonight. You're welcome to join us."

She was ignoring his request. It was a silent warning to leave it alone. There was more he wanted to say, but he didn't want to push his luck. So he didn't. It was her choice, but if he found out that greasy Shane put his hands on his woman, he would find a way to get him back. No one had to know.

# Chapter 5: I'm Grown

"Hello?"

"Hey Ms. Kindness. How are you doing this evening?" Money almost sounded civil. Almost.

"Better than yesterday."

"Well that's good to hear. So, are your bags still packed?"

"Yes. They've been packed ever since you told me to. But my mom is starting to get pushy and suspicious. I'm afraid she'll follow me to the club if I continue to stay here."

"I guess this call is right on time then."

"The apartment is ready?!"

She was excited and scared all at once. It would be a relief not to have to face the humiliation of watching parents who once adored her look at her like she was a stranger. Especially when comparing her old life to this one, they were right in doing so.

"Yea the apartment is ready. But are you?"

"As ready as I'll ever be!"

"I can't argue with you there." He chuckled, then voice turning sinister again. "How are you going to break it to mommy and daddy?"

Kindness ignored his evil demeanor. Her mind was too exhausted to process his spirit and all of the instructions he gave, plus her parent's anger, the fact that she was disgracing God and most of all, the fact that Money still had not let her speak to her brother. *What if he's not even alive?!* It angered her to think about that possibility, signified in her answer.

"Mommy and daddy are just going to have to get over it! I got to do what I got to do!! They ain't doing nothing!"

"Ain't? Is sweet little Kindness conforming to the street life already?"

"I guess I am. I have no choice. It's a shark tank in there. If those girls smell blood, it'll be a feeding frenzy in the dressing room!" He laughed.

"I like that. You know what, I like you. One day we'll have to meet."

"I'm sure," she rolled her eyes, voice dripping with sarcasm. He laughed again.

"Well run on and tell mommy and daddy, because I expect you to make the move tonight."

"You mean right now!?"

"Of course! What part of tonight don't you understand?!" He sounded like an angry little boy sometimes. *Just petty and rude!*

"I understand. I just thought I could move out tomorrow after I've had some sleep."

"Nope! It's either now or sever your brother's body into pieces for a special delivery in the morning!!"

"Okay, okay! No, I got it! I-I-I'll grab my bags and I'm leaving right now!!"

"Good girl. I'll see you soon!"

He hung up, as he was always inclined to do. Kindness took a deep breath and began to gather her things. *Well, here goes nothing!* She peeked her head around the corner from the stairway. No one was in sight. *Good! Maybe I can get most of my things in the car before anyone notices I'm leaving.* The trunk was almost full. All she had remaining in the house were memories. *Time for the change of my life!! Not what I imagined moving out of my parent's house would be like but it is what it is!* Deep in thought, she didn't see that her mom was sitting in the living room reading her Bible.

"Where are you going now young lady?"

"Mom? You startled me."

"Mhmm. Answer my question." She said blankly, spiritually and mentally drained from the past few weeks.

"I don't have time for this today!"

"You've been saying that for two weeks now."

"Maybe it's because I really don't have the time!"

"Why not? What are you doing? Where are you going?"

"Mom! Please!!"

"Not until I get some answers."

"Like I said, I do-not-have-the-time!!"

"Well, it's **time** you make time Kindness!"

"Mom, I'm tired and I don't want to argue okay. Just let me leave," she whined.

"If you are so tired, why do you keep going out late at night? Every night!!"

"Because I can!"

"Oh, really! And what bills do you pay around here Miss Thang?!"

"Mom, stop being so dramatic."

"I'm not being dramatic, I'm being a mother!"

"Same difference." She muttered under her breath.

"What was that?"

"Mom, you went from calling me young lady to miss thang in a matter of seconds."

"I know things are not the same in this house, but your father and I still have rules and we expect for them to be followed!"

"So, am I a young lady or miss thang?!"

"Don't patronize me! And don't try to change the subject. I was trying to be polite at first, but it seems you don't appreciate that kind of response, so we can go street if you want to!"

"Ha! What do you know about the streets?"

"Enough!"

"I'll bet!" She said sarcastically. "Miss Perfect! You walk around here like you've never been through nothing, judging people, like you came out the womb with Jesus in your heart, saved, sanctified and Holy Ghost filled!" She gestured with her hands up to God mock praising.

"I never!"

"Oh yes you do. I hear you on the phone when you think no one is paying attention. Sounding like a cackling hen with your sisters from the church!"

"I'll admit, I do express my opinion about what others are doing when I talk to my friends. But I never judge another person by my opinions. It's the Word of God that judges and it never fails Kindness. He is always right! So, if I judge by the Word of God, I AM RIGHT in doing so!!"

"Yea, whatever."

"And do you sit here and smugly mock God?"

"I didn't mock God. I mocked you!!"

"Kindness, what has gotten into you?! Apologize!"

"Nothing's gotten into me. I was trying to go handle **my** business. You are the one who stopped me!"

"What business do you have to handle?"

Kindness didn't respond. She was so tired, it was all she could do but to stand there and listen to her mother rant and rave. Rolling her eyes, Kindness tossed her bag over her shoulder and reached for the door handle. Angela stepped in front of her.

"I asked you a question!"

"Well, I didn't answer!"

"You'd better!"

"I don't have to! I'm grown!!"

"Well since you so grown you think you don't have to answer to me or your father, and you got so much business to tend to every night, then maybe you should move out!"

"Maybe I should!" She shoved past her mother and opened the door, but before it closed Angela was right there, back in her face.

"Don't you walk away from me young lady!"

"Oh, so now I'm young lady again?!"

"Stop skirting the issue!"

"There is no issue mom, except that you won't leave me alone so I can go!"

"Go where?"

"This new place on the Square called 'Nunya Bizness'!" She laughed.

"Are you high?"

"Not high enough." She muttered again.

"I heard that!"

"So!" Kindness shoved past Angela one last time. Her mother did not pursue, but continued to yell until Kindness was in her car.

"Ever since your brother came up missing, you have been acting irrational. Your father and I are worried about you. Please, when you get home, we have to talk about what is going on. Kindness? Do you hear me?"

Of course, she heard, but if she didn't get on I-20 soon, she would be late to work. And there was no way she wanted to spend any more time in Big Boi's office. His advances were beginning to be too much. Disgusting was an understatement. He literally made her stomach cringe. The last time he was so close to her she could smell the grease and cognac on his breath. She began to wretch and ran out of his office towards the bathroom. *Aww girl, you know you want this!* She could hear him saying before the door closed behind her. *Ugh!*

With her mother behind her, the ride to work seemed short. Too short. Memories of her and Jay running around the house getting on their father's nerves. And how their mother always played the mediator. She longed for those times. But those days were long gone. They would never be **that** family again, *if* they ever found Jay. *Maybe my focus needs to be on who this Money is and not finding out where my brother is... Maybe!*

"Girl, where you been? Big Boi been back here three times looking for you!"

"Not you too!"

"You know you up first!"

"Yea, I know, I know! Get off my case, aiight!!"

"Uh-oh, what happened? Yo mama gettin in yo junk again?"

"You guessed it! Can we get a Pulitzer over here for Chance the Great!"

"Oh, no. See what we not gone do," Chance got in her face and pointed between herself and Kindness, "is this! I don't do back and forth!"

"Well, I'll tell you like I told my mama. Get out of my face and we'll be fine!"

"Fine!"

"Good!" Chance felt sorry for Kindness, understanding all too well how hard this must be for her. She knew Money forced the move today and expected the girl to be stressed. She grabbed her bag and sat next to her naïve friend.

"Girl, you need a drink or a blunt or something. You have to chillax."

"Had both already. It doesn't seem to work for me anymore. Now I'm just angry."

"I'll bet if you hit this cush, you won't be angry no mo!" She laughed as she lit the cigar.

"Ew, you know I hate the smell of those things. Where is the bong?"

"We'll do that before your next dance. Right now, this is what we got so hit it. I soaked it in honey so it'll burn slow. And it has a sweeter taste. Here, try it."

Kindness took a long puff and held it until her chest burned, then let the smoke out for re-entry through her nose.

"French kiss! Girl, now you smokin like a pro!"

"Mmm, that's good!"

"Told you. You'll be better in no time."

"Karisma! Karisma, you back here yet!! I done been down here three times looking for you and you'd better be here!"

"Uh-oh, here come King Kong!" Chance laughed, hitting her chest.

"More like King Wrong!" Karisma joined the laughter. "Cush kickin in just in time too."

"Karisma?!"

"What?!!"

"What? What you mean, what?" He stomped around the corner, bursting through the door.

She looked at him long and hard before repeating slower, "Whaaat?"

"I'm gone ignore your ignorance for now because we got something special for you tonight baby. Someone has asked for a private dance in the VIP and they want you."

"What's the occasion?"

"Money!" Chance's head snapped up before she realized he was talking about money the trade and not Money the man. "Money is always the occasion and don't you forget it cause I want mine on time!!"

"Anyway, what else I need to know?"

"Nothing, except they'll be here at 11:30 and they said you can pick one girl to go with you and that's it."

"I'll do it but…"

"You'll do it but what? That was not a question or a request baby, it is what it is. You gone do it, period!"

Karisma totally disregarded his comment and continued as if he had not spoken.

"I'll do it **but** I'm taking two girls with me. Chance and one of the other girls after I go make this announcement. We'll see who wants it bad enough!" she laughed.

"Karisma you gettin real cocky. You can dance! I give you dat, but you don't run nothin up in here!! Remember dat!"

"Yea, whatever. You just go tell whoever asked for the dance about the changes. Hurry up Chicken butt!" Chance giggled.

Big Boi looked back over his shoulder but did not protest any further. Karisma was making him so much money, he dared not push her or Chance too far. He couldn't afford either of them quitting. Besides, Money would have his head, literally!

"Whatever! I got a new girl I'm about to hire tomorrow. She fine too! And I hear she can dance better than you."

"Who cares! Nobody cares Big Boi!!"

He kept walking and muttering. They could hear him all the way up the ramp.

"Ooh, I can't stand him!"

"Well, he loves you!" Chance pushed up on her friend and made kissy noises.

"Eww, get away from me. I hate it when you do that." She pushed the girl away and they shared another laugh.

"We'd better get dressed and ready. The doors open soon!"

"Agreed." Karisma slid off the counter top and finished the blunt before getting dressed.

The doors opened early for the VIP party, and all the girls were trying to catch a glimpse of the ballers. Chance did the same, but with a bigger purpose in mind. She was good at spotting the sucker! Then there he was, her worst nightmare. It was Money and his gang. *And eww, Jug is here! Oh no! I can't do this!!* She started to hyperventilate and pace. *Calm down, Chance. Calm down.*

"Hey, are you okay?"

"Cotton Candy, girl I'm not feeling well. Can you please ask Peaches to take my spot in the VIP? I've got to go home right quick and get my nausea medicine."

"Are you sure? Cause you know she would break yo hip to take yo spot!" Chance managed a smile.

"I'm sure. But jus- just, take care of it for me okay."

"O-kay. Do you want me to tell Big Boi anything?"

"No! I'll be right back and I'll just dance in Peaches spot."

"Girl, do you know how much money you missin out on? It's some ballers in here tonight!! Heeeey!"

"Yea, none like I ain't never seen."

"Aiight cool. If that's what you want. Let me go tell her to get dressed."

"Thank you."

Talking to Cotton Candy was like pulling teeth. She was as sweet as she could be, and just as dingy. *That girl don't have the sense God gave a rock, but at least she's dependable.* Besides she needed to jet fast. Big Boi was bound to rear his greasy head at any moment.

"Chance? Where is Karisma?" *Speak of the devil!*

"Uh, she,--" Wait. Why was she afraid of Big Boi? The one to fear was in the VIP section, waiting to prey on her mental psych. Torturing her with his eyes. And if he got drunk, there was no telling what he would say... or do! Chance quickly regained her composure.

"Uh what? You better not be playing with me Chance! Ion have time fa nunna yo junk!!"

"She's in the dressing room putting finishing touches on her make-up. Why?"

"Why? Because these ballers ready to start they private dance and spendin dat cash, that's why!" He looked around like someone was about to attack him, and Chance understood. They shared the same fear. "Um, who is dancin with y'all?"

"Oh, I'm not doing the private dance. Karisma chose Peaches and Cotton Candy to dance with her."

"Aww, is there trouble in Paradise?!"

"Shut-up! There is no trouble. She just chose someone else. I'm cool."

"Mhmm, well you go tell them to get they butts up this ramp right now cause it's show time!"

"Okay, I will Big Boi. Thanks." He turned and looked at her suspiciously.

"Is everything alright? Why are you being so nice to me?"

"What?! No, I'm not being that nice. I just don't feel good, so I'm going to step out and get some nausea meds. I'll be right back okay."

"Mhmm, well you'd better be back in time to dance for Peaches and Cotton Candy!"

"Three dances! Big Boi, please not tonight!"

"Yes tonight. You can thank yo arrogant friend fa dat! She took two of my dancers instead of one. I figured she would take you, but since she didn't, you have the luxury of taking their spots. Happy birthday!" He said turning and walking away.

"It's not my birthday, you idiot!"

"It never is!"

"Urrgh!" Chance took off her heels and ran for the back door, bag in tow. Then remembering Karisma used her key to open a gift in her dressing room. "Dang, I got to get my keys!"

She tiptoed into the dressing area. "Psst! Pssst!" No one looked up.

"Psssst! Bubblicious?" The girl looked around before spotting Chance behind a curtain.

"What are you doin?!" She frowned.

"Nothin. Look, did you see Karisma go up the ramp yet?"

"Yea. Her and Cotton Candy **and** Peaches. Why you ain't doin that party in the VIP?! Shoot girl, I woulda jumped on dat fa real doe!"

"Because, uh, I'm not feelin' well. Yea, that's it, that's why."

Bubblicious was looking at her like a pumpkin was growing out of the side of her face.

"You sound scared to me."

"Scared? What? Whatchu mean?"

"Scared is what I mean."

"Hunni, you don't know whatchu talkin about! I ain't scared of nuttin'!"

"Mmhmm, whatever! My baby daddy is a convicted felon, and even though we ain't together no mo, when he out on bail or sumthin, I be afraid fo my life. So, if there's anything I know, it's scared! And you is scared!!"

"I told you, I'm not scared of nuttin'!"

"I heard you lie the first time. What you scared of? Or should I say who!" The girl didn't stop to take a breath. "I hope it's not Big Boi. I mean he disgustin and all but he aint no bear. Girrrl, he aint nothin to be scared of. I remember..."

"Bubblicious, will you shut up?"

"Excuse me!"

"I mean, just take a few deep breaths or somethin." She looked around nervously, "Look, I got to go home for a minute. If I'm not back will you cover for me?"

"Yea, if..."

"If what?!"

Chance was getting very annoyed with the girl, but she needed her right now. There was no way she could do a private dance for Money, and with Karisma! She was sure to put things together. Eventually, they would all have to face each other, but not right now. Not tonight!

"If, you put in a good word with Big Boi so I can have one of the small areas in the big changing room." She looked around the dressing area, "It's messy in here and it stank! I swear suma dese girls don't bathe they..."

"Okay, that's enough. I get it! I'll talk to him." Chance shouted over her shoulder. "Hey I gotta go, but I'll try to be back before I have to fill in for Cotton Candy. She usually goes next to last."

"Wait? Wait! So I got to dance three times?! If so, I'm borrowin one of yo fits..."

Chance did not answer the girl. She grabbed her bags and slipped out of the front exit to the ramp and out the back door. *I don't know how I'm going to explain not coming back to Big Boi, not to mention Money, but I can't... I can't be in the same room with the two of them, not yet! Maybe after I get used to Karisma a little more I can lie better! I'll work over next week. I'll even take a beating! But I can't stab my girl in the back right in her face. Not yet! She'll never forgive me.*

Money knew she would bail if she saw him. But she was not the reason for the visit so he didn't care. He would deal with her later. It was Jug's birthday and Money decided to surprise him with a little action. Besides, it would give Karisma some experience with private parties. She would need it before all of this was over.

"Jug?"

"Yes Mr. Money sir."

"What have I told you repeatedly to call me?"

"Uh, Boss? Mr. Money sir."

"If you know, why do you keep calling me Mr. Money sir?"

"I dunno Mister... I mean Boss."

"It's your birthday, so I'm gone give you a pass. But try to work on it before I see you tomorrow okay?"

"Sure thing Mister... I mean Boss."

Money looked at him with contempt, but he didn't have time to be petty right now. He had to go visit his mama, and he didn't want to keep the queen waiting.

"Jug? I have to go. But the limo will take you and whichever one of these girls you want back to my apartment at the Twelve. It's yours until tomorrow evening."

"Thanks Boss!"

"Very good Jug. Your stupidity leak is closing up!" He smiled and immediately left, right as Karisma and the other girls entered the area.

"Hey fellas! I hope yall buckled in tight cause it's gonna be a looooong ride."

Jug grabbed Cotton Candy and sat her on his lap, while Karisma and Peaches worked the rest of the men. One thing Lady K had picked up from Chance is finding the weak link in a group of men. Usually they are the innocent, naive one that just tagged along because everybody else was going. He didn't really want to be there, but when Karisma started grinding on him he loosened up.

"Hey daddy."

"Hey love."

"You got some candy for me in your pocket daddy?"

The young man quickly pulled out a wad of cash from his front pocket. Peaches eyes lit up! There were no small bills. Nothing but big faces! She wished she had picked the young man until she noticed they all came stacked. *Good thing Chance got sick! I would hate to miss all this cheese!!* While Peaches was drooling over the men and their money, Karisma kept her cool and stayed in character.

"Mmmm, yea. That's what I'm talkin about daddy. I wanna taste of that sweetness!"

Karisma noticed the pole located in the middle of the room and went to work. Before long, she had everyone's attention including Jugs. Normally, jealousy would arise but not tonight. Lady K promised them 25% of the take after Big Boi's cut, and from the way the hundreds were flying, they would easily come away with $3000 a piece. Cotton Candy let Jug watch Karisma and he paid her to sit beside him looking beautiful. She was used to it. Rarely did she have to perform tricks just because of her looks and skin tone. Men went crazy over her and treated her like a possession, but to her it was just a part of the job. As long as she made enough money to take care of her kids, she didn't really care. Tonight, they hit the jackpot and she could rest easy for the rest of the month. No sessions in Big Boi's office because she didn't make quota. And no visit to the ER. *Who has a quota to meet in a strip club anyway? My money is my money, and your cut is your cut.* She remembered saying to him. But that didn't stop him from penalizing her. If it happened again, she vowed to report him to anyone who would listen. *But who?*

# Chapter 6: Broken Heart

"Mom?"

"Who else did you expect?"

"Mom, why are you calling me so early in the morning?"

"Early?! It's almost 12!"

"Well it feels like 3am."

"What time did you get done with your **'business**?'"

"Ugh, mom don't start! I have a headache okay."

"Oh?! Mama's baby got a hangover?"

"WHAT DO YOU WANT WOMAN?!"

"Calm down lil girl! I am still your mother!!"

"I'm sorry, Mother! What do you want?"

"I want to know where you are? And why your room is empty?"

"Duh. You haven't figured it out yet?"

"Well, from the looks of it, you moved out."

"And the Pulitzer goes to..."

"Oh, cut the crap Kindness!! Where are you? It's obvious you didn't come home last night and your dad is worried sick. He will not leave me alone until he knows you're okay. And he wants to know when you will be coming back. Look..."

Angela's voice trailed off into the distance. Hearing her old name made Karisma's stomach turn. She knew that would never be her character again. Karisma was the name, but to her parents Kindness would always be their innocent little princess. After everything she had been through, Kindness was far from princess or innocent. She would never be that sweet, naive, timid girl who first walked into Queen City only a few short months ago.

"Kindness?! Kindness?!!! Do you hear me?"

"Mom, how could I not. You've been ranting for at least five minutes straight."

"If you heard me, why didn't you answer the question?"

"I'm sorry what question was that?"

"I thought you said you were listening."

"No, I said I heard you. But I kinda zoned out after a while. Your voice is pretty annoying."

"Kindness, I don't know what's gotten into you but wherever you are picking up that attitude you can give it back. I will not tolerate..."

"Tolerate?!! I am no longer your affair woman. I am my own! I got my own!! I pay for my own!!! I don't need your help or dad's!! So, if you would excuse me..."

Karisma hung up the phone. Immediately it rang again. She knew it would. Her mother always had to have the final word.

"What?!!!"

"Don't you what me young lady!"

"Dad!"

She was surprised. He usually was out scouting new properties. There were at least two projects he was sure to close on in the next few days. What was he doing home? When she spoke again, her entire demeanor changed.

"Yes, it's me! And where do you get off hanging up on your mother like that?"

"Dad, like I told mom. I have my own space now, and..."

"And what?"

"Your house is no longer my home."

"No. No! I will not lose you too. Now Kindness, you get..." he paused to regain composure. "I need you to get your things and high tail it back this instant so we can talk things out."

"Dad, I know this may be hard for you to hear but..."

Really it was hard for her to say. Talking back to her mother was one thing, but this was her daddy. The one she always ran to for protection. The one who she could confide in at all times.

They were so close. It seemed wrong on too many levels to disrespect him.

"What? But what Kindness?"

"I'm not coming home."

"No, no, no! Baby please. Please don't say that." He was sobbing and sucking back tears. "You're my little girl. I can't... Please I can't lose you too!"

"I'm sorry dad, but I'm not your little girl anymore. I don't know if I ever will be again."

"No, you will always be my little girl."

"Dad! There's no sense in dragging this out." There was a long pause. "Goodbye!"

She heard him begging at the top of his lungs for her to come home. "Please come home! Please, please!! Don't hang up! Kindness..."

"Dnng!"

It was by far the hardest phone call she ever had to end. Even talking to Money didn't hurt that bad. She knew her dad's heart was broken. They're relationship would never be the same. She got up out of the bed. Neither sleep nor rest would come easy after that call. Her mind would be preoccupied with the sound of his voice and thoughts of what he might be doing to find her and her brother. *Maybe now they'll do something and we all can go back to some sort of normalcy. Hopefully...*

"Oh well. Guess I'd better call my girl and see if she can bring me some gas. Tired of being sad." Reaching for her cell phone, a hazy recollection came into view. "But wait..."

She remembered. Chance left a blunt in her bag for after the big party. However, Chance never came back to celebrate. *I wonder what made her leave so suddenly anyway. I'll have to be sure and get a good explanation tonight.* Karisma found the gift tucked away in a side compartment. Chance put it in a cigar case so it wouldn't get broken. She lit the blunt and sat back in her recliner, turning on the television to catch up on a few of her favorite shows. DVR was a life saver.

Memories of sitting in the family room with her brother and parents flooded her mind. She could hear her brother's laugh. It was infectious. If he laughed, no one had to know what he was laughing about in order to join in. She missed them all. Tears were a regular occasion now and since no one was around, she let them flow. So much had changed. She had changed. *Lord you must be disgusted with me right now. I'm sitting here getting high, talking to the Most*

*High. You must think me to be pitiful! I think I'm pitiful. How can I ever come back to you? To the church? After showing my body to all these men for money, drinking every day and getting high all day everyday... How could you ever want me back? I'm such a mess!*

"Knock, knock, knock!"

It could only be one person at the door. The only person who knew she moved out of her parent's home. Her one and only friend. But just in case she put out the blunt and hid the evidence. She thought to grab her bathrobe but ended up at the door in nothing but a t-shirt.

"Cha-- Oh, you're not... I mean. Um, how may I help you?" She stammered.

It was the landlord and a maintenance man. There was no need to try and hide her legs. They knew where she worked and the t-shirt was more clothes than she ever wore on stage.

"Don't be alarmed. We're just here to welcome you to the neighborhood and make sure there are no repairs that need to be done."

"Miss..." The maintenance man was trying to hit on her but replied dryly.

"Karisma."

"Ms. Karisma, have you done a walk through yet?"

"No. I got off pretty late last night. Well, it was more like this morning. I probably wouldn't be up this early if I hadn't had a very unpleasant phone call."

"Boyfriend?" The maintenance man was still drooling. He couldn't help but notice the smoothness of her legs and the curves which the skimpy little tshirt could never hide.

"No. I don't have a boyfriend." Hope gleamed from his eyes until she added, "I'm gay!"

"You're a lesbian too?! Shoot, all the good ones want each other!!" She couldn't help but stifle a laugh.

"Like she would have you anyway!" The landlord, on the other hand, laughed out loud.

"Whatever!" he growled at the lady. "Look Ms. Karisma? We gone take a look at the closets and windows, the bathroom and the kitchen. Once everything checks out, you'll have to fill out a work order for future repairs. Understand?"

"Yea, it doesn't sound too hard Einstein." She rolled her eyes, turning back into the apartment.

The man didn't realize he had been insulted until it was too late. She was gone, disappearing into her bedroom to change. She was quick. *One day that quick tongue gone get you hurt girl!* He wanted to choke her. None of these hoes get away with talking to him that way. In any other case, she wouldn't be breathing. He looked in her general direction, loathing her very existence, but Money gave strict orders to only watch. So he pretended to look around knowing full well there were already wires in the house and repairs were done prior to her arrival. There would be no reason for her to call for maintenance. And if she did, he would be there to oblige her. Some kind of way, he would get her back for that snide comment. Revenge was a game he was good at.

No one heard Chance approaching. She was leery about walking up the steps. Karisma's door was wide open, but she didn't hear any voices, just a noise here and there. Someone was rambling through the cabinets and drawers, looking for something. But what? She tiptoed up the last few stairs and flattened her body to the wall. Pepper spray in hand, she took a deep breath and jumped into the doorway. The landlord flinched so hard, she nearly peed in her pants.

"Eeeeyaaw!"

"Oh, I'm sorry ma'am."

"Sorry?! You almost scared me to death!!"

"Like I said, sorry!"

"And who is you?" The woman returned the girl's sarcasm.

"She's my best friend. Is that a problem?"

"No, not at all. I was just making sure she was in the right apartment."

"Mhmm."

"Are you gay too?!" The thug maintenance man joined the fiasco.

Chance's jaw nearly hit the floor. *Oh my God! It's one of Money's thugs pretending to be a maintenance man. I just can't get away from his malicious presence! He seems to be everywhere.* That is the impression he wanted to make. He wanted the girls to feel like he was always watching, whether indirectly or directly. Money was truly a worker of the devil and his thugs were like demons and minions doing his bidding. Chance knew she had better watch her tone with this criminal. They called him "The Choker" for a reason. Finally, she managed a response.

"Huh?! Who me? Nope. Nope, I'm as straight as they come."

"Well maybe you and me can hook up."

"Maybe…"

Karisma was looking at Chance like there was a hole in her forehead. When she noticed, she tried to spice up her answer, but not too much.

"Maybe, you can come by the club and buy a dance."

"I'm not paying you to grind on me! I can get that for free!!"

"That's the only offer you get from me!"

The man was totally fuming. He couldn't get a number. Not even a flirt. But that's okay. He would get his opportunity for revenge soon enough. Now that he knew where to find them, they both had better watch their backs or they just might find themselves in a sleeper hold. Chance knew it, but her friend was still a little naïve, having no idea who she was dealing with. It was a good thing the thug was new. He didn't know her face yet, or he could have spoiled everything.

"Ha, I guess she told you!" Still steaming, he added nothing. Karisma gave a victorious nod in his direction before turning to the landlord.

"Are you about done? We have somewhere to be."

"Yea, I guess so. If you find anything else, leave a message on the maintenance line and Debo here will come fix it for you." She cringed in disgust.

"I'm at your service young lady," he mocked a gentleman's bow. But there was nothing gentle about him.

"Hopefully, I'll never need **that** service." *That smart mouth, little girl, could end your life with one tight squeeze!* He was vehemently watching the girl.

"Hey, look at the time. We'd better get going."

Chance jumped in before the man became too heated. It was as if she could see the steam rising up from his head. If he reached out and touched Karisma this gig would be over for all of them and Money would find some way to blame her. It was her job to make sure Karisma was delivered to his house at the designated time. Money wanted her a little more relaxed and experienced first. It would not be much longer because Karisma was finding her niche. She was more comfortable in this skin than in the previous one. *Exactly what Money wanted!*

"Okay, fine. If I need you, I'll call. Now can you go?"

The landlady said nothing and Debo only grunted as he strutted past the girls like a peacock. They watched them walk down the stairs before closing the door.

"What was that all about?"

"Oh nothing. Just some extra stuff from when I moved in. I guess it happened so fast they must have missed something."

"Hmm, well I don't trust it. Your apartment is spotless. What could they have possibly been up here doing?" She looked around trying to see if there were any visible cameras or wires. Money was sure to have them placed strategically throughout the apartment. Nothing or no one was safe. He could hear and see everything. *This might be my last time coming to visit...*

"What's the matter?"

"Nothing. I'm just looking around." She lied. "What you got to eat in here?"

"I haven't been grocery shopping yet. I just have some chips and cookies in my room."

"That'll work." Chance darted into the room. "Perfect munchie food!"

"Hey bring the rest of that blunt from my jewelry box too," Karisma yelled.

Chance emerged with everything in hand and made herself comfortable on the couch. She put a cookie in her mouth and pulled out her lighter.

"How you gone fire up my blunt that I asked you to bring to me?"

"This is not yours!"

"How you know?"

"Because it's one of my honey blazes. And I grind my herb and cut my blunts like a pro. If you had rolled this, there would be seeds poppin' and everything." She laughed as she took a drag.

"Forget you. I'll get better." She pretended to be nonchalant, but it kind of hurt her pride that her friend thought her to be so naïve. *I'll just have to practice. That's what I'll do. I excel at everything. I will be the best!!*

"Chill out. Don't get your panties in a wad." Chance pulled a mesh bag out of her duffle and threw it in Karisma's lap. "Here."

"What's this?"

"A housewarming gift! Just open it." Karisma unzipped the bag to find a grinder, a scale, a box of Columbians and an ounce of gas.

"Oh wow. Just what I've always wanted."

"I knew you would love it. Now you can practice."

"What makes you think I want to practice?"

"Cause I know you. And I know you always want to be the best! That's how you earned the nickname GOAT!" It was the truth but not a topic of discussion right now.

"Mhmm. What you doing over here so early anyway?"

"I got a lot of sleep last night."

"Oh yea, I was bout to call you. What happened to you?"

"What you mean?"

"I mean, why you leave all that money for our weakest dancers to steal?"

"I wasn't feeling good, that's all."

"You was aiight earlier."

"It was a sudden case of the bubble guts okay."

"Ewww. I know that feelin'. You can't dance like that."

"Yea, I had to go home and take some meds and then I was better."

"Why didn't you come back though?"

"You know, by the time the meds kicked in it was about 3 o'clock, so I counted it a loss."

"Mhmm."

"For real. Anyway, that's one of the reasons I'm here so early. I got to run some errands for Big Boi before my shift. You wanna tag along?"

"Ion see why not. Let me pack my bag so we don't have to double back."

"Bet. Ima pull the car around and meet you on the curb."

"Aiight!"

Chance couldn't tell Karisma that Money paid her a visit last night. He must have pulled out right after she did because he met her at her front door.

"What you think you doing?"

"Money!!"

"Yea, it's me. Why you aint at the club doing yo job?!"

"Um, well I'm not feeling well so I got some of the girls to fill in for me."

"Don't be stupid! You know that's not the job I'm talking bout!!"

"Money, she'll be fine for just one night. I promise. She coming into her own."

"You'd better hope so. And what you doing getting sick? This is the street baby, you don't have time for sick!"

"It's just a little stomach ache. I'll be alright tomorrow."

"You sure that's it?"

"Yes I am."

"You sure you didn't see me and Jug at the club? And then decide it would be too hard for you to face all of us in the VIP?!"

"I'm positive. I would never skip out on you like that Money." She knew to keep her voice calm and cool.

"You'd better not!!" He grabbed her face with one hand, squeezing. She felt like she was choking though his fingers only grazed her neck.

"I promise. I promise, Money. Just let me go and I'll take my medicine and sleep it off. I'll be fine."

She managed to speak through the tight grip he had on her mouth. He looked down at the drug store bag and decided for once she might be telling the truth. He squeezed one last time before *mushing her face into the door.*

*"Let me get out of here before you give me your germs!"*

*He wiped his hands on his shirt like she was a contagious disease. The look he gave was pure hate and inwardly Chance returned the abhorrence. However, she managed a smile.*

*"Thank you, Money."*

*"For what?!"*

*"For believing me."*

*"Don't get too happy. You gone make it up early in the morning."*

*"Whatever you want."*

*"I know that." She rolled her eyes.*

*"So, what do I have to do?"*

*"You get Karisma and come over to Xavier's house. I have a package that needs to be delivered."*

*"And what do I get out of it?"*

*Normally Money would have slapped her, but they did have a business arrangement. Everything she did went towards her bill. He knew she wanted to be rid of him but he had her on a tight leash. Every time she got close to being paid off, he found a reason to add more. But she always hoped for the best. Freedom!*

*"You know what? I like your spunk. You messed up but you still want your cut. That's the street I put in you. So, I'll let that one slide and take 25% off your bill."*

*"Twenty-five percent?! Really!"*

*"You like the sound of that huh?!"*

*"Yea. I mean it would be nice to just make money so I can stack. Get me a nice place downtown. Are you really going to give me 25% off?"*

*"Yea. Sure. If you can get Karisma to Xavier's house on time and get the package delivered by 2:45, you got it?"*

*"Bet!"*

*"See you tomorrow."*

*"You're going to be there?"*

*"Aww, had enough of me already?"*

*"No. That's not what I meant."*

*"What did you mean?"*

*"I just don't know if it's the right time for Karisma to meet you, that's all."*

*"You said she was ready!"*

*"She is almost ready. Just give her a couple more weeks."*

Really, it was Chance who needed more time. Karisma would get the shock of her life whether tomorrow or a month from now. It was Chance who would stand to lose it all. Best friends were rare. Where in the world would she find another so pure? She needed more time to come up with an out and a story that Karisma would believe. Hopefully in the end, the truth would stand.

*"Relax Pumpkin. I'm always watching. Daddy will be there but you won't see me."*

*"Will Karisma see you?"*

*"Maybe. Maybe not. But it's none of your concern. I decide when she's ready and when the gig is up! Understand?!"*

*"Yes Money. I do."*

She began to worry as he walked down the steps. So cool. So sly. So hypnotizing. So deadly. How does a man that looks as good as he does, and is as educated as he is become so evil? She always wanted to know. There was no way of knowing what his intentions were in totality. All she knew was that he couldn't ever be trusted. He was always conspiring. He called himself God but really he was more like the devil himself.

"Hey? You about ready up there?" She yelled from the street. "I got a schedule to keep!"

"Hold your horses! I'm coming!!"

Karisma was always dressed so cute and classy. The other girls called her a square because she treated the job like a job. She always responded, *"This job will not take over my life. I make the money. The money don't make me!"* The girls would laugh. They liked living the fast life, all day, every day. Short, tight, skimpy clothes suited them. Only Chance looked up to her friend. When she finally bought her freedom from Money, she would change her identity and emulate Kindness.

"Girl, you is cute or whatever."

"Thanchu hunni!"

"Get in. We gotta roll." Karisma threw her bag in the back and hopped in the front seat.

"Why we rushin again? What you got to do that's such a rush? Big Boi aint no bear. He might be big as one but he don't scare nobody!"

"I just don't have time to hear his mouth okay."

"Chance, we all have our day to bring toiletries and cleaner for the dressing room. What's the big deal?"

"I know, I know. But today I got to make a couple of other stops and I can't be late."

"Wait? Are you sure I wanna be riding with you right now, cause I'm not?"

"Girl, you'll be fine. The less you know the better. Besides, you're here now."

"Mhmmm, I'm gone start asking more questions before I ride with you again Chancy!"

"Ugh, why do you call me that?"

"Because sometimes gettin mixed up with you is chancy. I'm taking chances with my life and freedom. It's bad enough I'm being forced into this..."

"Forced into what?"

"Nothing."

"Naw, tell me! What's up?"

"I can't. I can't tell you."

"Now who's taking chances? If you can't tell me and I can't tell you, then we both just gotta trust each other and be there for each other, right?!"

"I suppose you're right."

"Good. Then we don't have to talk about it until we both are ready to talk."

Karisma didn't know, but Chance knew her whole story. And at least when the time comes, she might actually believe. Money was Money. He would be evil no matter what. And if she had some conversations and run-ins with him already, she was sure to know that. *Yea, she'll believe me. She won't be too heartbroken over a hoodrat like me. By that time maybe she will have her brother back and this will be nothing more than a bad memory.*

"We're here."

"Where is here?"

"My friend Xavier's house."

"Xavier? I've heard that name before."

"Me too. I know a lot of Xavier's." Chance said, getting out of the car.

*Hopefully Money has not set me up for failure. If he has mentioned Xavier and his business of X pills to Karisma, she was sure to know that her friend was in on this masquerade.*

"I don't know Chance. I think I might need to stay in the car."

"Why? It's more dangerous out here than in the house, trust me."

Karisma looked around. She saw drug dealers and addicts on the corner. Kids with guns at the store across the street. And here she was looking all cute and naive. There was nothing hood about her. She got out of the car.

"If you had told me we was coming to the hood, I would have dressed differently."

"It still would've been more dangerous out here. Clothes don't change that."

"Yea, but at least I would look the part."

"Well, I'm sorry. I'll tell you how to dress next time."

"Gee, thanks!"

Karisma took another look around. There were a lot of junk cars lining the road. A few nicer looking vehicles, but one stood out. It was a black Escalade on 26" rims. *Nice ride!* That looks like the same truck my brother was dragged into. *Nah, it couldn't be?* But it could. It was the moment that had brought her to where she was today. Her eyes searched closer, hoping to catch a glimpse of someone who might resemble Jay.

"Girl, you better come on."

"Oh right."

"Hello ladies." Xavier King met them at the door.

"Hi Xavier." Chance hugged the good-looking young man. Tall, dark and handsome. *Yea, it looks a lot safer in here.*

"Aren't you going to introduce me to your friend?"

"Of course. Xavier this is my best friend Karisma. She works at the club with me. Karisma, this is Xavier."

"It's a pleasure to meet you sweetheart."

"The pleasure is all mine." She replied sweetly, as he held on to her hand.

"Hmmm, you work at Queen City?"

"Yes, I do. Why do you ask like that?"

"I dunno. You just don't seem the type."

"I'm not. But life can throw challenges your way and you have to rise to the occasion. Ya know?"

"I do." He was debonair and his smile matched his character. Their eyes were glued to each other. He kissed her hand again and she giggled like a little girl.

"Okay, okay. Enough flirting." Chance broke the hand shake. "I am on a schedule, so if I can see you in the back for a minute Xavier."

"Of course, my dear. Karisma, I will be right back so don't you go anywhere."

"I'll be right here." She smiled just as sweetly as she spoke.

Chance and Xavier disappeared into a back room, and closed the door. *So many secrets. She had secrets. Chance had secrets. It probably was best that they keep certain things to themselves. It seemed they both had enough problems on their own.* Karisma looked around the foyer and began to walk the length of the hallway. Pictures of Xavier and some other young men lined the walls. She admired them, touching some. He was really a good-looking guy. She didn't notice how far down the hallway she had come until she heard noises. The closer she got to the end, the more she realized others were in the house. It sounded as if they were playing video games. Yep, they were definitely playing video games. Suddenly a voice rose out of the chaotic male displays of egos.

"Oh no. I'm killin you boy. I'm killin you!"

*Jay!* There was no mistaking his voice and definitely not his laugh. Her walk turned into a trot. The hallway seemed to be too long to reach the end. She opened the door and there was a group of young men, but her brother was not there.

"Hey beautiful. Come on in and grab a stick!"

"Oh, I'm sorry. I'm in the wrong room."

"No. You're in the right room. You was obviously looking for me."

"I got a stick you can grab right here!" One of the other boys grabbed his crotch.

"Shut up fool. Can't you see she's a lady! Save dat talk for dem hoodies."

The young man looked to be the same age as her brother, but his voice nor his laugh matched what she heard. The second young man quieted in the corner, grabbed the joystick and continued playing with his friends. She looked around and saw that all of them were Jay's age or maybe even younger. It was obvious Xavier's was the hood hangout. Either he was keeping them off of the streets or putting them on. At any rate, Jay was not there.

"Actually, I'm looking for my friend Chance. Since she's not in here..."

"Karisma? What are you doing?"

Chance startled her, but mostly she was devastated not to find Jay. Tears began to roll down her face in abundance.

"Hey, are you okay?"

"No. I mean, yea. I just, um..." She was trying to hold back the tears and emotions. "I don't know. I just, um... Can we go?"

"Yea, sure."

Chance worried about her friend, looking around for the devil. *What happened? She was only gone for a few minutes, long enough to get the package and instructions Money left for her.* Xavier, on the other hand, was disappointed but did not add any flirtatious comments. She was hurting for some reason. And he could only imagine what it was, considering Money had her under his finger just like he had them all. Back in the car, Chance grabbed her friend's hand.

"Are you okay?"

"Yea. It's just that, I miss him Chance. Where is he?! I heard those young men from down the hall and I would have bet my life that I heard Jay laugh. I could have sworn it! Sometimes I hear it in my sleep. It be like he is right in the room with me."

She broke down in tears like a baby needing her mother and Chance doubted she had the right equipment to console the girl. Though, she        said and did all that she could.

"I can only imagine Lady K." Chance cranked the car. "Look, we got to deliver this package, but after we dance tonight you can stay at my house and we'll do each other's hair and talk. Okay?"

Karisma did not respond. She couldn't. Her heart was broken. There was no amount of talking to heal what was hurting inside. She couldn't tell Chance. For all she knew, her brother was at home with her parents, missing her too. Telling her would be a burden to an already hectic and problematic life. Kindness was fighting a losing battle. It was hopeless. Money had her on a string, an evil puppet master and only God could sever that relationship. Suddenly things that used to be hidden became truth. She now understood how a person could be driven to insanity by another and she craved deliverance. *Lord however you have to fix it, please HELP ME!*

# Chapter 7: Girl's Night Out

"I can't believe it's only been a few months since I met you. It feels like a lifetime."

"Yea, it does. One filled with excruciating pain and irritatingly long phone conversations." Chance sipped her cocoa. "Mmm, this is so good."

"Oh, and let's not forget having to see yo ugly mug every day! Ugh, I'm exhausted just thinking about it!"

"You too?"

They fell out laughing. Rarely did they have a day off and on the same day. *God must still love me!*

"I needed this."

"We needed this. Someone in the Universe was looking out today."

"Jesus."

"Jesus, what?"

"Jesus was looking out today, not the universe."

"Now Kindness, I know you're a Christian..."

"Used to be." She said solemnly.

"Okay, I know you **used** to be a Christian, but don't go preaching to me okay. God is a part of the universe. It doesn't matter what his name is."

"It does matter. Jesus matters, whether I'm living right or not. He matters."

"And what is living right anyway? We have the right to live however we choose."

"I never said that we didn't. It's the gift of choice, it is a gift given to all mankind. But we have to face the consequences of those choices too."

"You're right about that."

"Jesus."

"Why do you keep saying that name?"

"Because it's the only name that saves. And I need a little salvation right now. A lot if the truth be told."

"Jesus name saves? How can a name save? And saves from what? When you get saved, what are you saved from?"

"Jesus' name has power. It is the only name that demons flee from. And when you get saved you are saved from a hard life. No protection. Sin. Death. Need I say more!!"

"Saved from a hard life?! Please! We all have problems."

"I didn't say a problem free life, just not a hard one. Jesus, His Word, His power is right there with you to help you through it all. My dad used quote a scripture that says that Christians would suffer many afflictions but God will deliver out of them all."

"Mhmm. Well, what is sin, anyway? We all are imperfect."

"Anything that leads to death."

"No matter how we live our life, we all gone die one day."

"You're right. But there's more than one way to die."

"What do you mean?"

"You told me your mom was an English major, right?"

"Right. But..."

"And she frowned on the misuse of words."

"Uh huh..."

"And she taught you that one word can have several different meanings too, right?"

"Yea."

"The same thing with death."

"Enlighten me!"

"Okay Ms. Smarty Pants, I will. Death can be figurative, natural, spiritual and eternal."

"Uh huh, continue."

"Let's take figurative first. If you lose a friend or a loved one because of an argument or some other type altercation between the two of you, your relationship ends. A part of you dies. All of the memories you made together linger and hurt because they were a part of you. When they are torn from your heart, figurative death takes place."

"Okay I get that. Like when I ran away from home."

"Exactly. And figurative death can also be the end of anything that once was, especially something good in your life."

"Such as..."

"A job when you got bills to pay. You'll need another job or you may lose some things, like your car or home. That is death, figurative death."

"Makes sense."

"Alright, so natural death is the end of someone's physical life. Have you ever lost someone close to you?"

"In these streets? All the time!"

"What about a family member?"

"I lost my grandma about a year before I dipped."

"Physical death hurts the living because we remember how wonderful it was to have that person in our lives. Someone to talk to and share laughs with. Someone to cook you food and take care of you when you're sick."

"My grandma used to make this vanilla cream pound cake when I was a little girl, every summer she made one just for me. I called it my "I made it through another school year" cake. Oh, and on my birthday, she went all out. Cakes, cookies, ice cream, all homemade. She even had a candy station so when my friends came to my party, they could create their own gift bags to take home."

"You miss her a lot, don't you?"

"Yea. She's the only one who understood me."

"That's how I feel about my dad. He still calls me his princess." The back of her eyelids started to burn. Chance saw her blinking back the waterworks.

"Uhn Unh. No tears. Not today."

"Gotcha." Karisma cleared her throat.

"So anyways, you were giving me a lesson. It was quite interesting. I'd like to hear the rest please."

"Are you trying to be funny or are you serious?"

"Half and half!"

"Aiight then. I'll only focus on the half that matters! Now, where was I?"

"Physical death."

"Right. I think we get the gist of that. Don't you?"

"Indeed."

"Now we get to the most important, spiritual death."

"Why do you say 'spiritual death' is the most important? When you die, that's it!"

"Because it is the one that requires the most commitment in order for change to take place."

"Huh?"

"You remember saying we all have the right to choose?"

"Yea."

"Spiritual death is the only one we choose for ourselves and the only one we don't have to experience. And to be honest, complete success depends on it. But if you die naturally without choosing Jesus you end up in eternal death."

"I don't get it."

"We all gone go through some things in life, lose some things, end some relationships, no matter who we are or what our background, nationality or status is. Figurative and natural death are going to happen to us all. But spiritual death is a choice."

"So, what does it mean?"

"It means you have no relationship with Jesus. It means you either never accepted him as Lord and Savior or you ended the relationship."

"Oh, I get it. Although I have no idea how to accept him as Lord and Savior." She rolled her eyes.

"It's simple. You choose Him and His ways over yourself and how you want to live and then you follow His instructions."

"What do you mean, His instructions? Like the Bible?"

"Yes, but even more so, the revealed word of God."

"And what book do you get that from?"

"You still get it from the Bible. The revealed word of God is tailor made for your current situation and must be heard through the man of God."

"So, I have to go to church and listen to the preacher to get the revealed word of God, but I can read the Bible for myself?"

"Not exactly. You can read the Bible for yourself, but God reveals the meaning He desires you to get from that word through the Pastor."

"So, I shouldn't try to read the Bible on my own?"

"No, you should."

"But why if God is going to reveal the meaning through the Pastor? I should just let him do all the work." Kindness laughed a little at her friend but hurried to continue.

"Because, God will give meaning of things that you read. You meditate on it and let it become a part of you. Often times when you read in your daily devotion, God will reveal more of the meaning through the Pastor."

"Why? Why doesn't he just reveal it to me and cut out the middle man?"

"It's divine order. It's the way God built the church. He reveals only certain things to us, but he reveals His secrets to the Pastor."

"Secrets?"

"Yes, secrets. Those things God only reveals to the Pastor to keep order in the land."

"Sounds complicated."

"It only sounds that way because you've never tried Him."

"Okay, so basically when you go to church, you getting the literal meaning and the revealed meaning of the word of God from the Preacher."

"Yes, basically."

"So, you saying to be saved you got to go to church."

"Not necessarily, but to stay saved and grow your faith in God, yes, you have to go to church."

"So, going to church is a part of being saved?"

"Yes."

"And if I don't accept Jesus as Lord and Savior, that's spiritual death?"

"Yes."

"And if I die spiritually dead, I will end up in eternal death?"

"Yes."

"Eternal death must be the place called hell, where my grandma used to say she hoped she never had to see."

"So, you know about hell."

"Nah, not really. She didn't go to church much. Well, towards the end, she went more and more. But I don't know about the rest."

"But do you understand the four different deaths?"

"I'm not sure if I understand it all, but that was a good teaching. I get it, kinda."

"You'll understand it more if you ever decide to accept him. Seeing is believable but testing is proof."

"Do you miss it?"

"Why do you ask that?"

"I dunno. You speak so highly of it like it was the best life ever."

"Yes, I do. I miss it and I miss Him. It was my life, and I was truly happy. Every day I think about how He must feel about me. I wonder if He loves me, even though I know He does."

"If you know He loves you, then why wonder?"

"Now you sound just like my dad!"

"Is your dad a Pastor?"

"He's an elder, but he does preach the word of God similar to the Pastor, just not on a weekly basis. The day my brother ran away, my dad was preparing to fill in for our Pastor the next morning. It was his first-time doing Sunday morning service."

"Why wasn't your Pastor there?"

"He had a previous commitment and the conference was only held on Sunday. But he said he'd never make that commitment again because a Shepherd's place is with his flock."

"Well, it's a good thing your father stepped in for him."

"Yea. He was so nervous at first, but you couldn't tell it from the audience. I just know my dad."

"You miss him too huh?"

"Of course. I'm daddy's princess. He must be going crazy without me being there."

They both remained quiet for a short time, that is until the silence became deafening.

"Okay. Well, that's enough of that!! Let's talk about what we are going to do today."

"I know what I want to do. I'm going to the mall to buy me some new fits and see if I can spot a fresh honeysuckle to sink my teeth into and after that, how about dinter and a movie?"

"Sounds like a winner to me, but leave me out on the honeysuckles."

"Why?"

"Cause they usually turn out to be honey suckers! They want you to buy them something!!"

"You right about that!"

"They see you got money to spend and start following you around, giving out compliments, hoping for a Chance."

"And they might get a Chance if they lucky. Cause I'm feeling a little freaky." She pinched her butt.

"Now I told you, I don't do women."

"Neither do I! But aren't you a little curious."

"Not really."

"Liar!!"

"Okay, maybe a little. But I know God is not pleased with that."

"I know you have told me a million times. He will allow you to choose for yourself but that don't mean He likes it. Got it!"

"Good. Then stop pinching my butt!"

"I can't help it. It's just so luscious!"

"Whatever. Keep yo hands to yoself!"

"If I ever did decide to try it, you'd be my first candidate!"

"Don't hold your breath!" Chance rolled her eyes.

"Anyways, what are you wearing?"

"I'm rocking the romper today and these new sandals Marcus sent to the club for me."

"I hope I get to meet this Marcus one day. You talk about him all the time."

"He comes to the club a lot, but I've only seen him once."

"Yea, your first night. You told me. I just don't understand why this negro keep buying you gifts."

"I think he likes me and he leaves me gifts with the bartender to let me know he saw me dance."

"Mhmm, well if I were you I would be very careful."

"Girl, I can barely remember what he looks like."

"I hope you do. He could be following you and you wouldn't even know it."

"That's true."

"Maybe we'll see him today at the mall."

"I hope so. Then I'll know who to kill if anything happens to you."

"Girl stop! Ain't nothing gone happen to me. That man ain't studdin me like that!"

"Whatever you say, but keep both eyes peeled. Evil could be lurkin around any corner."

"Here, you can wear this dress."

"Okay girrrl! This is ca-ute!"

"You want it?"

"You better know it!"

"It's yours!!"

"Kindness, you really are the kindest person I've ever met."

"Aww, thank you girl. But can you please stop calling me Kindness. It's Karisma til I say othawise."

"I forgot. Look, I'll just call you Lady K, then that way it won't matter to which name I am referring."

"And stop using so much proper English. You making me sick!"

"Oh, how the tables turn!"

"Speaking of turning. Time is ticking! Come on, let's get dressed. I can't wait to get out of this house!"

"Me too!

Kindness went into her room and Chance changed in the bathroom. When they came out, both were dolled up and ready for the ride.

"I'm so glad you have a car. I'm tired of riding the bus."

"Why didn't you keep the car you had?"

"I told you. I didn't want anything connecting me to my parents. The police are looking for me. I can feel it. A car, is a dead giveaway."

"Why don't you buy you a new car?"

"I told you. All the money I make has a purpose, and when I reach that goal, I'm done."

"Mhmm, that's what they all say. But this money is hard to come by with a regular job."

"Yea, but at least I'll have peace and protection. Anyway, let's get going. I want to get some good shop therapy in before the movie."

"What we going to see anyway?"

"I dunno. We'll check it out once we get there."

They got dressed and headed for the mall. It was Saturday and as usual, the place was packed. Chance's eyes glistened at all the honeysuckles perusing the complex, however Kindness was focused. There were a couple of shops she had been dying to spend in.  Neither one noticed they were being watched, but he was no honeysuckle.

"Hello."

Chance froze when she saw who spoke. Money didn't look as deadly and fierce as he was. To Kindness he was a harmless patron named Marcus, who often bought her gifts and gave her compliments.

"Marcus? Is that you?"

"Yes, Ms. Karisma. The one and only."

"It's so good to see you! How have you been?" She gave him a brief hug.

"Excellent baby, always excellent."

"My girlfriend and I were just talking about you."

"You were, were you? And what did you and your **girlfriend** say about me?" He cut his eyes in Chance's direction but she didn't utter a word. She didn't dare move a muscle.

"Honestly, it was mostly me. She just said she would like to meet this Marcus who keeps sending me gifts."

"She did?" He turned to Chance. "And what does she think about Marcus now?"

"Oh, you-you seem cool to m-me." She stammered.

"So you approve of my gift bearing to your **girlfriend**?"

"No... I mean, yes, I-I do. But she's not my girlfriend. I mean, she, we are not gay. We are just two girls who are friends. That's it."

"And you're not jealous? Because you seem a little jelly to me."

"Oh, no. Why would I be jealous? We are friends and she likes men. We both do."

"Chance? Are you okay girl? You look a little pale." Karisma was concerned about the drastic change in her friend's behavior.

"No, I'm f-fine. I just realized I didn't eat any breakfast. Um, can we go? I mean, uh, can we go to the food court? I need something to eat."

"Sure, let's go."

"I'll go with you." Chance's heart sank into her stomach, but thankfully Karisma saved the day.

"I wish you could, but today is Girl's day. Girls only. Sorry."

"Yea, it's just me and my girl today." Chance was trying to sound nonchalant but it came off as a nervous, jittery wreck.

"Maybe some other time then."

"Yea, if I ever have another day off."

"I'm sure Big Boi will find it in his big, fat, greasy heart, to give you guys another day off together. That way we can hang out and your friend will see that she can trust me with you."

"That's a big, fat maybe."

"Wilder things have happened. Right Chance?"

"Yea, at the club! W-wild things h-happen every day! You know, like, huh, yea. Um, so can we go? I need to sit down a minute."

"Sure thing. Goodbye Marcus!"

"Until we meet again! Chance, I'll catch you later."

"Huh, yea. L-later."

When they were out of ear shot, Kindness couldn't help but to question whether Marcus and Chance knew each other.

"Have you ever met him before?"

"Who?"

"You know who!"

"Oh, M-Marcus. Yea, well no, not really. I mean, he comes in the club sometimes, but I didn't know his name was Marcus."

"You seem a little nervous, scared even. Have you ever had any dealings with him?"

"Who? Marcus?"

"Yes, Marcus!!"

"Unh Uhn. Nope. I've never had any dealings with Marcus."

"Are you sure?"

"Positive."

"O-kay. Well, let me get you a table and then I'll buy us something to eat."

"Sounds good."

When Karisma walked away from the table, Chance began to look around, searching to see where he was. She knew he didn't leave. He had to have been following them all morning. Her phone buzzed in her hand. She looked at the caller id. *It was Money!* She didn't answer. Her phone buzzed again. It was a text. *Answer the phone you stupid trick, before I get my girls to show you some new new. I know you had fun with my lesbian clique. Yea, you won't try that again will you!! ANSWER THE PHONE!!!*

"Buzz, buzz! Buzz, buzz!"

"What!"

"Oh, now you're brave! A few minutes ago, you were shaking in your little cowgirl boots!!"

"Money, what are you doing here?"

"What do you mean, what am I doing here? Trick I can go wherever I please!! This is my town!!"

"You know what I mean. She's going to figure it out eventually."

"Figure what out?"

"That you are not Marcus."

"Awww, Pumpkin. I'm just having a little fun."

"Urrgh, I hate it when you call me that!"

"And?" She let that go for now. As long as he knew she hated it, he would call her by the nickname as much as possible.

"What she do anyway?"

"Never you mind that Pumpkin. And why do you even care? You gettin extra for helping me out with her to go on **your** bill, and you still haven't met the halfway mark! You worry about that!"

"This girl is a good person. She doesn't deserve to be in these streets like I do."

"Since you like her so much, **you** can pay her due."

"No! I-I can't!! I'm working night and day to pay my own due, and you know it!"

"Then you'll work extra hard, because if for some reason she can't meet her expectation, I'm holding you responsible!!!"

"Money! You can't do that!! I'm already exhausted as it is! Working at the club and running X and..."

"You get no pity from me trick. You need to learn to watch that smart mouth of yours before you wind up with a gat in it or somewhere stankin in a ditch!"

"Okay, okay. I'm sorry."

"Ooo, always apologetic after the fact, huh! You forget! You always seem to forget that I-AM-THE-BOSS!! Well, you better start using your brain to think first and ask no questions because foolin around with me can get your life twisted! Remember dat!"

"I'm sorry. M-Money? Hello? HELLO?!" Karisma caught the tail end of the conversation, hustling to the table to help, or ease drop. But she missed the juicy details.

"Chance, what is going on?"

"Nothing."

"Naw, I'm not buying it! What's going on?!"

"Like I said, nothing. It's just my boyfriend. He's trippin about this Girl's Day and missin alla dis." She motioned her hands the length of her body in a dance. Kindness noticed some young men close by who were entranced by her grace. But that would have to wait.

"You never told me you had a boyfriend."

"I didn't. Girl, I'm sorry. I mean, we have been having some problems. On again, off again. I guess that's why I haven't said anything. But we've been trying to get back together too." She lied.

"Sounds like you're better off without him."

"You're probably right."

There was no probably to it. She was exactly right. Life without Money would be like the salvation through Jesus Christ that Kindness always talked about. If being in debt to Money was like sin then she definitely needed salvation! Kindness reached into the bag and pulled out the food, placing a clear container in front of Chance.

"Here, I got you a salad."

"A salad?!"

"Yea. You looked pale. I didn't want to get you nothin heavy."

"Well, I aint no salad type of chick! I am a carnivore; I need some meat!" Just then a fine, six foot plus, chocolatey specimen of a man walked by. He looked back and licked his lips. "Ooh, and some de-ssert!"

"You're hopeless!" Karisma laughed.

"Unh Uhn, I got hope. I hope he walk back by so I can get a handful of meat!"

"Front or back?!"

"Ei-ther one! Mmm!" They laughed.

Kindness noticed her friend was back to normal, but she hadn't eaten one bite yet. Hmm, something fishy is going on here. Although she was very suspicious, she said nothing else on the subject. She was just glad girl's day was still on and that she could have one day of familiarity. *Sin is kickin my butt!*

"Hey, let's do something wild."

"You know I love wild. What you wanna do?"

"How about **we**, not drink anymore alcohol or smoke any more weed for the rest of the day?"

"You call that wild?"

"Yea, considering we always do it. Wild is something out of the ordinary."

"Lady K, you crazy!"

"No, I'm serious. Just one day. I mean, we can survive just one day without being high and drunk, can't we? Our lives aren't that bad that we have to live behind a curtain of haze."

Chance was staring at her like a flower was growing out of the top of her head. But when she realized the girl was for real, she shook her curls.

"I don't know what life you lookin at but from where I sit if it got any worse, I'd be dead!"

"We don't want that."

"No we don't. But if you want to skip the high and the buzz, that's on you. More power to you. I just can't do it."

"If you don't, I can't."

"Why not?"

"Cause if I smell it, I wanna hit it!"

"You got that right! And speaking of **it**!! Wanna go in the bathroom and fire up another honey glaze?"

"Yup! But what we gone do with this food?"

"Put it back in the bag."

"Unh Uhn. I ain't takin no food in the bathroom with me. That's nasty!"

"Fine. How about we smoke in the car?"

"Now that's what I'm talkin about. Besides I got a couple more malls I wanna hit before we see the movie."

"What movie we goin to see any who?"

"I told you, we will…"

"Decide when we get there."

"Exactly."

"Okay. Let's go!"

The girls grabbed their bags and headed for the escalator. Suddenly Chance was aware that they were being followed. But it wasn't Money in person. It was one of his thugs. The very one she could not bare to see… Jug! He looked like a jug, big and empty-headed. But he was loyal to Money. Number one dumb thug. Jug was the only one who knew everything Money was mixed up in. He went with him every where, except to get his hair cut. For some reason, Money never let anyone go to Curls salon. He even drove himself. It was the only place completely off limits. And she was the only woman in his circle not under his rule. *Maybe that was the reason. Maybe…* She already didn't want to go back to work tomorrow and she could tell Karisma was growing tired of of the lifestyle. It was about time for the final stage of this gig. *I'm not looking forward to this!*

# Chapter 8:  Firm Foundation

Growing up in the church was very easy for Kindness.  She loved God and her family so much.  When she was a little girl, her mother used to tell her that God gifted her with countless talents because He created her intelligent and with a kind heart. He knew she would use the gifts wisely.  However, she did not feel very wise right now.  Just five short months ago she was a minister in training and leader over David's Daughters Dance Ministry at Greater United Baptist Church.  She loved to dance. It was like a stress reliever.  When she felt down and out, all she had to do was put some worship music on and start to move.  Soon an entire dance was choreographed and she felt enlightened, like she did not have a care in the world.  That is, when she used to dance for the Lord.


Now her name had been changed to Karisma and she was dancing at Queen City in Atlanta, and though she hated it with a passion, it was necessary that she continue.  It was literally a life-or-death situation, for herself, her brother and possibly even their parents.  If she did not move forward and bring in the big bucks to pay off her brother's kidnappers, they promised to kill him then hang him from the church steeple. After which, they would hunt her down like the dog they assumed she was.  Kindness had no idea where the abhorrence for her and her family was coming from. She only knew that if her brother never came home again, her parents would be devastated.  Their prayers and fasting may not be enough to save Jay from this mess, so she had to do whatever these villains asked of her, at least until God came through.

Karisma sat on her stool in the dressing room, reflecting on the last time she saw her brother face to face.  It was the same day he and her father had gotten into a fist fight.  She was on her way home from Dance and Worship, so amped from their productive practice that she just had to give God the praise. After all of that worship, she needed to get her praise on Holy Hip Hop style.  It was time to turn up.  She was listening to Kingdom Business by Canton Jones, bobbing her head to the beat and singing along when she saw her brother trotting alongside the walkway.  He was looking from left to right and behind him as if he expected someone to jump out and grab him any second.


Kindness pulled into the gas station on the corner, and turned around to check out his odd behavior.  When she reached him, she noticed he was very angry and seemed a bit disoriented, even frightened.  She tried to talk to him and ask what was going on with him but he immediately shut down, as he was prone to at the time.  So, she just spoke from the heart.

*"Lil brother, you know I love you right?"* He nodded though he did not return her intense gaze.  He could never look her in the eyes when she was being sincere; it made him emotional and he was too hard to be acting weak.  That's what Marcus would have told him if he saw the tears welling up in his eyes. Jay blinked hard and fast trying to fight back tears and Kindness used the opportunity to continue her speech.

*"I've noticed that you have not been the same lately, and I want you to know that if you need to talk, you can still come to me.  No matter how bad the situation may seem, I will do all that I can to help."  She paused, and reached to turn his face towards hers and said, "I Promise!  I'm here for you.  Do you hear me?"* Tears started to roll down his cheeks and he felt like a little boy all over again. She always did this to him but he never hated it as much as he did right now. Firmly wiping away the evidence, resentment returned to his spirit, which was made evident in his voice.

*"Yeah sure! I hear you!"  Jay took a deep breath and turned his back to Kindness and said in an anxious tone, "Well I gotta go. I'm late for an appointment."*

*"An appointment? With who?"* Kindness was astonished. Who could he have an appointment with and about what? She waited for a response but he gave none.

*He started jogging away in the same direction he was headed before, yelling back to her, "You wouldn't know him!" Not yet anyway...*

Kindness looked on helplessly as he disappeared into the distance. The feeling that she should run after him or follow him or something, overwhelmed her, but she did nothing. She stood statuesque, frozen solid in reflection, until the bubble guts started coming on like it did when she was a little girl in trouble with her parents.  Something in her spirit felt heavy and the need to dance swept her over once again.  She had to get away but her body felt like it didn't want to move. *I should do something!* She didn't know what to do but crying was not an option. Dismissing the urge, she questioned herself.

*"What is wrong with me? Maybe I'm just being over protective?"*

Slowly she regained some composure. Walking back to her car, she weighed the options of what to do next.  She really wanted to go in search for her brother but thought better of it for now, but definitely had to do something to release this heaviness threatening to steal her joy.  Settling back into the car she ejected her praise CD and searched for some worship music.  She needed to talk to the Lord and get her peace back. And all though the music was relaxing, there was only one thing she knew of that successfully lifted up her vive. The decision made, she headed back to the church for some much-needed P&D.  The necessity to pray and dance had become a regular ritual for Kindness. So regular in fact, that she gave the event the nick name P&D, Prayer and Dance.

When a car passed by going the other way, she realized her windshield was filthy and wished she had sent her car to be cleaned earlier that day when the opportunity was given.  *I could take it to one of those automatic car wash thingys* she thought, but she really needed to get to the church and release this stress that was increasingly building up inside her belly. She reached for the windshield washer button and thought she saw something out of the corner of her eye. Through the hazy film on the windshield, she could have sworn some guys were forcing a young man into the backseat of a black Ford F350, double cab, chromed out.

*Nice ride, but I've never seen it around here before.  I wonder who that is and what they are doing in the suburbs?* It was obviously a hood type of vehicle, the way it was tricked out. Despite the slight distraction, Kindness stayed her course. Yet she couldn't help but wonder if she should have stopped him and asked questions.  Suddenly she got woozy and her stomach clinched with fear.  The light clicked on in her head just as bright as the morning sun. *Oh my God, that was my little brother they forced into that truck!*

Returning from a horrific reflection to the harsh life which had become her reality, seemed a bilateral move, neither one any better than the other, inadvertently Lady K murmured under her breath.

"It happened so fast.  I should have done something.  There had to have been some other alternative than to end up stripping in this hell hole to save him."  She dropped her head and tears started to flow. "I don't want to dance anymore, not like this! Lord, Please help me!"

Her head was still bowed, body shaking violently as she cried. She was very near a nervous breakdown.

"This life is not a life I would have ever chosen for myself," she continued through the tears.

Chance had been standing in the doorway watching her, not knowing what to say to ease the pain. She remained there in silence for a moment then she started to walk away. Karisma was totally unaware of Chance's presence, until the floor creaked under her feet as she turned. Her head jerked up abruptly catching her friend in mid stride. She called for her through drunken tears.

"Chance?"

"Dang," Chance said softly under her breath, turning around to re-enter the room. It wasn't that she didn't want to help, she just didn't know how.

"Yeah, it's me Lady K." It was her nickname for her friend. She always told her she was too much of a lady to be dancing for Big Boi. Chance came in, sat her bag on the table and commenced caring for her friend as best she could.

"What's wrong with you today?"

"I don't know. I can't really put my finger on it. I'm just tired." She lied, tears rolling.

"Tired? I don't know. I mean, I've seen you upset before, especially in the beginning when it was your turn to dance, but today you seem a little hysterical, ya know? Out of control! Maybe if you take a vacation, or at least the night off, you'll feel better."

"No, no, no.... I can't. I can't afford to take the risk of not meeting my mark for this week. I have to work every day just to get close. If *I* miss today, I surely won't be able to come up with the money before Saturday."

Chance had befriended Kindness when she first came to the club, showing her the ropes. She taught her every dance trick she knew to make the big bucks. Kindness's background in dance helped her catch on pretty fast, and since she was 'fresh meat' the money started rolling in quickly. So, fast it scared her. It scared her even more that she didn't hate the fast cash flow! Well, at least in the beginning she didn't have a problem with it. It was becoming addictive. But all too soon the glamour vanished and there was nothing left but pain and low self-esteem. Before long she couldn't even approach the stage without a little help. It started with a couple of drinks, then escalated to smoking marijuana and hitting a bump or two 'just to loosen up' Chance explained. But now she had to get drunk and high just to walk out on stage or to even want to dance. Today her routine did not change, but something had changed, something on the inside. She was more than tired! She was spiritually drained!!

"Karisma, you are on in five minutes," the voice blared over the intercom. "I hope you're drunk and high enough to make it through the night, because it's going to be a good one! I don't know how this new girl is going to work out so I'm counting on you! She did okay last night, but consistency is the key to a good business. She aint proved that like you have! So, get yo butt up the ramp and make that money!"

The voice loomed over the dressing room intercom like a ghost in the night tormenting her soul. Big Boi was not like the devil himself, but definitely one of his minions. He was an associate of Money's. Evil company loves evil company. But he was the lesser of the two evils. Thoughts of the first time she heard the epitome of evil in her holy ears came rushing back. The night they took her brother.

Kindness had gone on to the church and prayed that Jay would try to contact her. She hoped he was okay and that he knew the people who pushed him into the car. God answered her prayers swiftly because as she was pulling up in the driveway of her parent's house, her cell phone rang. What she heard next confirmed her earlier convictions that it was her brother who had been stuffed into the backseat of that truck. The words, "***WE GOT YOUR BROTHER***!" cut into her soul fiber like a double-edged sword.

Swallowing hard to calm her nerves, she tried to sound as nonchalant as possible replying, *"What? Who is we? Who is this?"*

*"Alright you got me. It's not really we, just me. It just sounds better when you say we, don't it boys?"*

Kindness could hear faint laughter and grunts in the background, then total silence at his command.

*"So, what do I call you?"*

*"You? You can call me Lover or better yet God!"*

The sound of his voice made her heart skip a beat and not in a good way. She ignored his name requests, brushing them off as absurdity and ignorance.

*"Can I speak to him?"*

*"Who?"*

*"You know who. My brother?"*

*"NO! Not until you call me Lover,"* he snarled.

She was overwhelmed by the fact that her brother was kidnapped, but couldn't bear saying the word. She couldn't? She wouldn't! But still she struggled to find what to say next.

*"I – I can't call you that. I don't even know who you are. And even if I did, I wouldn't want to call you- that!*

*"Well, if you can't do that for me then I can't do anything for you."*

*"Well, if you won't let me talk to him, how do I know you have him?"*

*"You don't! You'll just have to take my word for it."*

*"Then why did you call me? And how did you get my number?"*

He gave an eerie laugh that made her skin crawl.  Sickness in the pit of her stomach worsened, however it was overshadowed by anger, an anger she had never felt before. She repeated in a much louder and determined voice.

*"Why did you call me?"*

The man stopped laughing speaking stony, cold and serious.  His reply was more of a command than an answer. She could tell he wasn't used to answering to anyone.

*"You, Kindness, not anybody else, will deliver $2000 every week to me.  You can't get it from your parents, your pastor or any of your friends, old or new.  You have to work for it yourself."*  Kindness stammered at the magnitude of his command.

*She stuttered in reply, "B-but I, I don't make that kind of money.  I only work part-time at the college."*

*"Then that leaves you in quite a dilemma.  The money has to be delivered on Saturday of each week."*

He didn't miss a stride. This man didn't care what she didn't have. All he cared about was getting done what he said had to be done. The sickness in her stomach started to increase. It felt like knots were literally forming there. Thoughts were jumbled. She couldn't think straight. Becoming frantic, she struggled not to panic. She had no idea how she would come up with that kind of money.  On cue, pure evil butted into her rambling analysis. He had a plan to solve her money problem.

*"Hey, don't get so down. Maybe I can help you find a way to get the money up every week. I have several friends who have their own businesses. Since you have no way of getting the money, here are your three options and you must choose one. So choose carefully!"*

*"No wait! I didn't ask for your help."*

*"And I didn't ask for your opinion!"* He laughed with evil delight, while Kindness morbidly contemplated possible choices.

*"Option number one,"* he continued, *"you can sell X pills for a young man I like to call X-avier. He has an entire building operating and there are even police guards, you know dirty cops."*

When she didn't respond, he maliciously continued.

*"Oh, you don't like that one. Okay. Option number two, you can turn tricks for my buddy L-Dog. He paruses a lot of establishments and has clients high end and low. I think he would want to reserve a little sweet thing like you for the high-end clientele. Don't you think?"*

She still said nothing. On the other end she was horrified. Who is this guy?

*"No. Okay. This is your final option but I think you'll find it a milder solution than the first two. I mean girls do it all the time and it counts like a real job. You can put this one on your resume."*

*Hopeful, she queried, "What is it?"*

*"Oh, finally you can talk again. Welcome back Kindness!"*

*"Just tell me what it is you bastard!"*

Her words hit home. He had a father, but one day he just stopped coming by to see him. It was a big part of the reason why he was the way he was.

*"O, ho, feisty little thing aren't you?"* She could tell he liked that side of her better than the innocent, holier than thou attitude, though she offered nothing more for kindling.

*"Fiery K!"* He said, prolonging the matter intentionally to annoy her.

*"The other option please."*

*"Your third and final option is you can dance at a strip club for this guy named Shane. The girls call him Big Boi. Now, I do know the man but he irks me, always trying to be my best friend and sucking up."*

*"And you don't like that?"*

*"No I love it, from beautiful, subservient women! But from a sloppy, hot wind eating, diabetes having idiot? No! I don't want to have any contact with him. And, here's the clincher. You'll go and he will be expecting you. All you have to do is mention my name and he gone put you straight to work. He'll be happy you can really dance. He might even try to solicit favors, but that's entirely up to you."* She cringed as he continued,

*"When you're hired, no one must know of our deal. If you rat me out to anyone, I will find out! I have eyes everywhere. And there will be repercussions. Your punishment will not be the death of your brother. Instead, there will be complete mutilation. I'll have my guys cut off every extremity of his body with a chainsaw while he's still alive and hang his torso from the church steeple, mailing the remains of his limbs, ears and nose to your loving and God-fearing parents. Do you understand?"*

*"I do."*

She was horrified but didn't want to prolong the conversation. There was no way she was going to allow her family to be hurt like that, especially her brother.

*"Aww, I didn't even ask baby, but maybe one day if you act right!"* He laughed once again.

He was trying to brutalize her mind, and it was working. Just the vision of her brother's torso hanging from the church steeple made her stomach churn. She was about to lose her dinner. Right in the nick of time she opened the car door and spilled the contents of her stomach onto their front lawn. She could hear him. He was laughing as the forceful retching brought her to her knees. Finally, she gasped for air. Praying for strength, she picked up her cell phone and faced her assailant. She could not speak but he could hear her breathing.

*"Are you okay? I mean, I need you to stay healthy so you can get that money. Your brother's life depends on it. So I ask you again. Are you okay?"*

*"Yea, as okay as I can be under these circumstances!"*

*"Great! So which option will you be taking, one, two or three? Remember these are the only choices you have so you better choose wisely. Just think of which one you would be better at because on every Saturday night you'd better have my money or on Sunday morning little brother will be the topic of every preacher's sermon!"*

For some reason she believed every word he said. Something in his voice. Hatred. Pain. Disgust. Betrayal. There had to be a reason why he was doing this to her and her family, but she couldn't come up with a valid reason to save her life.

She wiped her mouth on her sleeve and coughed nervously before muttering, *"I like to dance. I can dance really well like you said."*

*"Then option number three it is. I will have my contact at the club talk to the owner and I will be in touch with you on tomorrow morning. You will start your new job on next Monday so make sure to tell mommy and daddy not to wait up! The big bucks don't start rolling in until after 1 o'clock am."*

The phone went dead and she sat numb in the car for only God knows how long. She tried to pull herself together before entering the foyer of her parent's home, but when she opened the front door she realized the issue was more complicated than she thought. Her dad was lying on the couch with bandages on his face, and her mother was scrubbing blood from the wall and carpet. She was appalled.

*"What have we done to deserve this?!!" she screamed.*

The tears started to flow again and she did not have to worry about explaining why her eyes were puffy. Running to her father's side, she knelt beside his head. She didn't ask any questions. She didn't say a word. She just hugged him and closed her eyes hoping that he would one day forgive her for what she was being forced to do. Kindness rocked her dad and cried with him until he fell asleep in her lap. Her mother stayed downstairs to keep an eye on him just in case he had a concussion, but insisted Kindness get some rest. She obeyed, but knew there would be no sleep for her that night. She paced and prayed and paced and worried and prayed some more. The night felt like an eternity. When her mother called that breakfast was ready, she declined for the sake of not missing the inevitable phone call that held her new assignment. Besides, she wouldn't be able to keep it down once she heard the putrid sound of his voice.

*"This man is crazy! How am I going to tell my parents? What am I going to tell my parents?" she muttered, pacing from her vanity to the window.*

The sun was just rising. Morning dew shined brilliantly in the light and the sky was a magnificent blue. If only she felt as wonderful as the day looked. The phone rang. She gulped and took a deep breath before answering.

*"Hello?"*

*"Kindness, is this you?"*

She was glad that she had not eaten breakfast because her stomach went queasy just hearing him again.  He was talking to her as if they were old buddies or something. Yep! Certified Lunatic!!

*"Yes, it's me," she replied relunctantly.*

*Once he was assured that the female voice was Kindness, his voice went criminal. "Good. I hope you haven't told anyone about our little deal?"*

*"No, I haven't but I am wondering how in the world to explain this move to my dad."*

*"I'm good at solving problems, maybe I can help you out."*

*"Like you did last night?" she interrupted.*

*"Yeah, like I did last night!" he mocked in an abrasive tone.*

*"I don't think I want to hear any more of your solutions." Her voice shook as she struggled to control emotions.*

*"Tough, because it has just been made a condition of our agreement!" he growled.*

Kindness collapsed on the bed. Her legs no longer having the strength to support her body. Who does this man think he is? He is not in control! God is!! Despite her thoughts, he still ranted commandments. And she had no choice but to listen. He had her brother and she was the only one who could get him back.

*"I have arranged for you to move into an apartment complex around the corner from the club. It wasn't supposed to go into effect for 30 days but it seems you need a place right away."*

*"You got me an apartment?" She was devastated. "I've never lived alone."*

*"Don't worry you won't be home and awake long enough for it to matter, since you will be spending most of your time at the club. It helps to be in close proximity. Wouldn't you agree?"*

*"I suppose so, but how am I going to explain my moving out to my parents?"*

*"Hey you have to figure out the answer to some of your problems on your own. But as far as your moving arrangements and work schedule, they are in the mailbox. You'd better go and get it before the parents find them. Then this thing could get really messy. Or that could be a solution for you. Let them find out the hard way that baby girl's innocence is about to be tainted!"*

*"But..."*

It was too late. He hung up. There were so many questions left unanswered, but she was sure he would happily solve any issues. Introspectively, she decided against asking any more questions. *I'll just do what he says and maybe he will let my brother come home soon. I hope!*

*She managed to live a double life for four weeks before the effects of the club became noticeably apparent to her mom and dad. She was falling asleep at church and becoming more and more irritable at home. Their concern and her seemingly lack thereof was the perfect escape. The answer to her leaving home, which was starting to feel more like prison. They argued for days before she finally told them she was moving out.*

*"I can't take the pressure of being in this house without my brother. I've got to get out of here!" she had said.*

Her parents were devastated. They had always had a firm foundation. Jesus was their rock and His Word always had the final say in the Johnson house. But right now, if anyone new came along, they would have no idea of the calm orderly life they once shared. Their family was falling apart. It had been only six short months ago since the walls started tumbling down, but it felt like a lifetime.

"Karisma are you ready!"

She grimaced at the sound of his voice, shaking her head instead of pressing the intercom button to give Big Boi an answer. He ran "Queen City" but even he had a boss. He was always telling the girls, especially Karisma, how his Boss watched every move they made inside and outside of the club. So if they were making any moves, they'd better be money making moves. *If I get in trouble, every tramp in here gone pay the price! Do-I-make-myself-clear!!* He always bellowed, never just talked to anyone unless he was trying to push up on them.

There was a legend on the streets about his Boss. Not many who had ever seen him lived to tell about it. He was ruthless and feared by everybody on the streets. He was the one person no one wanted to cross. They all worked for him in one way or another. He owned the streets and used the people in it like pawns. When he was done with them, he discarded them in different ways, stripping them of power, money and often their lives. Treated like no more than trash in the gutter. Big Boi was mean and devilish, but Kindness Money was behind every move he made. He had to be if he owned the streets and every worker in it.

"You better pull it together and respond to that fool! You don't want him coming down here looking for you. You know he wants you, **baaad**!" Chance over exaggerated the word to signify just how much Shane wanted Kindness in his bed.

Chance continued, "Don't give him a reason or an opportunity. Get up!" she warned.

Kindness didn't budge. She just sat on the stool in a drunken stupor. *The liquor and weed were working fast tonight. A little too fast!* Chance rushed past her in disgust, pressing the intercom button and reassuring Shane that Karisma would be ready. "Uh, she's in the bathroom Big Boi. She'll be ready in five minutes."

"Well, she goes on in two so she'd better speed things up!"

She wet a towel and put it to Kindness's face. "Girl, you better get a grip. You up next!"

Chance pulled her to her feet as she gulped the last sip of her Brandy and Cranberry juice. Finally taking steps, she stumbled more than walked to the ramp, even with Chance holding her up.

"It's a packed house tonight girl," Chance spoke eagerly. "Fine time for you to make all that money you so desperately need." *Desperate? Kindness thought. She doesn't even know the half.*

"Karisma! Karisma! Karisma!" The crowd had fallen in love with the sassy and talented girl. But she didn't feel like either tonight. *Something is not right!*

"Now for the vixen you all have been ranting for. The vivacious, the curvaceous... Karisma!"

All the people in the club were clapping and cheering, already making it rain on the stage. When she stepped out her eyes wouldn't focus. The lights were so bright she couldn't see a thing and could barely stand up straight in her stilettos. She had to think fast but her mind was not cooperating and neither was her body. She was going down whether she liked it or not, so instead of falling, she used the pole to slide down onto her hands and knees and began to crawl like a panther preparing for the hunt. The crowd went silent. She thought... *I'm not going to make much money this way*! So she kneeled on the floor and started shaking and gyrating.

"Get this drunk skank off the stage!"

The rest of the audience joined in booing and jeering. She wanted to care. She wanted to dance. But it was all she could do just to move and breath. Dancing had never been a struggle but this was more than drunkenness. *Something has gone terribly wrong!* Her breathing was becoming labored.

"I want my money back," one of the patrons screamed, reaching for money off the stage, but security made him think twice about that. More guards were called in for fear of rioting. Karisma brought in a lot of supporters and a lot of money to the club. She was one of the best they'd had in years, which was why everyone was so upset and astonished. Even Chance looked in bewilderment. *Oh my God. Something is not right!* Chance rushed to her aid and pulled her off the stage. They both fell a few times before making it behind the curtain which invoked a shift in the atmosphere from rage to laughter. Glad to be out of sight, Chance toiled to help her friend to a more secure area. It seemed like forever, but she finally managed to reach the dressing room with Karisma almost on her neck.

"Whew girl you heavy!" She sat her down on a bar stool. "Sit tight I'll be right back. Maybe you just need to cool down. Your body is on fire!"

She ran to get another wet towel and something cool and non-alcoholic to drink. When she returned Kindness was in the same place swaying back and forward, singing a gospel song, almost toppling over with each sway. *She must have had too much to drink or something.*

"We shall overcome. We shall overcome. We shall overcome, someday-ay-ay-ay-ay!"

"You'd better overcome **today**! Do you have any idea how mad Big Boi is right now. Once he quiets that crowd, you know he's coming for you don't you?!"

"We shall overcome, some..."

"Karisma? Get a grip!" She shook her friend who grew more silent with each jerk. "Now tell me, what happened out there?" Chance inquired.

Kindness could hear her talking but did not have the energy to respond, besides she had the faintest idea what happened. All she knew for sure was that she felt downright weird, past drunk and high. Her body was not responding as it should and she couldn't keep her eyes opened. Her strength was failing so she knew she couldn't try to stand. Chance continued talking making suggestions to Kindness on how to get it together before Big Boi Shane found her.

"You need to just take some time off and rest your body. From the looks of it you are fatigued. You can hide in my car for now and I'll give you a ride home after my show if you......"

Her voice trailed off into the distance. It seemed that Chance's chatter was lulling her into a lethargic state. She was blacking in and out and had to strain just to decipher the words being spoken, apparently at lightning speed. The words sounded jumbled together, like she was sticking her head out of a moving car and words rushed past her ears like scenery. Soon she couldn't even make out Chance's voice. She was losing control. She felt like the life was being drained from her soul. She was dying! *I need to get back to Jesus and fast!*

"I don't wanna go to hell!" She finally managed to say, stunning her friend to silence. There was a sudden need to jump up and run. *Where? There's nowhere I can run to escape this fiasco imprisoning my life!*

"Jesus, help me!! I don't want to go to hell!!!" Karisma screamed!

The urgency to spring forth was denied by reality. She should never have tried it, but unfortunately, she did. It was all her body could do to stand up straight. With the residue of strength, she had left, she came to her feet, and then it happened. She completely blanked out.

Chance watched in horror as her friend fell straight to the floor like fresh cut timber. Her body did not collapse as most do when they pass out, instead her knees locked. There was no buckling of her legs to ease the fall. Terror struck Chance's heart when she realized Kindness was too close to the solid glass table which doubled as a mirror for the girls on rush nights. She reached for her but unable to consolidate a hold, Kindness slipped right through her fingers head first into the table. The corner of the structure sliced into her right temple and slivers of glass went everywhere. Blood was running profusely from her head. Chance screamed. She hated the sight of blood. She had been given the opportunity to nurse once, but hating needles and blood led her to Queen City. No way was she going to steal and falsify records just so Money could kill at will, and no telling what else he was hiding.  Prostitution was out too. The only thing left for a young girl to do, in the eyes of Money, was to deliver and dance.

"Heeelp! Help me! Please! Please don't die Karisma! Ple-e-ease!"

The only person who heard her cry was the new girl, Bossy, who was just finishing Karisma's set.  Her striptease was coming to an end, so she was already heading to the dressing room when she heard Chance's ear-piercing shriek.  The young lady took off her heels and rushed to see what was going on.  When she reached the dressing room, Chance was kneeling beside Karisma in tears.  Her head snapped up when the floor creaked under Bossy's feet. The girl looked unsure if she wanted to enter.

"Please," Chance managed to yelp through the trickle of tears and sobs, "Call 911!"

# Chapter 9: Evil Workers

"I'm so sorry Lady K. I'm so sorry. This is all my fault!"

Chance kept repeating over and over how sorry she was as if what happened to Karisma was really her fault. One EMT was working on Karisma the whole way. When the ambulance came to a halt, Chance kissed her on the cheek before the driver opened the door. In an instant they whisked her off to surgery. She had lost a lot of blood and even stopped breathing for a short time, but the paramedics revived her. They didn't understand why she stopped breathing though. It was like she didn't want to live, like she wanted to give up on life. Though she had sustained a nasty gash to the side of her head, it wasn't enough to cause death. Chance replayed the event in her head over and over again while sitting in the waiting room.

"I need a drink, a smoke or something!" she said to herself, or at least she thought she was inaudible.

A pregnant woman and her husband were sitting nearby waiting to be taken to the maternity ward, and they overheard her statement. The man was trying not to stare, while his pregnant wife looked at her with disgust, pulling her husband near. Chance had forgotten she was still dressed, or half dressed, for the club. Any other time she would have cursed the both of them out, but she was too worried about Karisma to even think of anything nasty to say. She just rolled her eyes and turned to sit facing the other way. There was a guy sitting on the floor with his back up against the wall. Chance noticed a pack of Newports hanging out of his pocket.

"Excuse me?"

He didn't respond. His eyes were closed, while he held his wrapped hand above his head. It was then that she saw the cloth was stained with blood. Chance sympathized but not too much. She needed something to take the edge off of her nerves, so she tried again.

"Excuse me? Excuse me sir, sitting on the floor, in the black leather jacket, with the cigarettes in his left pocket?!"

The young man slowly opened his eyes to slits so that she could barely tell they were opened. He had been ignoring her because of the pain in his hand and was terribly annoyed at her persistence. At least until he got a good look at her. Suddenly he was energized.

"Well, hello!"

"Hi," she said, humoring him for the sake of the cigarettes.

"What can I do you for miss lady?"

"I see you are in a lot of pain and I am sorry to ask this question, but could I bum a couple of squares until…" she had forgotten for a split second that she left all of her stuff back at the club.

"Until when?"

"I was gonna say until I go to my car, but I forgot I rode in the ambulance with her. She fell and hurt her head real bad. Got a huge gash down the right side from her temple to behind her ear, and my nerves are so shot right now I just need some nicotine or something to calm myself you know."

"Oh sure, no problem. But you gone have to come get em. I'm in so much pain, I really don't wanna move."

"Gee thanks." She moved quickly grabbing the pack and his lighter, disappearing out of the sliding doors before he could think to protest.

He didn't care. Jeff just wanted to get a closer look at her and maybe even a whiff. And he got both and found his assumption to be true. She looked and smelled beautiful. He couldn't help hoping to see her again. Maybe she wouldn't thieve the entire pack, then she would have to bring back the remainder of his squares. He laughed to himself. Beautiful…

Chance chain smoked all but two of the young man's cigarettes while waiting on the verdict of her friend. When she walked back into the waiting room, he was gone. Probably, finally getting to see a doctor for his own affliction, he hoped she would steal the whole pack. It was never her intention, but from the looks of the men and the hate from the women, she didn't know how much more waiting she could take. However, since she was acting as next of kin, she stood her ground. At any rate, she almost lost it when she could no longer hide from the gaze of the older gentleman beside her who had been making goo goo eyes the entire time. She cringed. Old men gave her the creeps. She had to deal with them so much at work, that outside the job, outside of work, she hated old men. They gave her the heebie jeebies, as Karisma would say. Some of them even made her stomach hurt and to think of being intimate with them or letting them touch her was sickening. She moved to a seat that was facing away from the man and felt momentary relief until he moved back into her line of sight. They had been playing this little cat and mouse game for about three hours and she was near to screaming when an angel called out to her.

"Miss?" It was the nurse and two doctors.

The bottom almost fell out of her stomach causing her to forget all about her ER episodes. *Please don't tell me she is in a coma, or worse, dead!*

"Yes ma'am, sir?" she queried nervously.

"Um do you know this young lady very well."

"No sir, not really. All I know is her name is Karisma. We -uh, work together."

"Well, I'm going to need to talk to her parents or a significant other about some things. And do you know her last name?"

"I don't know her parents or her last name. And she's not married. I only have her address. She stays in a one-bedroom apartment right around the corner from the cl-, our job."

"Please Miss, think. Is there anyone you could call who may know how to contact the young ladies' parents?"

She knew someone, but dared not call him. He was the reason they all were caught up in this mess. If only she could tell Kindness the whole truth, but they both were safer without her knowing too much. It's too soon. In due time, the truth will come out.

"Look Mister Dr., you are scaring me! Just tell me if my friend is okay and we can talk about the rest later."

"Alright. I understand this must be hard for you. We had to give Karisma two pints of blood during surgery and we still couldn't get all of the glass out of her head. There is a sharp sliver stretching behind her eye sockets, threatening to sever both of her optical nerves. We could go in and try to remove it, but there is a possibility that she will be blind once the surgery is complete. We can't do the surgery without her parents' permission, or that of a next of kin. Now, I relieved the pressure behind her eyes but she's going to be in a lot of pain. Until we hear from her parents, we will continue the Dopamine drip in her IV, but if we haven't heard from them within four weeks, we are going to have to operate. To rest her optical cavity, her eyes will remain wrapped. And..."

"And? And what!?"

"I don't want you to panic, but we had to induce a coma, until she heals a little more. She'll come out of it on her own in time. However, if she awakens and you are there, please don't let her take the wrap off. It's going to be hard enough on her as it is. Oh yeah, and don't tell her about the potential risks of surgery. Let me handle that. Okay?"

"No problem. You don't have to worry about me blabbing. I wouldn't know how to go about it anyway. I mean what would I say? How would I even begin to tell her about things I'm not even sure of myself. You know what I mean? I mean, um..."

"Miss, it's okay. You'll be fine and so will your friend. I just need for you to calm down, okay." The nurse said sensing Chance's agitation and confusion. Dr. Harris walked away.

"Okay."

"What's your name?"

"Chance."

"Chance, I'm Nurse Abbey and this is Dr. Reid, the ER doctor." She grabbed her by the hand, "Would you like to see your friend?"

"Yes please. Thank you so much."

"You're welcome. And Chance, can we count on you not to disclose any of the information we've discussed about Karisma?"

"Yes ma'am. You can trust me. I mean I wouldn't even know what to say..."

"Good." She cut her off before any more babbling could take place. "Follow me."

Remembering one more puzzling piece in this case, Dr. Reid stopped the two of them to inquire of Chance.

"Miss, uh..."

"Chance," Nurse Abbey reminded him respectfully.

"Right. Ms. Chance? Do you have any knowledge that Ms. Karisma was on any drugs?"

"No sir. I mean, we, all the girls at the club drink and smoke weed from time to time. And maybe a little bump here and there. But honestly, I don't know what Karisma was on tonight."

"Do you remember her behavior? Did she act weird?"

"Yes, as a matter of fact she did. I was horrified. I kept trying to help her out but she seemed to be hallucinating. And she was talking to herself and swaying. She couldn't keep her eyes opened and she was weak. Oh yeah, and her body was on fire! I put cold rags on her and gave her a cool drink but nothing helped."

"Mhmm. Okay thank you." He turned to walk away.

"Um, Mr. Dr. Why do you ask about her behavior tonight?"

"I'm not usually supposed to discuss narcotics information to anyone except family and police, but since you're her friend and I'm concerned you may get hurt, I'll tell you. Ms. Karisma had traces of Rohypnol in her blood, commonly known on the street as roofies. It wasn't enough to claim dependency, but someone definitely slipped her a Mickey. Rohypnol has been associated with date rape, and has also been called the "Forget Pill," "Trip-and-Fall," and "Mind-Erasers." In combination with alcohol, it can induce a blackout with memory loss and a decrease in resistance. Girls and women around the country have reported being raped after being involuntarily sedated with Rohypnol, which was often slipped into their drink by an attacker. The drug has no taste or odor so the victims don't realize what is happening. About ten minutes after ingesting the drug, the woman may feel dizzy and disoriented, simultaneously too hot and too cold, or nauseated. She may experience difficulty speaking and moving, and then pass out. Such victims have no memories of what happened while under the drug's influence. Some effects of the drug begin within thirty minutes, peak within two hours, and can persist for up to eight hours. It is commonly reported that persons who become intoxicated on a combination of alcohol and Rohypnol, have "blackouts" lasting eight to twenty-four hours following ingestion. Disinhibition, or losing your social inhibitions, is another widely reported effect of Rohypnol, when taken alone or in combination with alcohol. Adverse effects of Rohypnol use include, decreased blood pressure, memory impairment, drowsiness, visual disturbances, dizziness, confusion, gastrointestinal disturbances and urinary retention. I know that sounds like a lot, but I feel the need to educate as many young women, especially in your profession, to be very cautious when accepting drinks from anyone, especially ones you didn't see being poured. Promise?"

Nodding, she said, "I promise." He could tell she was thinking so he waited to see what she would add.

"Now that you mention it Mr. Doctor, there was some strange thangs going on during her dance. She was on hands and knees, prowling like a lioness or something."

Nurse Abbey snickered a little before recovering. "I think the doctor means that a person who has ingested Rohypnol could very well hallucinate, as you stated your friend did."

"Oh yeah. She did that too," Chance said, a little embarrassed. *Is she trying to show out in front of the doctor?*

In reflection, she did remember seeing Shane at the bar. He slipped the tender a couple of bills. She didn't miss a thing especially when it comes to money. It wasn't the first time she'd seen him do that, so she thought nothing of it. But since Big Boi had been trying to get into Karisma's pants since she arrived, this could very well be his doing. *Wonder if I should mention it to the good doctor?* He broke into her thoughts.

"Ms. Chance?"

"Yes Doc."

"The behavior you spoke of, was it out of the norm for Ms. Karisma?"

"Yes, very! I mean she's a really good dancer. She brings in a lot of tips... a lot!" She nudged him a little, "...if you know what I mean."

He didn't feed into her insinuation that he may have been to the bar before, but he had. He remembered seeing both girls. And Chance was right. She was a really good dancer. Before mentioning any of this to the police, he decided to do a little test at the club.

"Is there anyone you know of who may have done this?"

"Not right off hand, but if you're going to investigate, I would start at the bar. During premium hours, there is only one bartender Big Boi Shane trusts."

"Okay great. After I run a few more tests, we'll have something concrete to tell the police."

"Rrrright." Chance may not have all the book knowledge but she was street smart and man smart. She knew how to survive and she knew how to read a man. The ER doctor knew he would have to use a disguise to hide from Chance and possibly wear a wire to get evidence that someone at the club was doing this to young ladies, mostly dancers. There had been a couple of rape accusations, but no name was given by any of the girls. It was like they were terrified of this man or of someone. I have every intention of finding out who!

"Mr. Doctor."

"Yes, young lady."

"What does adverse and inhibition mean?"

Nurse Abbey couldn't help but snicker again, trying to relieve the inquisition.

"Chance, Dr. Reid is very busy and really needs to get back to work. Why don't you Google those definitions instead of weighing on the doctor? Unless you have something else to add that would help this young lady's case that will be all!" She said sternly. *Oh, so you wanna show out huh!*

"Sooo, Doc, as I was saying," she got right in between the doctor and Nurse Abbey then turned her back to the woman. *Oh no this heifer didn't!!* "Care to elaborate on those definitions."

Doctor Reid couldn't help but to get tickled. But he needed to diffuse the situation because he did have work to do, just not at the hospital. He wanted to jump right on his new assignment. *I always wanted to be a detective.*

"Ms. Chance, adverse just means an unpleasant result and inhibition means self-consciousness. Your friend experienced something that took her completely out of her character, that's why she acted strangely and passed out."

"Oh, okay. Thank you doctor."

Nurse Abbey was fuming but only stood by in silence with her arms folded. She had hoped the doctor would back her up on the Google comment, but instead he obliged this disrespectful little twit. He must have good reason. The doctor smiled at the young lady as he turned to walk away, which didn't help Nurse Abbey feel any better.

"Remember, this is confidential information. Got it!"

"Yes sir. I won't tell nobody. I mean who would I tell. They'd only find a way to blame it on me anyway, like they always do. And,"

"Good."

The doctor left at the confirmation that Chance understood not to blab, though Nurse Abbey was not so optimistic. Still upset, she led Chance down the corridor of the ER in silence and they disappeared through the double doors.

Jeff watched her walk cautiously behind the nurse, trying not to be sexy, as if she could hide it. A blind man could see her sex appeal.

"Chance." He muttered as the double doors shut behind her.

On the other side of the doors, Nurse Abbey led Chance to Karisma's room then proceeded back to the nurses' station. Chance couldn't believe all that had happened. She looked at her friend with her head all wrapped up, blood seeping through the gauze.

"Oh, Lady K," she muttered.

Taking a deep breath, she continued to talk to herself.

"I wonder who I should call first? Or should I call anyone? They just gone blame me for everything anyway." Chance mumbled.

Her phone rang and she jumped. It took her a little off guard, but even before looking at the caller id, she knew who was on the other end. It was Shane! *That pig!!* Chance cleared her throat before answering.

"Hello?"

"Don't hello me stupid trick! Why haven't you called me? You were supposed to call as soon as you got to the hospital. That was five hours ago!"

"I-I'm sorry Shane! I forgot you even told me to call." There was no recollection of him being anywhere near the EMTs when they came to pick up Karisma. Matter of fact, he disappeared.

"I didn't! It's like an unspoken rule fool! Get your butt back to the club. Y'all making me miss my money. If it had not been for Bossy, both of y'all's butts would be in a sling! But don't think you getting off easy and Karisma better get ready once she can leave that hospital. Y'all working overtime until you pay me back for last night and any other time you miss! Got it?!"

"Yea. Um, Shane?"

"What?!!"

"I don't think she is going to be coming back anytime soon."

"She'd better! She owes me a thousand dollars for that glass table she busted with her head!"

"She passed out Shane! She's in a coma! I'm looking at her right now laying in this bed unconscious!!! And from the looks of it she may not be back for a real long time!" *This idiot is ridiculous!*

"Who you yelling at?!"

Chance wanted to say, "*You!*" but all she said was, "No one."

She couldn't afford to mess up this gig. Shane was a hand full but right now he was the least of her worries. There were bigger, darker predators in the ocean, harder to kill than a shark like him.

"That's what I thought! Now get your butt back here and make it snappy! Until your girl gets well, you working double shifts!!"

"Big Boi! Now you know that's not fair! I had to come with her. Somebody had to ride and make sure she was okay, besides I got some news for you."

"What?" He waited nervously.

"The doctor said someone had to have put something in her drink. Something called roofies. Anyway, they call it the date rape drug and,"

"I know what it is Chance!"

"My bad Big Boi. You sound a little worried. Any reason why that is?"

"I'm not nervous, I just want her to get better so she can come back and help me make this money." He was probably sweating like a Hebrew slave. *Breathing makes him tired!* She laughed at the thought. Karisma was a trip. She always found a way to make the girls laugh after one of Shane's non-pep talks.

"Alright Shane. I'll see you tonight. And don't be nervous. They don't know you put that pill in her drink."

"I didn't- You tramp! Ugh!"

Dnnnng. The dial tone was a joy compared to the obnoxious sound of his voice. He sounded like he had a mouth full of hot potatoes and was about to pass out from lack of oxygen. Probably was true as obese as he was. He looked like he was always stashing away food for the winter, even in the winter. That's what Karisma used to say about him. *And he always smells like fried chicken! Who smells like fried chicken? And in the middle of the night? Hmph! Hmph!* They laughed all night about that one. Already she missed her.

"Girl, I hope you are okay in there."

She whispered in her friend's ear, kissed her on the cheek, grabbed the bag Nurse Abbey gave her to put her skimpy clothes in and walked out of the sliding doors in scrubs and hospital issue socks. When she stepped off of the sidewalk to cross the street, a stretch limo cut off her path. She wanted to bolt but was too afraid of catching bullets in her back. The door opened and she stood rigid, terrified to move. Out of the darkness of the vehicle, one of Money's ruffians jumped out and dragged her into the car before the chauffeur sped off into the sunrise.

"Chance. What's up baby? Nice threads!!" He snarled.

"M-Money..." It was all she could think to say. She knew she should have called him as soon as the ambulance pulled into the hospital, but being so distraught she fell out of protocol.

"Now Chance. What was our agreement?"

"I set up the interview with Shane for Kindness and you give me a $5000 bonus and $1000 per week if I keep her out of trouble."

"Aaand?"

"And, I'm supposed to watch out for her and make sure she gets paid so you get your money."

"Aaand?"

"And, if anything goes wrong, you are the first person I'm supposed to call."

"Ooh!! You do remember!"

He turned to look at the ruffian who still had Chance hemmed up by the arms. After the last time he had to grab her and she nearly scratched his eyeballs out literally, he knew he had better hold her arms firmly.

"She remembers!" he said to his bodyguards. Then back to Chance. "So why did you not do it?"

"Do what?"

"Do wh--, yall dumb tricks are really getting on my last nerve! Let her go!" She had been struggling to get free from the guard but when he let go, she found herself wanting him to grab her again. At least it felt safer in his grasp. She sat still on the seat across from Money.

"Come here."

"For what?"

"Because I said so ho!! Now-- Come- Here!"

"What are you going to do to me?"

Without hesitation Money pulled out his .357 Magnum, pointing it right at her chest and said, "If you do not come here right now, you won't have to worry about ever questioning me again!!"

He didn't have to ask again. She slowly half stood and slid over to the opposite side of seats. As soon as she sat down, she caught a backhand to the right cheekbone that knocked her onto the floor. Her face stung so bad it felt numb and she thought about staying on the ground, but remembered the time she tried that before. He stomped her unconscious. She had to miss two weeks of work. Chance hurried at the thought and jumped right back up onto the seat like a spring board, praying he would not hit her again. Her nose was bleeding. She quickly grabbed a napkin out of the bag, but before she could find them, she caught another backhand to the cheekbone. This time she could taste blood in her mouth and it was leaking from her nose like a faucet. She tried to get up and explain, but he hit her again.

"Okay, okay, okay! I'm sorry Money! I promise it will never happen again! Just please don't hurt me!"

"You promise what will never happen again?!!"

"I promise, I will never disobey you again. I will never forget the rules again. I promise!"

Eerily he turned sweet, like he was always accustomed to doing.

"Come here baby. Let me wipe your face." He snatched the napkins from her bag and proceeded to wipe blood from her nose and the corner of her mouth.

"Jug,"

"Yes sir, Mr. Money sir."

"What did I tell you to call me?"

"Uh, Boss?"

"Well, when you gone start Jug? Tomorrow?"

"No sir. Im gone start today Boss."

"Very good. Now, put some ice in a towel and give it to her. It'll help with the swelling. Geesh Jug, where are your manners?"

"Right here Boss. Right away Boss!" He rushed to gather the ice into a cloth rag and passed it to Chance. She dared not move from the floor until Jug gave her the towel, then she slowly got up and sat as far away from Money as she could.

"Don't be afraid baby girl. Come here."

He was trying to be nice, like he had manners, but she knew better. Money was like a dormant volcano. He could explode at anytime, and even when nothing was moving, if you get too close he would still burn you. She slid closer, slowly, until she was right next to him. He smiled at her and stroked the side of her face, the same side he had struck twice.

"Are you okay?"

"Yea I'm okay," she whispered the lie.

"Good. Now don't make me hurt you again. You know how I hate that."

He touched the places that had already started to bleed again and swell.

"Look at what you made me do."

"I'm sorry. I know it's all my fault."

"You better believe it's all your fault!"

He grabbed both sides of her jawbone with one hand and squeezed as hard as he could. Chance couldn't hold back the grunts and grimaces. He ignored her plea.

"Don't you ever forget that it is always your fault. And you better not ever do it again. I'm bout tired of you anyway!" He gave a short pause. "You know what happens to ya'll tricks when I get tired don't you?"

She nodded her head signifying full comprehension before he mushed her face, pushing her back onto the floor.

"I know you do! Now stay down there where dogs belong! And don't you get up until I tell you to, okay Fido!!"

Money's henchman laughed at his corny jokes, as usual. She thought them to be stupid. Every one of them was bigger and stronger than him, but they were all scared. They jumped to do anything he said. *Pitiful!* Chance sank into silence thinking of a happier place and a more beautiful face. A picture of the guy sitting on the ER floor, the one who gave her his whole pack of cigarettes, came to mind, bringing her a sense of peace. Momentarily, she forgot she was in the face of evil, that is until the limo came to an abrupt halt.

# Chapter 10:  Take a Chance

Jeff watched through the bars of the gate's entrance. Two men dressed in all black got out of the limo, preceding a gentleman who had on so many labels, his outfit alone cost more than Jeff had seen in a while. He suppressed a longing for street life and a time where he was that man everyone moved for. Waving off the thought, he waited to see if she would emerge from the limo. Bodyguards stood with the door open, talking and laughing. But there was no sign of Chance anywhere.

*Maybe I have the wrong limo. Did I lose them on the freeway?* He contemplated returning to his car and leaving, until the well-dressed gentleman leaned back into the limo, said something to someone and then slammed the door.

"She's got to be in there. I know I kept up with them pretty good." He affirmed himself. "And from the way she was dressed in the ER and the way this man is dressed, he has to be her pimp or something." *Why do I even care? Getting involved in street drama can turn deadlier than falling into a pit of vipers!* Though Jeff questioned his own intentions, he couldn't help but to continue in pursuit of the limo. *Those look like some serious vipers! I hope Chance is okay.*

The limo took the ramp from GA 400 to I-285S. Jeff figured they were headed back towards Douglas Health Center until they got off at I-20E, West End exit. On the highway it's easy to disguise when you're tailing someone, but on main streets it was different. Keeping a safe distance, Jeff watched each turn the limo made before following. When it was obvious they were getting close to their destination, he parked in a closed shopping center and walked, never losing sight of them. That's when he saw her. Chance emerged from the backseat, along with one of the henchmen. He was holding her around the waist and it looked like she was graciously refusing his advances. Finally, the bodyguard released her and she walked inside Queen City. *I knew it! She's not a prostitute but stripper is not that far from it.* A lot of male clients still treat women like a piece of meat or property. *But at least she's not sleeping with men for money. I hope...*

He wanted to leave but his street sense told him to watch for a while. In less than ten minutes, he found out his gut was right. *What an escape artist!* Looking between the buildings, Jeff saw Chance dart across the back parking lot and duck behind a dumpster right next to a wooded fence. She was hiding from someone other than the rich pimp and his henchmen. *What in the world is this girl really mixed up in?!* He had to see where she was going so he planned to follow. She didn't move. He waited a couple of minutes before running over to the dumpster, not wanting to spook her more than she obviously already was. When he got there, she was gone but he saw how she had eluded him. There was a plank missing. He slid through the small opening, immediately spotting the beautiful vixen who'd stolen a piece of his heart. He trotted until he caught up with her.

"Where you going so fast?" She almost punched him before realizing who he was.

"Where did you come from? You scared me to death!"

"Hold it young lady. I'll be the one asking the questions here."

"Oh really! Who you sposed to be?"

"Well, I'm trying to be a friend."

"Too late. I have enough friends."

"If you're talking about the rich guy in the limo or the bodyguard who couldn't keep his hands off of you, it looks to me like you need some new friends. Good ones!"

"How did you know who was in the limo? How long have you been following me?"

"Since you received curbside service from yo pimp!"

"My pimp?! Hey nigga you can get off yo high horse before I knock you off! Aiight!!Don't think you have any idea who I am or what I do!! And even if he was my pimp, who are you to judge! Looking like you just got released yesterday!!!"

"That's almost the truth!" he laughed.

"Figures,' she muttered under her breath. "Chance you sure can pick 'em!'"

"I'm sorry, I couldn't hear that last part." He was leaning in so close she could smell his soap. Clean, Irish Spring fresh and all man!

"Nothing. I was just talking to myself."

"That's evident. I'm just trying to figure out why you would do that? I'm right here." He sounded so sincere. Chance wanted to believe that a man could genuinely be interested in her and be kind too.

"Yea you right here, uninvited might I add. Why don't you go away? I got to go to my apartment and get ready for work."

"Can I watch?" He smirked.

'NO! You may not!!" They were joking around with each other already. It felt easy and right and good!

"I meant can I watch you dance, not watch you change yo clothes. Geesh, lighten up!"

"Oh, well the answer is still NO!"

Finally, a smile, and happiness looked so beautiful on her. He wished he could keep a smile on that face always.

"You don't mind me tagging along to make sure you're safe, do you?'

"I guess not," she drawled.

"Good."

"And that being said, we are here at Donnelly Garden Apartments. It was nice knowing ya Jeff." She turned to walk away.

"Nope. You not getting off that easy. Besides, I'm worried about you." He grabbed her hand, turning her back to face him.

"Why are you worried about little ole me?" She jerked her hand away. "You don't even know me!" she reiterated. They were flirting hard. But he was so serious. Jeff touched the bruises on her cheek and her swollen top lip.

"They'll heal." She whispered under his gaze.

"But not tonight! And you got to go to work! How is that going to play out?"

"Man, do you think this is my first rodeo? I've been here several times."

"More reason for me to be nervous! You act like you're okay with it!!"

"I'm used to it, but I'm so not okay wit it!" She shrugged her shoulders. "It's my life."

"Well it's time to change dat don't you think?"

"Yea, I always think about it. But it's never gonna happen."

"It'll happen if I have something to do with it. They just got you scared to move that's all. Once you see there's nothing to be afraid of, you'll change your mind."

"Hmmph, if you knew who I was dealing with, you'd be scared to move too!"

"I've dealt with worse. My broth-" He stopped in mid sentence. Samuel would be livid if he knew his brother was telling his testimony, especially if it wasn't being used to glorify God.

"Your brother what?"

"Oh nothing. Let's just say I've dealt with worse."

"You did say it, like thirty seconds ago."

"Moving on," he said in an attempt to save his dying ego. "What time do you have to be at work anyway?

"Oh, my goodness! I'm gonna be late!!" She said running up the stairs with keys in hand. "I have to work doubles to cover my shift and my friends." She fumbled through the keys finally finding the right one. "This is all your fault!"

"My fault? You were already at work. Why didn't you just stay?"

"Look Big Boi has this thing for Karisma. He probably will have someone over here watching the place before long. I just wanted to pack up some of her things to take to the hospital before he starts asking questions. I got to cover her butt and mine!"

She opened the door and rushed into the bedroom. Knowing Money, he'd have someone watching her every move too. There was no way she could come back here or go back to the hospital.

"Hey you live near Douglasville, right?"

"Actually, I live in Carrollton. But my brother ministers to people in the ICU and ER at hospitals in Carroll and Douglas counties."

"Okay, okay. I don't need an autobiography."

"What do you need?" He looked over his shoulder towards the bedroom to see if he could get a flirtatious response. *No such luck!* She was too wired to flirt now.

"I need a favor. I was wondering if you would take this bag of Karisma's things to the hospital for me. Then that way I can keep her out of all this madness."

"How is she?"

"Right now, she's in a coma. Medically induced the doctor said, which means she'll come out of it in her own time. Hopefully when she wakes up she won't remember the nightmare that is her life." She tossed the bag in his lap.

"Wait. I never said I would do it?"

"You never said you wouldn't, besides aren't you the guy who was begging to help me a little while ago."

"I don't know. Was he good looking?" Still trying to make moves.

"He was aiight and he looked a lot like you!!" She batted her eyes and pouted, "Please! Will you help me?"

"How could I say no to such a beautiful face? Sure, I'll take a **chance** on you. No pun intended. You know, just to help a sister out, **if** you give me your cell phone number."

"Just to help a sister out, huh. If you really wanted to help me out, you would just do it. No strings attached. No conditions."

"Look, I'll do it anyway, even if you don't give me your number. But I'd feel better about leaving you right now if you just gave it to me. That way I can call and check up on you later. You know, make sure you're safe."

"Alright, fine! You win!"

"No, we both win." He grinned. *How could this handsome man be a thug? I guess that saying is right, 'never judge a book by its cover'.*

"Okay, I'll take that but I have to hurry. My shift starts in ten minutes." She was still rushing around trying to find something to put on, like she didn't know where anything was.

"So what is it?"

"What is what?"

"Your-phone-number?"

"Oh yea. It's 404-555-7887." On cue, her phone rang. *It was Shane!!!*

"Thanks Jeff." She grabbed the bag and took him by the hand, quickly walking both to the door.

"I really appreciate your help, and give this to Karisma for me." She gently kissed his cheek, he stepped out onto the porch and before he could take another step the door shut.

"I'm on my way Big Boi!" He heard her conversation trailing off as he walked down the stairs and back towards the parking lot to his car.

Jeff sat waiting, just to catch one more glimpse of the beautiful Chance before he took off. While he waited, he thought about the man he used to be, who could buy her nice things and take her away from this life. But that would only put her into another level of the game, out of the frying pan and into the fire. He let his thoughts run wild, thinking of a better path for the both of them until finally she appeared from behind the club. She had made it to work. He watched with amazement. You could barely see the swollen bruises. But that's not the only reason he watched her. She was so graceful, and her body was banging. *I'll bet she would look gorgeous in a sundress and sandals!*

# Chapter 11: What's Up Doc?

Chance walked into the dressing room cautiously. She knew he would emerge eventually, but she had no desire to see him first off. He turned their stomachs. All of the girls hated the sight and sound of him, but it was a part of their life. They made the best of it, having to deal with him on a daily basis. *Hmmm, maybe I should do some investigating of my own.* The girls' hatred of Big Boi gave him motive. And he sure did sound guilty over the phone. *There has to be someone willing to talk. And I am going to find her.*

"Hey girl. How's Lady K?" It was Bossy. She had this gleam in her eyes, like she was power struck or something.

"Not too good right now, I'm afraid. They're keeping her until she gets better."

"Oh okay."

"I know they'll take really good care of her."

"I hope so, but in the meantime, maybe somebody **else** can make a thousand dollars a night!"

Some of the other girls agreed, hearing the conversation. Or maybe they were just cosigning because they were afraid of Bossy. *Nah...* She brushed off the thought.

"Well, y'all might be happy she's gone, but I'm gonna miss her."

"Speaking of miss. I don't wanna miss this money! Big Boi put me on first in place of Karisma. Only in her absence of course, but more money for me!!" She laughed, walking to the door.

"You evil whore! Money? Really?! That's the only reason you even asked about Karisma. You wanna make sure she's not coming back no time soon!"

"Honey, you can call me all the names you want to, but the reality is, as long as she's gone, I'm gone get these coins." Bossy walked right up into Chance's face. "You got a problem wit it?"

Chance didn't have time to argue with this conniving snake. She said nothing but she gave her that don't mess with me look. Then she realized Bossy had spotted the bruises under her makeup. She ran her finger down Chance's cheek.

"Seems like you have enough problems as it is. Next time use steak on those bruises and some concealer and bronzer. Foundation and face powder doesn't hide the shine good enough."

*I can't believe she just threw me under the bus like that! Oooh, it is so on!!* And to make matters worse, she smiled like she hadn't said anything snide. Chance looked back at the other girls who hid their faces and pretended to look through their bags, preparing for their next dance. *No one is going to stand with me against this new girl? Something fishy is going on! All the scrappers in here, and no one is standing?!*

"Fellas, you're in for a real treat tonight. She has charisma, she's a woman of style, and boy can she dance. I know she may not be what you're used to but please take a chaance on Boss-yyyyy!"

In a flash, she was on the ramp and out on stage. No one said a word about her afterward. All the girls kept pretending to get ready. *Yep, I can smell a dead fish from a mile away! Something stinks! And that heifer used my name and Karisma's name in her introduction. She got to get it! I'm gone find out what the problem is and when I do, that Bossy is mine!! Ima take her back to Chi-town!*

"I'll be back girls."

"Wait Chance! Where are you going?"

"I'm just going to the bar to get a drink. I'll be right back."

"What do we do if Big Boi comes?"

"Tell him I'm at the bar! Duh!"

"Oh right. And if you're not back in time for your dance?"

"Take my spot and I'll take yours, like we always do."

"Okay. Okay."

*Why does everyone seem so nervous? I gotta get to the bottom of this or I'm gone explode!*

"Cotton Candy?"

"Huh?"

"Are you okay? What's going on around here?"

"Um, nothing. It's just that after Karisma passed out last night, Big Boi started acting strange. He was talking to himself and pacing. And when any of us would try to talk to him, he yelled at us."

"But he always yells at us. What's so different now?"

"Chance, you weren't here. He had this wild look in his eyes. You…. You just had to be here."

"Did he raise his hand or try to hit one of yall?"

"No, but who knows what today will bring!"

"Well, I'm heading to the bar. Send him to find me if he comes in yelling for me okay. I gotta see this for myself."

"Okay, girl. Whatever you say."

Chance peeped around every corner before making it to the bar. By the time she reached the showroom, Bossy was done with her dance. But she didn't go back down the ramp. She walked through the audience and headed to the back room. *Now, who in their right mind would intentionally go anywhere near Big Boi's office?!*

After whispering the change in the lineup to the DJ, Chance discreetly headed to the back of the showroom where Big Boi's office was located. There was yelling, a lot of yelling. But ironically most of the yelling came from Bossy. *What does she have on him? She got to know something for Big Boi to let her talk to him like that? Too bad I can't make out what they are saying, but sooner or later it's gone hit the fan!*

She proceeded back into the showroom just in time to see another familiar face. He was in disguise but she could recognize a big tipper anywhere. It was something in the eyes. She always looked into the eyes of the big tippers. They liked to connect with you while you dance for them, like having sex. He was usually in the VIP Showroom, but today she had a feeling he'd be heading straight for the bar, and she was right. She tried to stay hidden until he rested on a barstool.

"Hi. Can I have a Scotch straight in a chilled glass, no ice please?" The man spoke short and fast, like he was on a mission.

"Yes sir, right away."

Darnell opened the chiller and pulled out a short glass, filled it half way then placed it in front of the man.

"That'll be $10."

He passed him a $50 bill and said, "Keep the change."

"Yes sir!"

It was a test to see if the tender would be moved by money. The second test was to see if he could get him to spill any dirt on anyone in the club.

"Who is this girl that's dancing right now? I don't remember seeing her the last time I was here."

"Oh yea. She's fairly new. Big Boi got rid of a lot of the older girls and replaced them with new faces. You know, to boost profits and what not."

"Yea I can understand that. What did you say her name is?"

"Cotton Candy."

"Mmm, sweet." They shared a laugh, then the gentleman continued.

"So, what can you tell me about... Cotton Candy?"

"I'm sorry. I'm not sure what you're asking me."

"I'm asking you is she good?

"Oh well, she's not the best but I guess she's an okay dancer."

"No. Not good in dancing, I mean good?"

"Oooo!" He smiled. "I never got to taste Cotton Candy. I'm currently in a slight, complicated relationship with Bossy."

"Bossy?"

"Oh right. You haven't been here in a while. She's new too. And a real knock out. She's good too. Almost as good as Karisma, but..." The bartender trailed off into silence. The man continued as if he had no idea what Darnell was talking about.

"Karisma? Who's she?"

"Man, how long has it been since you came in here?"

"Hmm, I'd say about nine months."

"Oh, that explains it. Well, Karisma's only been here a few months, but boy did she rack in the tips. All the girls were a little jealous, except Chance."

"I guess those two must be really close."

"I suppose so."

"Are those two ladies dancing tonight?"

"Chance is, but I don't think Karisma will be in for a while."

"Why not? Did she get sick? Or worse, pregnant?!"

"No, nothing like that." The young man looked as if to reflect on a tragedy, then snapped back to reality. "Um excuse me."

Darnell disappeared behind the bar. The gentleman had a feeling the boy needed a stiff drink. He knew something, and he was going to spill it all.

"What's up doc?"

*No, no, no! What is she doing here? She's going to spoil everything!!*

"I knew you'd show up here tonight. And I knew just where I'd find you."

"How? Did you Google it?" He smirked.

"Ha, ha. Very not funny!"

"Scram. You're going to blow my cover."

"Why you say that? Have you found out anything yet?"

"I'm about to, if you don't mess it up for me, now beat it!" He turned his back to her, hoping she would leave. No such luck.

"Well, I got a little information of my own to share."

"Spill it!" he said, slightly turning his head to give her the side eye.

She was about to tell her story and do a little dance for the doctor. He was very still as she turned the stool around so that he could see all of her moves. Her hand was on his chest as her lips grazed his cheek. But just then, the young man reappeared from behind the bar stand, and sure enough his breath smelt of hard liquor. *This is going to be a piece of cake!* Dr. Reid was excited in more than one way, but right now he was on a mission. He was going to catch whoever was drugging these girls. And maybe when it was all over, he would have his **Chance**.

"Well," Darnell said, coughing a little, "I see you've met Chance."

"Oh yea, we are getting well acquainted..." He looked at Chance like, get out of here and she took the hint.

"Yea, but I have to go and get ready for my time to shine. Mr. Reid is it?"

"Yes it is."

"That'll be $100."

He rolled his eyes, pulled out the bill and stuffed it into her g-string.

"Thanks. I'll catch you later and maybe get some more of that candy out of yo pocket daddy."

"Indeed, you will." She sauntered away, disappearing through the stage doors.

"Man, I always wanted a piece of that. Tell me how good it is cause I know it's good."

"How can you tell?"

"By the way she moves. You'll see in a few. She dances next I think."

"Oh yea, I'm going to enjoy every minute of this."

"Me too!"

They shared more laughs and drinks before Chance came out to dance. By the time she was done, both men were mesmerized. Dr. Reid broke silence first.

"You mean to tell me, Karisma is better than her?"

"Oh yea, ten times better."

"I would love to see that."

"Too bad she's in the hospital. You know she fell last night and broke a glass table with her head. There's no telling how long she'll be in there. And..."

He looked around to make sure no one was coming, namely Bossy or Big Boi. When it looked as if the coast was clear, he continued.

"And I heard someone put something in her drink. They think it's Big Boi but you never know around here. It could have been a customer or even one of the girls."

"Man, that's some drama for you huh."

"Bruh, you don't know the half. These girls be backstabbing and jabbing in here. It's real cutthroat."

"I'll bet."

Dr. Reid tried to act nonchalant about the conversation, but he was finally getting what he wanted from the boy. And it only took $200 worth of drinks. He kept buying alcohol so the boy wouldn't disappear every time the getting was getting good.

"So, Darnell. What do you think? Do you think one of the girls did it to try and throw her off of her game? Or do you think Big Boi did it?

"You know it could go either way, but I'd put money on Big Boi. The girls hate him but he's always trying to push up on em, especially Karisma. Everybody wanted her, shoot, I wanted her! Man, that girl is finer than wine. I'm a bartender. I know! And she don't be in here twerking and doing tricks like the rest of these hoes. She really can dance. Man, I wish you could see her dance."

"Maybe one day I will."

"Yea, if she gets better. But maybe she'll go back home and patch things up with her parents. You know they fell out about some disappearance. I think it was her brother, either ran away or got kidnapped or something. Anyway, she may never step foot back in here once they find out what happened to her."

"Do you know her parents?"

"Naw man, but I think Chance has an old address or some mail or something. I don't know. These girls tell me so much when they're drunk, I can't piece together whose story is whose."

He chuckled a drunk laugh, and missed a step. Just when Dr. Reid thought all was lost and that was all the information he had. The boy gave him the best piece of information into Karisma's true identity.

"Oh yea, I think her dad is like an elder at Greater United Baptist Church. Elder Johnson I think."

"Are you sure, or are you just talking off the top of your head?"

"I don't know. I think I'm pretty sure." He scratched his head. "Yep, I'm sure, Kindness told me that herself. Oh- yea-... Her real name is Kindness. Kindness Johnson."

"Well young man. I think you've had enough for the night. I know I have."

"Oh no, I don't get off until we close. It don't matter how drunk I am, as long as I count the money right, Big Boi says I can drink as much as I can handle. I just can't let the customers see me drink. That is unless the customer is buying."

"Great. Now you tell me!" The doctor said sarcastically, sliding off of the barstool.

"Goodbye Dr. Reid."

"Bye Darnell!" Then the doctor gasped. *Did he just call me Dr. Reid? Oh I know it's time to go. I done drank and talked too much myself!*

"Where do you think you're going?"

"Home!" He said unquestionably.

"Well, don't you wanna hear the information I found out."

"I did at first, but I think Darnell gave me all the information I need to get to the bottom of things."

"Betcha he didn't!"

Dr. Reid was drunk and really tired. But tomorrow was his day off. And though he was on call, he would still have time to sleep and get over his hangover before heading to the police station.

"Okay Ms. Beautiful, let's go for a cup of coffee and you can tell me what you know."

"Sounds good."

Chance took him to a popular after club hang out called Beautiful. She ordered chicken and waffles, but the doctor only had coffee. He watched her devour most of the food, taking short sips of the black concoction before him.

"Okay Ms. Chance, I've been patient while you satisfied an obvious hunger for this place. Now spill it."

"Right. I'm sorry. I was a little hungry." She said, mouth half full.

"You act like you haven't eaten in months."

"It's been a few days since I really settled in to eat a meal."

"Now you can't be that busy!"

"No, not too busy. I'm used to busy." She shrugged with a heavy sigh. "More like worried."

"What are you worried about? Big Boi?"

"Big Boi is a pain, but he is the least of my worries."

"So, what **are** you worried about?"

"I can't say much about it, but just know that even right now I'm being watched and you need to watch your back."

"Why would I need to watch *my* back?"

"Because, he has eyes everywhere. No matter what happens, he always finds out."

"Who?"

"I can't tell you that, but I do have to let you know that we've got to check into a hotel under your name once we leave this place."

"Why would *we* do that? I have a perfectly good condo in Midtown. We can just go there?"

"No we can't!"

"Why not?!"

"Because, *he* is going to expect me to give favors and get paid! And Johns don't take tricks to their homes!"

"So, for this information you have to offer, I've got to not only pay for a room, but I've got to give you money too."

"Yes. To him, you're just another trick and tricks pay for their treats."

"Hey, now wait a minute. That's not what I'm here for."

"I didn't say it was. It's just that I know he's watching and I'm telling you what he expects."

"What if I don't do it?"

"Then, I'll get more of this." She touched the bruises which he only noticed once she pointed them out. He softly touched her hand.

"Chance. You've got to get away from these people. They're killing you little by little."

"It's my life." She shrugged nonchalantly, as if to have accepted her fate.

"It doesn't have to be. You can change your life with only one decision."

"I dunno. I mean I have nothing else. I have nowhere to go."

"How about home?"

"I ran away years ago. That's how I met Mon-, I mean this guy. And furthermore, I don't even know if my parents live where we used to live. But listening to Karisma talk about her brother and how much they all miss him makes me want to go back and try."

He reached his hand out and touched the bruise at the corner of her mouth. "I think that's a good idea."

"Maybe, but there is the chance that they won't have me."

"Look, here's my card." She took it and quickly stuffed it into her pocket. He noticed but there was no need to ask why. Whoever had her bound had put the fear of death into her.

"Hey, it's okay." He spoke slowly. "Everything will be okay. Just try and go home. And if you get there and your parents don't want you, I'll pay for you to come back. And I'll even help you find a job and somewhere to stay, away from these evil people."

"You'd do that for me?"

"Yes." He kissed her on the cheek.

"Why?"

"I get the feeling you deserve better, you just don't know it."

"And that's it?"

"If you really want to know, I'll tell you."

"I want to know." He breathed slowly. His eyes had a far away look.

"My little sister was a victim of a street hustler. She was ten years younger than me." He motioned to the waitress to refresh his coffee and she obliged.

"What happened to her?"

"She died."

"How? What happened?"

"He killed her."

"Wow. I'm so sorry to hear that."

"Yea me too. It happened when I was away in medical school. When mom called and told me the news, I was devastated. My grades began to fail."

"It must have been hard to not be able to protect your little sister."

"That was my downfall."

"You must have turned it around. I mean you are a doctor now."

"Yea, one of my professors motivated me to write my dissertation on drugs used to incapacitate people to do what criminals wanted them to do."

"And that did it?"

"Yep. He was so impressed; he talked the Dean into throwing out all of my failing grades due to temporary emotional instability."

"And he agreed?"

"Not at first. But when he read my dissertation, he deemed it pure genius. He said there was no way I could have failed those minor tests having written such a masterpiece."

"Wow. You must be real smart, huh?"

"Let them tell it. But they were a little disappointed when I decided to be a ER doctor as opposed to a surgeon."

"Why did you choose to be an ER doctor over a surgeon?"

"My sister died in an ER room because they were understaffed. They didn't know she had been drugged until it was too late."

"They probably thought she was just another junkie prostitute."

"You get that a lot?"

"I did the other night!"

"I suppose so, the way you were dressed."

"Yea, people walk by sight and judge based off of what they see before they get to know one thing about you."

"We are terribly opinionated."

"Yea, especially your Nurse Abbey." He chuckled.

"Sorry about that."
"It's cool. I think I taught her a lesson, and if I didn't it was sure fun trying." He laughed a little louder.

"You remind me of her."

"Who, your sister?"

"Yea. Maybe that's why I have a soft spot for you."

"Maybe."

"Come on, let's go to a hotel. We can get a suite and I'll sleep on the pull-out sofa."

"No funny business right," she joked.

"Absolutely no funny business!" He smiled. "You're my little sister now, right?"

"Right!"

"Okay, let's go."

Chance was relieved. The doctor was handsome **and** rich, but he was no Jeff.

"Besides, you still got to tell me the juicy details of your findings."

"Oh yea, right! This was supposed to be about Karisma, not me."

"It sounds to me like it's about the both of you. And it's time for freedom!"

"I don't even know what that means anymore, or how it would feel."

"You will. I promise."

He laid a one-hundred-dollar bill on the table and they walked towards the door. The waitress saw the money and called after him.

"Mister, don't you want your change?"

"Keep it. It's your tip." He called over his shoulder.

"Oh wow, thanks mister! You can come back and I'll wait on you anytime!"

On the way to the hotel, Chance told Dr. Reid what she overheard Bossy and Big Boi talking about, stating that she couldn't make out everything but one thing was for certain. Bossy had a hold on Big Boi. Whatever was going on, they were in it together and maybe even Darnell had something to do with it. She told him about how terrified the girls were of Bossy. But that she didn't fear the *skank*, as she put it. And when she got the chance, she'd take her to the streets! He laughed at how comical she made the story and thanked her for corroborating a lot of what Darnell told him. The case against Big Boi and Bossy would be open and shut once they found out who put the date rape pill in her drink. All they needed were a couple of witnesses and he knew exactly how to find them. *Hospital records!*

# Chapter 12: Who am I? Who are you?

Minister Samuel James often made visits with the occupants of the ICU at Douglas Health Center, dispersing his free time between hospitals in and around Carroll and Douglas counties. However, he had taken a hiatus a month ago to tend important matters at his church in Carrollton. In his absence, Nurse Abbey spent most of her shift with Karisma, talking to her and reading to her. But fearing she would soon get into trouble, she put in an emergency call to Samuel. Good thing for Nurse Abbey, he was already in the hospital. He'd been working in the ER all night but just had not made it around to the ICU area.

It had been two weeks since Karisma's accident. Physically, she was normal except for the medically induced coma. All of her vitals were stable. The doctors couldn't figure out why she hadn't recovered from the coma, but decided to allow the medicine to take its course. Nurse Abbey, on the other hand, pushed for a reversal of the medicine. She was quickly rebuked by the Administrator and decided to continue to keep the young lady as comfortable as possible. For some strange reason, she developed a strong connection with Karisma thinking she just didn't seem like the type of girl to be dancing in a strip club.

That concern is what really led her to ask Minister James to visit. Like a parent afraid to leave their newborn in the care of others, Karisma's visits came with specific instructions to read uplifting scriptures only and to pray over her at least twice a day. Samuel accepted the challenge after hearing the girl's background, or at least all that Nurse Abbey could tell him. He felt like any woman in that predicament needed some spiritual guidance. When he first saw her face, he thought she looked like an angel. Most of her sweet face was exposed. Only her eyes were wrapped, and Sam could tell someone had been keeping her up nicely.

"I see you've been clipping her nails and keeping her skin moisturized."

"Yea, well I have. But I do that for all of my invalid patients."

"Mhmm, just not on this level." He walked over to the bed and raised the young ladies' hand. "And you've been polishing nails too!"

"Yea, well I want her to look pretty when we find her family."

"Nurse Abbey. You're not *fooling* me! You've taken a liking to this young lady, more than your *other* invalid patients. For this beauty, you've gone the extra mile."

"So what if I have! Is that a crime?!" She defended.

"No, it's not a crime. But it is unusual, especially for someone who's usually so by the book."

He looked at her for a moment, sizing her up. "What is it about this girl that's different?"

She breathed in a long deep breath and released before replying.

"Minister James, have you ever met someone and without having said a word to them, or they having said a word to you, you know that somehow this person is special?"

"I can't say that I have, Abbey."

"Well, that's how I feel about this young lady. I know I told you how she came to be a patient here, but the story just doesn't sit right in my spirit. But I do believe she's here for a reason."

"Why do you say that?"

"I did a little research and found out the club is several miles from here. And there are several hospitals between here and there. But she ended up here."

"And you being the God-fearing woman that you are, feel that God led her to you?"

"No. I believe he led her to us."

"To us?"

"Yes. To us! This girl could've ended up at any of those hospitals but she's here. I have been taking really good care of her, doing some things that I could be suspended for and yet I did them without hesitation. Then when I could no longer continue, I called you..."

"And I just happened to be in the ER."

"Yes! Of this hospital. You could have been anywhere between here and Carrollton."

"To be honest Abbey, I don't really know why I decided to come last night. I've been done with my work at church for a few days now, but I needed some time to myself. However, last night I hopped in my truck and started to ride. Before I knew it, I was on I-20. When an ambulance passed me on the way, I followed them here."

"Oh right. I heard about the accident with the SUV full of teenagers and the transfer truck. Is everyone okay?"

"Two of the kids are critical, one is still in surgery and the other kid died on impact."

"Oh my, I'm so sorry to hear that."

"So is his mother. He was her only child, and they just lost his father two years ago."

"Oh wow. I can't even imagine the pain."

"Yea. She's taking it really hard. I prayed with her and consoled her until her sister showed up. Her car ran hot trying to get here and that was the reason her son had to catch a ride with the other kids."

"Was anyone drinking?"

"All of them, except the kid who died. He was simply catching a ride home."

"Oh no Sam! That poor woman must be devastated!"

"She is, but after we prayed she said she felt peace about the entire situation. Her son just started going to A Place of Refuge church and joined their Youth and Young Adult ministry. He went to the altar just last Sunday."

"Ain't that just like God. He knows how to pre-fix a situation."

"Yes He does. Bishop calls it a setup."

"You see all of the things that led us all together on this day. God set it up this way. It's not for no reason Sam. I can feel it in my gut."

"You know what Abbey, so do I."

They talked for a while as they always did before she left him to his new assignment. In the meantime, Jeff was flying down I-20 West, thinking of the promise he made to Chance and wondering how in the world he was going to avoid his brother at the hospital. *Maybe I should just call him. He might be the best person to get Chance out of trouble.* Being saved didn't mean he had lost all of his connections. It had only been eight years since he found Jesus. At first Jeff and the rest of his gang said he was only "jailhouse" saved, but Sam never gave up. His last contact with the crew was three years ago. Although they were not in agreement, they respected his decision. And that respect still stood. If he called, they would come running. Since Chance was mixed up with some hood fellas, there had to be a way to fight fire with fire. *There just has to be!* No matter how holy he tries to act, I know he still can pull some strings to help Chance and her friend at the hospital. Obviously, they were in way over their heads. *I'll wait to talk to him in person.* Jeff finally decided that asking his brother face to face was the best option. The matter was too critical to leave in the hands of a hospital page that his brother may never hear anyway.

"Whoot-whoot!"

The blue lights were blinding. *I should've known. Just another day in the life of Jefferson Nicodemus James...* Jeff pulled over onto the shoulder of the highway and rolled down his window to save time. The officer opened his door, slowly moving toward the car. He saw that Jeff's hands were on the steering wheel and his window was down. *Oh so we have a habitual violator.* He approached the vehicle, shining the flashlight right into Jeff's face.

"Do you know how fast you were going young man?" The officer was black. *Yes! I may be able to talk my way out of this one, and by telling the truth. Or at least some form of the truth.*

"No sir."

"85 in a 55! You mean to tell me you were going thirty miles over the speed limit and you didn't notice one bit?"

"I guess I was preoccupied sir."

"With what? Are you dying?"

"No sir. I'm perfectly healthy except this busted hand I got when I had a misunderstanding with a brick wall."

Jeff watched as the officer made a note on his pad: *Has anger issues! May have priors...*

"You say you rammed your fist into a wall?"

"Yes sir." He could've elaborated a little, but there was no need. Get this done and over as soon as possible is all he was thinking.

"You headed to the emergency room?"

"Uh, yes sir!" It wasn't a lie. He was headed to the hospital and his first stop would be the ER just to keep the statement honest.

"Uh huh. Let me see your driver's license and registration please sir."

"Sure." Jeff leaned over and grabbed his insurance sleeve, where he kept all of his driving credentials, and passed them to the officer.

"You sit tight. If everything checks out, I may let you go with only a warning. But make sure you get that hand checked out."

"Yes sir!" *Wow, my brother was right. Who knew this truth stuff really works*. The officer was gone for only five minutes before returning.

"Mr. James, I'm going to need you to step out of the car."

"What? Why, Officer..." Jeff looked at the man's badge, "Cofield? What happened to letting me go with just a warning?"

"That was before I found out there is a warrant for your arrest. It seems you had another ticket three months ago and you failed to appear in court. And you know how that goes. I mean of course you know. You got a rap sheet a mile long. Now get out of the car please sir!"

"Dang! I completely forgot about that ticket. My PO is going to hang me!" Good thing Officer Cofield didn't hear him. Maybe it was because he was too busy opening the door so Jeff could step out. Assuming the position, the cop put cuffs on him and placed him in the backseat of his squad car. After radioing for a wrecker to pick up Jeff's '75 Mustang they took off down I-20W towards Douglas County police station.

"Mo' problems, mo'problems." Jeff mumbled.

"What you say young man?"

"Nothing really. I was just saying the more problems you have the more problems come."

"Like my nine-year-old says, 'It be like that sometimes'. I mean not for me but yeah for people like you."

*People like me!* Jeff wanted to add another smart comment but considering the circumstances, figured he was in enough trouble already. So he just rolled his eyes at the officer who had been talking while looking at him in the rearview mirror. Jeff held his peace.

In the holding cell, at the jailhouse, Jeff used his only phone call to call Chance but he must have entered a number wrong or either she gave him the wrong number, because he got the operator instead. W*hy would she do that when she showed me where she lives? Unless she doesn't live there.* That's when it dawned on him. *She was packing clothes for her friend, but it was not her apartment. It was Karisma's. Ugh!! How could I be so stupid!* He sat down on the bench in the cell, lost in thoughts of the beautiful temptress, whom he couldn't forget, despite the fact that she was also a liar.

Samuel had been sitting with Karisma every day, shutting out all other invites and requests. There were others who could pray for families in need. As long as this angel needed him, he would make himself available. And that's what she looked like laying there with her eyes wrapped, her chest rising and falling subtly, almost undetected. Whatever spell she cast on Nurse Abbey; he had also fallen victim to. He had grown very fond of her, too fond. He knew he should just walk away, end the visits, let someone else take over, but he couldn't do it. He couldn't abandon her. It was like they were bonded together by some unforeseen purpose or force. But his feelings were simply feelings of compassion. That's what he kept telling himself. But, no. No matter how much he tried to deny it, there was something more personal going on. Not love? *I can't love her. I don't even know who she is and she has no clue I'm even here.* He grabbed her hand and kissed it right as Nurse Abbey walked in the door. They both froze and then Nurse Abbey continued into the room, checking Karisma's breathing equipment and tubing before addressing him. Without looking at him, she began to speak.

"Minister James, I think it would be best if you go home and get some rest." She paused and looked at him to drive her point, "By then I will have found someone else to come and pray with Ms. Karisma." He shook his head in agreement, half because he had just got caught kissing someone he didn't know, even if it was just on the hand, and half because he had no idea what to do with these feelings. Nurse Abbey was right. He needed sleep and time to sort out his emotions.

"Nurse Abbey, I- I am really sorry about what you just saw and I hope you can forgive me."

"Me forgive you? You'd better hope that young lady you just violated can forgive you."

"But she's in a coma. She has no idea what just hap-"

"Mr. James. It is obvious you have no idea what goes on when a person is in a coma. They are asleep but they can still hear, think *and feel*. I wouldn't be surprised if she didn't remember you when she wakes up."

"Wakes up? Remember me?"

"Yea wake up and yea remember you! She's not gonna sleep forever. And when she wakes up, more than likely she will remember you. You, the one who's been talking to her and holding her hand for the past few days. All day, until somebody kicks you out. Then you're back the next morning." She said, smirking.

"You knew?"

"Yea I knew. You may think you are hiding, but Nurse Abbey is always watching. Trust and believe me." She said walking towards the door. "You just make sure you go home and get some rest. Maybe I'll let you come back once your thinking clears."

"Yes ma'am. And if it's okay with you can I recommend someone from my church to come and visit with her?"

"Sure." She said seeing the concern in his eyes but standing firm on her decision to replace him. "Just make sure it's a woman okay! We don't want nobody else falling in love!" She teased. "Don't be long now."

"Yes ma'am. I'm right behind you."

Suddenly the bed sheets rustled and Samuel realized Karisma was moving. She reached for her eyes grimacing because of the pain. Slowly she began taking the wrapping off. Samuel was frozen for what seemed like an eternity. He couldn't wait to see her eyes. But then he remembered what Nurse Abbey said about Karisma not taking off her bandages.

"She's waking up! Nurse Abbey, she's moving and unwrapping her eyes!!" Nurse Abbey ran back into the room with her stethoscope in hand. Karisma groaned as the endearing woman comforted her back into a relaxed position. Immediately she began checking her vitals starting with the sound of her breathing. Nurse Abbey was so excited. She couldn't wait to find out who this girl really was.

"Minister James, I know you must be just as excited as I am but I'm gonna have to ask you to leave right now."

"B-but..."

"Mr. James. I will call you later and give you an update on her status okay." He hesitated for a moment before replying.

"Okay."

"Okay, talk to you later." She followed him to the door and closed it behind him, turning her full attention to the young lady that had everyone intrigued.

"Now baby, we gone have to wrap your eyes back up. Doctor's orders."

"No. I don't want to be in the dark anymore. I won't let you!" Her voice was raspy but strong.

"Fiesty little thing aren't you! Alright for now we won't put the wrap back on, but when Dr. Harris makes his rounds he may recant."

"Well then, I'll have to make sure I'm awake so we can talk about how and why that is not going to happen." She winced at the brightness of the light above her head and Nurse Abbey immediately dimmed them.

"Better?"

"Yes ma'am."

Nurse Abbey smiled thinking if this mystery girl had that much boldness to tell a doctor what to do and not to do, she'd be just fine. While she was tending the machines, Karisma tried to make sense of how she came to be in the hospital. She felt like she had been away from home a very long time but didn't exactly know where home was.

"Miss Ma'am?"

"It's Nurse Abbey dear."

"Nurse Abbey?"

"Yes baby?"

"Who are you?" She said to the nurse, rubbing her eyes, still grimacing from the brightness of the natural light in the room. "No, don't rub your eyes Miss Lady. You'll make it worse."

"Make what worse?"

"We'll let the doctor explain that to you when we have more information about you."

"Okay. But you still didn't tell me who **you** are."

"Why sweetie, I'm Nurse Abbey, head nurse at the ICU department of Douglas Health Center."

"Is that where I am?"

"Yes'm, it is."

"Well how did I end up here? What happened to me?"

"You fell and hit your head on a table. You were in surgery for a few hours. When we finally got the bleeding to stop and stabilized your vitals, we let your friend Chance in and-"

"Who? What friend?"

"Chance. Your friend from down at the club where you girls dance."

"I'm a dancer, at a club? Is it ballet?" She was so excited when she said ballet. Nurse Abbey almost laughed but cut it short because she noticed how serious the girl was.

"Uh, no ma'am, I don't think so. Especially seeing how you two were dressed, or should I say barely dressed."

"So I'm a stripper?" The girl looked confused.

"I'm afraid so."

"Okay, okay. Okay..."

Nurse Abbey understood she was trying to wrap her mind around the truth. She wished she could lie to her but a person coming out of a coma can be an extremely delicate situation. Some don't remember their life very well before the incident that sent them into a coma. Some are blocking it out for one reason or another. Others have total memory loss, while the rest just need time to adjust until the memories start to flow again. Nurse Abbey had found it to be best to tell the truth little by little, as the patient asked questions.

"So, I am a stripper who was hurt at the club I work at, and my name is...." She stopped short, thinking extremely hard. Nurse Abbey waited intently to hear some truth of her own. Karisma was obviously her stage name.

"My name is... um? I don't know." Nurse Abbey was holding her breath, but exhaling, she extended what she knew to help console the child.

"Well, like I said before, your friend Chance gave us the only name she knows to call you. She says it's on your lease and the little mail you receive at your apartment."

"What is it?"

"Oh I'm sorry baby. It's Karisma. Your name is Karisma."

"Karisma. Sounds like a pretty decent name for a stripper but, for some reason I don't feel like that's my name. It doesn't sound familiar at all."

"To be honest baby, I don't think that's your real name either. However, it is the only name we got for you as of yet."

"You said there was mail at my apartment. Was there a last name on that mail?"

"Chance, your friend, said she was going back to your apartment and was supposed to have called me when she knew more, which she has not done. She was gonna try to provide your last name so that we can find your parents or at least some relative. Do you remember anything about your parents, siblings... church members?"

"No, I don't remember."

Nurse Abbey was fishing. She wanted to know if the girl was saved or belonged to a church more than anything else. Karisma just didn't seem like the kind of girl to willingly become a stripper. She was too kind and gentle. And she mentioned ballet. Maybe we can find out a little more about her background and start putting the pieces together because what we have now just doesn't fit.

"Who was that man that you ran out of here earlier?"

"You sure do have a lot of questions," Nurse Abbey was stalling. She really didn't want to tell her about Samuel yet.

"I have been in a coma. I'm just trying to figure some things out."

"Understood sweet child. Alright, I'll tell you whatever you want to know."

"Who was he?"

"That man's name is Minister Samuel James."

"Why was he here... in my room? Does he know who I am?"

"I'm afraid not sweetie. He's just a minister who comes and prays with patients in the ICU and ER departments of the hospital."

"Oh. I was hoping... I mean it just seems like I know him. He seemed like a really good guy."

"He is a really good guy. And he's not too bad on the eyes either!" They both laughed.

"He's not? Wish I had got a better look at him!" They laughed harder, but the laughter was too much for Kindness because for the first time she realized the origin of her injury. "Ow!"

Back into care mode, Nurse Abbey rushed to her side. "I guess that was too much too fast. Here, lay back and take it easy. You need to rest."

"No disrespect Ms. Abbey but I believe I've had enough rest for a long time."

"You might be right but you need to relax just the same."

"Yes ma'am," she said reluctantly.

"Here, why don't you watch a little television. Let's put it on the news so you can at least catch up on current events."

"Okay," she said sullenly.

*(In the background: The newscaster is standing with a man and his wife talking to them about their missing son. The couple offered $20,000 reward to anyone with information leading to the whereabouts of their son. – A picture of the boy posts on the TV and Nurse Abbey glanced up at him for a short moment before walking around the bed to continue her conversation - And then the couple sent a message to their daughter. – A*

*picture of Kindness posts on the screen for a second, but Nurse Abbey did not see. Kindness looked over the nurse's shoulder while she checked her IV drip, just in time to miss the picture of herself but she did catch a glimpse of the couple. Her heart went out to them as they spoke words filled with hurt and love. 'We love you Princess. Please call us so we can work out our differences. We have no idea where your brother is and the thought of losing you both is too much. The man breaks down trying not to cry and his wife hugs him walking him away from the news reporter. Tears were streaming from Mrs. Johnson's eyes through the entire message).* Nurse Abbey looked up at Karisma.

"What's the matter darling? Why the long face?"

"I miss him."

"You miss who?"

"The minister that you ran away. Will he be coming back?"

"Wait, you miss him? You don't even know him."

"I know but I feel like I do. I feel like he's been with me this whole time. His voice called to me in the darkness while I slept. My desire to live was dying until I heard his voice. I mean I know Jesus brought me back to the light, but he uses people a lot of the time in order to do that you know."

"Why yes I do sweetie. I do know." *I knew she had a relationship with Jesus, or at least she used to. And from what I can tell it hasn't been too long ago.*

"So is he coming back?"

"Probably not."

"Why not?"

"Because I told him not to."

"Why did you do that?!"

"Calm down child."

"I'm sorry. I just, I want to know."

"Well... It's because I caught him holding your hand. I witnessed him doing it several times, but today he did something different."

"What was that? What did he do differently?"

"He kissed your hand!"

# Chapter 13:  See You Later Then

Chance was exhausted. She was barely getting four hours of sleep a day working doubles to cover Karisma's debt to Big Boi *and* Money. *I hate to leave you hanging girl, but I got to get out of here.* Chance had thought about going back home to Chicago before, but now that her plans were almost complete, she might actually go through with it. *I'll leave after I get a few hours rest.*

She tried to sleep but guilt is a beast. Before ditching town, Chance's conscious wouldn't let her go without saying goodbye to Karisma. She'd stopped in a couple of times but that minister was always there praying for her and reading to her, and Chance didn't need nobody questioning her or trying to preach to her. Besides, he looked like he was making himself pretty cozy by her bedside, holding her hand and kissing it, laying his head on the bed beside her. Once she thought she saw him kiss her on the cheek. But he could have been checking an alarm or something. *Maybe.*

Approaching Karisma's door, Chance realized she was nervous. *Why am I nervous? Karisma can't hurt me no more than anyone else has!* Then she heard it, a very familiar voice. *Karisma! She's awake!* A real friend would've rushed right in and given her a hug, but instead Chance lingered in the hallway, unconsciously backing away, unintentionally bumping into someone. When she turned around, she saw another familiar face.

"Going somewhere?"

"For your information, I am!"

"Where have you been?"

"I've been around. I even came to visit once or twice but I thought it would be rude to interrupt prayer." Nurse Abbey wasn't buying it. She was highly upset to hear this girl had been to the hospital but didn't bother to come in and talk to her friend.

"You mean to tell me you've been here and didn't bring the information you promised AND you didn't come in and talk to your friend? Do you know voice recognition can help coma patients recuperate faster? If you weren't so irresponsible and cowardly-"

"Hold up old lady! I've had as much as I can take from you. Everybody wants to blame Chance for Karisma's problems. Well guess what? I have my own problems trust me and for what it's worth, Karisma is better off not hearing from me. She's better off not remembering..."

"Remembering what?"

"Never mind. For your information I sent someone to bring the mail because I had to work. I wasn't sure if he made it here or not."

"I don't believe so."

"Well, I did. I also went in one time and talked to her. I even read a passage out of the bible Minister love Jones left in her room."

"Really. What did it say?" Nurse Abbey folded her arms with anticipation.

"I don't remember it all but one part I will never forget."

"Oh yea, and what's that?"

"Vengeance is the Lord's! And I hope it's true because there are some really bad guys holding some heavy weight over her head **and mine**. It's going to take a miracle to get her out of the snake pit she's in!"

"What are you talking about honey? Please tell me."

"I'm sorry, I can't. I've already said too much. But look, here is some of Karisma's mail. It has her real first and last name on it and I found some other stuff that may help you find her parents." Chance hands Nurse Abbey the information and walks past her towards the elevator.

"But what about you? Where are you going? Are you sure you don't wanna go in and talk to her? She has a lot of questions."
"I'm sure of only one thing Ms. Abbey. That is that Karisma will be better off not knowing the truth until she's ready to face the consequences of remembering."

"Maybe you're right young lady." Nurse Abbey held out her hand for Chance to shake. "Goodbye Chance. You be careful, okay hunni."

"Yea, sure.  As careful as an accomplice and a victim can be anyway!" she said walking away.

"What you say, hunni?"

"Nothing," she said shortly, speed walking down the corridor looking back to make sure Nurse nosey wasn't in pursuit. Chance ran out of the hospital, almost tripping over a smokers ash tray, falling into the arms of a man. *Jeff*.

"Fancy meeting you here!"

"I knew I shouldn't have grown a conscious today!" She all but screamed as he placed her back on her feet.

"And what's that supposed to mean?"

"Exactly what I said." He brushed off her comment, pushing on to a more pressing subject.

"Want to know where I've been?'

"Not really." She said dryly.

"Jail."

"Jail?! What did you do this time?!!"

"I was speeding. You see I was so eager to help a friend in need, I forgot to watch my own back. Turns out, there was a warrant for my arrest because I failed to appear in court for a previous speeding ticket."

"Oh wow. I'm really sorry Jeff." She sounded apologetic and he might have believed her if she hadn't been proven a liar.

"Well hold on baby, it gets even better. While I'm in the holding cell right, trying to figure out who to call with my one-phone-call, I remember that this beautiful stripper I happened to meet by **chance** owes me a favor. So I call 404-555-7887, and what do you know? A woman answers, but it's not you, it's the operator telling me I have the wrong number. Go figure?"

"Jeff look. I'm really sorry!"

"Oh, I'm not done baby!! So, my PO found out I was in jail and revoked my probation. The only reason I'm out now is because one of my brother's old associates knew one of my cell mates and paid my ticket, bail and probation fees. So, what do you have to say for yourself?!!"

"I did it to protect you okay. I didn't want you to get hurt because of me. What if you called me and I was with Money or Big Boi and they found out who you are and how I met you. I would be in danger and so would you and Karisma. I wouldn't be able to live with that!!" She was pacing.

"Who is Money? Is that the guy in silk who stepped out of the limo in Buckhead?"

"Yea. He's the one you should really be watching out for."

"I ain't afraid of nothin and nobody."

"Well, you should be! Money aint nobody to play with Jeff."

"Neither am I."

"Really." She said sarcastically.

"Girl, I used to run these streets."

"Money still does!"

"I'll bet he never ran into me or my brother."

"Maybe not, but he got connections everywhere."

"So do we."

"Okay, this is not a match to see who's the most dangerous."

"Ion know if I believe you anyway!"

"It don't matter if you do or not! I'm out of here!!" He grabbed her arm.

"Alright, alright, alright. You know what?"

"What?!"

"For a liar you sure are pretty convincing." He believed her but he wanted to keep making a fuss. Her guilt could work out in his favor.

"Thanks for your approval. I so live for it!" She jerked her arm away. "I asked for your forgiveness. You ain't gotta..."

"Okay, I'll forgive. But on one condition?"

"What's that?"

"You have to give me your real number right now! Deal?"

"Deal!"

*That was easy!* He still didn't trust her so he called her phone while she stood and waited. He wanted to make sure she didn't conveniently leave out or misplace a number again. Once the number was confirmed, she kissed him on the cheek and said goodbye.

"No goodbyes, I'll see you later."

"Aww, you are so handsome when you're blushing."

"So, will I?"

"Maybe."

"See you later then."

Chance nods in agreement, holding back the tears stinging her eyelids. She nodded despite the fact that there was doubt she would ever return to Atlanta once she left. Chance got in her car, speeding away headed towards I-285 South. When she reached the Marta station in East point, she got out just as she planned. She stood, clutching the airplane ticket in her pocket. It would be safer for her to get a jump on Money by not driving herself or taking the bus. He was sure to have spies. Sending the ready for pickup signal on her Uber app, destination, Hartsfield Atlanta Airport, her mind wandered to a happy place and Jeff was there.

# Chapter 14: Daddy's Here

"What are you doing here?"

"I uh- I came to see you."

"I haven't seen you in weeks and now you just decide that it's okay to show up while I'm working?"

"Man, you ain't working! You probably up here trying to see who you can get over on!! I should've known you wouldn't help me anyway. I'm out!!"

"Wait. Jeff, wait." Jeff turned back around giving his brother a challenging look.

"What?"

"Wha-," Samuel almost had a flashback and raised his hands, nearly grabbing the boy. But instead turns his back for a second to regain composure.

"Look, I'm sorry for letting my emotions get the best of me again." He sighed, "I'm glad you're okay. So what's up? What kind of help do you need?" Sam wanted to add, *'this time'*, but knew that would send his brother right out the door. He didn't want that again, at least not until he heard him out.

"Do you really want to know?"

"I'm asking you ain't I!"

"Yeah, you are. But sometimes people ask questions just to be nosey."

"To be honest, I am a little curious. You seem to always find me when you need me, but I can never find you when it's time to take care of business."

"Look, are you going to help me or not?"

"Jeff, I asked you what you needed help with because you are my brother. My only sibling. So, if I can help, you better know that I will do my best. You know that, right?"

"Yea, I guess I do."

"So, tell me, what kind of help do you need, this time?"

"Okay," Jeff paused to breathe knowing he had to make this story good or his brother would blast him out. "So, the help is not for me. It's for these two girls I know. Actually, one of them I know a little and the other is a patient here at the hospital."

"Sounds interesting. Tell me more."

"Well, a few weeks ago I met a young lady in the ER named Chance. When I first saw her, I was drawn to her and not just sexually. I wanted to meet her. You remember? It was the same day that you told me to get lost. But I hesitated leaving. I was so angry at you that I needed a moment to breathe. I walked the halls and took the elevator to the first floor which led me to ER. As I sat on the floor, she walked in. Scared, make-up smeared, tears streaming down her face, nervous and beautiful."

"Ooo, I get it. You like her! So, you walked up to her?"

"No. I just played it cool. I let her come to me you know. Trying a different approach," arrogantly spoken like a true player.

"Uh huh. And how is that working out for you?"

"Oh, it worked! She played hard to get at first but eventually she came around."

"What did she say? How did **she** approach **you**?"

"Well, she got up, pulled down her mini skirt, as if that would do any good. And then she walked, no strolled over to me. Then she bent down and put her hand on my pack and told me how much she needed what I have. And-"

"Boy stop lying!" Sam said, holding his stomach laughing uncontrollably. "You really know how to pour it on thick!"

"What? I'm telling the truth though!"

"Yea more like embellishing the truth! You're hysterical!! Now tell me, what really happened?" He was still laughing a little.

"You always know how to ruin a moment, especially when it's my moment."

"Hey, don't go there," he warned. "Just get back to telling me the truth, the real truth, about why you feel these girls need **my** help. And no funny stuff!"

"Alright. You win!" he said, picking up where he left off. "So the young lady grabbed my pack like I said and proceeded outside to the smoking section and disappeared."

"Why didn't you go after her?"

"Remember? It's my new approach!"

"Oh right, I almost forgot." Not wanting to get off the subject he diverted the dialogue back to the need. "So what happened after she disappeared?"

"The nurse called my name to go back and have my hand checked out."

"Wait. Why in the world did you have to see the nurse? When you left me-"

"You kicked me out!"

"Okay, I'll give you that. But I didn't lay a hand on you."

"No you didn't but on the way down here I had a little run in with a wall, fist first and…"

"I got you. You knew you couldn't hit me so you took it out on something that couldn't hit back."

"Are you calling me a punk?"

"Naw, but that was a punk move."

"Maybe it was. I'm just trying to find new ways to deal with my anger besides doing things that get me locked up."

"Like punching walls that can't hit back so you don't beat 'em half to death?"

"Yea, but for something that can't hit back, that wall sure packed a mighty punch!" He flexed his hand, which still carried remnants of the pain from that night.

"Mmhm. Well after you had your hand wrapped did you get your head examined?" Jeff just looked at him with mock disgust, continuing the story.

"Anyway, after I had my *head examined*, I figured the girl would be gone once I got done. But I waited around just in case, you know, cause I wanted my pack back."

"Mhmm."

"Just when I was about to give up hope, and get in my car and leave, I saw her walk out to the curb. And then this limo pulled up. I could see the fear in her eyes. She froze like she wanted to bail but couldn't move. The limo door opened and reluctantly she got in."

"Her pimp."

"That was my guess too."

"So what did you do?"

"The only thing I could do. I followed them."

"Are you sure you're not making this up?"

"No bruh, I promise on mama's grave."

"This story is just too interesting to be real."

"Yea well it is. I'm sure Chance wishes it was a lie! Shoot, I wish it was a lie."

"So what happened next?"

"I kept following them! What do you think?!"

"I meant, where did you end up boy?"

"Oh right. And don't call me boy."

"Mhmm, back to the story."

"We ended up in Buckhead, at this beautiful fenced in mansion. I,"

"Do you remember the address?"

"Will you stop butting in?"

"Sorry! I'm sorry. It's just... Nothing. Continue."

"To answer your question, no I didn't get the address but I remember how to get there. Now can I finish the story?"

"Please do. But come on inside. We can sit in the conference room. That way we can relax and drink a cup of coffee while you get to the point of why these women need my help. If what you're telling me is true, we gone have to have a plan and an army to help these girls."

Sam put his arm around his brother's neck like he did when they were younger and they walked into the hospital. Jeff proceeded to explain the rest in full detail.

"So why are you just now telling me all of this."

"You want the truth?"

"Always."

"A few hours after Chance had to be at work, I was headed back this way to find you and I got pulled over by the cops. I forgot about an old speeding ticket I got while driving your truck. There was a warrant out for my arrest and my license was suspended. My PO threatened to revoke my probation but luckily, he only let me stay in for fourteen days. I had the money on me to pay the ticket so the judge let me go."

"When was this?"

"Two weeks ago, fool! Didn't you hear me say that like three seconds ago?"

"Yea I did. I just don't understand why you didn't call me."

"I wanted to, but I'd already used my one call to call her, only..." Jeff went silent, embarrassed to finish the sentence, but Sam knew the ending.

"Only she gave you the wrong number, right?"

"Right. Bruh I was madder than a rattlesnake in a hornet's nest. But I just saw her a few minutes ago and she explained she didn't want to see me get hurt. She don't want me mixed up in her mess. She's worried I can't handle myself against her *friends*. The dudes these girls mixed up with are the real deal bruh."

"Yeah? Worse than you and me?"

"I don't know about that now. Maybe cut from the same cloth though." He got quiet. Anytime Jeff was quiet he was plotting.

"What are you thinking of doing?"

"Nothing. I'm just thinking of what we can do. I've already been back to the house in Buckhead and to Chance's apartment but I hadn't seen her. I even went to the club and didn't find her. My last hope was to find her here and what do you know I did. Only she was in a rush. She kissed me and said goodbye, and I told her I would see her later. But the way she said goodbye seemed final, like she was leaving town or something."

"Oh no! She can't! We need to find out who she really is and what she knows!!!"

"Woah, now you wait! You don't even know her, do you?"

"No, but from all you just told me and what Nurse Abbey said to me, her friend is a girl named Karisma. She just came out of her coma a couple of days ago."

"And you haven't been here preaching to her? What's wrong with you?"

"Nothing."

"Oh no. You can pull that act on somebody else, but not me buddy. What happened? What did you do?" Sam took a deep breath knowing his brother wouldn't settle for anything less than the truth. *Like brother, like brother…* He taught him well, besides, they could always tell when the other was holding something back.

"Bro, I'm not sure how to tell you this because it has taken me almost exactly 48 hours to be honest with myself. But," he took another deep breath, "I believe I love this girl."

"Love? You?" Jeff laughed incessantly, still ranting. "You have never loved a woman in your life except mama. Forever the player. Even since you've been saved many a woman has been hurt because you—you don't know how to love! You don't have a clue!"

"You're right. That was me and has been me for years, so many years that I didn't know how to begin to love a woman. And then it just snuck up on me. I didn't even recognize it myself. God had to reveal it to me. I still don't know what to make of it!" Samuel was pacing back and forth.

"Bruh? Chill."

"I'm sorry. I got lost in the truth. It seems so surreal!"

"Man, you're really serious about this huh? I just can't believe it!"

"Yes, completely serious. That's why when Nurse Abbey kicked me out for catching me kiss her hand, I was kind of relieved. I needed time to, to..."

"Breathe! Wow, this girl done got in your head. What did she do to you?"

"Nothing. She was in a coma. Whatever it is, it's got to be divine. That's the only explanation I can come up with."

"Bruh these girls got us gassed, for real!" Then Jeff's thoughts had to double back. "Wait? Did you say you kissed her hand?"

"Yea, I did. And I got caught. It's a good thing she didn't come in a few minutes before."

"Why not? What else did you do?"

"I kissed her on the cheek and the forehead and..."

"No Sam! Please tell me you did not kiss an unconscious woman who you have yet to speak to of your love on the... lips!" His words trailed off into the distance as Sam's attention was whisked away by emergency vehicles fast approaching.

"Whooo! Whoo! Whoo!" Sirens whirling loud and coming fast, but it didn't sound like an ambulance. It was a police detail escorting someone to the hospital. But who's that important they need a police escort.

"What's all the commotion bruh?"

"I don't know, but I'm sure about to find out." A lot was about to be revealed. Samuel James didn't know the half.

Suddenly, the hospital was swarming with cops, news reporters, journalists, innocent bystanders and some not so innocent! Ever since the day he picked Chance up, Money positioned some of his workers to stake out at the hospital, the club, her house and at Karisma's apartment. He had worked too hard to make sure things happened according to plan. There was no way that little tramp was going to get off the hook that easy. His evil workers had been instructed not to approach anyone or ask any questions. They were only to observe and report. Everyone inside and around the hospital seemed to be waiting on the main attraction, talking amongst themselves but no one was filming or taking pictures. The police were scouring the area as if they were looking for someone in particular like a celebrity.

Elder Johnson and the church had paid for extra security since unknown enemies decided to wreak havoc on their calm and peaceful, Christian life. Dramatically, reporters rushed to the door as the police formed a walkway for the approaching vehicle. A Porsche Cayenne pulled up and two valets opened the doors for Elder and Mrs. Johnson. Elder Johnson walked to the back of the car to meet his wife, grabbing her hand and walking swiftly. Without answering a question or breaking his stride, they entered the hospital. Cameras were flashing, reporters and journalists were hurling out question after question despite the lack of response. Several police held back the crowd until the couple had a chance to reach the elevators. Sam and Jeff watched from the opposite hallway.

"Who is that?"

"I don't know brother, but I think I have a pretty good idea."

Once inside the elevator, the couple remained nervously silent, looking at each other from time to time. The last moment they spoke to Kindness, it was more like a yelling match in which everybody lost. Led down the hallway by police escort, Nurse Abbey met them at the door on guard like a female pit-bull guarding her last pup.

"Mr. and Mrs. Johnson, I tried to prepare Karisma for your arrival but she still doesn't remember you."

"She's our daughter! She'll remember, I'll make sure of it!!"

"I understand she is your daughter Mr. Johnson, but I have been taking care of her for the past few weeks and I know how sensitive she is right now. She beats herself up every day wondering why she can't remember. I watch her blame herself for things she doesn't know the origin of, so I am now telling you, not asking, telling! Be delicate with her. Don't overwhelm her by trying to force her to remember before she's ready. Let her ask the questions and you answer them as honestly as you possibly can. Remember, our job right now is to be unselfish. Memories are what she needs to trigger her brain so we all will know what it is Karisma's running from."

"Kindness."

"Kindness what Mr. Johnson?"

"Her name. Her name is not Karisma, it's Kindness!" He was gritting his teeth at the audacity of this woman to stand and pretend she knew more about this girl than he did. *I am her father!!*

"Oh right. Sorry about that. I-, we have been calling her Karisma for so long, it kinda got stuck you know."

"Well get it unstuck—"

"Walter!"

"I'm sorry Angel."

"You need to be apologizing to the Nurse who has taken such great care of our daughter, even in our absence. That's rare! Usually if a person has nobody on the outside that cares, those on the inside could care less."

"You're right." Walter turned to Nurse Abbey and grabbed her hand. "I truly am sorry Ms. Abbey. You just don't know how grateful I am that you've acted in love towards my little girl."

"Our little girl!" Angela interjected.

"I mean our little girl. We've been under a tremendous amount of stress and... that's no excuse. I'm terribly sorry."

"I understand Mr. Johnson. I forgive you!" Nurse Abbey turned their attentions back on the nature of the visit.

"Remember, don't force her to remember. Spark her memory with your words."

"Okay we will. Thanks Nurse Abbey, for everything." Angela nudged her husband on into the room. She couldn't stand the anticipation any longer. The couple entered the room and stood at the foot of the bed, not really knowing where to begin. Kindness helped them.

"Hi."

"Hello Princess." Walter chimed right in.

"Hello baby," Ms. Johnson followed her husband.

"How are you guys doing?"

"We're as well as can be expected," she said with tears in her eyes. "Actually, we **have** to believe that we are better than can be expected because we know God is in control."

"I could tell you guys were God fearing people when I saw you on the television the other day."

"You watched the news?"

"Yes, I saw the picture of my brother too."

"What else did you see?"

"I saw you guys crying and I sensed the sincerity of your words. My heart went out to you. I hoped that you would find your son and daughter very soon. I guess we're off to a good start huh."

She smiled that heart melting smile her daddy couldn't resist. Before he realized it, he had her in his arms in full blown tears. Her mom followed suit approaching from the opposite side. They sat there holding each other and crying for a while before Walter loosened his hold a little to take one hand and tuck Kindness's hair behind one ear.

"I know this has been toughest on you Pumpkin, but I don't want you to worry anymore okay. Daddy's here! And I won't let anything else happen to you, okay.

"Okay," she whispered, holding on to her parents. It was the safest she had felt in a very long time.

"Ms. Johnson?" It was the police addressing Kindness.

"Yes sir?"

"I know you don't remember much but I have a few questions concerning the night of your accident."

"Sir, if I could help you I would. But I don't remember anything. I don't remember the club, anyone in it, the accident or how I got here. I'm sorry..."

"That's okay." He turned his attention to Elder. "Mr. Johnson, if your daughter happens to remember anything, please don't hesitate to call us. Any information will be pertinent to our case against the owner and a couple of her co-workers."

"I will call as soon as she can tell us something."

"Wait, you think someone I work with had something to do with my accident?"

"Well Ms. Johnson, that's exactly what we're trying to find out. It has been reported that a couple of other girls have come through the ER with similar symptoms as you had the night of the incident."

"I hope I can remember soon then."

"We do too! No one else should suffer the way you have."

---

"Hey Pumpkin!"

Chance was stricken with fear. She knew that voice. No matter what, she knew that voice anywhere. It was distinct unlike any other she could recollect.

"How did you—"

"Find you? Oh dear, I think you underestimate my power. I have many, many resources. There are not too many places you can hide where I don't already have eyes."

"But I just got here like thirty minutes ago. Who could have told you where I was that fast?"

"A little birdy told me!" He said in jest. But wanting to speed things up a little he got serious. "Did you know I am part owner of Uber in Atlanta?"

"No. I didn't," she said solemnly. *I just can't get a break. Freedom is what I seek!! I just want to be free!!!*

"Yea, just one of my many investments. See, I put out an A.P.B. on you when I couldn't find you last week, especially when you didn't show up for work. I was worried about you, Boo!" He was nearly whispering, lips almost touching her ear like a lover's taunt, then his hand eased up her arm and rested near her collar bone. She held her breath thinking he was going to choke her right there, but instead his hand stopped cold.

"Where you been?" She gulped hard, knowing that nothing she told him would suffice but also knowing that if she didn't tell him something it would be ten times worse.

"Money, I really didn't mean to miss work.  It's just that I was so tired from working doubles trying to pay my debt and Ki-Karisma's," she stammered hoping he didn't hear her almost call Karisma by her real name. "I fell asleep and missed my shift. After the first day, I was scared to show my face. I knew if Big Boi didn't get me, you would. So,"

"So, you tried to run away from all of the pain and suffering. I know it's stressful but you can't run away from your problems. You have to face them head on. Why can't anyone see that besides me?!" He was getting upset, but the anger was geared towards someone else. Once upon a time somebody hurt him really bad and he was hell bent on taking it out on everyone he could.

"Money please calm down. You don't want these people to get the wrong impression of us." He stood, looming over her now with a bone chilling gaze.

"So you're not leaving?"

"No, I'm- I'm not leaving. I'm just- glad you're not mad at me. That's all I- I was afraid of," she stammered all over her words, lying.

He turned sweet as he always did, "Aww, my poor Chance. You have nothing to fear now, daddy's here." Money pulled her into an embrace. "Lay your head on my shoulder. There, there," he said, rubbing her back. "Everything is going to be alright!"

Chance knew that was not the end of it. She would soon have to answer for her behavior. Money had taken her clothes before dropping her off at the club so he was sure to find the plane ticket with her intended destination. He liked having plenty of ammunition before a drive by. Thank God he didn't take her phone though. They'd made love and he seemed fine, as fine as Money could seem. But she knew, this night was her only shot at making it out without very serious injury or death. She was going to have to ditch the club but with extra security to watch over her to ensure her "safety", she wasn't going to be able to escape alone. Hopefully Jeff thought enough of her to be her knight in shining armor once again.

## **Chapter 15: Face to Face**

It's Saturday. The day Money always went to the barbershop. Since he called himself the King of Queens, no one except a woman could shape him up. He met his stylist, Curls, at a hair show in Atlanta and liked her so much he kept in touch. He fronted the money for Curls to open her shop and even offered to buy her a house in Buckhead, but she was too smart for that saying, *"Naw baby! We can be business partners only. I don't need no man trying to run my house. No man will ever have that much power over me! What you trying to do? Buy me like one of your high-priced hoes? Please! Curly don't get down like that! I don't need to be kept! I can take care of myself."* Money admired her boldness, honesty and intelligence, but only to a certain degree. He still wanted his way. He had to keep tabs on her somehow so he made her his stylist/barber. Turned out she's the best at what she does. No one kept his dreads fresh and tight like she did.

Curls catered to him from the time he walked in to the time he left. No matter who was in the shop, the television closest to him was his and anything else he wanted. There were girls serving cold non-alcoholic beverages and bringing cool towels to the patrons under the dryer. She even put a massage parlor in the back to help patrons relax while waiting on their chair to be called. There was a mani/pedi room and a nail bar. Her setup was one of excellence. She paid off the loan a few years back despite Money's repeated refusal. *"This is my shop and mine alone. I don't need nobody else's money hanging over my head. That's some overhead I can do without! Thank you!"* All Money could do at that time was laugh, take the check to the bank and hope that it wouldn't clear. But it did!

"Hey baby girl. What you been up to?"

"Great things baby! Great things!" she gave a hearty laugh. "Why don't you climb on in my chair and I'll tell you all about it! But what can I do for you in the meantime?"

"Turn the television to Channel 5 News if you don't mind lovely."

"Anything for you daddy!" Curls was loud, hard-working and independent. Money had grown fonder of her for being who she was and yet he despised her for the same reasons. Curls would flirt with him but wouldn't date him declaring, 'I don't date my clients, not past, present or future.' It was her way of letting him down easy. She knew his type. Controlling. Obsessive. Possessive. Abusive in every way. They were good to you for as long as they needed to be, but when they feel you love them unconditionally, everything changes. When she got out of the last relationship, she promised herself *never again*.

He wanted badly for her to be on his team but settled for a date in her chair once or twice a week. He listened to her and laughed at her humorous encounters. That is until breaking news crossed the screen. Money's laughter turned to fury. It had been years since he'd seen his dad up close, but now there he was. Smiling. Happy to see that his precious little girl was okay. *You just hold on, old man! This is just the eye of the storm! The worst is yet to come!*

He listened as Elder Johnson told of his daughter's condition. How she still didn't remember who he or his wife were yet. But how it was good to see her alive and well. Elder Johnson told how the doctors were preparing Kindness for eye surgery the next evening because some of the glass was still lodged behind her eye.

*"There's a slight possibility that she may lose her eyesight, but we are all hopeful. Our family is just ready to move forward, find our son and get on with our lives. We firmly believe that God is in control of all things!" The newscaster came back on and closed out the interview. "I'm Amy St. John, Channel 5 News."*

Money could not hide his anger. He rose up in the chair. *Oh, so baby girl don't remember. Well maybe I need to make a personal visit. Let's see if she remembers the voice of the one she loves to hate.*

"What's the matter honey?!"

"What you mean?"

"I mean why you muggin my TV like that?"

"Oh, I was just thinking about something I need to do, that's all."

"Mmhmm, well from the looks of it, you don't need to be doing it nowhere near Curly's. But like I was saying..." her voice trailed off as Money sunk into a pit of dark thoughts. He hadn't heard a word she said.

"Money? Money? Do you hear me talking to you?"

"What?!!" He said in a violent tone, but when he saw her face he recanted. "I'm sorry baby girl. My mind is so preoccupied right now," he said sweetly.

"About what? You were fine when you came in the door, or at least until you started watching the news. What is this sudden change in attitude about?"

"Nothing. Hey look. We gone have to finish this another time alright."

"Okay, but let me at least touch you up. Curl's name is on the line here baby, so you can't leave my shop looking nothin but clutch! You feel me?"

Money sat impatiently for another fifteen minutes before she was done. When Curls took the wrap from around his neck, he kissed her on the cheek and was gone. She watched with amazement. He never moved that fast. Always smooth, cool and laid back. He had hired hands to do the running and fetching. *Something is wrong with that man! Some deep, dark secret is haunting him, she thought.* Then shaking her head she turned to the next patron.

"Come on up here baby and let Ms. Curls fix you up."

On the way to the hospital, Money made a phone call to one of his stooges for some feedback on what's been going on with the lovely Karisma. The information he was told acted as a catalyst to urgency. There were no henchmen driving him today. He always went to the barbershop alone. Despite the fact that he continued to surpass the speed limit, Money made it all the way to Douglasville without getting pulled over. Then the inevitable happened. Money knowingly pulled over on the side of the highway, his story already together. The officer tapped on his window. With tears in his eyes, Money obliged.

"Is everything okay?"

"I'm sorry officer. I know I was speeding but I just found out my sister is in the hospital. She's been missing for months. Now I'm told she fell on a glass table and broke it with her head causing amnesia. They got most of the shards out except a large sliver behind the eye sockets. It's laying across the nerves of both her eyes and," his lip quivered as he feigned a struggle to continue to speak.

"I heard about that on the news. I'm sorry to hear about your sister, Mr." the policeman looked at Money's license, "Johnson. But I'm going to have to check your license and registration. I promise to make it quick so you can get on to the hospital. If everything works out, I'll escort you there myself."

"Thank you, officer."

The cop was gone for about ten minutes. Losing patience, Money pretended to get a phone call. He made it look urgent by yelling out the window to the officer.

"Excuse me, the nurse just called and said they are about to prep my sister for surgery. I would really like to see her before she goes. She may never get to see me again." *And not to mention, it means the world to me to see fear in her eyes. Ooh I hope she recognizes my voice! Not right away, but before I leave...*

"Well Mr. Johnson, everything checked out. Just make sure you slow it down on the way to the hospital." Money started to ask about the police escort but retracted. He really didn't want it anyway. The officer made a U turn and went back down the ramp onto I-20E. *Good riddance.*

The night shift nurse approached Kindness's room but stopped to check her lip gloss before entering. Satisfied with the result, she opened the door. The patient was asleep

"Hello Mr. and Mrs. Johnson." Then the nurse turned deliberately towards the minister and said seductively, "Sam." Delaying for a split second just in case he couldn't tell she was interested.

"My name is Nurse Patrice and I am the night shift charge nurse. I just wanted to let you guys know that we will be prepping your daughter in about ten minutes for surgery so if you would please get ready to leave the room, we can get started."

"What about me? Do I have to leave too?"

"No, Minister you can stay until I get my paperwork ready."

"Why does he get to stay?" Elder was upset.

"Because Minister Samuel is her spiritual advisor!"

"Well, I'm her father AND her spiritual advisor of twenty years! Can't I stay too?"

"No!" She disappeared without waiting for a reply. Nurse Patrice was not as nice as Nurse Abbey. She either did things strictly by the book or she did them her own way. Today she was being extra pushy.

Angela turned to her husband and said, "I thought they were going to wait until in the morning."

"I guess the doctor changed his mind."

"We'll see about that Mr. James!" Elder rushed out of the room demanding to speak to the doctor.

"I'm sorry Mr. Johnson. Dr. Harris is in the middle of another surgery right now."

"You'd better let me know as soon as he's available! If anybody lays a hand on my daughter without my knowledge, I'll sue him and this whole dadgum hospital for malpractice!!"

"Mr. Johnson,-"

"ELDER Johnson!!"

"Okay, *Elder* Johnson, I'm gone have to ask you to leave before I call security!"

Angela stepped in, "Come on Elder. Let's go wait in the lobby. I'm sure Nurse Abbey—"

"Patrice."

"Forgive me. Nurse *Patrice* surely will let us know when Dr. Harris is available. Isn't that right Nurse Patrice?" She gazed at the both of them as if neither of them had spoken to her. Elder grunted in agreement with his wife, not Nurse Patrice.

"Okay, I'll go. But if anyone comes to visit my daughter, you call my cell. No one sees her without my approval! You got that?! And when the doctor gets here, you'd better let me know!" Elder barked.

Patrice looked at the man with disdain and only nodded before giving a little deceitful smirk. Elder wanted to lay hands on the girl, and not to heal her either. Angela sensed his tension, hooking her arm into his, gently she pulled him away.

Minister James had just finished praying over Kindness with her parents in agreement, but was so thankful her parents were gone. She was stirring and he decided to wake her up. He hadn't had a moment alone with her since she requested his return. But now that they had some privacy, he didn't know what to say to her.

"Sooo, how are you feeling?"

"Considering I have a prism in my head, I guess I'm doing pretty good."

They both laughed slightly before she cut it short.

"I'm so happy to finally be alone with you. My parents, though I'm sure they mean well. They are getting on my nerves a little bit."

"Kindness, that's not a nice thing to say."

"I know, but it's how I feel." Samuel simply shrugged in compliance.

"I guess this has been overwhelming for everybody. I mean I still don't have any memories of them. But I do have memories of someone, or at least his voice." Samuel took a deep breath and sunk deeper into the chair.

"Who would that be?"

"I'm not sure. Sometimes I think it's you. Then at other times I think it could be someone else. It may be two voices altogether that I'm hearing."

"Why do you say that?"

"Because your voice is kind and warm and inviting. I just want to melt in your arms and,"

"Maybe we shouldn't be having this conversation right now."

"Why not? Now is as good a time as any. I have no time to waste Sam. I don't remember my life before this hospital. Can you blame me for holding on to the one person I do remember?"

"When you put it like that, I guess not. Continue."

"As I was saying, your voice makes me want to melt and love. But this other voice gives me an eerie feeling sometimes and other times I feel protected. Unless you have multiple personalities, there has to be two people I'm remembering."

"How does that make you feel?"

"It makes me feel weird, like this other person from my past may hold the key to putting my entire life back together."

"Maybe he does."

"Minister Samuel, we need you to step out now. The doctor is about ready for Ms. Kindness. Gotta get her prepped ya know!"

She liked Sam. He was fine and she secretly wished he'd ask for her number, but Nurse 'Crabby' was always there. Fortunately, tonight was her night off. But she still had to worry about Nurse Flatty'.

"Alright, I got you." Samuel grabbed Kindness's hand and kissed it. "I hope you find all the answers to your questions and all the pieces to your puzzle. Soon."

"Thanks Sam." Kindness looked deep into his eyes and held the gaze without reserve, gripping his hand a little longer than usual. *Is she flirting with me?* They both looked into each other's eyes, until Nurse Patrice butted in clearing her throat.

"Uhkumm! Sometime today Minister James!!" Obviously annoyed. Jealousy sparked a sinister thought. *I hope Money kills this hoe!*

"Oh sorry." He let go of the beautiful seductress's hand, walked to the door and looked back. She was still watching him. Minister James was baffled again.

*This has never happened to me before. I thought I had these feelings in check. Just when I was doing so good, she had to seduce me with her eyes, her sultry voice and those beautiful pouty lips and the curves she can't even try to hide. Not even under that hospital gown. Mmm... I wonder what she looks like under... Whoa! Chill! Calm down! Don't go there! You can't go there! You're a Minister at Living Word. Though I would love to go th- Ahhh! Samuel get a hold of yourself!! I gotta get out of here.*

He released a heavy sigh, walking quickly and silently, reflecting on previous events. Samuel hadn't really been watching where he was going, walking on auto pilot, talking himself out of trouble. He didn't notice the clean-cut gentleman wearing silk shirt and designer slacks approaching the nurse's desk until he nearly knocked him over. Money tried to stay cool.

"Hey boy! You better watch where you going! You never know who you're bumping into!!"

"Hey man, I apologize alright! It was an accident."

"Be careful! I don't have an accident of my own!"

Money was gritting his teeth. He wanted this pitiful sucker to make a move. Samuel didn't realize just how close they were to blows until he heard her voice.

"Gentlemen please! This is a hospital. If you want to box, take it outside."

Patrice's words betrayed the look on her face. She seemed eager for action, eyes glistening with suppressed excitement. Sam was suddenly disgusted with her and without saying a word, turned and walked off. She let him. A better option had shown up anyway.

"And how may I help you sir?" She said, her eyelids fluttering like butterflies in the spring wind.

Money leaned on the countertop, meeting her gaze with fierce intensity. Immediately calmed.

"Yes, I am looking for a friend of mine."

"I hope that friend's name is Patrice."

"Who's Patrice?"

Pointing to her name tag, saying seductively, "I'm Patrice."

"Umhm."

Sam looked back before turning the corner and noticed the two of them getting pretty cozy as if they already knew each other. He shook it off. *She aint none of my business.* But something in his spirit kept nagging him. That man all dressed up in designer clothes. He kind of matched the description Jeff gave of the guy who beat up his friend Chance. Mr. GQ being in *this* hospital, on the *same* floor as Kindness, made Samuel experience a fearsome eeriness. *You just paranoid Sam. Being overprotective is what got you in trouble with the law in the first place. Let it go!*

Nurse Flatness returned to the desk after making her rounds, disturbing Patrice and Money's flirtatious encounter.

"What's going on here?" She said with a knowing smirk. Not waiting for an answer, she kept talking. "You know we have a strict policy about personal matters while on the job."

"Oh, this isn't a personal visit. I don't even know this man."

"You could have fooled me!"

Patrice rolled her eyes, defending herself. "Oh wow, you're overreacting as usual. I was just about to show mister…"

Money chimed in on the queue, "Johnson. Marcus Johnson."

"Well Mr. Johnson, let me show you to the patient's room."

Nurse Flatness folded her arms asking, "Why can't you just tell him the room number? That is what we are supposed to do."

"Because, Flatty, I don't want him to get lost. Don't he look like a man who has servants doing his bidding. Answering his every whim?"

"So, you're volunteering I see!"

"No! But I am going to show him to Miss Johnson's room."

Patrice walked around the desk, summoning him with her fingers. "Follow me sir." Money was enjoying her servitude as he always did. She really knew how to treat a man, in every sense. She was a professional in more than just nursing.

"Hi, Ms. Kindness. There is someone here who would like to see you."

"Who is it?"

"His name is Marcus."

"Do I know him?"

"I don't know. I'll let you two talk out the details. I'm just showing the man to your room. Besides I got work to do."

She left, but not before running her hand down the front of Money's shirt. He shot her a quick smile and she disappeared. *Ugh! That woman is a hot mess!!* Kindness thought to herself.

"Now it's not that bad is it?" Money said, sitting in the chair closest to the door.

"What do you mean?" She said unenthusiastically, not knowing how to respond to this man she wasn't even sure if she knew.

"I mean that disgusted look on your face," he said sweetly. He had to be careful and precise in order to get the answers he needed.

"Oh. Naw, I just don't like that nurse. She is a mess!"

He laughed. "She didn't seem that bad to me."

"Oh she seems to be good with men but not so much when it comes to being a nurse."

"She's got to be pretty okay to work at the hospital, don't you think."

"I guess. Or maybe someone she knows got her this job!" She laughed.

Money knew how good Patrice was with men and how good she was not in the nursing field. He helped her get the job just as he had so many other women, positioning them like pawns at hospitals and establishments all over the Atlanta area. He snickered a little at her amazing perception, all at the same time hoping she didn't remember him. Not just yet.

"So how are you doing Kindness?" She just looked at him like *'who are you?'* Money read her mind.

"Okay. You're right. Introductions are in order. I just hoped that you would remember me without me having to tell you who I am," he lied. "It's so formal for friends, well relatives really."

"You're a relative of mine?" She perked up a little.

"Yes. We met at the club."

"We did?"

"Yes, we did." Kindness cringed.

"So, what do you know about that part of my life?"

"Well, I know you hated it at first, but then you started to like the money and thought it was okay. You said *'It pays the bills.'*"

"Yeah, well I don't think I ever want to go back to doing that." The disgusted look returned and it gave Money a morbid sense of pleasure to see how horrible the thought made her feel. *Oh, you going back!*

"Yeah, I know what you mean. But aside from that, I thought you were pretty good. Better than most. It was like you could tell you loved the art of dance and not just the money."

Her eyes lit up. "I do. I love to dance!" She surprised herself. "Oh my God! I remember dancing!! I remember how to dance. I remember heading to the church after seeing..." She paused, trying to recall the memory.

"Seeing? What did you see?"

"I'm not sure."

"What was the last thing you remember before you lost the thought?"

"I think I left my house to pick up a member of my dance ministry. We had to call an emergency practice because my dad was preaching the next day and mommy asked me to do a dance presentation during praise and worship. She always said I wasn't just gifted to dance. *'You're anointed to dance'* she'd say." The remembrance of her mother's love made Kindness smile. "That is what I remember."

She sat on the bed in shock. It was the first reflection from her past and it made her feel a sense of happiness and hope. But the thought of remembering what led her to this point, in the hospital, heading to surgery in a couple of hours, made her countenance fall. Money interrupted her thoughts.

"Is that all you remember?"

"I-I- I think so. I think the rest is too gruesome for m- me to even want to remember. Every time I-I try I get a m-migraine," she stammered. Money mocked excitement.

"Well, I'm glad you are okay and that you are beginning to remember. You can't know where you're headed until you know where you've been."

"Maybe you're right Marcus." She sighed a long sigh, realizing she still knew very little about this man.

"So, Marcus, who are your parents."

"Dorothy is my mother's name," he spoke truthfully. "I really didn't get to know my dad."

Just thinking about *Walter Johnson Sr.* made Money's skin crawl. He absolutely abhorred the man and would not rest until Walter felt every inch of pain he had caused when he abandoned him and his mother twenty-two years ago.

"Now I know it's not that bad." She replayed his words back to him.

"Oh naw, I just sometimes wish he would have stuck around to see what a wonderful person I have become. You know?" She just looked at him, not really knowing what to say.

"No, you don't know, do you? You don't know the pain of abandonment because your parents have been together probably since before you were born and no one left."

Kindness didn't know what to say or how to console him. So, she grabbed his hand and cupped it between both of hers and said, "I may not know what it feels like to be abandoned, but I'm here for you if you need to talk." Right on queue Patrice popped her head in, looking anxious.

"I'm sorry Marcus, but it's time for Dr. Harris to come in and examine Kindness before surgery." Money looked at her like, not now!

"Oh no. Can't I have a few more minutes with my cousin? We're really getting a lot accomplished in here." He jerked his head back trying to urge her to get lost but she used the same gesture telling him it is time to go!

Kindness cocked her head to the side trying to remember if she'd ever seen or heard the two of them together before. Looking at the both of them silently arguing gave hints that they have known each other for a while. Patrice was the first to notice her staring and quickly tried to clean up their faux pas.

"I wish I could give you more time Mon-, I mean, Mr. Johnson," she smiled sheepishly, "but Dr. Harris just called. He's on his way up and Mr., I mean Elder and Mrs. Johnson are with him!"

She seemed pretty nervous about the whole matter. Too nervous! Something fishy was going on here. *I have amnesia but I'm not stupid.*

"Oh. Well I guess it **is** time to leave then."

"Yea," she spoke in an '*I told you so*' tone.

But Kindness didn't really want him to go. He was the only person who had provoked a memory. Maybe if they talked long enough he could help her remember more. And she could get some answers about that silent argument with Nurse Patrice.

"No. I want him to stay."

"Well he can't!!"

Kindness turned to Marcus, ignoring the comment.

"Please stay. I'll ask Dr. Harris if it will be okay. And I'm sure my parents would love to hear how your mother is doing!"

Money looked at his Dolce & Gobbana watch. "You know what? I didn't notice how late it's getting. I forgot I have a date. Sorry, I can't stay!"

"A date? With who?" Patrice asked with noticeable jealousy.

Marcus and Kindness both looked at her with astonishment, each for different reasons. Patrice quickly gathered herself, hurriedly walking away from the door.

"Um, what was that about?" She asked curiously.

"I have no idea. You tell me and we'll both know!" He laughed it off.

Kindness shrugged but the look in her eye said she knew he was lying and that there was more to the two of them.

"Hey look, I really must get going but I'll call your room tomorrow to see how the surgery went."

"So, you're not coming back to visit?"

"I might. But if I don't I'll definitely be calling you soon!"

"Is that a promise?"

"Oh, it's not just a promise love, it's a guarantee!" She smiled as he walked towards the door.

"Oh okay, sounds good. I'll look forward to hearing from you."

Money walked hastily out of the room and almost ran right into Patrice as he rounded the corner. Just the person he was looking for. Kindness could slightly hear their conversation, though she was straining to make out the words. But it was obvious that Patrice was angry and jealous about Marcus's date.

"So, you have a date, do you?!"

"Yeah, I do! And that means it's time to go."

Patrice knew by his tone, that she should leave it alone, but she was really troubled.

"No! Not until you tell me with who!"

"Girl!" Money growled. "You are pushing it! Money don't answer to nobody, especially some D+ barely passing nursing school student who I had to donate $10,000 for just to get this job!! It's an embarrassment to even call you a nurse! But remember this and don't you ever forget. You owe me so I own you!! Now get out of my way!!"

Patrice politely moved; feelings hurt but mostly scared for her life. She knew who she was dealing with more than anyone else. She was one of his first girls. But when she got pregnant, he sent her to school instead of forcing her to continue to work the streets. She thought that meant he felt differently because of his son, but it didn't. Sure, he had a heart, but it was still a cold one and made of nothing but stone.

"And get back to work," he shouted calmly over his shoulder halfway down the hall.

*I'm still getting pimped! Never should have thought I was special just because I'm not on the streets anymore. Same game, different setting!*

*Sooooo! They do know each other! And it seems like their relationship runs back some years. I knew it! Well that's it, neither of them can be trusted, but I can use what I know against them if I play my cards right. Something tells me I'm going to need to get the upper hand before everything is said and done. Marcus and Patrice, if those are even their real names!*

Money passed Dr. Harris and the Johnson's going down the corridor. It took everything in him not to lay Walter out when he nodded a silent hello. *This fool don't even know his own son when he sees me. He doesn't even know who I am! But soon... soon he will! All of them will!!*

"Well Ms. Kindness, everything looks good. Your optical nerves have recovered enough to move forward with the second surgery. How does that sound?"

She said nothing. She was staring into outer space, thinking about Marcus and Patrice and how they knew each other. And what else they were hiding? She wondered if they were who they said they were.

"So many questions..." she muttered under her breath.

"Kindness? Do you have any questions for me?"

"Oh no. Sorry, I was talking about something else."

"Excuse me? What do you mean Ms. Johnson? You don't have any questions?"

Dr. Harris had not heard what she muttered as she had originally thought. She recovered quickly.

"Um, just one. Do you think I will get my complete memory back after the surgery?"

"Well, that's hard to say. The surgery is to remove the glass shards threatening to sever your optical nerves. Your memory is psychological. I'm afraid there is no surgery for restoration of memory."

"Oh."

"But I can tell you what we can do. After your surgery, we can schedule a psychiatrist or a hypnotist to come visit. I've heard that it can help to talk to them about things you may not want to with anyone else. Do you want to do that?"

"I guess it's worth a shot. That is if I don't remember after the surgery."

"Okay then. We'll talk about it when you wake up. So, are you ready?"

"Yes sir."

"Good. I'll have an anesthesiologist come up. In the meantime, Nurse Flatness will get you all prepped."

"Dr. Harris? I do have one more question."

"Okay. What is it?"

"Am I gonna have to cut off all of my hair?"

He sighed, "I'm afraid so, unless you wanna rock a shag."

She laughed. "No, I don't think that would be a good look for me."

"I agree. I'll send your parents in now. I'm sure they have some things to say to you before we roll you down."

"Yes sir. Thank you."

"No problem Ms. Kindness."

Elder and Mrs. Johnson rushed through the door before it could close behind the doctor.

"Hey Princess."

"Hey daddy." Then she looked at Angela with tears in her eyes. "Mommy!"

This was different and a little bit weird. Kindness had always been daddy's little girl. Now she held her arms out to her mom. When Angie walked to the bed, Kindness grabbed her and buried her head into her mother's torso.

"Shhh. It's okay baby. Everything is going to be okay. You know what I always say. Trust..."

"God!" she finished her mother's quote. "I do mommy. I do trust God. I just remember..."

"You remember? Remember what baby?" Angela looked up at her husband nervously.

"What do you remember Kindness?" she said, still looking at him.

"Your love."

"My love?"

"Yea. And I want you to know that I appreciate you." She held her head up to look at her mom. Angela pried her eyes from Elder to meet her daughter's gaze. "I appreciate your strength. You have held this family together mom. And I don't think I have ever acknowledged you for it and I haven't thanked you for it. I just want you to know how sorry I am."

Angela reached for Walter's hand to join the hug, but he just leaned back on the wall watching his daughter become someone he didn't know anymore. Or maybe that she always had been he just couldn't see past himself. But he was beginning to see that hogging her attention created a wedge between mother and daughter, and it was time for that wedge to be dissolved. He let them have their moment. Angela dropped her hand. Her attention was restored to Kindness.

"Shhh. It's okay. I know you're thankful."

"That's just it ma. You never receive adulation but you are always giving it, to God, to daddy, to me and…"

"And who baby?"

"My brother," she whispered. "Where is he ma!? Where is he?" Her body was jerking with tears.

"It's okay baby. He's in God's hands. Everything is going to work out I promise, because God promised. And what He says, He will do. Has He said one thing and not made it good? He can do anything baby. Always remember God is able!" They were all crying, and finally Walter walked over joining the hug.

"I appreciate you too Angel!" He kissed her on the cheek then Kindness on the forehead.

Nurse Flatness stood in the doorway holding back tears watching. She didn't want to interrupt, but time didn't permit a prolonged therapy session. However, she could tell the Johnson family just had a moment of healing.

"Elder and Mrs. Johnson?" Walter broke away first.

"Yes, Nurse Flatness?"

"I have to prep Kindness for surgery. Can I ask you guys to step into the lobby?"

"Sure." Walter looked at Kindness and said, "We'll be right here when you get back."

"Okay daddy." Angela wiped her tears and gently kissed her cheek.

"My precious little girl."

She didn't want to leave. They'd always had a distant but loving relationship. Currently, Angela was experiencing a deeper, more profound love for Kindness. She had never felt so close to her daughter than she did right now. Reluctant to depart, Angela kissed her daughter once more before joining Walter at the door.

"I'll see you guys in a little bit." At the same time both her parents did a half turn, and her mom spoke for the both of them.

"Yes you will darling. Yes, you will."

As they headed to the lobby, Elder fell into his own thoughts and a peaceful silence engulfed the pair. Finally! Finally, his family was coming back together. Angela and Kindness are getting closer, which he had to admit to himself, was going to take some getting used to. He felt a twinge of jealousy when Kindness reached for her mother first. The fact that she remembered her mother's love but not his took him aback. However, it was great to see the two of them healing together. Elder didn't remember a time when they had shared that type of affection. It was breathtaking and a little overwhelming. But that is how change happens. He remembered the words his Pastor had preached that past Sunday.

*"A trial is only God's opportunity to show us how much we can be in our own way and that we need to get out of our own way so that He can move for us. God cannot move for us if we are standing in front of Him. He won't run us over. And He won't force us out of the way. But He will allow things to happen to get our attention with the hope that we will see more clearly that He is God and He alone. We just need to trust Him and stay in His way. Stay in His way by following His way! Let Him lead!! And just Let God be God! Let Him have His way!!"*

God knew how much he needed to hear those words then and how comforting remembering them would be today. Now all they had to do was find Jay so that God could work on that part of the relationship also. Elder had to believe that God was already working on their son and so he waited in the lobby in peaceful silence with his wife. Healing.

Nurse Flatness closed the door behind them. "You ready to go ahead and get this over with?"

"Yes ma'am, as ready as I'll ever be."

"Good." She was cleaning the clippers and testing them. Fear was all in Kindness's face.

"Sweetheart, it's going to be alright. Dr. Harris has performed these type surgeries many times. He's the best you know."

"No, it's not that."

"Well, are you worried about your hair? You know it will grow back faster than you think."

"No, it's not that either." Nurse Flatness put down her tools, placing her hands on thin hips.

"Well, what is the matter then child?"

"I don't know exactly. But I got a feeling that after this surgery everything is going to change in my life. Or maybe it will go back to the way it was before the injury."

"And that frightens you." It was a statement not a question.

"Yes ma'am."

"Well don't worry about it so much. God is in control like your mother said. You believe that right?"

"Yes ma'am."

"Hmm, you don't sound too convincing but I'll humor you." She walked closer and sat on the bed. "Look, if you just believe that God is in control, He will work everything out."

"I suppose so." She said quietly.

"But you're still frightened?"

"Yes."

"I'm going to tell you what my Aunt Ruby used to tell me. 'Baby, when you get stuck and you want to move but you can't, sometimes you have to go back to the beginning. You have to go back to the beginning...'"

"So, you can move forward!" Kindness finished the sentence.

"O, so I see my Aunt Ruby wasn't the only wise woman, or person. Do you remember who said that to you?"

Kindness smiled. "My dad." Nurse Flatness smiled as Kindness finished the memory. "The first time he said that to me, I was sitting on his lap crying because I couldn't find my favorite stuffed animal. We searched and searched the house but it was nowhere to be found. So, he scooped me up and sat down on the couch consoling me. That's when he said it."

"Kindness, do you realize you are getting your memory back."

"Yes ma'am. That's why I'm a little scared."

"When was the first time you started remembering?"

Kindness's eyes lit up. "Today. It was when my cousin Marcus came to visit."

"What did you remember?"

"Well, he was talking about me dancing at the club. And I said I don't think that I'll ever go back there. Then he said he understood my not wanting to return but that I was good, better than most. That's when it happened."

"What did you remember?"

"I remembered my mom telling me that I wasn't just good. 'You're anointed!' She had said."

"Was that all you remembered?"

"No. I remembered how much I loved to dance, how it made me feel all light and free. I remembered my mother's love when she spoke encouraging words to me. And..."

"And?"

"And then the memory starts going black. The last thing I remember is heading to dance practice and seeing..."

"And seeing what? Who?" Nurse Flatness was getting excited right along with Kindness.

"I dunno. I think it was a black SUV with 24's on it. I passed it and I turned..."

"You turned? Go on." Nurse Flatness tried to guide her through the memory.

"I. It- It was after I talked to my brother! He was upset! I think with my father, but..." Kindness got lost between thought and words for just a moment. "But I don't know about what."

"Is that all you remember dear?"

"No ma'am."

"Then what's the matter dear?"

"What I'm remembering is all jumbled up. I need time to figure out what's real and what's not." She lied.

"I understand." She said rubbing her back. "You just take all the time you need."

"Knock! Knock!"

"Is everything clear to go?" It was Dr. Harris.

"Yes Doctor. I'm getting ready to shave her now."

"Well Ms. Kindness, are you ready to get this over with."

"I suppose so, but I have to admit, I am a little nervous still."

"Oh, don't worry about the hair. It'll grow back."

She laughed before answering. " It's not the hair I'm worried about."

"Well, if it's your eyesight, then you can trust me. I've done this type of surgery a few times before and I have a 99% success rate."

"That's good to hear."

But that was not at all she was nervous about. She was starting to remember everything. The events, the voices, the smells, the fear, and after desiring to remember for so many weeks, for the first time she wanted to stay right where she was in the thought process. *Why can't I just love from right here and move forward with my life? Why can't I just love Sam and get to know my parents more and find my brother and live happily ever after?* Then she heard the eerie voice that had been plaguing her mind in her dreams. *'Life is not a fairy tale princess. You got to prove you can make it just like everyone else. And no one is going to come and save you, not even daddy!'* His laugh was even more disturbing than his voice. Voices were separating in her mind and being matched with memories and events.

"Kindness? Baby, are you okay?"

"Oh, yea sure!"

"Well, you don't look like it."

"No, I'm fine."

Dr. Harris moved closer. "Kindness, if you want to postpone the surgery we can. It may be a few months before I can get you back on the schedule though."

"A couple of months? Why so long?"

"I'm going out of state to do a series of surgeries where interns will be studying my techniques."

"Wow, what an accomplishment Dr. Harris!"

"Thank you, Kindness. I've been waiting on this day for years and I'm just grateful to have been chosen. But before I bore you with the details and to get back on subject, would you like to wait?"

"Wait? Wait for what?"

"Wait to perform the surgery, remember?"

"Oh yea, the surgery. No let's continue. I trust you."

"Are you sure?"

She took a deep breath. "Yes, I am sure. Whatever is bothering me, I may as well face it and get it over with. It's not going nowhere until I do. Besides, I have a feeling that I will have even bigger fish to fry soon enough. But I also feel that everything is going to work out too." She paused. "So come on, Nurse Flatness. Shave me and let's get this show on the road!"

# **Chapter 16: Back to the Beginning**

"Kindness can you count backwards from twenty for me?"

"Sure Doc! Twenty, ninthteen, eighthdeen, seventyteen, hahaha! I can count really I can!" she said drunkenly. "And backwards too! Uh let's see, where did I leave off? Oh yeah six teens, fif--, fif--, a fifth of vodka please and I'll be good to go! Hahaha!"

"I think she's almost ready," Doc Harris said comically to his partners, but Kindness became suddenly serious.

"No! No, I'm not ready yet! I'm not drunk enough to go out there!! What if they laugh at me? This is not the kind of dancing I do!!"

"Her heart is racing doctor!"

"Kindness?"

"Hmm," her chest was rising and falling too rapidly.

"Kindness, I need you to calm down for me okay."

"Calm down? Who are you?"

"I'm Dr. Harris. Remember?"

"Are you a regular? Or are you new? Because I only give discounts to the new faces," she whispered. "But don't tell Big Boi. He don't like me giving discounts to nobody!"

"Kindness, I'm your doctor and we are getting ready to perform eye surgery okay."

"Really? You a doctor? So, you gone give me some good tips huh! If you do, I'll let you play a game of operation and you can start right here with my heart!" She snickered.

"Yes Kindness, we are going to operate, but before we can begin, I need you to calm down and lay flat on the gurney okay?"

"Lay flat! Oh no, I don't do that!! I done told you Big Boi, it aint that type of party!!!" She was fighting the doctor and two of his assistants.

"Give her 50 more cc of Diprivan stat!"

Nurse Kelly prepared the shot and pushed it into her IV while Dr. Harris continued to calm her down. After about one minute, her head was bobbling again. His voice was soothing and peaceful. The more he spoke, the more tranquil she became.

"Kindness? Can you continue counting backwards where you left off?"

"Sure!" she said, forgetting her earlier rantings. "Um, what number was I on again?"

"Fifteen."

"Oh yea, a fifth of gin and I'll be good to go."

"Repeat after me Kindness. Can you do that?"

"Sure! Anything for you Dr. Harris."

"Well at least she remembers my name this time!" He said to his colleagues, who were laughing silently.

"Well at least she rebrembers my lame in time!" She snickered drunkenly.

"Oh, sorry we are supposed to be counting, aren't we?"

"Yep! You first! I'm repeating asta you now rebrember!!" she laughed. Dr. Harris stifled a laugh, focusing on the not so easy task of sedating this young lady.

"Someone has a high tolerance," the nurse whispered near his ear. He only nodded, prodding Kindness to follow earlier instructions.

"Repeat after me. Fourteen."

"Fourtheen."

"Thirteen."

"Thirsteen? Yea I am kinda thirsty! I'll take a bottle of Patron to go please!!" She laughed again and it took everything for Dr. Harris and his crew to remain serious and not outwardly join in the laughter. He let her finish laughing but continued compelling her to count.

"Twelve," he said, hiding a slight giggle.

She said nothing.

"Twelve," he repeated.

Again, nothing.

"Finally, we can get started," he said adding, "That girl sure does have a high tolerance!" They laughed as he made his first incision.

Kindness was out. But just as instantaneous as her body went limp, her memories sprang to life. It was like a movie going on in her head. She saw herself driving down the road the day Jay went missing. She was talking to him, reasoning with him but he didn't want to hear it. She remembered, and could even feel the overwhelming helplessness as he fled her presence. The portrait of her brother being pulled into a black Escalade with chrome everything was so vivid it was like she could touch it. Then she was trying to regain the peace she once had, and it worked for a minute. Dancing always left her feeling serene. But the more she danced the more questions arose. She worried about her parents and how they must be feeling, speeding down the highways and side roads to get home. Only to find her parents in disarray, blood all on the walls and carpet, but not before being commanded by the dark sinister voice of a devil. She didn't have a choice but to comply. Her brother's life depended on it. The heavy weight on her shoulders seemed such a small price to pay for the safety of her family. But... Why? Why was this tragedy happening to them? Then her mind flashed forward a few weeks to her point break. She couldn't take it anymore. She couldn't come home to a lifeless house. She could no longer face the silence without Jay. And why weren't they looking for him!

"Why aren't you out looking for him?"

"Princess, we've looked!"

"Look again!"

"But where do we start? We searched everywhere we know to look! There are  no new leads!"

"I don't know! Start over! Maybe you could start at the corner where I told the police I saw him being abducted! Search for a black Escalade! I don't know!! But you can't stop until you find him!"

"Baby girl! I know you're upset and hurting but now is the time to pull together!"

"How daddy!? How are we supposed to pull together when everything around us is falling apart?!!"

"Our family may be knocked out of our comfort zone, but we are not falling apart."

"You're in denial!"

"Young lady, you better watch how you talk to me! Now I know things are a little tough for us right now, but I am your father and you will respect me!"

"No, I will not! I won't watch how I talk to you! I will not respect you! Not until you find my brother!!"

"Kindness, please calm down. You're being irrational."

"And you're not being irrational enough!!"

"Do you think it's easy for me to be patient and wait on God? I pray every day for insight, to know what to do, where to go. He hasn't spoken anything to me. And even when God is not speaking, He is still answering prayers. He's telling me not now. It's not time to move."

"Prayer alone will get you nowhere daddy! I remember a scripture that says we are to watch and pray, but it seems all you do is pray and sit!!"

"You'd better calm down young lady, and **watch** your tone!" She was still angry but she did relax, curious to see what he would say back before she left.

"Watch, doesn't mean I have to do anything other than what God has told me to do. If he doesn't tell me to move or where to go, then I'm just out there fighting against the wind. It won't accomplish a thing."

"Yea dad, maybe you're right. But it's also true that sometimes when God doesn't speak it's because you're asking Him to do something you're supposed to be doing. Maybe he hasn't given you an answer because you're looking in the wrong places. Maybe the answer to where to start is inside of **you**!"

Kindness walked towards the door, expecting her dad to stop her, but he didn't. So she continued.

"Your heart dad. We've looked all over this city searching for my brother and there isn't one clue that would give us a glimpse of hope. I don't know why but I feel like there is something deeper going on with my brother. And since he is your twin, maybe the answer lies in **your** heart."

She stopped in the foyer, picked up her bag and reached for the doorknob.

"Baby please don't go!"

"Mom, I have to. I can't stay here without him. It's too hard!"

"Whoever said life was going to be a bed of ease? God will allow things to happen in your life to see how you're going to deal with them."

*"Then I guess I fail this challenge, because I'm not dealing with this very well..."*

*"If you know that, then the only person who can change your course is you baby."*

*"I know, but I can't..."*

*"Yes you can. You're the only one who can!"*

*"But mom, you just don't understand! I can't! I have to leave!"*

*"No you don't..."*

*"Yes I do!!"*

*"Why Kindness? Why do you have to leave?"*

*"I can't tell you. And even if I did, it wouldn't change anything!"*

She walked out of the door, slamming it shut. But immediately the door opened as she knew it would. Her mother always chased after what she loved and her father never did. He let things and people go when he should not have. It was something cold in his eyes when he did so.

*"Mom, I have to go..."*

*"Okay baby. I'll let you go but I want you to know that I love you and God loves you. And you can always come home."*

*"Yes ma'am." She turned and got in her car and vanished. Like father like daughter. Like mother like daughter.* But after a few days at Chance's house, she returned. Money was still working on her apartment. She apologized to her parents. They were glad she came back home, but it only made the inevitable more difficult. Eventually, she would have to leave for good.

Kindness could feel herself stretching though her eyes were still closed and her mind half dazed. She blinked a few times hoping for a clear view once her eyelids opened. But when she did, she couldn't see a thing. *No, not again!* Panic was on the rise. Her voice cracked a little from the stress.

"I can't see! Why can't I see!?"

"Kindness, baby. Calm down okay. The doctor wanted your eyes to stay covered for at least 48 hours so your optical nerves can rest and heal."

"But can I see?" She said bluntly, almost rudely.

"I'm not sure baby. We won't know until they take the wrapping off."

"And when will that be exactly?"

"Dr. Harris said 48 hours Pumpkin. Don't you remember your mother just told you?

"Of course, I remember dad! I'm not stupid!"

"Sweetheart what's the matter? You seem a little upset."

"Well, aren't you a regular Einstein!"

"Kindness! What has gotten into you? Apologize to your father this instant!"

"For what? I didn't do anything wrong. Y'all the ones that lost my brother!"

She looked toward her father, then her mother. "And mom, wipe that ghastly look off of your face! I can't see it, but I know it's there. You know we are not the perfect family so let's just stop pretending!! Okay?"

Both parents went silent, not really knowing how to respond.

"And dad, would you please, pl-ease stop calling me all these sugar sweet names! Princess, Pumpkin, Sweetheart! Ugh! It's getting to be a real pain in the butt!"

"But you used to love it when I called you Princess. You're daddy's little Princess!" Elder was tearing up.

"Not anymore! Take a look around daddy! I haven't been innocent in months and I'm not a little girl anymore! I've grown up! Fast!"

"But Pumpk-, I mean Kindness-"

"The name's Karisma!!" She butted in. "And don't you forget it!"

"Kindness! Why are you acting like this? Before the surgery everything was fine!"

"No! Everything was not fine! I didn't know what everything was then and I still don't know!" she lied. "But what I do know is I'm sick and tired of seeing your faces! So I'm out of here!"

She pushed to get off the bed but lacked the strength, though determination was well intact.

"Your eyes are covered up baby. You can't even see our faces!" Angela rushed to help Kindness back into the bed.

"Well Mother, I don't want to see your faces when the wrapping comes off! How about that!? So, I'm leaving!"

"Kindness, you're in the hospital. You can't leave!" Walter ignored her ignorant behavior and tried to appeal to reason. Angela was still trying to calm Kindness back to a resting position.

"Mom! Stop fussing over me!!"

"She's just trying to help you see why you can't leave. You're not strong enough to stand yet."

"You know what, you're right daddy dearest. I can't leave, but you can. So, go! You guys can leave! As a matter of fact," she pressed the nurse call button.

"Yes Ms. Kindness?"

"Um, the name is Karisma! And could you please have security come and escort my parents away from here. I'm tired of seeing them!"

"But ma'am, they're your parents. They have waited all night without sleep to see you and talk to you and make sure you're okay. Why would you want them to leave?"

"Didn't I say I'm tired of seeing their holier than thou faces!"

"Yes you did say something of that sort. But,"

"Alright then. DO YOUR JOB!"

"Yes ma'am. I'll call them right away."

Walter and Angela were already on their feet, coats and bags in hand.

"There's no need to call for security Ms. Karisma. We can find our way out!" Walter said, stunned that his little girl was acting so horribly.

"Good! Bye!!"

Angela was speechless as well. She had so much to say but no words could express the hurt. She took one last look at her daughter's face before leading the way out of the room. When they reached the double doors, Angela turned to her husband.

"What just happened in there?"

"I'm not sure, but I have a feeling our daughter is getting her memory back."

"Well, if you're right, things will more than likely get worse before they get better."

"Do you really believe things will get better and that we'll find Jay and that all will go back to normal?"

"No."

Elder stopped and looked at his wife like a stranger so she clarified his suspicions.

"No, I don't just believe that things will get better. I know they will. But they'll never go back to the way they were either. And you know what?"

"What?"

"I'm glad! It's time for a new beginning. Come hell or high water, me and you, we got to stick together and be honest with each other. Don't you agree?"

"I do. I've agreed with that for 27 years. Why would I stop now?"

"Hi Mr. and Mrs. Johnson. How's Kindness?" It was Nurse Flatness coming in early for the night shift.

"Uh, you may want to see for yourself."

"Huh? What do you mean? Why can't you tell me? She's okay, isn't she?" Her head was snapping back and forth between the two of them.

"Physically, I think she's fine. But she's not the same Kindness she was yesterday."

"Yea, today she's not even Kindness at all. She's Karisma! And you better make sure you call her by the right name too." Walter said with a hint of disgust.

"I see. Is she getting more of her memory back at all?"

"Not all at once, at least I don't think so. It seems she's going back to the beginning of things."

"So, she can move forward."

"I guess so."

"You know, she said that last night. After her cousin left, she told me you used to say that to her just like my Aunt Ruby used to say it to me."

"Cousin? What cousin?" Walter interrupted.

"His name was, um, um," it was on the tip of her tongue and Elder wanted to shake her until it fell off. He was giving her a look like he would do it too, gazing with fierce intensity! Then she finally remembered.

"Marcus. That's his name. Marcus Johnson."

"Honey, that's your name. Walter Demarcus Johnson."

Nurse Flatness was watching them like a soap opera, as they looked at each other, one with confusion and one with recognition.

"No. It couldn't be."

"It couldn't be what?" Angela was getting a little agitated considering they'd just made a pact of honesty. She repeated herself.

"It couldn't be what, Walter?"

Elder looked over at Nurse Flatness. "Uh, can you excuse us for a moment please?"

"Oh right. Sorry. I'm going to be late for my shift anyway!" She reluctantly pulled herself away and headed towards the sliding doors wishing she could be a fly on the sidewalk. Their life was better than any soap opera she'd ever seen. And she'd seen lots.

Once the nurse was out of sight, Angela continued her interrogation.

"Elder Johnson, if you don't tell me what is going on right now! I promise you; it'll be a long time before I will ever trust you again."

"Honestly Angelface, I don't know."

"Well, tell me what you think is going on then, because you know something! I can see it in your eyes."

"Honey, let's go home. If I'm going to tell you what I think is happening, we're going to need a couple of pots of coffee, some comfortable seats and a little bit more privacy!"

"Alright then. Let's go!"

# **Chapter 17: A Married Man's Truth**

"Baby?"

"Don't baby me! Why haven't you told me about this woman who says this child is yours before?"

"She was crazy, threatening your life and mine! I didn't want her to hurt you and mainly *I* didn't want to hurt you Angel!"

"Oh I feel like Karisma now! Don't call me none of those sugar sweet names and think that's going to make it all better! You've been doing that for years!"

"Angel please calm down."

"Maybe I could have been more calm ten years ago, maybe even twenty. But it's too late for turn down now baby! I'm all the way turnt up!"

"You need to sit down and shut up!"

"What? What did you say to me?"

"You heard me! None of this ranting and raving is going to change anything. It's not going to make things better!! It's not going to put our family back on track. So why must you continue?! And using slang at that!"

"Because I feel like it! And it feels good to let all the pain out! I've been holding it in for way too long Walter! Way too long! Forever the loving, forgiving, understanding Christian wife! So for as long as I want to rant and rave and ask questions, you will listen! And you will answer!"

"Yes ma'am! Whatever you say Mother Teresa!"

"What?"

"Yea, that's you, the Saint! The only one who has never made a mistake in this whole entire family!"

"Don't try that with me! I've made my mistakes but at least I own up to them. I apologize and I make things good again! But you! You're full of secrets, empty promises and broken vows!"

"What do you mean? Everything I have done was to protect you and our kids. I didn't want to hurt you! None of you!"

"I'm sure the only person you cared about hurting besides yourself was Kindness. Daddy's little girl. Remember, she's the only reason we stayed together after the first two years anyway."

"Yea, I remember. I can't help but remember lately because you keep reminding me. I thought we'd gotten past all of that madness. But, now in our latter years you want to bring the drama back!"

"I didn't bring the drama back baby! You did that thirty years ago, when you slept with that tramp."

"Angela, it was when you and I had broken up. You divorced me and were gone for almost a year. Everyone from church questioned me in your absence! It was humiliating! And I ended up being consoled by a newcomer, someone who didn't know you and wasn't trying to judge me!"

"Oh, so now the truth really comes out. You didn't just sleep with her one time. Ya'll was making love, huh?"

"Maybe she thought we were, but I was just relieving myself of some stress! Look, I'm not proud of what I did, it's just the ugly truth!"

"Umhmm! Did you wear a condom?"

"Yeah, I wore a condom!"

"Every time?"

"Well maybe I forgot once or twice! But I-"

"Exactly what I thought! Ya'll was in a relationship and no matter what you called it then, that's what it was Walter!!"

"Angel! Please?"

"Don't Angel me! That woman had every right to expect you to be there for her child, hmph, I would've come after you too!"

Walter had nothing left to say. He just stood in front of her, helpless, looking like a man who'd lost his last ray of hope. There was more to be told of the truth, but if she was this mad now, he could only imagine how she'd act when everything comes out. He knew it would eventually. It had to in order for his family to be functional again. In the meantime, he let her vent. Angela stood up and started towards the steps.

"And what kind of a man leaves his son for years! Never talk to him! Never see him! Lord, what kind of man did I marry?! That kid's probably grown up to be a broken mess of a man by now!"

She stormed up the stairs still muttering things to herself about this man she married but obviously did not know! Walter could hear her stomping to and fro, gathering up things. Then she yelled from the top of the stairs.

"I won't let the sun set on my anger, so I forgive you for my own sake! But I will not sleep in the same bed with you tonight!! Your bed is the couch until further notice!!!"

He didn't respond. He did the only thing to be done in times like these. Pray.

*"I'm a changed man! I know I am. It's just going to take some time for her to believe me, that's all. That man, the boy trying to be a man was selfish and full of pride, but I am no longer that man! That's not who I am, not anymore. You got to help her to see. She's mad right now and I can't blame her, but anger is clouding her thinking. Clear her mind, please Lord."* He talked to the only one he could always talk to, Jesus.

After prayer and meditation, suddenly Walter got the notion to make a couple of house calls. He needed answers, sure answers, because in the morning he knew she would have much more to say. He didn't call her name to let her know he was heading out, he simply wrote a short note: *Gone out. Be back soon! I love you! Walter*

---

"Ring, Ring!"

Kindness looked at the phone, not sure if she wanted to answer. Reluctantly, she picked it up on the third ring.

"Hello."

"Hey, how are you doing?"

"Who is this?"

"You don't remember me? I just came to visit you last night."

"Marcus?"

"Yep."

"Hey man, what's going on?"

"I can't call it. I'm just keeping a promise.

"To who?"

"You silly."

"Oh, you made me a promise?"

"Yes, when I came to see you last night I promised to at least call and check up on you."

"Oh right, you did."

"So, how are you?"

"Well, I can see if that's what you mean."

"Yes, that is part of what I meant. And I'm happy you're better, but I wanted to make sure you were feeling okay mentally too. Surgery can take a toll on the mind you know."

"You got that right! But, I'm good. I just need a break from everyone, especially my parents."

"Yea, I understand. Parents can be a real pain sometimes."

"Tell me about it."

"So, where are your parents? Are they in the room?" He asked, trying to sound distantly interested.

"No. They are not here. I just kicked them out!"

"What? Why would you do a thing like that?"

"I don't know. I guess I'm not myself today."

"Mhmm, maybe. Or maybe that surgery **is** affecting your attitude."

"You know, you could be right. I did act like a jerk towards my parents."

"I can't believe you threw them out of your room!" He sounded concerned but secretly he was enjoying every detail. *Daddy's little princess done turned on her king!*

"I must admit now, looking back, I was kind of harsh."

"Kinda?"

"Okay, a lot harsh. I guess I need to apologize."

"Yea, I agree. But if I were you, first I'd get some rest. There will be plenty of time for apologies tomorrow."

"You're right. I'll call them in the morning." Right on queue, Nurse Abbey walked in.

"Miss Johnson, it's time for your X-ray."

"Oh right. I completely forgot."

"Let me say goodbye to my cousin." Nurse Abbey shot her a confused look, but said nothing. Kindness turned her attention back to Marcus.

"I'm sorry, I have to go."

"I heard. Go ahead. Like I said, you need your rest anyway. I'll see you soon."

"You're going to come and see me! When?!" She was excited to have someone to talk to besides her parents. *A friend.*

"Maybe later on today, but I have to check my schedule first."

"Oh," she sounded disappointed.

"Okay, if I don't come today, I'll come first thing in the morning."

"Great!" She perked up, "I get up at nine."

"Then I'll be there around 9:30."

"Sounds good."

"See you then."

"Okay. Bye Marcus!"

"Bye!" His stomach churned as he tried to match her excitement. It felt good to be back in his own reality. *The snowball is in motion and gaining momentum!*

Nurse Abbey remained silent until Kindness hung up the phone, but questions were whirling around in her mind. She had to know who this *Marcus* was!

"Um, you don't mind if I ask who that was?"

"Oh no, of course not. It was my cousin Marcus. He's the only person who knows me from the club."

"Really? What did he tell you?"

"Last night when he visited with me, he told me I was a good dancer. And he said I hated it at first, but I made a lot of money."

"You said he was your cousin. Did he tell you that too?"

"Yes ma'am."

"Do you have any proof that he's your cousin? Any memories of him at the club?"

"I don't have any proof. And to be honest my memories are few." Nurse Abbey could hear the distress in Kindness's voice and decided not to push any further.

"It's okay baby. That doesn't matter right now. All that matters is that you get better, so let's go get that X-ray, okay."

She was trying to lighten the young lady's mood, but it wasn't working out very well. Kindness lackadaisical allowed Nurse Abbey to dress her and help her into the wheelchair, though her mind was somewhere else. She was searching. Searching for a clue, a sign, proof that she had met this man before. There was only one. His voice.

---

---

"Knock, knock!"

"Hold on, I'm coming."

Walter stood outside of a place with vague familiarity. The address was the same, but the house had been remodeled adding a basement and second level to the once shotgun home. A sick twinge in his stomach developed at the thought of having to face his past under duress, but it had to be done. He was not looking forward to talking to her and somewhere in his heart he hoped she no longer lived there. However, a knowing in his spirit told him that Dorothy Hayworth was about to open the door to more than just the past. His future and the future of his family were at stake.

"Who's knocking on my door this late at night?"

"It's Walter."

"Who?"

"It's me, Walter Johnson!"

"Who?" Dorothy couldn't believe her ears. There must be some kind of mistake. It couldn't possibly be the man she'd grown to detest over the past 27 years.

"You heard me right. It's me. Walter Demarcus Johnson, Sr. Can you open the door? I need to talk to you. It will only take a little of your time, then I'll go."

Hearing his full name drove all doubt from her mind. Slowly, reluctantly she began to unlock the door, but froze before opening it. *I must look a mess!* She took off her head scarf and ran a comb through her hair, grabbed some lip gloss from the stand in her foyer, somewhat struggling to gain composure. Finally, she opened the door.

There he stood, with the eyes of one she used to love dearly but who also committed ultimate betrayal. Both looked at each other for a while, neither knowing how or where to begin. But since Walter didn't have time to waste, he initiated the conversation.

"So, are you going to let me in?"

"I dunno. Do you think you deserve it?"

"Dorothy, I'm not here to get back with you or to try to make amends."

"Then why **are** you here?"

"It's a little bit of a story, not long but very intriguing. Can I come in so we can talk about it?"

"After all these years Walter, you show up on my doorstep. You have no idea how long I've waited for you to come! And your son-,"

"My son, is the reason I am here..."

"Why? What happened? Have you talked to him? Have you seen him?"

"No, I haven't seen nor talked to him, but my daughter is in the hospital and I think he went to visit her yesterday."

She asked questions like she hadn't seen him in a long time and sounded a bit worried. That was none of Walter's concern at the moment. Right now, he needed answers.

"Visit her? Why would he do that?"

"I don't know. I was kind of hoping you could shed some light on the subject."

"How would I know? And, what makes you think that it was Jerard?"

"Because the night shift nurse told me and my wife that a young man who was my daughter's cousin came to visit her right before she went into surgery."

"So what does that have to do with Jerard!" she reiterated.

"I distinctly remember you telling me that if I walked out on you that you would officially change our son's name to mine and purpose **your** life to making **mine** a living hell!"

"Yea, I did say that. But I was just young and angry and hurt. I never intended on doing anything about it. It was just talk. Besides I didn't have the money to do it anyway. And if I did, then I wouldn't have wasted it on that."

"Then someone with the same name as mine visited my daughter, or else someone is playing some sick joke. Where is Jerard? Does he stay here with you?"

"He used to, but Walter I haven't seen Jerard in months. He got a new house in North Atlanta."

"Do you have the address?"

"Sure, but I want to know what you're going to do before I just hand it over to you."

"I just want to talk to him."

"I don't believe you. Something big is going on or you wouldn't be here in the middle of the night instead of at home with your precious Angel."

"You're not still mad about that are you?'

"Child, I stopped being *mad* a long time ago. I don't want to see my son get hurt, that's all. He's been through too much already!"

"You're right."

"I know I'm right. Now tell me, what is going on?"

"Okay, fine. Now, this is just a hunch. I'm not sure if any of this is true but,"

"Walter, just tell the story!"

"Okay. It all started the day my son went missing, or maybe even before. Our life isn't perfect but the children living under my roof have always been respectable. But a little over a year ago, Walter Jr. and I started having a lot of verbal fights. He would come home and attack me for no reason, or at least for no reason I could fathom. The same day we had the big blowout where he knocked me off of my feet and ran away from home, my daughter started acting strange. At first we thought she just missed her brother, but then she started staying out all night and sleeping all day. She was even falling asleep in church and you know I wasn't having that. Anyway, after several confrontations she finally stopped going to church all together and moved out. Angela and I heard stories about her prostituting and being strung out on drugs, but we couldn't bring ourselves to believe that our little Princess would be doing such things. Yet the truth has a way of being revealed."

"Did you confront her?"

"I was looking for her but finding my son took precedence since he was underage. His teachers were starting to ask about him so we had to get the police involved. The church set up an account to reward anyone who had information about the disappearance of my son. So if you know anything about it or if you hear anything, the reward is up to $25,000."

"Oh, I'm not hurting for no money baby. My son sends me a weekly allowance check to cover my expenses and the house is paid for."

"What does he do? It's not nothing illegal is it?"

"I don't know and I don't care!"

"You got to care. What if something happens to him? The streets are ugly Dorothy."

"He's prepared for that. I raised him in the streets, besides he's been hurt so much, hurt should be his middle name. And these days he don't hurt as quickly as he used to." She looked at him to confirm that her words did stick. "Why do you care?"

"Well he **is** my son!"

"You picked a fine time to come around daddy! But I regret to inform you that your son has grown up into a full blown man, and without your help might I add!"

"Now wait a minute, I gave you what you wanted."

"You had no idea what I wanted then nor now!"

"Oh, yea and what did you want?"

"You! I wanted you Walter!"

"Oh, I knew! But we went through this Dorothy! There was no way we could work. I was still in love with Angela!"

"Your precious Angel! What made her so much better than me, huh? She left you! And I was there for you! But as soon as she came back, you dropped me like a ton of bricks. Do you have any idea how that made me feel?"

"I do."

"Naw! You may think you do, but how could you. You were the one who came out sitting pretty. You had someone to hold and comfort you when you were lonely, and then someone to wife because she was more acceptable to your congregation!!'

"No that is not it! We, me and Angela, had to suffer with the congregation before the eyes stopped rolling and the rumors stopped spreading! It was years before the tension ceased! So, before you talk, you'd better get your facts straight."

"Whatever Walter?"

"It's true! And you got what you wanted! Since you couldn't have me you took the next best thing. Money!"

"Money never made up for you being gone and having to see your son's face while he sat in the window everyday hoping one day you'd come back."

"You told me not to remember! You said I would cramp your style if you ever got a new man. Remember?!"

"I was only trying to make you jealous... But obviously, it didn't work."

"And I remember there being a little issue of blackmail."

"Blackmail?"

"Yep. You said as long as the money came, you wouldn't expose our child to the church! And so, I paid up!"

"Do you think that I didn't want you to have a relationship with your son? If you did, you were wrong! I only said those things to protect my heart, our hearts. I figured you would never come back anyway, may as well get some security out of the deal!"

"Many times, I wanted to come and see Jerard, but after letting so much time pass by without Angela knowing, it became harder and harder to think through. After a while, it was a distant memory filed deep in my mental rolodex. But that's no excuse. I should've come. I should've come."

"But you didn't."

"No. And now I fear my entire family is suffering for it. And I have a good feeling Jerard is the key to putting us all back together."

"How you gone blame my son for your mishap?"

"I'm not blaming him, but I do believe he has something to do with it. And it's high time I go visit *my* son."

"Ooooo! Now he's your son, when you need him to repaint your perfect picture."

"He's always been my son. I was just selfish and stupid. But I won't avoid the inevitable any longer. It's time I go visit *my* son!"

"Does Angel know you have another son?"

"I told her you said the boy was mine but we never had a blood test performed."

"Still covering up your faults huh?"

"Yea, I guess so. But that is all over. The truth has to come out! The whole truth! So I have to talk to Jerard and figure this whole thing out."

"Okay. Hope you find him?"

"You're not going to give me the address?"

"No, I'm not. I won't partake in hurting my son again. You're on your own!"

"Dorothy, jealousy will get you nowhere. Just give me the address."

"Jealousy might not get me nowhere, but how about this?" She dropped her robe, under which she wore nothing but skin.

"Woah, now I know it's time for me to go!"

But he didn't move. He was looking and he still liked what he saw. She was still the beautiful seductress and it had been weeks since he and Angela were intimate. Dorothy walked towards him and cupped his cheek in her hand.

"You don't really want to go. This is why you came over here for real, isn't it?"

Elder was breathing stiff and his heart rate was increasing rapidly. He still did not move.

"No Dorothy, this is not the real reason I came."

"Why'd you come then?" she now cupped his other cheek. Her breasts were less than an inch from his chest. He couldn't take it anymore. Elder grabbed both of her hands and put them at her side.

"I am a happily married man of God, and if I got to do all that for the address, then I'll find Jerard another way."

She looked into his eyes for a long time. He still held her arms. Finally, she sighed. "Alright. I see some dogs do learn new tricks."

She walked to the kitchen fastening her robe. In a couple of seconds, she came back with a piece of mail with her son's address on it. Halfheartedly, she handed it to him.

"Thank you, Sunshine,!"

It was the nickname he gave her for changing his dark clouds and giving him joy again during the time Angela went M.I.A.

"You're welcome." She said, trying to sound dry but it was apparent her mood had lightened, simply because he called her Sunshine. He hadn't forgotten. "Now get out of here."

"Yes ma'am," he said gladly.

Dorothy walked him through the door and onto the porch. "It was really good seeing you
Walter."

"It wasn't so bad seeing you either."

"If you ever get lonely you know where to find me."

"I doubt I'll ever be that lonely again." He waved his hand to her as he got in his car and quickly pulled away.

# <u>Chapter 18: Down Goes Big Boi</u>

Seduction was just finishing her dance when the police entered the club. She saw them and was so happy this fiasco was almost over. When Dr. Reid called her, she was eager to comply.  Though the money was good, she could no longer stand the abuse. Besides, Big Boi was taking more than sixty percent of their tips now that Karisma was gone. She wanted to leave this dangerous life months ago, but for the same reason she wanted to go, she stayed. Fear! The fear of Money had been spoken into their hearts for so long, none of the girls dared leave. That is until the day Karisma fell. All of them knew something shady had taken place that night, but none was bold enough to go to the police with any concrete information. They talked amongst themselves who they thought would be attacked next. Some of the girls vowed never to talk about the situation again. 'Just pretend none of this ever happened,' one of them said. Only a handful resolved to tell the whole truth if anyone came asking.

In the meantime, Dr. Reid kept digging until he found a few of the girl's ER records for sexual abuse and rape. Finally, Nicole Shaffer, Seduction, Cynthia Randolph, Peaches, and Carla Chivers, Cotton Candy, all came forward with the truth. Big Boi paid Bossy to get Darnell to put the pill in the drinks, but he was supposed to wait until after the girls danced. Then Big Boi would call them into his office for a critique session. At least that's what he told them while they were on their way. However, once behind closed doors, he talked to them until their words were incoherent. After which, he did whatever he wanted to them. Bossy had some of the instances on video and was using them for blackmail. Ever since she showed him a copy of one of the DVDs, she acted like she ran the place and Big Boi didn't argue. He let her say and do pretty much what she wanted. She created the lineup and manning for each day, giving herself only prime time spots. It all was becoming too much. That's why it was such a relief when Dr. Reid and the detectives called. They were all about ready to start new lives.

As soon as Dr. Reid found the witnesses and provided the results from Kindness's tests, the police had enough evidence to arrest and prosecute. Darnell had already been questioned and fingered Bossy and Big Boi as the ring leaders. It was he who called and told the police both Bossy and Big Boi were in the front office. He promised to testify against them for a plea bargain stating he only complied because he feared for his life. He even told them about Money, but when asked had he ever seen him, the answer was always the same as with everyone else who mentioned him. 'No.' If no one had seen Money, then there was no way the police could go after him. That left only the suspects at Queen City.

The police had the building surrounded. Only a few patrons were at the club so it was easy to get them out without causing a commotion. There were several officers in plain clothes staged throughout the establishment. And one officer was on either side of the door where Big Boi Shane and Bossy were consorting. Detectives Bradford and Kelly knocked.

"Knock, knock, knock!"

"Go away, I'm busy!"

"Shane Whitman?!"

Big Boi looked at Bossy and whispered, "Who's calling me by my gubment?"

She shrugged, looking just as bewildered as he did.

"Hey, we're having a meeting. If you'll give the bartender your name and number, Big Boi will call you back at his earliest convenience."

"I'm sorry Ms. Heart, but we need to talk to the both of you. Can you open the door please?"

Neither one of them moved. They knew it was a detective or the police or someone with some authority. *But they don't have anything on us, do they?*

"Who is it?" Shane yelled.

"It's Detectives Bradford and Kelly, Mr. Whitman! Ms. Heart! If you don't open the door, we'll be forced to open it for you!"

"Okay, alright, here I come," Big Boi stated before reaching under his desk and pulling the .38 caliber from its case. He placed it under his gut.

Shane looked at Bossy and spoke defiantly, "I ain't going to jail. Are you?" She said nothing. Once he made it to the door, she tucked herself into the furthest corner. He looked at her, shaking his head before proceeding.

"Hey detectives! What can I do you for?"

"You can put your hands behind your head! That's what you can do!"

"For what detectives? I've done nothing wrong!"

"We have evidence that states otherwise."

"Oh yea? What kind of evidence?" *Oooh, if I see that Chance again, I'm gone kill her!! I know she did this!*

"The best kind! The kind that sticks!" Detective Bradford smirked. Kelly couldn't help but to chime in.

"Yea, the kind that gets you 10-20 and the kind you don't have enough money to buy your way out of! That kind!"

"But officers?"

"Detectives!" They both roared.

"Right. That's what I meant. Detectives…"

"What?!" Detective Bradford struggled to fit the cuff around Big Boi's obese wrist.

"What is this all about? Ouch!"

"You should really consider losing some weight. The cuffs only have so much give in them!"

"I already lost some weight."

"Did you measure that in grams or ounces?" Both of the detectives laughed, however Shane was not amused. He didn't retort though. He knew his size would work in his favor this time. That's why he hid the gun under a roll of fat.

"Are you going to answer my question or what?"

"Sure I don't see why not. Kelly, tell him a little bit about our evidence while I keep working on these cuffs."

"Well for starters, are you familiar with the drug Rohypnol?"

"I mean I have been known to get a little wasted, but if I ever took that drug, someone must have slipped it into my drink cause I don't remember," he teased.

"Someone did slip it into a drink or two or three, but not yours wise guy."

"I don't know what you're talking about."

"Yes you do Big Boi!" Bossy came out of the corner, makeup smeared and snot running down her lip.

"You conniving trick, get back in that corner!"

"Ms. Heart. How nice of you to join us!" Detective Kelly took out his cuffs and walked towards Bossy who immediately broke down to her knees.

"Please, please! It wasn't me! It was all Shane!"

"Liar! I don't even know what a Ro-hip-nawl is!!"

"Yes, you do. Remember the Roofies you purchase from the X man? You had them delivered here by one of your girls!"

"Oh, Roofies. Yea, I heard of those. But what has this got to do with me? I don't use them!"

"You idiot! Don't try to lie!! You paid Darnell to put one in the girls drinks after their set and had me call them into your office for a little "critique" session. Only, you did some nasty things to the girls without their consent!"

"I did not! Every one of those girls wanted it! You told me that dancing and gyrating all over that stage made all of yall hot and bothered, and the girls wanted me to put out the fire! It was..."

"You snake! Don't you dare try to blame this on me!"

"I'm not just tryin' you slut, I am! You did this! You set this all up! From the pills and the drinks, to the videos and the critique sessions! Even poor ole Darnell!! And Karisma's fall! It was all part of your evil, twisted plan!"

"Evil and twisted plan is right, but it was yours not mine. Yes, I did set up a camera in here to get dirt on you so that I could use it against you because you had all of those sweet girls afraid of you. And I got tired of it. Most of these girls have been used and abused by you and Money, and the rest of yalls gang, not to mention most of the men in their life before coming here. I had to do something to try and take yall down."

"Alright, we've had enough of this back and forth. We'll figure out the real story in court!"

Bradford was still trying to cuff Big Boi, but his size forced him to cuff the man in front instead of behind. His girth put too much strain on the cuffs and his wrists. They didn't want another lawsuit. Whoever was guilty here, no one needed to get off on a technicality.

"Officer John," Bradford called for help.

"Yes sir?"

"Take our portly suspect to my squad car and read him his rights, while we take care of Ms. Heart."

"Yes sir."

When Officer John reached for Big Boi, he pretended to accidentally fall. He was buying time to hear what they would ask Bossy and to see if he could reach his gun. She was going on and on, spreading the lies thick. Fury was boiling inside of him. *How could she betray me?! It was our plan! I wanted the girls and she wanted to be on top! It was perfect, until Darnell got drunk and forgot when he was supposed to put the pill in the drink. He didn't even know what they were. He just did whatever Bossy told him to do. Poor fella. Or maybe she put the pill in Karisma's drink. Ambitious trick! She wanted the number one spot from the time she came in the door, even before. I should never have hired that girl!!* At any rate, she wasn't going to get away with this, not by a long shot. The other officer stepped in to help his partner with Shane and they finally got him to his feet. That's when it happened. The gun fell out. Big Boi fell on top of it and grabbed it with his left hand, though he was right-handed. *Ten to twenty years! Uh-uh, not me!* He aimed at Bossy and fired two shots, but missed by a couple of inches. She ducked and crawled out of the door. All the men were working to get the gun from Big Boi and did not notice her escape.

The rest of the police outside heard the shots and ran in to help their colleagues. Bossy saw them coming and blended in with the rest of the screaming strippers, acting astonished while simultaneously making her way to the dressing room. She made it. *Now to get my things and get out of here!* Rummaging through her new dressing room and make-up station, Bossy raked all of her belongings into the Prada duffel bag Big Boi bought for her, grabbed her purse and headed for the back door. *Hopefully all of the police are inside by now and I can get away!*

"Going somewhere?" It was Chance. Bossy recovered from fear nicely. *This lil girl don't scare me.*

"What's it to you?"

"Oh, a lot!"

"Nah, I don't think so! I think you'd better get out of my way or..."

"Or what?"

"Or I'm gone run over you, drag you out the back door and throw you in the dumpster like the trash I always knew you were!"

"Try me!"

That was all the invitation she needed. Bossy dropped her designer bags and charged. In her haste to catch up to Bossy, Chance forgot to take off her boots. But in the five seconds it took to cover the space between them, she had the boots off and was ready for whatever Bossy could throw. Bossy tackled her into the wall, but Chance knew that move. Her brother always told her to spread her legs creating a center of gravity, that way no one can knock you down unless you want them to. She planted her legs and slammed Bossy on the floor.

"Get up ho!"

She got up slowly, but this time she did not charge. She waited to see if Chance was coming to her. And she did. Bossy had a little buck in her. She shot Chance two right jabs then a left, knocking her off balance. Chance rubbed the inside of her jaw with her tongue and tasted blood.

"Hmmph, not bad. But not good enough! Whether it's your blood or mine, blood only feeds the fury honey!"

She punched Bossy so fast, the girl didn't have time to blink. Chance hit her with the one two about three times, then an upper cut. Bossy spit blood for a second. Not sure if she wanted to continue this bout. But if she had any chance of making it out the door, she had to get past Chance.

"Face it Bossy! There's no escape!! You may as well stay and face the music!"

"I'm tired of music! I'm tired of dancing!!"

"Music I can understand, but dancing. You better get used to it cause where you going you gone end up being some butch heifer's trick!"

Chance hit her again, but Bossy pushed up and out, kicking her with a round house.

"Whew, I haven't had to use that move in years."

"You proud of that weak move? Come on, I know you can do better than that!"

"I guess you think you bad 'cause you got a few lucky shots in, huh! Well it won't happen no mo'!"

She ran for Chance again. This time she stood like she was going to take the charge, then simply moved out of the way and let her stumble into the plants in the corner.

"Ole!" She laughed at how easy this was. Moving a little closer, bending down to put her hands on her knees, she added, "I thought you were going to be a challenge! I love a good challenge, but beating you is like taking candy from a baby!"

Bossy was furious, but it seemed she was only good at using words. In action, she was nothing more than a coward and a weakling. When Chance got her hands on her this time, she commenced to giving her the Chi-town beat down she promised was coming. It was a good thing the officers came looking for Bossy or else Chance may have killed her.

"Miss! Miss!! Get off of her, or we'll have to take you in too!"

"That won't be necessary Officers. I'm one of the informants. I waited for her just to make sure she didn't get away with the videos and DVDs."

"You have them?"

"No, I put them back in her locker."

"You watched them?" Bossy asked through bloody tears.

"Yes. And I'm sure the officers will find some very interesting conversations between you and Big Boi Shane on some of them."

Bossy couldn't do anything except cry. It was all over. All of her hard work was down the toilet and she didn't have a friend in the world to help her. Not to mention she just got her butt handed to her on a platter. As if to read her mind, Chance walked by and whispered in her ear just before the police hauled her off.

"And that whoopin' was from all of us girls! Especially Karisma!!"

The officers cuffed Bossy, grabbing her bags containing the additional evidence. She was trying to get away with the videos of Big Boi which also contained some self-incriminating content. It looked like they both were going down for conspiracy, rape and sodomy.

# Chapter 19: Veil of Amnesia

"Ring! Ring!"

"Hello Jug."

"Hello Mr. Money."

"What you got for me?"

"Man, you never gone guess who just left your mother's crib."

"My dad."

"No, Karisma's dad."

"Like I said, my dad!"

'Oh right. I forgot about that."

"Ooh you so stupid! I need some new bodyguards! Ones who aint so dumb they forget who to shoot because they forget how to shoot. Just pull the trigger man!" He laughed.

"Okay boss, you got jokes!"

"Yea, sometimes!"

"So what we gone do bout this daddy situation?"

"We're going to take care of it, like any other problem. I knew he would start putting two and two together after a while. And then he would have to go see my mom to find me."

"But **how** we gone take care of this daddy situation though? What you plan to do?"

"I think it's about time to make another visit to my dear little sister."

"What about Chance?"

"What about her?"

"Can't we stop in and make a visit on her?"

"For what Jug?"

"Uh, I don't know."

"Jug, if I didn't need you, I'd probably have to kill you!"

"Stop playing Boss! But for real though, Karisma might feel more comfortable if there's another female there. They can talk and stuff. And that'll make it easier to get information from her befoe you drop tha bomb on her."

"Hmmm. Not a bad idea. Why didn't I think of that! Make it happen."

"Okay Boss."

"And for the record Jug, for a stupid fellow, you aint too dumb!"

"Gee, thanks Boss."

"Dnnnng..." Money hung up just as fast as he'd picked up, but Jug wasn't done. He had more questions.

"Ring! Ring!"

"What's the stupid question?"

"Heh-heh-heh! Actually I don't have *a* stupid question, I have two."

"Go ahead. Ask away but hurry up!"

"Okay. Okay Boss. First, do I need to go get Chance now?"

"Well yea, that's the plan isn't it?"

"Yea, okay Boss."

"What's the second stupid question?"

"Uh,"

"Uh what?"

'Uh, are you going to visit Karisma right now?"

"Well yea, that's the plan Jug."

"Okay Boss. I just asked in case you need back up or body guarding? You know the police are all over that place right now like ants on a picnic. We don't want to get caught up."

"You're right Jug. Once again, you've proven me wrong. That's twice in a lifetime! So, why don't you go pick up Chance and then swing by to pick me up before we go to the hospital. Then we can send her in to get Karisma."

"Okay Boss."

"Oh, and Jug."

"Yea Boss."

"Don't be too long okay. This is kind of important."

"Right. Sure, thing Boss."

"Dnnng!"

"Ring! Ring!"

"What Jug?!!!" He all but snarled into the phone.

"Awww, is that any way to talk to your mama?"

"Oh, mama! Hey, what's up?" Jerard was nervous. He wanted their plan to run as smoothly as possible. He had to show her once and for all that he could handle himself in the streets, no matter what the situation.

"You know what's up! Your boy has been at my house every night for the past two weeks. Spying on me!"

"Well, that's what you told me to do, so that's what I ordered."

"I know. You did good son."

"Thanks mama."

"Now I sent your old sorry daddy to your house in Buckhead. You got everything ready?"

"Uh, not quite." He had traded places with Jug all of a sudden.

"Not-quite? What do you mean, not quite!"

"Well mama. You know how you wanted Kindness,"

"Karisma!" She blurted in.

"Uh, yea right! Karisma…"

"By the time we get through with that little heifer, there won't be a kind bone in her body! Go on!"

"Right. Um, well, you know how you wanted Karisma to be there at the same time her daddy got there?"

"Yea."

"Yea, well, she just had surgery."

"And?"

"And, she aint healed yet."

"So! Who cares? You?!"

"Naw mama!"

"Then what's the problem?!"

"I just don't know if we're going to be able to get her out of the hospital tonight. There are some by the book nurses up in there and it may not be easy."

"Well, you better make it easy!!!"

"But mama!"

"Look! Don't but mama me! I need you to get the job done! That's it! I didn't spend all that time trying to make sure things go according to **my** plan to hear that you're too much of a wimp to make it happen! You scared baby?"

"I," he turned from timid Jerard to fearless Money, "I ain't never scared!"

"That's my boy! Get it done!"

"Dunng!" They both hung up at the same time. Like mother, like son.

Walter was on I-285N about to ramp off exit 27/GA-400N, Buckhead/Cumming. He had no idea what he was going to say or do. All he was certain of was that he had to face his past if he ever wanted to have a productive future. Jerard… Jerard was the key. It wasn't hard for Walter to empathize with him. He could still remember like it was yesterday how the boy stood in the doorway the last time they saw each other. He had overheard his mother yelling that Walter would regret ever leaving her and his son, and that one day he would pay for it with his life. Walter fought back to have the right to visit with his son but Dorothy refused.

*"You won't be over here acting all holier than thou, cramping my style. What if I want to get a new man? Uh-uh! Naw, if you really wanna see him, take him to your house to visit!"* She was furious and saying a lot of things Walter hoped she didn't mean.

*"You know I can't do that Dorothy! Angela would never understand! Especially now that she's,"* he couldn't finish the phrase. This was not how he wanted to end things.

*"She's what? Pregnant?"* Dorothy gave a nervous laugh. If Angela was pregnant, she and Jerard could forget everything she'd dreamed for them. Her life with Walter was over! There's no way he would leave his wife now. Walter remained silent.

*"Well, is that it? Is that why you acting shady? Huh? Huh?! Answer me!!"* She was slapping him in the face and chest.

He finally broke his silence, trying to fight her off without hitting her. *"I'm not acting shady. I just can't do this anymore Dorothy. The double life is not for me. It's too difficult. It's time for me to be real."*

*"So, you choosing her and her child over me and mine?"*

*"No, that's not it at all!"*

*"Then what is it, because that's sure what it seems like to me!"*

*"I'm choosing right over wrong Dorothy! That's it!"*

*"No, you're choosing her over me! And her child over mine! Jerard was here first!! Why should we have to suffer? Tell me, huh! Why?!!"*

*"I'm sorry Sunshine!"*

*"Don't you call me Sunshine! And your sorry don't mean nothing to me! Absolutely nothing!"*

He said it again. *"I'm sorry! This is just what I have to do. It's the right thing!"*

*"Right for who? You? Cause it sure don't feel right for me and Jerard!"*

*"If I choose you or my wife someone gets hurt either way!"*

*"So, it is a choice between me and her, just as I thought!"*

*"No, it's not. It just seems that way. Look, I am married. And marriage is sacred to God! It's a gift! I've got to do right by my gift."*

*"Oh, now God is in the picture! I don't remember you consulting with God before you laid me down! But I do remember you mentioning him somewhere in the middle and definitely at the end!"*

*"Stop trying to water down **my** commitment to God. This aint about you! Yea, I made mistakes. We all do. Nobody's perfect! But now I got to do better!"*

*"What about, what about your child? I recall something in God's Word saying that children are a gift too! What about your son, huh Walter?!"*

*"Dorothy, you know I love my son. He's the reason I still come around!"*

*"Oh, and don't forget about the perks too baby!"*

She sauntered by him and slapped her butt. He said nothing because he couldn't. She was right. Walter knew he'd been playing both sides of the fence, lying to his wife and giving Dorothy hope. In some sorted way, he did it all to be in his son's life, no matter who got hurt. But after the message his Pastor preached on Sunday, he knew the time had come to put an end to the lying and cheating. Well at least some of it.

*"Dorothy, it's over!"* That was all he said. But it wasn't over, not until she had her last say. She jumped up in front of him.

*"You think I'm just gone let you walk out of our lives with nothing to show for it. Naw, you gone pay child support and you gone visit with your firstborn child, or so help me God I will make your perfect life with Angel a living hell."*

Walter knew she would try but he didn't care, nor did he respond. He kept stepping away from her and closer to the door but she circled him, continuing to taunt.

*"It may not be today baby, and it may not be tomorrow, but I promise you, the day will come!"* She got as close as she could without kissing his lips and added, *"Soon!"*

*When she said the word, her lips grazed his. Afterwards she slowly stepped out of his way and let him choose the future of his family. If looks could kill, he would be dead but he kept calm and remained silent. He simply hugged and kissed his son goodbye saying, "I love you son. I always will. And I will come back for you soon." Afterwards, he walked out of the door in a daze. He didn't know how he was going to live without him, but he couldn't deal with Dot anymore.*

*Dorothy continued to scream threats to his life and his other families' lives but he didn't turn back to debate with her. Once he stepped into the safety of his car, Walter looked back to see his son standing in the doorway. He waved at the boy but Jerard didn't wave back. He came out and sat on the top step and watched his dad until he disappeared around the corner and out of his life.*

Now that he was there, it was more difficult than he thought it would be to drive up to the gate and press the buzzer, as he originally planned. He had to admit that fear was trying to grip his heart. But it wasn't fear of Jerard or what he'd become, it was fear of facing every past indiscretion. His whole life was at stake here, not to mention Angela and their kids. And Jerard?

The damaged soul he left behind, how could he face him after all these years? Where should he begin? How would he justify leaving and never fighting for him? But all these things had to be addressed. He didn't have a choice now that Angela had some idea of what was going on. The whole truth had to come out. If only there was some way for everyone to be in one room at one time, he wouldn't have to repeat the ugly truth too many times. *That would be worse than torture!* He had arrived, but instead of stopping, Walter drove right past Jerald's Buckhead mansion. *Lord Please! I need a miracle!! Help me walk on water in the middle of this storm.* He parked on the next street and got out.

---

"Okay, okay! You don't have to push!!"

"Get in the car tramp! Money is waiting!"

Jug and Chance always had words no matter what the occasion. He constantly found reason to pick a fight with her. It was clear to Chance that he liked her but she couldn't see how in the world he would think she'd have him. *Never!*

"But what do you need me for?" she continued. "I've done everything he told me to do." The limo driver turned and gave her a knowing look.

So, she solemnly added, "Lately."

"Well, you know Money. He always got a plan," Jug said stuffing Chance into the front seat before fitting himself in snugly beside her.

"And he doesn't always include everyone in it. We just do good to do what we're told. You feel me young lady!"

Mr. Simmons was the nighttime limo driver and full-time butler. He was older than the rest of Money's henchman and wasn't as rough but what he lacked in brawn he made up for in street knowledge and wisdom. Chance secretly admired his advice and took it to heart even when she pretended not to listen.

Silence. They had been driving for half an hour and the silence was eating her up inside. Knowing that at the end of the drive she would have to face the devil had her nerves on edge. Music! I need to hear some music. She grabbed her cell phone from her purse and connected it to the USB port on the radio. Surprisingly neither of the men protested. She clicked the volume to 15 and laid back against the seat trying desperately to relax. The soothing sounds of Lauryn Hill helped sort of. 'Ex-Factor' was one of her favorite songs ever, but she never realized how sorrowful the words were before. They made her think of Jeff. *Hopefully he wouldn't treat her like this, if they ever had a chance to be together.* If only he knew she was still in town. If only she'd called him to let him know how much he meant to her. Maybe tears wouldn't be filling her eyes at the moment. Why did she have to play so hard to get and make things so complicated? *I should've called! Now I may never have the chance to see him again!!* She looked at her phone and before she knew it she had pulled up her contacts and selected Jeff's number. The phone was ringing.

"Hey, whatchu doing?" Jug asked.

"Nothing!" She quickly depressed the end call button.

He reached for her phone, but she snatched it away. "I'm just listening to music!"

"That's all you better be doing!!"

"It is!"

"It'd better be!!"

"Didn't I say..."

"Hey, now both of yall shut up." It wasn't a question; it was an order. However, Jug wasn't good at taking orders from anyone except Money. He looked at her sideways to put his last two cents in.

"No phone calls!' he growled through clenched teeth, "Or this old man will not be able to save you next time! Got it?!"

Though she looked directly at him while he spoke and clearly heard every word, she didn't acknowledge him with a response. Rather, she leaned forward towards the radio and somberly clicked the volume to 20, sat back into her previous relaxed state and lost herself in thoughts of a knight in shining armor. Mr. Simmons turned the volume back down, shaking his head. She had earphones. Why didn't she use them? He knew she was trying to prove her point with Jug without speaking. They were the last two people he ever wanted to have in his front seat together. *Never again!*

In the midst of thought and music, Chance didn't notice the limo was slowing down. And that's when she saw him. It was Money. *Uh oh! Here we go!* She quietly unhooked her phone and placed it down the middle of her bra. No one knew but her that listening to the music was a part of her plan to charge her phone before this ordeal was under way. It felt like it was going to be a long night! A very long night! Jug got out and opened the back door for his boss, but before getting in Money stuck his head in the front.

"Hey Pumpkin! Do you mind joining me? I get lonely back here by myself."

She started to move but didn't say anything. "Oh, you don't wanna sit with me? You look pretty cozy all hugged up with Jug in front. Maybe you'd rather finish your ride with him?!"

"No! No, I'm just tired Money."

"Well come on back here and relax with Big Daddy, that way we can talk about your next assignment. I know you're wondering what's going on. And I'm the only one who can tell you."

She put a lot more pep in her step to dispel any thought that she may prefer anyone else's company over his. Besides, the invite wasn't an invite, it was a command.

"That's a good girl."

She climbed in the back and Money followed. Once Jug got in the front, Money banged on the divider to give the go ahead. Mr. Simmons immediately cranked the vehicle and took off.

"Do you understand the assignment?"

"Yes, I do. You want me to go and convince Karisma to leave the hospital. Then get her into the limo so that she can go to your house under the false pretense that her life will go back to normal."

"No. That's wrong. It's not a false pretense! Her life will go back to normal, just not the normal of her childhood. It'll be her new normal."

"Right. She'll get to go back to stripping and drugs and making all that money she rarely gets to spend."

"Careful Chance!"

"Yea, I know. Careful I don't get slapped in my smart mouth. Right?"

"Slapped? Naw, more like punched!"

"Slapped. Punched. What's the difference these days?" The fight with Bossy had her mind in a different place. She was ready for whatever. *Game on!*

"You pushing it lil girl and about to graduate to the kill level!"

"I know." She knew that Money didn't threaten; if he was going to hit her, he just did it. Why was he holding back today? Something wasn't the same about him.

"You know, and you don't care? You're not scared of what's to come of you if you keep poking the monster?!"

"I guess not. Not as much as I did yesterday."

"What you say trick?"

"I said I'm not scared! I'm tired Money. I'm tired of running. I'm tired of doing your bidding. And I'm tired of living in fear of what you will do to me if I don't do as I'm told. I want my life back! And not the new normal either!"

"Umhm," he thought intently on how to respond. He couldn't lay a hand on her. He needed her to look her best when she went inside the hospital. Although he was fuming, he had to play it cool.

"I tell you what. I'll give you your life back if you do this last thing for me. If you can get Karisma out of the hospital and into this limo and this night turns out just as planned, I will set you free! I'll even give you this plane ticket back!"

She knew he found it. He was waiting on the right time to bring it up. He liked holding things over her head, torturing her with thoughts of what could be and would be. Chance decided not to address the ticket specifically. She only addressed the promise of freedom.

"Do you promise?"

"Promise. And you know I keep my word."

Chance didn't trust him but at this point she had no choice. She knew he would say anything to get her to act right. It wasn't the first time she got tired of this life, but it would be the last. No matter what, after this she was done. Dead or alive. She knocked on the divider like Money always did.

"Let me out of here! I got work to do!!"

"That's my girl."

---

"Knock, knock!" Chance pushed open the door before Karisma issued approval to enter.

"Who is it? Who's there?"

"It's me Karisma. It's your friend, Chance."

"Chance? Is it really you?!"

"Yes. I'm here!"

"Where have you been? I've felt so lonely in here with all these squares. You got to get me out of here!"

*It couldn't be that easy, could it? I mean, if I can get her to leave I'm free from Money. I would have thought after having surgery it would be close to impossible to get Karisma to leave, but here she is offering to leave willingly.* Chance had to play it cool.

"K, I can't get you out of here. What about your eyes? What if something goes wrong?"

"I'll take the blame for it, besides it's my choice. Everybody has been choosing for me all my life. It's my turn to decide my path."

"It doesn't matter! It doesn't matter if you take the blame. Everyone will still blame me! I can't let you do it K!"

Karisma had begun to put on her street clothes. "You don't have much of a choice! I'm leaving with or without your help. Seeing you has given me motivation. This place is cramping my style. I'm ready to get back to living."

"Living? You mean stripping seven days a week to pay some debt to a dude holding the life of your brother over your head! You call that living?!"

"My brother? My brother. How did you know that? I never told you that! And until you said it I didn't even remember." She lied. "But how did you know?"

Chance was quiet. She'd stuck her foot down her throat and was kicking herself in the stomach. *How could you be so stupid and careless?* Money would be furious. She gave a hearty sigh. *It's time for the truth.*

"K, there's a lot you don't know. And to be honest I don't know how to tell you."

"Just tell me Chance. If you have information that could help get my brother back, that's priceless! Then I'll really be able to get my life in order."

Chance remained silent.

"Chance!" Karisma screamed. The nurses came running down the hallway.

"Is everything alright in here?" Nurse Flatness spoke.

Patrice just stood back and watched. She looked at Chance and gave a short nod then turned to walk away. Nurse Flatness however was another story.

"Is everything alright Karisma? We heard yelling."

"Yes Nurse. I was just getting reacquainted with an old friend."

"And what are you doing getting dressed? Are you going somewhere?"

"Nah, I'm just tired of my butt hangin out the back of that gown."

"Mhmm. Okay, if you say so." She said reluctantly, giving Chance a good once over. "Well, if you need me, don't hesitate to call."

"I won't Nurse Flatty." The lady started to walk away then looked back rolling her eyes at the insult before returning to the nurses' station.

"Ooo I can't stand that woman!"

"Me too!!" They both laughed.

"Uggh, I really miss this," Karisma managed to say between giggles.

"Really?"

"Yeah. I mean, I've always been surrounded by plenty of people but not many I could honestly call friends. And most were church folks. That's a different kind of friendship, you know what I mean?"

"No, I don't know but I can only imagine!"

"Don't get me wrong, some of the people are great. I mean there are some really good people in the church. There's this one old lady that my mother can't stand. She always has a story to tell, and even though people try to shut her up, she just goes on and on. You see, they try to hush her because most of what she tells is the truth. It's just the truth that no one wants told. And—,"

"Karisma?"

"What?"

"You've got your memory back."

"Oh. Well not really. I mean it comes at its own will and leaves just as suddenly." She gave a fake snicker, but Chance wasn't buying it.

"No, it's not coming and going. You remember, don't you? You remember everything!"

"Let's just say I remember enough."

"So you know."

"So I know what?"

"You know that someone has your brother and is black mailing you for his life."

Karisma was silent. She didn't want to reveal what she really remembered, which **was** everything! Chance hit the nail on the head but could she trust her? It would be nice to have an ally. She was going to try to use friendship but it looked like honesty was going to be her best bet. It would be better for both of them.

"You know, don't you?"

"Okay, okay! You got me. I remember everything. You happy?"

"No. No I'm not."

"Why not? You the one keep hounding me for information and now that you have it, you're still not satisfied?"

"No, I can't be. The amnesia was going to be a buffer for your mind and mine."

"A buffer? For what?"

"I didn't just come to visit you. I was sent to- uh. I mean I came to see if you wanted me to help you get out of here."

"That's it! Why would I need a buffer for that? What's really going on?"

"If I tell you everything it would take too long and we don't have much time."

"Much time for what?"

"Like I said there's too much to tell!"

"Okay. Well tell me the short version!"

"Fine. If you want the ugly truth here goes. I was sent to lure you into the Lion's Den!"

"Lion's den? This ain't a story out of the Bible girl! You better speak English and you'd better be clear!!"

"Ah, now there she is. The Karisma I know!"

"Yea, it's me! Kindness and Karisma all rolled up in one, the best of both worlds. Now tell me the truth!"

"Alright! Money, the guy who's holding your brother hired me to mentor you and make sure you make the money to pay him every week. For the opportunity, I get an extra $5000 per week and the occasional fist in the face when things don't go according to plan."

"So, wait. You've known all along that this man, this Money, has my brother?"

"Yes."

"And you knew about the blackmail?"

"Yes!"

"So, you were just pretending to be my friend?

"YES! YES!"

"Really?!"

"Yes! At first it was all a lie. It was a job! And just in case you don't know, every person involved in this is in a life-or-death situation, not just you!! You've never met Money!" She lied. "For some reason he's saving your encounter for something real special!"

Chance neglected to tell her that Marcus Johnson and Money were the same person. She would have to see that for herself. Karisma took the rest of the wrap from her head. It was almost gone from earlier when she kicked her parents out. She was dressed and ready to go. Deep down, she felt this moment coming. She didn't want her mom and dad to be a part of it. No way would she bring danger to them. It was the reason she left home in the first place and the same reason she must stay away until this man, this Money, can be stopped!

"Something real special, huh?"

"Yes. And today it seems that special occasion has finally arrived."

"Now I get it. That's why amnesia would be a great buffer. It would be better if I didn't remember until the right time."

She grabbed the wig her mother bought for her and went into the bathroom. Moments later, she came out with it glued down. She was glossed, lined and ready to go.

"Well, if it would be better for me not to remember, then amnesia is what I'll hide behind. Let's go to the Lion's Den."

Placing the special tinted glasses Dr. Harris left for her on her face, Karisma scooped a bag from under the bed and turned to her friend.

"And Chance, you can hide behind my umbrella too. I'll protect us both."

Chance smiled at her vote of confidence, but doubted very seriously that neither Kindness nor Karisma could protect them from this evil. It was going to take more than amnesia. It would take a miracle! Chance sent a text to Patrice and Money to let them know they were on their way out the door.

# Chapter 20: We Shall Soon See

Patrice spotted the two young ladies coming out of the room and immediately began distracting Nurse Flatness. Karisma saw every deliberate movement to screen their escape. She didn't miss a thing! *I knew that woman was shiesty and probably my 'cousin' has something to do with all of this too. We shall soon see!*

In the elevator, they discussed who everyone in the limo was and what their function was in correlation to Money. Though she couldn't act like she knew them, Chance thought it would be good for her to know the crew. She had also made a few personal calls, asking favors of a few key associates. So much was at stake here. A lot of lives were going to be affected by the outcome of tonight's events. If their plan didn't work, they both were going to be in some very serious danger, not to mention Jay. She filled her in as much as she could during their walk knowing any shared information could only increase their chance of survival.

The walk from the door to the limo was just as staged as Money's plan to lure Karisma into danger. They feigned a sense of nonchalant camaraderie, laughing and talking all the way to their chariot. But this was no fairytale. This was real life. The night was young, and the promise of danger was imminent.

"Wow, a limo! You didn't have to get a limo for little ole me!" Karisma was over exaggerating but hopefully her sweet lies were good enough to fool Money into believing she only remembered her former self, before the accident and after leaving her parent's home. That's the girl he wanted to see first. He heard the voices of young ladies and opened the door from the inside; however, he didn't dare show his face for fear of sparking a "before surgery" memory. Not until she was secure inside the limo anyway.

"Ladies, would you please join me in the back?"

"With pleasure Big Daddy!" Karisma was laying it on pretty thick but so far Money was eating it up. Women appealing to his narcissistic ego was right up his alley. Besides he would pretend to believe anything to get his way, especially since he had to answer to a higher power. Chance however said nothing. She simply climbed in after her friend. Comfortably seated on the plush cashmere covered seats they all settled in but it seemed no one knew where to start the conversation. Of course, Money viewing that as a sign of weakness needed to be the first to break the silence. *"You must always establish authority,"* He could hear his mother's words loud and clear.

"Chance, why don't you do that thing that gets us all moving?"

"Huh? What thing?"

"You know!" he said lightly, motioning that she should knock on the divider.

"Oh, right." He shook his head at the poor, ignorant child.

"So Kindness, how are you feeling today?"

"The name's Karisma!" she said darkly.

"Oh, excuse me." He held his hands up in a stick-up position.

"Yea, just don't let it happen again." It was a test and she knew it was the first of many. She couldn't fail!

"Well, it sounds like I've ruffled a few feathers."

"I don't like to be called by someone else's name."

"I see. Soooo, Kindness," he said deliberately, "do you know who I am?"

She didn't respond.

"Did you hear what I just asked you?" he said nonchalantly.

She still didn't respond.

"I understand you've been through a tough time in your life, so I'm going to give you a second chance. Do you know who I am, Kindness?"

She looked right at him but still said nothing. He was getting upset but was a little intrigued. Chance feared the worst for Karisma, however she remained stoic, and fearless. When his arm flew up she didn't even flinch. She just loo

ked at him. Impressed, he lowered his arm.

"You're not scared of me?"

"No."

"Oh, so you can talk."

"Yes, I can talk. I was talking when we walked up to the limo, remember? I answer when I want to."

He didn't respond but continued to question her. He always had to let whoever he was talking to know that he was in charge.

"Okay." He rubbed his facial hair like he always did when he was furious and struggling to stay calm. "Well, if you can talk, why didn't you answer my question?"

"Because, you weren't talking to me. My name is Karisma."

She was calm. It was almost scary. She reminded Chance of Money, the way she was nice and calm one minute and fierce and deadly the next. Money looked like he was about to explode, then he did something he rarely did. He started laughing. He laughed until tears were rolling from his eyes. It was a while before he could continue talking. Through sadistically joyful tears, he finally spoke again.

"You know what? I like you."

"I like you too, but um…" she was looking around until she spotted what she was looking for. Found it!

"But what?"

"I'd like you better if you offered me a drink!" she said motioning towards the cooler with her head.

He laughed again before replying. "Help yourself."

"I will!" she said seductively, then turned to her friend. "Chance, pour me a drink."

Without waiting for an answer, she turned back to Money and started flirting with him. *Did she just pimp me?* Chance wondered while carrying out the command. "And pour the gentleman one too!" No more need for wondering. *Yep, she's pimpin me!* But I owe her that much and more.

"So Big Daddy?" She scooted closer and put her hand on his thigh. "Is this really **your** limo?"

"Why yes, it is!" He was very amused.

"Mmmm, well you must make a lot of money huh?"

He laughed at the understatement. "My mom would say I make enough."

"Enough that you could share some of that candy in yo pocket and not miss it!?"

He looked intently into her eyes and replied, "Oh yea! I can stand to part with more money than you can count and still not miss it. What did you have in mind?"

"It depends."

"On what?"

"On where you're taking me."

"Mhmmm."

"So, are we going to the club," she pulled herself closer to him and him closer to her simultaneously, "Or are we going to your house?"

"Oh no this is a private event. We're going to my house. Everything should be set and waiting when we get there."

"Excellent!" She said guzzling the cup of liquor in her hand. "Hit me again Chance!"

"Okay, but don't you think you should slow down. That was Ciroc, straight."

"You let me worry about that. Besides that good be smooth anyway, as smooth as new Money!"

Money was lapping up every bit of her sugary sweet fabrications. He looked like a ravenous wolf watching Karisma's every move. And she reciprocated his emotion. It was almost like they were the same person. Both lying, vicious, smooth as honey and dangerous.

"So, Mr. Smooth! What is your real name?"

His attitude turned dark and his voice aggressive.

"Most people say I'm their worst nightmare, right Chance?"

Chance, nerves on edge, continued to pour drinks with no response, and Money knowingly didn't push. Not this time. He turned his attention back to Karisma.

"But you, being the intriguing woman, you are. You can call me Money!"

Then it dawned on him that she made a reference to his street name earlier. *Does she know? Couldn't be! It's just a coincidence. If she's playing me, I'll wring her neck! No, that wouldn't please mama. I got to keep my cool. Stick to the plan Money!*

"I believe I will."

"You believe you will, what?"

"Call you Money. I love Money!"

"I'll bet you do," He smirked.

"Ring, ring!"

*Ugh! Who is ruining my moment?* Money pulled his arm from behind Karisma to check his phone. *Mom!* Immediately his demeanor changed. He started fidgeting and fixing his hair like he was going to be analyzed for everything he did and spoke. Whoever was on the other end of that phone call was the person they really needed to be afraid of. *Money looks like the king, but he's just a pawn.* She was staring at him with a disgusted look on her face and he knew he needed time to get himself together. He couldn't take this call in the presence of Karisma or Chance. Privacy was mandatory. He beat the divider twice and the driver started slowing down and pulling over. When the limo came to a halt, Jug got out and opened his door.

"Thanks Jug. Would you mind keeping the ladies company while I take a call?"

"Sure, thing Boss."

"Oh, and Jug?"

"Yes, Boss?"

"Be a gentleman will you. These ladies are special to my dear heart."

"Of course, Boss. Sure thing."

Jug opened the front door and waited until Money was safely in before closing it. He knew this may be the only opportunity to devise a plan that included the girls. But he couldn't act anxiously. Money always picked up on mood swings, though he seemed terribly preoccupied at the moment. *Must be Mommy Dearest!*

Chance shuttered at the sight of Jug entering the back of the limo. Usually, he saw that as an opportunity to engage in an argument, but he said nothing. It was like he was waiting for something, almost like he was a different person.

"What's wrong with you?"

"Shhh!" He shushed her abruptly.

"Don't shush me! And why you acting so weird?"

"Shhh!"

"If you shush me one more time!"

"Lil girl, will you please sit down and shut up." He was almost whispering but she could still sense the seriousness of his words. And he hadn't made a pass at her once. They sat in silence, until Karisma couldn't take it anymore.

"What in the world are we doing? Sitting here in silence..." She slid closer to Jug. "When this fine specimen of man meat is here and I'm so hungry!"

Jug snickered out loud. "Girl please. You don't have anything I want."

"Yea, that's only because you spend your days and your nights dreaming of being with me. Well, I hate to bust..."

"No. Look, I hate to bust your bubble, but I don't want either one of you."

"Man stop playing. You been trying to get with me since Money hired you two years ago."

"Chance, that was all an act. It's all been an act. But I don't have time to explain everything. And right now, I can't say much."

"What can you say?" Karisma's detective skills were in full fashion.

"Well, I can only begin to tell you what needs to happen tonight."

"So, what are you waiting for?" Karisma spoke candidly.

"Yea, cause you freaking me out!"

"If Money isn't coming back here to keep you ladies company the car will start moving again soon. Then and only then can I tell you more. So can we please sit in silence?"

"No, I think we need to make some noise. Money is used to hearing us argue. If he doesn't hear something soon..."

"You're right, he'll come back here. So, start an argument. And make it believable."

"Yea, believable. But it can't be about you and me getting together, or not. It can't arouse anything in him to make him angry or jealous. It has to be evil."

"Okay. I'll start then."

Jug reached and grabbed a bottle of liquor and poured a glass for the two of them. "Here, sit over here with Karisma." She obliged.

"This is weird."

"What? Us getting along."

"Yea. You're a pretty good actor."

"Hmph, if you think that's weird, then you just hold on. The night is young."

"Okay so about this argument."

"Throw your drink at me."

She sat for a minute and he began sipping his cup. "Ah that's good." As he was taking a second swig, her glass came flying at him hitting him on the forehead.

"What the... You stupid trick! You almost hit me in my eye!"

"That's what I was aiming for! Not such a stupid trick after all, huh!"

Jug moved over to her and slapped her in the face.

"Why did you hit..."

"Shhh, believable remember." He whispered. Then speaking louder, "You'd better be glad I didn't shoot you. But the night is full of promise, baby!" He snickered.

Suddenly the divider opened and the voice of what Kindness remembered as the devil emerged. Without hesitation, confidence gave way to fear. She knew it was him when they were face to face, but to hear his voice without an image, her imagination was getting the best of her. She sat frozen.

"Jug?"

"Yes Boss?

"Is everything okay back there?"

"Sure Boss. I got everything under control. I just need a little time to teach this slut some manners."

"I understand. Take all the time you need."

"Thanks Boss."

"We'll even turn up the music so you can have more privacy. You know, like all the other times you have to teach these filthy beasts a lesson."

"Yeah," he laughed.

Money almost closed the divider, but then remembered Karisma was in the back.

"Hey, send Lady K to the front with me."

They all froze. Jug had to think fast. The plan would only work if both girls knew what to do. He didn't have time to think of a Plan B. He played his favorite card. The one that had gotten him this far. *The Stupid card!*

"Aww, Boss."

"Aww Boss what?"

"I want both of em to stay."

"Why Jug?"

"Because I never had two before."

Karisma hadn't prayed in a long time. But at this very moment she was asking for God's favor. If she had to sit beside that man one more time, he would feel the fear radiating from her heart. *'Never show weakness Kindness. Demons thrive on fear! But our God did not give us the Spirit of fear!'* She could hear her daddy's voice and it brought temporary comfort for which she was grateful. They were all waiting on Money to answer. And though she heard her father preaching, terror still threatened her mind.

"Come on Boss. Let both of em stay."

"Why don't I come back there and ask Karisma myself?"

She wanted to scream but thankfully Jug came to her rescue. *Thank you, Jesus!*

"No disrespect Boss, but you owe me. Besides after tonight I may never have another chance to love on these two beauties."

"Let's get this straight dummy, I don't owe you anything! But, you're right about one thing. This may be your only chance to have them both at the same time. So, I'll let you have them. But you don't have but thirty minutes before we reach the house."

"Ok Boss. Thank you, Boss."

They all sighed a huge sigh of relief as the divider closed. Karisma was silently freaking out but she was trying not to show it.

"Are you okay?"

"Yea, but I could use another drink."

"I believe we all could use another round," Jug agreed. "Chance?"

"This time, I'll be happy to!"

She moved over by the mini bar and picked out a bottle of Tito's. Money always kept a fresh bottle, being that he was a Cowboy's fan. He fancied himself a true Texan. *You's from Georgia negro.*

"Yea, that's fine. But that's not what I wanted to ask you."

"Oh," pouring three drinks she said, "what is it then?"

"When you're done pouring drinks, you both need to take off all your clothes."

"What?! Why?!" Karisma asked before Chance had the opportunity, but the look in her eyes cosigned.

"Ladies. I am not going to sleep with you, but we do have to make this believable. Money has to believe that we did and we now have less than thirty minutes before arriving at the house."

"But do we have to get completely naked to make it believable?"

"Yea, like can't we be, like half naked," Chance chimed in.

"Hey, whatever makes you happy, because it is your happiness that matters the most, right?"

"Okay, I see your point. You don't have to be sarcastic about it. But we still not getting all the way naked."

"Fine. Do what you do but do it now!"

While the girls got half undressed, Jug told them the plan. He talked about Mommy dearest and the fact that Money never had a father and how all of this played into his character. He spoke of someone named Dirty Black that his agency had been investigating for over fifteen years. By the time they arrived at the house, Kindness knew about Money's dad leaving his mother when he was only five and not being around much before that and none after. She learned all the different avenues Money had income streaming and who ran those businesses. Jug also knew about her brother Jay being held in the basement of the mansion. But mainly the plan for tonight was to stay calm and play dumb no matter how much was revealed. Jug needed information, evidence. He had been here much too long and this life was clouding reality. It was hard to remember who he was before becoming Money's head man. But being the head dummy had advantages. He knew things the others didn't, but it still wasn't enough to take him down. He owned too many police officers and judges. They needed a fearless witness. Money's plan was to shock and awe Kindness with surprise after surprise. He was trying to break her and her family. The only dark area was why he was trying to break them down. Jug questioned the intrusion from the beginning.

"Why this family Boss?"

"Well Jug, I figure this family is as good as any. If I choose another family, would that make you happy?"

"Oh, I don't care either way Boss. I was just curious."

"You know curiosity killed the cat. Are you that cat?"

"No Boss."

"Then don't ever ask me that question again!"

"Sure thing Boss. Sure thing."

Jug always kept a cool head, even when he was being threatened. It was the main reason he earned Money's trust in the first place. Every week that passed, he showed Jug more and more of his operation. He didn't know all of all, but he knew some of everything. Everything except why this family had been chosen for mental anguish. It was the first time Money had ever done something of this nature. Finding out the truth with at least one living witness was the goal. Jug had planned to use Chance as a witness and bust Money months ago, but when he started in on this family, the case was put on hold. 'Find out what he's up to!', were his strict instructions. Jug was so ready to return to his life and his family, but the truth was more important. He had waited long enough. Tonight, finally the whole truth was about to come out. Then he could go home.

The limo was slowing down and taking several turns. Jug knew they were close to Money's house. He gave the girls an encouraging look and they started putting back on their clothes, but not all of them. Their shirts and shoes they saved until Money opened the door. Hair mussed, make up smeared and teary eyed, Chance looked as if she'd been forced into the cat fight of her life. Kindness had a red mark on her face but no tears. She looked fearless. When Money saw them, he seemed to be pleased.

"So, how did everything go Jug?"

Jug arrogantly jumped out of the limo with his pants and shoes in tow. The smirk on his face indicated he'd gotten everything he wanted. And Money was satisfied that the horror had begun early for the girls, especially Karisma.

"Karisma?" She walked over to him. "How has your time with Money been so far?"

"Not so bad," she lied. "But I hope you have something more enjoyable in mind for the remainder of the evening." She looked at Jug, "Besides being bullied by this big oaf!"

"Oh, Jug. You mean you didn't get your threesome?"

"Nah, not really. That one right there is too feisty, and I didn't have time to beat her like I wanted. Besides, she's the star tonight and seeing her delicate situation, I didn't want to mess that up. So she just watched us while I watched her."

"Ok. Alright. That's almost as enjoyable isn't it? Being watched."

"Yea, it was Boss."

Money slapped the back of his head. "How do you know Jug!? You've never done either!"

"I'm just guessing Boss, since it was very gratifying."

"Oh wait. Don't hurt yourself using them big words now Jug!" Money laughed and turned attention back to Karisma. He circled her.

"Fiesty!" He walked around her a few times. "You never cease to amaze me!"

"It's a gift!" She said sarcastically.

"What other hidden talents do you have?"

"Oh, it's too many to number," again sarcastically spoken.

He laughed that dark sinister laugh. "We shall soon see!"

# Chapter 21: Friends on Both Sides

Money led everyone into the foyer of his mansion. Ms. Pearl met them at the door as she always did.

"Mr. Money. Is there anything that I could get for you and your guests?"

"You can draw a bath for the lovely Karisma here for starters."

"Yes sir. Right away." She grabbed the young lady by the hand. "Come with me dear."

She embraced the absence of Money. The charade was getting old and tired fast, but after what Jug told them, she knew it was just getting started.

"What about me? I would like a bubble bath too. I feel extra dirty right now!" Chance said, directing her comment towards Jug.

"Oh, you'll get a bath, but only after my nurse examines you."

"Examine me for what?"

Usually, Money didn't tolerate anyone questioning his actions, but this time he welcomed the inquisition.

"I'm glad you asked. You see, something didn't feel right when y'all were in the back," he looked at Jug, "alone. Something about Jug's story didn't fly with me. He sounded desperate instead of stupid. Desperate signifies more intelligence than he is supposed to have." He turned back to Chance, "So I called Nurse Patrice and told her to meet us here. Now, go on up the stairs and get undressed. When she arrives Ms. Pearl will bring her to you."

Chance was backing away into the living room, breathing noticeably hard. *Too hard.* Jug was afraid Money had her cornered. You could see her cowering under his evil scowl. She looked to Jug for some sort of relief or encouragement or something, but he showed no emotion whatsoever. She was about to lose it! *If there is a God, I need your help now!*

"Go!"

The boom of his voice caught her so off guard, she fell backwards over the couch almost striking the coffee table with her head. Money darted forward and tried to catch her, but he was too late. She scarcely missed the table before plummeting to the floor, knocking her head violently against the hardwood.

"Oh no. This aint happening again! Another ho trying to get out of debt with me because of a personal injury!" He said out loud.

"Ow!" Chance was rubbing her arm and head, sobbing. She couldn't move her left arm but her fingers were still tingling. Hopefully that meant nothing was seriously injured. But the incredible migraine was all too serious.

"You're alright. Get up tramp!"

Money was rounding the side of the loveseat. She knew that if she didn't get up now, she may never have the opportunity again. Head pounding, slowly she pulled herself up and onto the couch with the strength of her right hand, tending her wounds.

"Ms. Pearl?!" Money screamed. Suddenly, almost instantly, she appeared at the top banister.

"Yes, Mr. Money?"

"Can you please take this, *girl*, upstairs and check out her arm? And make sure nothing's broken?"

"Yes sir."

"Oh, and she hit her head pretty hard on the floor, so check that out too," he commanded.

"Yes sir. I'll be right down."

Ms. Pearl disappeared, and then a few minutes later you could hear her descending the spiral staircase. Chance hobbled over to meet the woman, avoiding being yelled at further. Money was watching her intensely as if to say, *'If you're hurt, I'll kill you!'* Though she could see him in her peripherals, she looked at no one except Ms. Pearl.

"Are you alright dear?"

"Yes ma'am, I think so."

"She'd better be!" Money growled. *At least he didn't shout...*

"Come along dear."

Despite the urgency in his voice, Ms. Pearl let Chance take her time. Both ladies noticed they were under close observation and both ignored, until they were out of view.

Money was beginning to look a bit frustrated but he had to keep his mind focused on the bigger picture. Tonight, was going to be a night to remember. And the star of the show was not Chance, it was Karisma.

"Genie?!" Genie was one of Ms. Pearls assistants, a second in command of sorts.

"Yes, Mr. Money."

"Will you please check on Karisma and make sure she has suitable attire once she's clean?"

"Yes sir! Indeed sir!"

"And make sure she uses that shea butter and coconut mix. I like the way that stuff smells."

"Yes sir!" She disappeared just as swiftly as she arrived.

"Jug go get changed. Everything is almost in place." Money sounded nervous and slightly excited. He looked at his watch from time to time as he yelled out several more commands.

"Jug?!"

"Yes Boss."

"What are you waiting for?! Go get changed like I said! Our guests should start arriving any minute now!"

"Right Boss. Sure thing."

"Ugh!" He said out of exasperation. "I don't have time for this Jug!!! Get a move on!"

Money rolled his eyes and stormed into his private room through the kitchen. Shortly thereafter, Jug could hear him talking on the phone. It was just the opportunity he needed in order to plant cameras in the foyer and living room. His crew, parked a couple of streets over, was waiting on their queue to move. But figuring out when that perfect moment would be was crucial. They needed to know who all was arriving and when, without making it obvious that their case was about to unfold. And with Money expecting Jug to be right at his side, there was no way he could give them the go ahead. Jug was used to being in sole control, but this time it was a must to depend heavily on his team. In order to bring down this operation it was going to take nothing less than a miracle.

---

"It looks like they already made it in."

"Yea, it does. So what are we going to do now?"

"What do you mean?"

"We planned to be here. At least we were hoping to be here so that we could tail them in, but since they've already entered. How are we going to get in?"

"I don't know yet."

"So we wait."

"Yes, we wait. I'm sure that a door will be opened at the right time. Don't worry, everything will work out."

"I hope so."

Minister James was stoic on the outside, but on the inside his stomach was turning flips. He had prayed all week for an opportunity to see and help Kindness, but he was starting to believe this was more than he bargained for. It felt criminal to be staking out this man's house to help someone he knew very little about. Oh, sure she seemed innocent enough laying in the hospital bed, but what if all of this was her fault. It was very possible that she and Chance were reaping what they had sown. Why would he jeopardize his safety and freedom for them? He looked over at his brother knowing full well why he was putting his life on the line... Jeff! Sam knew that if he refused to come, Jeff would have tried to save the day all alone. There was no way, after all the sacrifices he made for his brother, that Sam would allow the streets to steal him anyway.

One of Sam's biggest enemies, Dirty Black, tried his best to frame Jeff when he was sixteen, but Sam took the fall. Though it was Sam he hated, he felt the only way to truly wound him enough so that he would come after him, was to go after the one person he loved the most. He'd tried to steal his women, cars, vandalize his homes, take over his territory, but Sam always survived and picked up the pieces. There were always plenty of willing subjects, so replacing women was easy. And because of the respect he had on the streets, he ended up getting some of Dirty Black's boys on his team, therefore getting his territory back and then some. It was infuriating. Then one day Dirty realized that the only reason Sam acquired any of those things was to keep his little brother out of trouble. It was the one option he'd neglected to try. And sure enough, Jeff was his kryptonite. It was a great day in the hood, the day he heard Sam was going to take the fall for Jeff. Without trying he killed two birds with one stone.

*"You're too young to go to prison! Besides if I don't take the rap for you, I'll end up killing that sleaze Dirty Black. I can't believe you got caught up with him! What were you thinking?"*

*"You wouldn't give me a spot. I was just trying to be tough like you!"*

*"Jeff, there's a difference between being tough and being stupid."*

*"Oh yeah! How can you tell the difference?"*

*"The difference is..." He walked over to his brother and put his hand on his shoulder, "Getting caught!"*

He said it with a slight laugh, trying to lighten the mood. And Jeff tried to laugh too but it was hard. One part of him felt relieved, but another part felt hopeless. Who was he going to depend on now? Who would be there the next time he did something stupid! Sam was all the family he had left. Their dad was killed in a gang war in Bankhead, so Sam had been more like a father than a brother. Then, when their mom past, and they went into foster care, Sam made a pact that he would get custody of Jeff once he turned eighteen. And he did just that. Their foster mom even helped him with the legal guardianship papers. Sam was always a man of his word. No matter how much Jeff tried to talk him out of it, he knew his brother would take the fall and the consequences. But before he went to prison, he made Jeff enroll in college courses and promise to give it his best shot.

*"Stay off the streets bro. I want to see you do better for yourself than I've done for me, for us. If you don't then all you can expect is more of the same, more trouble, more fighting, more jail time, more problems."*

It was the last thing he said before the police took him away. He was right again. Jeff did get his Bachelor's degree in Business but he never completely got the streets out of his system. Though none of the charges he accumulated were as major as drug trafficking and possession with intent to distribute, for some reason the bad boy image seemed to always follow him. Jeff was repeatedly presented with confrontation and had to prove himself simply because he was the brother of Uncle Sam. That's what they called Sam on the streets because he demanded the utmost respect and he was widely admired for helping those in need, standing up for the underdog and taking the rap for his little brother.

Bangers often considered Jeff weak because his brother stood up for him so much. It became a necessity to establish his manhood. Many of them admitted to being hired by Dirty Black, his ex-street boss, of course the confessions only came after one of Uncle Sam's beat downs. It had been eight years since they worked together, but Jeff still had to fight for his life. It was the reason he came to the hospital to see Sam, the same night he met Chance. Barely escaping a mob of Dirty's ex-goons, he begged his brother to round up some of his old associates and take care of the gang once and for all.

*"Bro, you don't even have to do anything. Just call some of your boys and tell them to meet me at the Marta station on Bankhead. I'll take care of the rest!"*

*"No."*

*"Sam, please!"*

*"I said, No! Look, do you think I risked my life and freedom just to see you follow the same path I did. I've done some really bad stuff, most of you have no clue! You know, they used to call me Black Heart when we did a hit. During the day, I was a fairly nice guy, as nice as a thug could be. But the night called for a different atmosphere. I hurt people and I loved it. It was like I didn't have a heart. So, you've got to understand why I can't do it!"*

Jeff didn't respond. Sam had already done so much for him, he couldn't keep asking him to fight street battles, especially now that he was a minister of the Lord. Yet, he persisted.

*"Sam, if you don't help me then who will. You're all the family I got. I'm so tired of these goons stalking me and hounding me. I don't know what else to do!"*

*"Bro, the only way I can tell you that works is Jesus. He saved me from the streets, not jail. When I gave my life to Him, He gave me a new outlook. It was like starting over. I was off of the streets long enough for most of my enemies to forget about me, and working in ministry propelled me forward. He will do the same thing for you if you choose Him. Other than that little brother, I can't help you."*

Jeff stormed out of the conference room, roaming the hallways, punching walls and kicking plants like a spoiled brat. When he reached the emergency room, his wrist was throbbing and knuckles were bleeding. The tough guy in him said, 'Leave! Your hand is fine.' But reality made him sign the sheet and have his hand checked out. The receptionist gave him some gauze to reduce the bleeding while he waited. And it's a good thing he didn't leave or he never would have met her. It was unclear exactly why, but something about her made him want to be good. She made him want to change and be better. Maybe she was God's answer to his brother's prayers.

When Chance called from the hospital and told him that Money was forcing her to lure Karisma to his house, it was easy to see that Jeff was totally committed. He was going to her rescue with or without Sam's help. And once Sam knew that Karisma was the focus, he was all in. So, there they were, two knights in shining armor. Neither one knowing exactly what the plan was, but there was no way quitting could be an option.

"Hey, isn't that the man the police escorted into the hospital to see your girl?"

"Yea. It's her father! Wonder what he's doing here?"

"Let's go find out!"

"Jeff, wait…" It was too late. He was out of the car and approaching Mr. Johnson.

"What's up old man?"

Elder reached for the .9mm hidden in a built-in holster inside his leather jacket. He had never seen Jeff before. For all he knew, he was one of his son's hired thugs. When Jeff was close enough, he put the gun right to his forehead.

"What's up is right!" He clicked the gun.

"Whoa, hold on! I'm on your side!"

"Elder Johnson! Don't shoot!"

Elder turned to see Minister James crossing the street.

"Minister James? What are you doing here?"

"Same reason as you, to help Kindness."

"And who is this idiot!?" He pushed Jeff's head with the gun.

"Oh yea. Sorry on behalf of the **idiot**, who is also known as my wild and **tactless** baby brother, Jeff."

"Mhmm," he said holstering the gun.

He didn't act like it at the hospital, but it was obvious Mr. Johnson trusted Sam a little. At least he didn't shoot his only family member, and he put the .9mm away. That's always a good sign. *Maybe he is seeing like I am, an act of God. From the looks of things we both are going to need allies!*

"So, what's the plan?" He hoped Elder had a better one than they did.

"Not much. I'm just going to walk right up to the gate and push the call button."

Jeff and Sam erupted into a quiet but noticeable laughter.

"Man, you gone die early tonight!" Jeff howled. Elder already didn't like the boy. He reminded him of his own egg-headed son.

"You know what? You remind me of my son Jay... Young and stupid!"

Jeff immediately stopped laughing but Sam was still chuckling. This time at Jeff. Elder turned his attention back to the minister.

"Since you're laughing at mine, do you have a better plan?"

"Naw. We've been sitting in the car trying to conjure up something, but all we can figure to do is just wing it."

"Like we always do!" Jeff chimed in.

"And how's that working out for you?" The comment was intended for Jeff, but Sam stepped in.

"It has worked before, on several occasions in fact, but I'm wondering how you figure your plan will work? You just gone walk up to the gate and ask to come in?"

"Yea, and you don't have to wonder. I know it's going to work. I can't explain everything but I have a hunch Jerard is waiting on me."

"Jerard? Who is that?" Jeff was determined and tenacious, two traits Elder admired so he answered the boy.

"He's the son of a woman I knew years ago."

"Did you and her have a thing going on?"

"You could say something like that."

"Player, player!"

"It was nothing like that."

"Hmph, okay. Tell me anything." Jeff gave a little smirk that Elder ignored.

"That's not what's important right now. I knew I had to see him as soon as possible, so I went to see the only person I knew who could help. In short, his mother told me where he lived."

"Mr. Johnson, you've been a bad boy tonight. Does your wife know where you been?"

"Minister James, will you please put a muzzle on this fool of a brother of yours before I forget why I'm here and shoot him instead!"

"Jeff, please leave Elder Johnson alone. We don't have all night to be playing around!"

"Alright, I'm sorry. He's just so easy to mess with."

"Cut it out!"

"Okay, I'll stop. You don't have to get testy with me because you're nervous for your sweet Lady K."

"Jeff! Shut up!!"

He didn't say another word, at that moment at least. Mr. Johnson's voice broke the silence.

"So, if you guys aren't here to see Jerard, why are you here?" His eyebrow raised at Sam this time as Jeff's comments soaked in.

"We came to save the girls from this thug Money. He's real bad news, and..."

"Wait. Girls? This don't have anything to do with no girls?"

"Yes, it does! They are the reason we are here! Aren't they the reason you're here?"

"Yea, haven't you been listening?!" Jeff added before he realized it.

"Maybe not close enough. I don't remember hearing anything about some girls. I'm here to see this punk Jerard and see why he went to visit my daughter two days ago!"

"Mr. Johnson, I told you earlier that we are here to save Kindness."

"And don't forget Chance!"

"But Kindness is in the hospital. How can you save her here?"

"It sounds like we got two versions of the same movie going on!" Jeff said.

"Yes, it does." Sam knew he had to try and explain. "Look Mr. Johnson, this is not going to be a walk in the park. In fact, it's very dangerous on the other side of that gate. No matter who you think this guy is, we are in a life-or-death situation. So, I think before we go in all willy nilly, we should step back, piece these stories together and come up with a workable plan."

"I agree," said Elder.

"Me too," added Jeff.

"Let's go back to my car and talk this through. If we are to get the girls and ourselves out of here alive, we gone need some divine intervention!"

They all walked to the car. Jeff sat in the back quietly while Sam and Elder figured out the details. One thing they didn't need, when devising a plan, was confusion.

# **Chapter 22: Change of Plans**

"Ms. Pearl?"

He entered the livingroom to find it empty and the house silent. *No guests yet! Something is not right.*

"Yes, Mr. Money?"

"Remember, just for tonight you are to call me, Jerard."

"Yes sir. My apologies, Mr. Jerard and I'll be sure to remind the others."

"Good. Has anyone arrived yet?"

"No sir, Mr. Jerard. No one has called from the gate."

"I wonder where he is!" He said under his breath.

Money was getting nervous. His mother would expect things to be well under way by the time she arrived. But no one had showed up. Patrice was on her way, but got held up in traffic. Maybe *daddy dear* was stuck in the same boat.

"Ugh!" He pulled out his cell phone to call his mom. When the voicemail picked up he hit the red button. "Nothing is going as planned!"

"Ding, dong!"

"Oh I hope that's the Great and Powerful Elder Johnson!"

He rushed towards the door but slowed in front of the mirror to check his appearance, refolding his collar and straightening his tie.  He was dressed to impress in a navy blue Armani suit with baby blue button down shirt, gold cufflinks and gold silk tie.

"Ding, dong!" Ms. Pearl was heading down the stairs.

"Mr. Jerard, I just let a man named Walter Johnson into the gate. Looks like the guests are starting to arrive."

"Yes indeed. Answer the door and send him into the living room. I'll wait for him there."

"Okay, but there's something you should know."

"Tell me later Ms. Pearl! Just answer the door and send him in!!"

She never argued. It wouldn't do any good anyway. Money was stubborn and spoiled, and the best teacher for someone like him was hard experiences. Tonight, he was about to get a rude awakening. She opened the door and led the first guest inside.

"Mrs. Blackmon, Mr. Jerard." As soon as Ms. Pearl announced his mother, she disappeared. Money jumped to his feet.

"Mom?! What are you doing here so early?" His voice squeaked like an adolescent teenager, but he quickly got a handle on himself. "I mean, I thought you were going to call me when you were on your way."

"Actually, I'm not early, it just looks like you're late, again!! It's a good thing I've been in the area for a while or I might have missed all the action. If there ever is any." She walked around and sat in her favorite chaise. He waited on her to speak again.

"So, how are things going? Has anyone arrived?"

"No but Daddy dear should be ringing the doorbell any minute now."

"Good. That's good." She nodded her head in approval, though he knew she was dissatisfied. "You know, you're just like him." *Here we go!!*

"Who? Walter?"

"Yes, your daddy."

"Mom, don't say that. I hate it when you say that."

"Well, you are. He's a slacker and you're just like him."

"Slacker? I know you're not calling me a slacker just because people are not here when YOU think they should be! I have a lot of power, mom, but I'm not God!" She stood up.

"Boy, who you yelling at?"

"I'm not yelling ma. You act like I'm never supposed to get angry and raise my voice and you can talk to me any old kind of way."

"That's because I can. Now, you better lower your voice and keep it there when you're addressing me. Understood?"

"Yes ma'am."

He was getting annoyed. *I don't know how much more of this verbal abuse I can take! I know she's my mom, but we've got to set some boundaries here!! And tonight, being an epic moment for parents, seems like the perfect time. Just not right now...* He took a deep breath to deliberately relax his tone.

"Aren't you going to head on down to the guest house? You don't wanna spoil the surprise before the audience arrives do you?"

"I guess not. But this seat is so comfortable, I think I'll sit here a minute longer. Anyway, I have someone I want you to meet first."

He dared not question his mother or push her to move until she was ready. She looked like a very calm and collected woman, but underneath was an extremely angry spirit. And she didn't play her radio, not with him or anybody else. He waited, impatiently.

"Mrs. Johnson, you can come on in." Money's jaw almost hit the floor. *What in the world was Mrs. Johnson doing here? No, no! NO!!*

"Jerard, this is Mrs. Johnson, your stepmother." She walked over to him and extended her hand. At first, he didn't know what to do. He couldn't move. He just looked at her.

"Hi. You can call me Angela."

He still said nothing, but he managed to pull his arm up long enough to solemnly shake her hand. Still stunned, he sat on the couch speechless.

"Ding, Dong!"

The look Money gave his mother was pleading, but she offered no explanation. She watched him to see how he would handle the situation.

"You look terrified boy." She uttered nonchalantly.

"No, I'm not." But when Ms. Pearl approached the door, fear filled his eyes.

"Ms. Pearl! No, don't answer the door. I'll get it myself!"

"Whatever you say, Mr. Jerard." She turned and proceeded to climb the stairs.

The atmosphere in the room was getting thicker and thicker by the second. No one moved. No one spoke. And Mrs. Johnson looked confused.

"Are we waiting on someone?" She finally said, trying to break the tension. But it didn't work. No one answered her question. She knew the answer herself and Dorothy shot her a look which she ignored as best she could.

"Ding, Dong!" Still, no one moved.

"I think this was a mistake, so I'll just go." Angela grabbed her purse and started to get up. Finally, Dorothy spoke.

"You're not going anywhere!" Immediately, Angie sat back down on the couch. Then Dorothy pointed to Jerard and with a stern, evil tone she said, "Open the door boy."

She almost never deviated from the plan, but Mrs. Johnson being here was news to him. And Dorothy hadn't disclosed that they would be having a private meeting with his dad. He was supposed to meet him alone and take him to the guest house, where the girls would be waiting. However, the look on her face said the plans had changed. Without another thought, he went to let in the next guest.

"Patrice?"

"Yea, it's me. And why haven't you been answering your phone. I called you like three times in the last ten minutes."

Now he was the one confused. *What happened to Walter?* Ms. Pearl said she buzzed him in at least fifteen minutes ago. He should have been here by now! Money moved to let Patrice in and looked around the front lawn. There was no sign of another car, or Walter. *What is going on?* Not to mention, Patrice was looking at him like he was crazy.

"Are you okay?'

"Yea," he said reluctantly. "I'm fine." He closed the door and re-entered the living room.

"Ms. Pearl!"

"Yes, Mr. Jerard."

"Take Patrice upstairs so that she can check on Chance."

"Yes sir. Come on child." Patrice followed behind still looking at Money. He heard her whisper, "What's wrong with him tonight?" But Ms. Pearl didn't answer. She never did.

He waited until they were upstairs and the door was fastened tight. He thought he heard it lock, but he didn't have time to wonder about such trivial things. His mother was ruining everything and she acted as if nothing was wrong. *Maybe she has a different plan. Plan B? Or maybe this was the plan all along and deceiving me was at the top of her list.*

"Mom?"

"What?"

"What are you doing?"

"Whatever I want!"

"But we had a plan and you're ruining it!"

"Boy, you don't raise your voice to me. Don't you ever!! Didn't I just tell you that not even five minutes ago?!"

"You're right. I'm sorry. But it's just that nothing is working out like we agreed."

"Yes, it is."

"How can you say that? You got Mrs. Johnson here. You didn't tell me she was coming. Then Ms. Pearl says she let in..." he looked at Angela, and she could tell he was changing his words to keep secrets but she felt like she knew more about the plan than he did.

"She let in who?"

"Um, another guest." He said hurriedly, "But that person has yet to ring the doorbell."

"Well, that guest has other accommodations at the moment."

"Really! And when were you going to tell me!"

"Let's be clear boy! I don't have to *tell* you nothing. And if you raise your voice at me one more time, it's gone get really hot in here." She patted her hand on her purse. He knew what was in there.

"Yes ma'am. I know."

"Then act like it!"

"Yes ma'am."

Angela was still sitting on the couch, processing all that was happening. When Mrs. Blackmon knocked on her door, she gave the impression that she needed help with her unruly son. But from what she saw, he was only second in command. Dorothy was the General. And since she had the boy completely subdued, Angie was left to ask all the questions.

"So, what do we do now?" She asked.

"We wait." Dorothy replied.

"On what?" Obviously annoyed, Dorothy gave her a gaze of finality.

"A phone call."

Angie said nothing else. If this woman would threaten to shoot her only son, surely she would kill anyone else. *Lord, what have I gotten myself into? And my family!?* When the silence was becoming unbearable, Dorothy's phone rang.

"Yes, Treybo."

*Treybo!? He's supposed to be out of town on business. What is he doing calling my mom? He works for me! Something fishy is going on here and I'm going to get to the bottom of it!*

Treybo was an old school thug, not as old as Mr. Simmons, but a little older than Dorothy. Money seemed to believe Trey liked his mom in more ways than one. He always licked his lips when he talked to her, as if to keep from drooling. Like a wolf, or better yet a hellhound. The only reason Money kept him around was because he was very good at his job. Torture was his specialty.

"Mhmm. Okay," she laughed a little before hanging up the phone. It was the softest she'd sounded all night. She put her phone back in her purse and when she looked up, Money was staring her down.

"What boy?!"

"I was just wondering, what's really going on here."

"You'll see soon enough. Let's go."

Suddenly he forgot about his current inquisitions and concerns. That could wait. *It's showtime!* He decided to let his mother deal with all the petty details, as long as he got to humiliate his dad and watch that whore of a sister of his squirm, he was good. For now,... But since Mommy loves surprises so much, he decided to give her a dose of her own medicine.

"Ms. Pearl!"

"Yes, Mr. Jerard?"

"Have Jug bring Girl #1 to the guest house, and tell Patrice after she's done examining Girl #2, call me. Oh, and tell Mr. Simmons to pull the limo around for me and the ladies please ma'am."

"Yes sir." He turned to his mother and Mrs. Johnson.

"Shall we ladies?" Dorothy gave a sinister laugh.

"I know *I* am. I've been waiting on this for too long."

She nodded at Angela who seemed relieved that the main event was on the way. Money thought there may have even been a signal between the two ladies, like a shared knowing. *Odd!*

# **Chapter 23: Private Dance**

"Did you see *that*?!" Jeff whispered loudly.

"Of course, I saw that fool! I'm right beside you! And be quiet!"

"So, what are we going to do?" He spoke slightly quieter. "From what I heard, *that* was not part of our plan!"

"I guess we go back to plan A."

"What was plan A?"

"We wing it!"

"Oh. Right."

"At least until we see where they're taking Elder Johnson."

"It looks like the coast is clear. The last thug just disappeared around the house. We'd better get a move on so we don't lose them."

"It'd be kind of hard to lose them Jeff. They're not leaving the property, unless there's a secret driveway in the back. The estate is completely fenced in."

"The way this guy is living, there very well may be Bro!"

"Well, whether there is or isn't, we are going to play it safe rather than sorry. Okay?"

"Okay."

"So, we wait a few more minutes before we head around back. And maybe, just maybe, we'll see something else that will give us a better view of what's going on."

"Maybe."

Jeff sounded doubtful, but Sam had too much hope to be thwarted by his brother's skepticism. There had to be more to this story. It was bigger than Kindness, Money, Jerard and even Elder Johnson. He could feel it in the pit of his stomach. Something big was about to happen.

"Jug, Mr. Jerard says it's time to bring Karisma down to the guest house."

He nodded and she closed the door to deliver the second message to Nurse Patrice.

"Karisma are you ready to do this?"

She smiled nervously, "As ready as I'll ever be."

He put his hand on her shoulder. "Just remember, I'll be right there if you get scared. Okay?"

"Okay."

"No matter what I say or what you see me do, in the end, I'm on your side."

"Okay." Kindness didn't realize how hard she was breathing. And her heart was racing a mile a minute.

"Calm down sweetie. Take some deep breaths."

"Okay, okay. A drink would do me better."

Jug thought about it a minute, then yielded. "One drink, then we must get going."

"Ms. Pearl?"

"Yes Jug."

"Will you get Karisma a double shot of vodka please?"

"Yes sir."

"Thank you."

"You should've told her to bring the whole bottle."

"No, I need you as sober as you possibly can be. There's no telling what surprises we may encounter tonight."

Jug didn't want to frighten her, but the night would definitely get a lot worse before it got better. If she could only get through the darkest part, her life would be that much closer to getting back to normal. Ms. Pearl returned with a large glass, half full of Tito's vodka and Karisma was thankful. She had no time to sip, so she turned the glass up. When she was done, she slammed the glass down onto the nightstand.

"I'm ready. Let's go."

He almost hated to lead her into the pit, but everybody's liberation was depending on her. She had to suffer so that all of them could be free from their own personal evil, whether it was Money, Mrs. Blackmon, self or whomever.

"Okay. Let's go."

They both stood and Jug headed to the back door of the bedroom, leading her down the stairs towards the guest house. The ten-minute walk seemed like an hour but finally they were outside the door. He reached for the doorknob, turned it and let Karisma go in first. When she stepped over the threshold, he gave a violent shove.

"Get in there trick!"

She stumbled a little, breaking her fall with both hands. If she didn't know any better, she would have thought two men were behind her. But Jug reassured her ahead of time that no matter what, he had her back. Yet, she still found herself hoping now that she could really trust him. If not, she was going to need some real divine intervention.

The room was quiet, and empty. Jug knew they were behind the double mirror; however, he couldn't give that bit of information away. They were watching her every move, and he knew they were watching him too. On cue, his phone rang. She knew who was on the other end, so she waited to see what the next command would be. *He was good at giving orders!* When Jug hung up, he grabbed Karisma by the arm and half dragged her to the bathroom.

"I'm told there's a special outfit for you in there. Change and come right back out. And don't take all day tramp!"

He slammed the door shut. Behind it, she struggled not to have a panic attack. Looking at herself in the mirror should have given her courage, but instead it had the opposite effect. She had to fight back sobs, while reaching for the stringed outfit on the back of the door. *What have I gotten myself into?*

"It may as well be nothing!"

"Did you say something in there?!"

"Uh, no. I was just talking to myself.'

"Well you and yourself better hurry up. Your guests are waiting."

"Okay. Just give me a few more minutes."

"You got five!"

It was hard to figure out where each string was to be placed on her body. She had arm strings around her leg and vice versa, and she couldn't tell which hole her head was supposed to go into. However, after three tries, she finally managed to get it on successfully. The alcohol was finally kicking in but she longed for a blunt. It was always easier to dance with dulled senses. She looked into the mirror with a little more confidence. *In a few hours, this will all be over. But for now, it's showtime!!* She opened the door to find a room full of men, all silent, all waiting. One was tied to a chair in the center of the room. His hands were cuffed in front of him and he had a black cover pulled over his head. She looked around the room and noticed that all of the other men had black covers over their heads with the eyes cut out, and they were dressed in all black. *I've seen a lot, but never have I seen anything like this...*

"Hello Beautiful!"

She jumped, startled by the voice that came over the intercom. *It's him! No, I can't do this!! I CANT!!* Her mind flashed back to the very first night she danced. She was sitting in the dressing room, contemplating escape until she heard **that** voice. He didn't yell. He never did in the beginning. His voice was tempered, controlled and deadly, a silent killer.

*"I know what you're thinking but it will not work. You can't run. I'll find you. I always find my runners and the end will not be pretty, besides you have your little brother to save. Remember? Now get ready to dance for the gentlemen who are not so gentle. And don't forget, if you ever get the notion to run, don't! I have eyes everywhere!"* He growled the last few words.

She grabbed both sides of her head, silently screaming, trying desperately to block out the memory but he was relentless.

"Hey, are you okay?" He snickered. His mother and Angela both stood in silence

*Where is he? Does he have cameras in here?* She was looking around searching for the answer and met Jug's gaze. He didn't change his facial expression, but his eyes reminded her that he was on her side.

*It doesn't matter where he is but...Okay, okay, okay! What do I do?! What do I do?! Don't panic! Calm down Kindness. You've got to do this, so relax. Don't be Kindness. Be Karisma! Be fearless! Take some deep breaths.* She inhaled deeply following her own advice and recalling some of an unlikely ally. *"Remember, no matter what you see or hear, I got your back."* She looked back at Jug one more time for reassurance. When she removed her hands from her head, she stood a little bit taller.

"Jug pour the lovely Karisma a drink and burn one to help her loosen up some more."

"Sure thing Boss."

He poured the drink first, reminiscent of Money's previous instructions. *I need her to be so far gone that she doesn't recognize her father or her brother until the right moment!* Karisma guzzled the liquor, and after Jug lit the blunt she puffed without sharing. Soon she was walking around the room, dancing, taunting, and enticing the men, who reacted like most men. They were whistling and throwing dollars. One man asked to cut one of her strings for $100. She obliged him. Then the other men chimed in, asking for lap dances and special tricks. Surprisingly, she was having fun. While being in a coma didn't take away all of her experience, she still felt like the new girl who hadn't seen more than $1000 at a time, ever. She had already piled up stacks of cash amounting to over $2000. But dollar bills wasn't the reason she was here. She came to get her brother back and that's it. Whatever she had to do to make that happen was exactly what she planned to do. *But I can have a little fun too!*

The party was live. Every man was getting exactly what they thought they came for. But everyone had to be wondering the same thing she was wondering. *What's up with the man in the chair in the middle of the room?* It was like she and Money had some kind of connection. He was always in her head, speaking her thoughts. It was weird and a little scary. Always when she was questioning things in her mind, no matter how she tried to disguise them, he answered.

"That's a good girl. Now walk over to the man in the chair."

She obeyed. But as soon as the words were uttered, the man in the chair became defiant. He could hear her walking over, and with every click of her heels, he was trying more desperately to free himself. Based on the muffled words he was **trying** to speak, it sounded like he was gagged. Every time she touched him, he cringed. *What's wrong with this guy? He's probably here under duress knowing Money? Or maybe he just doesn't like strippers? Either way, it's time to put him to ease and change his mind! And Money, I'll show him too. I'll show him who the real master of deception is. I'll show all of them. By the end of this night, everybody in this room will know who I am!* Money turned on the music and her body followed his commands like a charmed snake.

"Good. Very good." He said in his own twisted way. She was his sister and still lust took him over. He licked his lips continuing to give her commands. "Now, show the man in the chair that there's nothing to fear. He needs a lesson in honesty and fun." He changed the song from a slow one to a rump shaker. He loved to see her dance to the fast songs. *If only she wasn't my blood sister...*

Meanwhile, watching Karisma grind on her own father was beginning to be more than Angela could handle. She wanted to hear the truth and it was the only way she could get Jay back in one piece, but now she was second guessing this method. Did she dare say anything to either one of them? If she said something to Dorothy she may get cursed out, and the way Jerard was acting he might punch her without even thinking. It was like she was a mouse surrounded by hungy vipers. No matter what move she made, she'd get eaten alive. Yet her family was at stake. Sure, Walter had lied on several occasions, and she was truly tired. But the road back from this would be a hard one if she let this madness continue. He was bound to find out soon enough. That was the plan anyway. No matter how many regrets she had, there was really no turning back now. *But this is getting out of hand!* She watched in disgust wondering how much more so Walter was feeling. *And where is Jay?*

"Okay Karisma. That's enough. Step back from him. I have a surprise for you."

He looked at his mother who hadn't said a word or even expressed any emotion. She didn't look at him but she knew the next step. Dorothy stood up, walked over to Angela and asked the dreaded question.

"Are you ready?"

*Am I ready?! Of course, I'm not ready!* This was one of the hardest trials of her life. She had to stand and hear the ugly truth from her husband in front of her daughter and new found step-son. Dorothy was looking at her like she'd better give the right answer and fast. Even though it was a lie, she answered.

"Yes. I'm ready." She finally replied solemnly.

Money walked out first, pulling out his .9mm to let the other men know the party was over. They left without any argument. One by one, they walked out. One by one, cars cranked up and drove away. When it was quiet outside, Kindness stood alone with pure evil, shuttering at the sight of him, knowing the inevitable was about to take place. It was the final step to this whole ordeal. The moment she'd been working towards since the day Jay went missing. *This is it!*

"Hi Sis." Karisma looked around for another female. There was none.

"Sis? I'm not your sister! Why are you calling me that?"

"Because, it's the truth." He walked a circle around her. She didn't move.

"No, it's a lie! I don't believe you!"

"I never expected you to Sis. That's why I brought proof."

"What proof?"

"Why don't you take a look for yourself?"

"Look where? You got some papers or something?"

"No."

"Well, what?! What could you possibly have as proof that I'm your sister?!"

He motioned towards the man in the chair. Kindness got a sick feeling in the pit of her stomach, kind of like the day she found out her brother was taken. She looked but couldn't move. It was the first time she'd actually paid attention to the man. He was the right height and build. *No, it couldn't be!*

"Don't be afraid. Go take off the mask."

He spoke calmly as he often did. But it usually meant that things were about to turn deadly. The unknown element was what she feared most about him. *But if he is my brother then he really won't hurt me, will he?* She looked at the man in the chair then back at Money.

"Go ahead. It's okay. Time to find out the truth."

She walked over and stood still, trying to muster the nerve to carry out the request. *I can't! I can't do it!* Her knees were weak.

"I can see this is going to be tough for you, so we brought you some help."

*We?* Simultaneously, two doors opened at once. Dorothy entered first with Angela walking directly behind her. And Jug slightly pushed a young man into the room before positioning himself in his normal spot near the main exit. Kindness didn't even notice her mom. All she saw was Jay.

"Jay!" She ran over and hugged him before realizing she was dressed inappropriately.

"Oh, sorry for the clothes," she said, a little embarrassed, "but I really don't care. I'm just so glad to see you alive and unharmed." She squeezed him tight, tears rolling uncontrollably. And she wasn't the only one crying. Kindness looked behind Dorothy and couldn't believe what she was seeing. A woman's uncontrollable sobs drew her attention.

"Mom?!" She loosed her hold on Jay, but grabbed his hand. Slowly, she approached her mother. "What are **you** doing here?"

"Hi Kindness." Angela tried to stay calm, wiping away tears.

"No time for tears now mommy!"

"I'm just so glad to see you both together again."

"Answer the question, mother. Why are you here?"

"Yea Angie," Jay said, releasing Kindness's hand. "Tell her why **we're** here."

Kindness looked from her brother to her mother. *Why do I feel like the odd man out? Everyone seems to know what's going on except me!* Seeing that confused look on her once innocent daughter's face, made Angela want to tell the whole truth, but she decided to sum it up. This was Walter's coming to Jesus party. It was his moment of truth! Everything else would make sense when he resolved to be honest.

"I'm here for the same reason you are here honey, for the truth."

As much as Money and Dorothy were enjoying this little family reunion, they needed to push things along. Time was running short. The main event, a surprise only Ms. Blackmon knew about. Dorothy nudged Angela and she slowly complied.

"Kindness, why don't you go ahead and take the mask off of the man in the chair."

"Why? Why do I have to be the one held in suspense?! Everyone seems to know what's going on except me! It's only fitting that one of you should unveil this mystery." She looked around the room at every individual before resting her gaze back on Angela. It's time for a little twist. Everyone was giving her orders... *My turn!*

"Mother, why don't you do the honors," she stepped aside, clearing the path to the man who was no longer struggling to get out of the chair. He was completely silent and still.

"I know who's under the mask, and so do your brothers."

*Did she say brother or brothers?* While analyzing the conversation, Kindness forgot about the masked man for a second. Dorothy was getting agitated and shot an unnerving glare at Mrs. Johnson, prompting her to act. Angie reluctantly moved towards Walter. Kindness was right. She knew her mother and brother, along with everyone else, knew who was under the mask. But Angela wasn't ready to face him. Not now. Not like this. In hindsight she realized her mistake of letting the devil deceive her into thinking this was the better way, the only way in fact to handle their issue. Walter had lied to her repeatedly over the years but until recently she'd never retaliated. *How in the world did I get so far gone with pride that I allowed this temporary trial to change who I am? How did I allow the voice of a stranger, an enemy, to sway me to do things totally out of my character?* She questioned herself and she knew these would be questions he'd ask her too, but she had no answer. She reached for the bottom of the mask, slowly revealing familiar features.

With the mask completely removed, Walter blinked looking around the room, trying to focus. His eyes finally rested on his wife. He was in utter disbelief. *How could my wife link up with this hussy who obviously wants revenge and could care less who gets hurt in the process!* He couldn't speak, but his eyes spoke volumes. If looks could kill... And speaking of deadly looks, Dorothy gave a few of her own pushing Angie to gear commands to Kindness. However, Kindness wasn't falling for it.

"Kindness, come and take the gag off of your father."

"You know I would mom, but you're doing such a great job. Why don't you do it? Besides, **mother**, it looks like **daddy** has a few questions for you!" She smirked.

"Yeah, well I have a few questions for him too!" She fought back.

Angela untied and snatched the gag from his mouth, stepping back a little, not knowing what to expect of him. Suddenly she had a flashback of the first time they met. He was a thug, strong and deadly. Remembering the man Jesus saved made her question her own sanity in pushing Walter to anger. He never broke her gaze. Spitting out the gauze, Walter spoke almost instantaneously.

"Woman, what in the world are you doing?!"

"I'm seeking the truth!"

"But this way? Why?"

"I've been asking you to tell me the truth for years, but you refused! So why not this way? Was there another way you'd prefer?"

"Yes, there is another way. We were working things out last night. At least that's what I thought!"

"Well you thought wrong! You were finally put in a position last night where you had no choice but to tell me the truth, all of it! Yet somehow in the midst of truth you managed to lie, as usual!!"

"You're right I didn't tell you the whole truth, because there were still some missing pieces for me. I came here searching for them, only to find out my wife has been working with the devil herself!"

"If you're talking about Dorothy…"

"IF?! Of course, I'm talking about her! She probably orchestrated this whole thing!"

Dorothy stood up to the challenge. She never backed down.

"Are you calling me out baby?!"

"I am not your baby!" He snarled, still tied to the chair so he couldn't really move or he might have choked the life out of her.

"Oh, that's not what you said last night when I dropped my robe."

Angela gasped at the thought. Walter looked at Angela.

"I didn't touch her sweetie, I promise."

"It's too late for your promises Walter. They're just words that mean nothing!"

"But it's true. I would never touch such a filthy beast! Especially after the Lord has forgiven and cleansed me!!"

"Your pulse and the bulge in your pants when I got close to you said you wanted me bad. And you sure got an eye full!" She laughed seductively. "And when was the last time you and Ms. Thang over here got hot and heavy?! Hmmm baby…"

"Now wait a minute…"

"Shut up and stay in your place!"

"My place?"

"Yes, your place! You agreed to this Mother Teresa, now deal with it!!"

"I agreed to finding out the truth! I never agreed to... to this!"

"The truth, right. Let's tell the whole truth from the beginning."

"No! I mean, that's not the truth I'm talking about. I just wanted Walter to be honest with me so that our marriage could get better. I knew he was lying to me but I just didn't know to what capacity."

"The only way to find out to what capacity, is to tell your own truth. How can you expect him to be completely honest when you're not." Angela didn't say a word. Dorothy was right but she was also a conniving, filthy liar. *How could she?*

"Ms. Angela, since it looks like you don't have the courage to tell your truth, I'll spill."

She walked over and stood by Walter, who was stunned to find out his wife had been consorting with this woman from his past. *For how long?* She now faced them all, with Walter at her side. Angela was standing alone, while Kindness held her brother's hand once again. Money stood in the corner, watching with glee. *I've waited to see the perfect family which I was neglected for fall in complete destruction. Today is not about Walter, Dorothy, Angela or Kindness. Today is my day! They needed a lesson in truth and my mom is the teacher.*

"Okay class today's lesson is about deception. Let's start with Ms. Angela. She looks like a perfect angel, the perfect wife. However, she has been talking with me for over a year about making this moment happen."

"I did no such thing!"

"Sure, you did! You remember calling my house and I told you about Jerard."

"Yes, but I only called you on a hunch. I've felt in my spirit for years that Walter had a child with you. And if so, I wanted our children to get to know each other."

"True, but how could they do that successfully without Walter introducing them."

"I didn't know how to tell Walter about our conversation so I didn't…"

"And so, when I called you back you told me where my son could find yours?"

"That is correct."

"Mom! How could you? You've known about this all this time."

"I knew."

"How much mom? How much of this tragic story did you have knowledge of?" Kindness was disgusted with the sight of her.

"I knew Jay was with Jerard and that he was healthy and safe. At least at first, but after a while of not being able to see him nor talk to him, worry and guilt started to get the best of me."

"And you just let me and dad go on thinking whatever we wanted to think."

"Yes."

"Why?"

"For a lot of reasons, Kindness! First of all, Jay needed a brother. He and you were too close. He needed a male figure in his life other than his dad and the pastor to teach him about life. He needed to know how the streets worked. And all your dad wanted to teach him was the Bible."

"And that's a bad thing?" Kindness huffed in abhorrence.

"Yes. In my opinion it is."

"Do you care to elaborate?" Walter was intrigued with the level of ignorance with which she was speaking. Now I understand Job's statement, "You been hanging with those foolish women!"

"Certainly. It's really simple. How can you apply the word of God if you're always in the church and never experience those types of opportunities, which bring me to my second reason. I always told Walter he sheltered you and your brother too much. He wouldn't let you guys make friends or acquaintances outside of the church. I saw it as an opportunity to witness to other kids, possibly unsaved kids. He saw it as a death trap, thinking that you and Jay are so much like he and I, that if we let you guys out there in the world, you'd become like the world and not vice versa."

"From the looks of it, daddy was right!" Kindness interrupted the stupidity.

"No he wasn't."

"How can you say that mom? I mean look at Jay and look at me! We're not exactly the poster kids for Jesus!!"

"That's the point."

"What's the point?"

"I needed your father to see that since we never allowed you guys to make such friends, that when you were old enough to make your own decisions, it was inevitable. And without us there to mold you while you made mistakes, you'd become trapped in the world."

"Wait? You mean you knew about the threat on my brother's life and choices I made to try and save him?"

"Yes, I did."

"Why didn't you say something?! Why did you let me leave home, think my brother was kidnapped and strip in a club to pay off his captors? Why ma?!"

"I didn't have a choice. The plan was under way and completely out of my control."

"Yes, it was out of her control by that time." Dorothy walked over to Kindness. "You see baby, your mother let you become a whore to prove a point."

"I did not let her become a whore. She chose it!"

"No! You both are wrong. I am not a whore, no matter what I look like. And I didn't choose it! I had no choice. My choice was taken from me when this villain called my phone and said that he'd kill my brother and hang him from the church steeple if I didn't do what he said. You see?! I couldn't let that happen!!"

"You mean, you did all of this for me?" Jay squeezed her hand.

She looked at him. "Yes, I did. I would give my life for you. You're my brother and I love you."

"Awww, how touching." Money finally spoke, holding the gun in his waist holster. "But who cares!" He walked around the group, pacing.

"What really matters is that 27 years ago, this womanizer," he stopped behind Walter and put the .9mm to his head, "helped to conceive me. Then five years later, he left my mother and me for all of you! Isn't that right dad?"

Angela, Kindness, Jay and Jug all were holding their breath, but Dorothy only smiled. She looked like the proud mom who had taught her son all he knew and finally he was stepping up to the plate. They all waited on Walter.

"Jerard? Stay calm now son."

"Son? Please! It's too late for the formalities. You should have been there to call me son when it mattered."

"I was there for five years."

"Oh, I'm sorry. You're right. Let me rephrase." He cocked the gun. "You should have been there for the last 22 years. Specifically, when I was a teenager and had questions that my mom couldn't really answer!"

"What about Dirty Black baby? He was there for you?" Dorothy maliciously interjected.

"Don't get me started on him ma! You know what he did to me! Yeah, he was there, but he was no father figure!" He pushed Walter's head with the gun. "And you should have been there to protect me from his hand!"

"Jerard, I am truly sorry. Please put the gun down so we can talk about this."

"What's the matter old man? Not ready to meet your maker?!"

Walter didn't respond. Naturally, he was afraid. No one wants to die, but to be absent from the body is to be present with the Lord. It is a blessed thing when those in Christ die, but at the right time by God's appointment. Not because this crazy hussy wanted to take vengeance into her own hands.

"Jerard, we can talk this out. All you have to do is ask and I will give the answers you've been looking for. That's all you really want is answers. It's your mom's crazy idea to create a violent atmosphere. I know you didn't want this. Let's just talk about it. Okay son?" Money seemed to think about what his father was saying, but only for a second.

"Uh-uh," he said, nudging Walter's head with the point of the gun, "it's too late for talking. It's time to smoke. Right ma?!"

"Right baby."

"Dorothy?" Dorothy ignored her plea. Angela was trying to hold it together, but emotions were rising.

"Dorothy?! This was not part of our agreement!" Before she knew it, Dorothy had her by the throat against the wall.

"Hasn't your pastor ever taught you not to make deals with devils?" She nodded in agreement.

"You should have listened!"

# **Chapter 24: Freedom**

"Hey isn't that Chance?"

"Yep, and I know the other one too. Nurse Patrice!"

"The nurse from the hospital?!"

"Shhh! Get down and be quiet!"

"Sorry Sam. But is that her?" He whispered loudly.

"Man you need to learn how to whisper."

"I'm sorry Sam. But is that her?" He spoke a little quieter.

"Yep. I knew I didn't like her for some other reason because she is fine. If she'd had a nicer spirit, maybe I would have tried her up."

"You're right about that bro."

"About what?"

"She is fine!" Jeff licked his lips, "But not as fine as my Chance!"

"From the looks of it, she's not only fine but deadly."

"Mhmm, and I'm not going to sit back and wait on her to hurt my beauty!"

"Boy, get down and shut up! Didn't she tell you to wait on her signal?"

"Yes," he said trying to whisper, "but she never stated what that signal would be."

"Right."

"So, what do we do?"

"We wait."

"Um, not to sound rude but that's all we've been doing... all night!"

"Yep, and we wait some more."

"Why!?"

"Boy, if I have to tell you to shut up one more time!"

"I'm sorry, but I can't just sit back and wait on them to hurt my girl."

"Just in case you didn't notice, the girl I love is in there as well. And there ain't no telling what they're making her do."

"Right. So what do we do?"

Sam looked at his brother in disbelief.

"We wait."

"Again?!"

"Yea again stupid! We only have one gun, and even though there's an undercover agent in there, he's just one man. Plus, we don't know how long it will take his team to get here. So, we have to wait until the right time."

"And how will you know when that will be?"

"Instinct. I've been in situations like this before. I'll know when the time is right."

"Okay Bro. I'll trust you, but if something happens to my girl..."

"Boy, ain't nothing gone happen to your girl! Oooh, get down. Here they come."

Patrice was approaching the guest house with a gun to Chance's back. She couldn't wait to give Money the results of the examination. She called like he told her too, but he didn't answer so she assumed things were well under way.

"C'mon sweetcakes, let's go tell Money what we found out about your little liaison with Jug."

Chance was stricken with fear. Money was going to kill her when he found out they lied. And there's no telling what he would do to Jug. *Good thing Jug is not Jug and has backup!* Patrice opened the door and pushed Chance to the floor, just as Dorothy slapped Angela. Startled, Jug pulled his weapon and pointed it at Patrice.

"What are you doing here tramp?!"

"I came to see Money." She said calmly. Unmoved by the fact that a red dot was on her chest.

"Money don't have time to see you right now!" he snarled.

Chuckling, "Oh he'll want to make time for what I have to tell him."

Money was growing tired of her, but her tone intrigued him. "What is it that you have to tell that would be of personal interest to me... right now?"

"The results of the examination?"

"Oh. Yes of course. To see if my right-hand man can be trusted."

"Boss? You checking up on me?"

"Don't take it personal Jug. It's just business."

"But Boss, when have I ever lied to you?"

"There's a first time for everything. Stranger things have happened."

For the first time in years, Jug feared for his life. If he didn't act fast a lot of blood would be shed tonight. He looked at Karisma, who had been staring at him the whole time. She knew what she had to do. But she wasn't the only one who was watching. Dorothy caught the signal too. Money was still trying to figure out what was wrong with Jug.

"Why are you questioning me? You know how I hate that! Do you have something to hide?"

Jug didn't answer. He simply waited for Patrice to tell the results.

"Go ahead Patrice. What did you find?"

"Nothing."

"What? You mean you came all the way down here to tell me you found nothing! That's supposed to be a matter of personal interest to me?!" He put the gun to her head. "You know what? I'm about tired of all yall hoes interfering with my life! I ought to just kill you right now!!"

Jeff and Sam found an opening under the house that kept them out of sight and in the hearing loop. They heard the threat on Patrice's life. Then Money cocked the gun for the second time tonight. He was playing a dangerous game of Russian Roulette. One of them was bound to make him mad enough to pull the trigger. Patrice was determined not to be the victim.

"No Money wait! Let me explain. Okay?" He released the trigger on the gun.

"Explain." He said calmly.

"Okay, so you know how you told me to examine Chance to see if she and Jug really had sex? Well, they didn't. This girl hasn't had sexual intercourse within the last 48 hours. So, shoot one of them, not me!" Money immediately turned his attention to Jug.

"Is this true my friend."

He said nothing. But fire was raging in Money's eyes. He reared back his arm and back handed Jug, who didn't budge.

"I almost forgot why I hired you. Your strength and high tolerance for pain has kept you alive thus far, but let's see you tolerate this bullet!"

"Freeze!" *It was Treybo.*

"Aaargh!" Money screamed. "I hate surprises!!" He cocked the gun and fired at Treybo. Everyone hit the ground except Dorothy and Jug.

"You missed punk!" Treybo taunted him.

"I did it on purpose! The next time I will-not-miss!!"

Dorothy ignored their weak display of manhood.

"You're late."

"I'm sorry Puddn. I got caught in traffic. It must be a game or something tonight because 75/85 was packed. And so was 400."

"Shut up! You are ruining everything!" Money screamed at his mother.

"Boy who are you talking to?"

He pointed the gun at her. "I'm talking to you."

"Aww, sweetheart. You wouldn't shoot your own mother, would you?"

"Why is he here ma? He's supposed to be on assignment in Washington D.C." He held the gun steady.

"I called him back for our special moment." She spoke calmly, but for the first time even she was frightened. *Bullets don't have eyes or emotions, only purpose, she remembered teaching him. Suddenly wishing she had been a kinder mom, or at least having a sweeter manipulative factor.*

"No one needs torturing here ma!"

"Aww, dear. Can't I torture your father just a little bit?" She motioned her fingers to a pinch.

"No! Not until I get my answers!!"

"From who?"

You could tell Money was confused. He didn't know whether to question Kindness, Walter, Chance or Jug. He grabbed his other .9mm, now having one in each hand. His mother continued to torture him with words, everyone else stood still and quiet.

"Who do you question first? What questions are there left unanswered? Everyone's truth has been revealed except yours."

She taunted him like she always did. Usually he would run away and hide for a few days until he regained composure. But tonight was just full of surprises. Dorothy continued.

"Jerard, honey. There's no one left to question. All has been said. The only thing left is to shed blood."

"No ma. You're wrong. There is one person left to question."

"Who is that son?"

"You!"

"Me? Why in heaven would you want to do that? I've always been honest with you."

"No, you haven't. Out of everyone, you hurt me the most!"

"You're wrong Jerry, baby listen. Everything I have done was for you!"

"Liar!!!" He almost pulled the trigger and she gasped. "I've been mad at my dad all this time because of you, but I remember ma. I remember the day he left and the things he said. He wanted to be in my life but you didn't give him a choice. You wanted him for yourself. I was a hazard. An unwanted result!!"

"That's not true. I loved you. I love you Jerard. You have to believe that."

"Naw, you manipulated me. All you ever wanted was a man. You're the blame!"

"Oh Jerry. Why do you want to blame mommy?" She was still playing the game, but this time he was tired. It ends tonight.

"Because you were always there and you never protected me. Not from Walter, not from Dirty Black and now you got this punk Treybo! What would you let him do to me to keep him in your life? Kill me!!!"

"Son, I was just trying to get you to stand up for yourself. You know, stand on your own two feet, be a man."

"Really? Well today you finally got your wish!"

He pointed the gun and a shot fired, hitting Treybo in the gut. This time he did not miss. The man hit the floor and Jug yelled at Kindness and her family.

"Move!!! I'll cover you!"

Chance and Patrice shot past everyone and exited beside Jug. Kindness grabbed Jay's hand and ran for the closest exit sign. Angela darted for the chair where Walter still sat gagged. Both of them fell to the floor. Frantically she untied his hands and feet. Treybo was shooting back at Money, keeping him occupied long enough for Kindness and Jay to make it into the other room. They were safely locked inside, but they could still see everything.

"Mom, watch out!" It was too late. Dorothy hit her target and Angela fell to the floor. It was now Walter who held a bloody spouse, praying to the Lord for grace and mercy.

"Please God! Please don't let her die!" He cried.

Dorothy looked up mocking his prayer. "Please, please white Jesus. Save my wife!" She laughed.

"You are such an evil woman!"

"I know. It's a gift."

"I hate you!!! What happened to you?! You were mean before but never this dark."

"Well, if you must know. After you left me and your son, I had to find a way to take care of us. I met this guy on Stewart Avenue. The streets called him Dirty Black. He married me and took care of all of our financial needs."

"But I was sending you money."

"Oh please, that money barely took care of Jerard. I needed some 'me' money! That's where Dirty came in."

"You had our son around that evil beast. No wonder he turned out the way he did."

"Yes, it's true. Dirty wasn't the best father, but neither were you."

"I would have been there for him, if you had not shut me out."

"Why would I want you around? You would've spoiled all of **my** fun!" She laughed.

"It wasn't about you Dorothy! I wanted to see my son, to have a relationship with him."

"I know." She drawled. "But if I couldn't have a relationship with you, why should he?"

"Because he's my father!" Jerard pointed the gun at her chest.

"Oh, honey. I forgot you were over there." She looked and saw Treybo out cold. It was hard to tell if he was breathing. For the first time in a long time, she felt truly alone.

"You always did forget I was there ma. All these years you've treated me like I was nothing. And now I know why." He was shot, but managed enough strength to stand. "You were jealous. Not just of Angela and Kindness, but of me."

"What makes you say that?" She didn't deny his allegations.

"It's the only thing that makes perfect sense. You didn't want me to have a relationship with my dad. You watched me suffer without him and you found pleasure in that. That's why you never stood up to Dirty for me! Watching me suffer was like watching Walter suffer."

The truth was more than he could bear. He loved his mother but she was nothing but evil, and she fed him negativity until he became her spitting image. His strength started to fail and he dropped to his knees and cried, still pointing the gun at her. Walter remained still holding Angela. He looked down at her finding that she was conscious and breathing. It gave him hope that everything was truly going to work out in spite of all. Kindness and Jay watched in awe.

"Is this really happening?" Kindness frantically whispered to Jay.

"Yea Sis, I'm afraid it is."

"Do you have a cell phone?"

"Yea."

"Call 9-1-1."

"I already did. When we were on the floor and the first shot was fired. I hit the emergency call button on my phone."

"Good. Now we just got to get mom and dad out of there."

Suddenly, a hatch opened under Money's desk. Jay jumped in front of Kindness ready to fight for their lives if he had to. Luckily, it was help.

"Minister James? What are you doing here?"

"You know this guy?"

"Yea. Actually, I know them both."

"Kindness, I'd like to tell you why I'm here. But it looks like there is a more pressing issue on the other side of this double mirror."

Money was in and out of consciousness, finally dropping the gun when he fell over. He couldn't take the pain. He knew he was losing too much blood when his thoughts started to jumble and decision making became too hard. It was all he could do just to keep breathing.

"Looks like my son is sleeping. Good!"

They all watched as Dorothy walked over to Money, picked up his gun and put two more slugs into Treybo.

"You were supposed to shoot first! Idiot!" Then she walked back over to Walter and Angela.

"Awww, I see we're still breathing," she mocked, "but obviously in a lot of pain. Don't worry. I'll take care of that. I'm gone send you both to the land of no more tears. I know you remember your pastor preaching about it. Streets paved with gold, mansions lining every street, no darkness. When you wake up, you'll be on the other side. Isn't that your goal?"

"Dorothy, you don't have to do this?"

"Dorothy? Who's that?"

"Woman you are crazy!"

"That I am!!" She checked the gun to see how many bullets were left inside. "Only four bullets left, but just enough to get the job done and blame it on my loving son." She reloaded the clip in her own gun and tucked it into her purse. Then she cocked Money's and pointed it at Angela first.

"Wait!"

"Wait? Why prolong the inevitable?"

"I'm just curious. If you're not Dorothy, then who are you?"

"You haven't figured it out yet. I'm Dirty Black!" The gun still aimed at Angela.

"But isn't he a guy. He used to be your man, after I left, right?"

"That's right. But after the feds got him, I was left alone to fend for myself. Sure I had a few coins saved up, but we lived lavishly, so I knew I needed more. I bought this house in Jerard's name and I paid cash for it. We've been using it as a front, while establishing several lucrative businesses along the way. But we never could have done it without the power of the name."

"Dirty Black." Walter said in full awareness.

"You got it holy roller! I became Dirty Black, paid a banger in the feds to kill him, so he couldn't reveal my secret to anyone. And voila! I had the juice, the power!" She laughed wickedly. "I don't know why you keep telling people they need Jesus. I know I don't need him. Take a look around. Things seem to always work in my favor." Dorothy leaned down to whisper one more thing in his ear before killing the perfect couple. "And Walter, don't worry about your kids. I'm going to take really good care of them."

Money saw Sam sneak into the room but Dorothy was in her own world. He didn't warn her of what was coming. He couldn't believe she did all this to kill the entire family and set him up to take the fall. And she and Treybo were going to live happily ever after. *Good thing I got that bum!*

"Say goodbye to your beloved Angel!" Angie looked into Walter's eyes one last time.

"I'm truly sorry Rock. But I'll see you on the other side." He kissed her hand. She hadn't called him by that nickname in what seemed to be forever. He couldn't believe that after all he had done to save them, he failed. He watched Angela peacefully close her eyes as if to be waiting to go home. Walter sat, helplessly. But just as Dorothy was about to shoot, Minister James pushed her arm up in the air.

"Mr. Johnson, get her out of here!"

Dorothy was stunned but didn't fall or drop the gun. She turned and pointed it at Sam. You could tell she was used to this kind of life. Minister James on the other hand was a little rusty. In haste, he realized he'd forgotten to grab Elder Johnson's gun from the bushes. But Jeff hadn't. He shot three bullets into the woman and Dorothy fell to the floor with a huge thud.

"Down goes Dirty Black!" He said, stepping over Dorothy, "And I don't miss like your boy!"

Money was losing consciousness. "Is she- is she dead?"

"Oh man. I almost forgot you were over there. But I guess you're used to that huh."

Jeff's tact never kicked in. You could always count on him to say something crass. However, in this instance, no one minded. He walked over to the boy's mom to check her pulse.

"No. She's still breathing. I didn't shoot to kill. Yo mommy's gone be around for a while to keep you company in jail."

"I'm not going to jail! Do you know how much money I have?"

"Bruh, it don't matter how much cheddah you been stackin! You've been investigated for a long time and finally there are enough witnesses and dead people to convict you and ya mama!

"What if I leave town?" His breathing was labored.

"Bruh, you ain't going nowhere!" Jeff laughed.

"Oh yeah! And who's going to stop me?"

"Nobody. But that bullet might have a say in it. You can barely speak, let alone run!"

"Jug!! Where's Jug? He supposed to have my back. But he seems to be more on your side than mine."

"It seems that way huh? You just keep getting a bad rap!" Jeff laughed again.

"Story of my life..." His voice trailed off into gibberish. Then Jug showed up.

"Where have you been Jug? You're supposed to be working for me!!" Money said sluggishly.

"Sorry. I've been cheating on you with someone else. Or actually more like the other way around. But we just reconciled and so I'm breaking up with you!" He poked fun into the seriousness of the situation. Money ignored him.

"And who are all these people?"

"These people are my first love." He turned to his lead man, "Take him into custody."

"What? Into custody? You can't!"

"Oh yes I can. I'm tired of this life. It was fun, but I got to go!"

"Who are you?"

"I am an undercover agent for the D.A. And I've been investigating you for almost two years."

"You're a cop!"

"More or less."

"How did I miss that? I usually can spot a cop a mile away."

"I dunno. Maybe it's because I have a past in streetology."

"If you so street, how did you become an undercover agent?"

"Change and hard work son."

Money's wheels were turning. *Maybe I can change my life too.*

"Maybe you can."

"Maybe I can what?"

"Change your life and make a difference in society instead of being a menace."

"You been around me too long! You reading my mind now?"

"I've studied you for four years. I just know how you think, that's all."

"Wow. Now that's power!"

"Yep Boss. Knowledge is power." He joked.

"I need to go back to school, get my knowledge up."

"Where you're going, you'll have plenty of time."

"Yea, I suppose so." Jug smiled at him. Then spoke to his team.

"Now get him out of here. And don't forget mommy."

"What about him?" Sam pointed to Treybo.

"Oh, there's no hope for him. He's gone."

"No, I mean aren't you going to call the coroner?" Jug chuckled a little and took a deep breath of freedom.

"The coroners on the way. The guys will just throw a tarp over Trey until the coroner arrives. You think I've been here so long I forgot how to do my job?"

"Maybe."

"Maybe you're right. That's why I'm thankful for my team. Y'all keep me sane."

"So, what are you going to do next?"

"On to another case. But not before spending some very much needed quality time with my wife and kids."

"You're married?"

"Yes. And I've been away from them too long."

"I hear you man. Enjoy your freedom for a while."

"Exactly what I was thinking." He looked around. "Hey, where's your brother?"

"Hmmph, I have a pretty good idea." Kindness and Jay emerged from the room right on time. "And I have the same thing in mind that he does."

Jug and Jay saw the look in his eyes when they rested on Kindness. Taking the hint, they backed off and gave them some privacy.

"Are you okay?" He asked, stroking the side of her face.

"As okay as can be expected, I guess. How about you?"

"I think I'll live…" They both laughed a little.

"So, now that you've saved your brother, what are you going to do with the rest of your life?"

"I'll probably go back to the club. You know, save some money up for my own place."

"You already have your own place. Why would you go back to that… life?"

"Because I'm good at it and it's the one thing I've done on my own that can take care of me and my brother."

"What about God?"

"I still love God. But right now, I'm doing me."

"No, you don't."

"How do you know?"

"If you really love God, you'll keep His commandments."

"Yea, that's what the Bible says huh."

"Yep."

"Well, I'm not ready to go back to church. So, until then, I'll be at the club." She turned to walk away but he grabbed her wrist, walking around to face her.

"That's selfish Kindness and to be honest, it's not you."

"And you know me so well?"

"I've watched you for weeks and you have a beautiful spirit. So, I know this is not you. Proud, selfish, hard? It just doesn't fit your character."

"And what is my character?"

"Kindness. Kindness is your character. And when a person is kind, they bring those around them peace, joy and love."

"Well, a lot of good it did for my family."

"You can't blame yourself for what happened here. It was out of your control." She didn't respond.

"I know you always want things to be perfect…"

"Not perfect. Just right. I want things to be the way they should. I want my family back the way we were, before all of the deception, lies and changes."

"I know you do. But let's be honest. Things will never be the same as they were. But that doesn't have to be a bad thing."

"Why do you say that?"

"Because instead of looking at it like it's the end of something good, think of it as a new beginning of something great, a clean slate." She looked at him with tears of hopelessness.

"But what if we can't make it work? What if our family is all screwed up now and there's no rectification?" He pulled her into his arms.

"That's the perfect time for Jesus to do the impossible. It is in our most impossible situations that He turns things around. Miracles are not meant for us to perform unless we do them by the power of Jesus. Without him things are impossible, but..."

"With him, all things are possible." She pulled back, managing a smile through the tears.

"Right, if you can only believe Kindness." Sam was rubbing up and down her arms, only to console her emotional side. However, it was activating something on the inside of him as well. He swallowed hard, wanting to kiss her and she knew it.

"So what about you? What are you going to do?" She took a couple of steps back, just out of his reach. He folded his arms, thankful for her insight.

"I'll keep ministering at the hospitals and working hard to please God."

"That's good. But what about your personal life?"

"I never had one until now." This time she pulled herself into the hug.

"Just in case you didn't know, I've grown fond of you. Don't you feel the same?"

"I can't lie. I do feel a connection between us."

"So, what are you going to do about it?"

"I haven't worked all of that out in my head. I mean it was just a few days ago that I realized that I lo..."

"What? That you what?! Love me?!!"

"I didn't want to use that word so loosely, but yea. I think I do."

"You seem uncertain."

"I am. Only time will tell if what I'm feeling is true."

"Well at least you're not alone. I'll be praying and working it out on my side."

"Working together."

"Yep. Together is the only way to make it work."

"Right. With the help of the Holy Spirit of course."

"Naturally. I mean Supernaturally!" They both laughed. It was a relief to be able to breathe, live and talk freely.

"So, are you going to give love a try?"

"I thought we just established that."

"We did. But I was speaking in reference to God."

"I know, but I was speaking in reference to it all. After all, we can't do this without God so I'd better get my act together."

"Kindness, I have one favor to ask of you."

"And what's that?"

"Please, don't be too hard on yourself. Losing your connection with God was a process, and so will be the reconnection. Give yourself the necessary time to heal, grow and move forward."

"I'll try my best Minister Sam. You know I'm a perfectionist."

"Yea, I can tell by how well you take care of yourself and how you dance."

"You've seen me dance?"

"Yes."

"Where? At the club?"

"No, but Dr. Reid did show me some videos of you dancing at the club."

"Really?" She was embarrassed.

"Don't be embarrassed. There's no need. I thought you were very graceful."

"And naked."

"He didn't show me the parts where you took off your top. Just the beginning of a couple of sessions. And I'm telling you, your gift is amazing."

"I never wanted you to see me like that."

"Well, if you ever change your mind on God again, I'm coming in that club and dragging you out over my shoulder. So, if you don't ever want me to see you like that, you'd better not go back to that club."

"You'd come and get me?"

"From anywhere!"

She looked at him, long and hard before planting a short, sweet kiss on his lips.

"You know I could get used to this."

"To what?" He cleared his voice. "To what?" He said again, a little bit clearer.

"To you. To looking at that handsome face. Your smile and your heart."

"Okay, don't get too mushy on me."

"Oh, so I see you can't handle a lot of emotion."

"I'm just not used to sharing my innermost feelings with anyone."

"It's time to get rid of that Mr. Samuel James. We're in a new beginning, remember!"

"Yea, I guess that does include me huh."

"If you want to be my knight in shining armor, then yes. It has to include you!"

"Okay." He blushed under her gaze.

"Now, I haven't seen a black man blush in a long time. Like, never!" She teased.

"Well, if you knew what I was thinking, you'd blush too."

"What were you thinking?"

"If we get married, would you mind showing me the whole dance, like what I watched from those videos? Kinda like my own private dance."

She snickered, but didn't blush. "When we get married Mr. James, you can see a heck of a lot more than that!! I'll always be your private dancer!"

"Mhmm." He said, grabbing her hand as they walked over to meet up with Chance and Jeff.

"God is and always will be the God of a second chance. He gives chance after chance after chance after..."

"Yea I get it. Until we stop breathing, we have an opportunity to get our lives right with God, to do what pleases Him and not ourselves."

"Alright, preach sister."

He smiled at the thought of newness and freedom. It wasn't just a fresh start for the Johnson family. God was doing a new thing in the lives of all the survivors, including Money and Dorothy. Sam was finally happy and open to intimacy. God was really doing amazing things inward and outwardly. Jeff, Chance and Jay joined them in the yard, and they all headed to the car.

"So, Bro, it looks like you're about ready to settle down."

"It's definitely headed in that direction," he looked at Kindness. "God sent me an angel to show me the way."

"Well, what do you know! He sent me one of those too!" He grabbed Chance by the waist and she pulled away from him.

"Um, not so fast buster!" Jeff threw his hands up.

"Hey, we still working on it but things are improving. At least I didn't get punched this time."

"Yea, that's definitely an improvement!" They all laughed.

"So, Sis, are you mad at me?"

"A little, yea. But I'll get over it."

"Then you forgive me?"

"If God can forgive me little brother, I have no choice but to forgive you. And," she let go of Sam to embrace her brother. "I want to. It's the only way any of us can be a family." She looked at Chance. "We have to be able to forgive ourselves and others. Everyone deserves a second chance."

"Even me," she got teary eyed.

"Especially you."

"Why especially me?"

"Because, despite the danger you were in, you remained loyal to me and my cause. I'll never forget that."

"But I'm the one that led you here."

"Chance, it was God's plan. You are a person he used to carry out His plan. And His plan doesn't always look right, but it always turns out right in the end. Just in case you didn't notice, you're free. We all are!"

"Free. I forgot how it feels to be free."

"Well get used to it. And you're moving in with me."

"Okay." She smiled so hard you could see the gums in the back of her mouth.

"Besides, someone's got to protect you from that octopus over there!" Jeff had been silently listening, but he recognized a jab when he heard one.

"Hey, I know how to be good. I'm her protector. That's the only reason I use my hands so much."

"Mhmm!" Everybody laughed.

"Man, I am hooongry! And I do mean hongry, with an 'o'!" Jay hadn't really eaten in weeks. But now that everyone was safe, he could breathe easy and munch on some favorites.

"Me too!" Jeff agreed.

"Boy you always hungry!" Kindness elbowed Jay.

"Well, we all can't be little bird eaters like you!"

"Hey, I don't eat like a bird. I'm well put together and I'd like to keep it that way, lean and fit. I have a dancer's frame!"

"Chance is a dancer and she is far from lean! M-m-m!" She punched him in the stomach this time.

"Okay, I deserve that." He said, feigning loss of breath.

"Yea, you do," she rolled her eyes, wiping tears and turning her attention back to her friend.

"I have to admit, I could eat too. But first we've got to go to the hospital and check on mom, and then we'll go wherever you want to go Jay."

"Sounds good KK."

"Um, can I please make a suggestion?"

"Sure Chance." Samuel confirmed.

"Can me and Kindness stop somewhere and change clothes or buy some? Cause I refuse to start my new beginning looking like this!!"

"Amen to that!" Kindness agreed.

"There's a Ross close to the hospital. I can buy you girls a couple of outfits and then we'll check on mom."

"Awesome!"

"Then we can eat?!"

"Boy we gone get to your stomach soon enough! Goodness, just selfish!"

"No, not selfish! Hongry, with an "o"!"

"You too much!" Sam said, before pulling off heading back to Douglas county.

---

"Well Mr. Johnson, it looks like your wife is going to be okay. The bullet went clean through. It barely escaped without rupturing her kidney, but luckily no organs were hit." The EMT looked hopeful which helped Walter to relax.

"Young man, luck had nothing to do with it. What happened here today was nothing short of a miracle."

"Well, it looks like God is still in the blessing business."

"Yes, He is! Um, can I see my wife?"

"Sure. We're about to head to the hospital. You can ride if you want."

"Of course, I want!" Walter turned to get into the ambulance when he heard a familiar voice call him by an unfamiliar title.

"Dad! Dad!" It was Jerard. Walter cleared his throat, slowly approaching the gurney. It was the first time he had addressed his father that way in years.

"Dad. I just wanted to tell you how sorry I am for all of this."

"It's okay son."

"No, it isn't."

"You're right, it isn't. But it will be."

"Even for me?"

"Yes, even for you. As long as you have breath in your body, you can change for the better."

"You're talking about getting saved, aren't you?"

"Yes, I am."

"There are a lot of ways to change."

"True. But there is only one true and absolute way to make a change for the better."

"Look, I don't know if I'm ready to get saved. But I do know I don't want this life no more. The streets, thugging, I did it all for mom. Now that she's going to jail, I don't know what I'm going to do."

"Son, you're a business man. You'll figure it out. From what I hear, you have some legit businesses. The others you can sell and liquidate, or count it a loss for your own good. Making an honest living will be easy for you. Living an honest life is another story."

"You know, I always knew there was more to life than just making money. My mom just pushed so hard for me to make a name for myself in the streets. She acted like that was the only way to live. And even though I know it isn't, it can be hard to see past what you know."

"I know the feeling son."

"Wait. You lived the street life?" Walter, looked over his glasses before responding.

"I haven't always been saved son. I had my day in the streets and I was a force to reckon with too."

"I'd imagine so. My mom always goes for the thugs."

"You're going to miss her a lot aren't you?"

"Yeah. She **is** my mom. The only solid person in my life. It's going to be strange without her presence. But I'm a little relieved."

"Relieved? How so?"

"I can finally make my own choices without the fear of disappointing her by becoming more like you."

"Your mother always had a way of powerful manipulation. I secretly hoped she'd use the gift to influence good in others."

"That never would've happened. And now it never will."

"It might. God has a way of touching people at their lowest point. She may turn her life around and help to save some other women in the prison she's going to."

"Well, I hope she can find her way. And I hope I can too."

"Me too Jerard. But look son, I know the EMT's have to get you to the hospital now, but I want you to think about what I said."

"About getting saved?"

"Yes. Salvation is the only change that can last forever."

"I just don't know if I can really come clean and live that holy roller life."

"Do you think it was easy for a thug like me to give over control to the Lord?"

"I suppose it had to be stupid hard."

"Stupid hard and then some!" They both laughed a little. "But I made it. Not without mistakes or flaws, but I kept going. I kept trying. I kept living. And when God sees your effort, he makes the ends meet. He knows you can't do it alone, that's why we need Him."

"I tell you dad, after today I know I never want to come back to this. I want to be better. I know I can be."

"I know you can too son. If I can, you can."

"I remember you..." he cleared his throat, though tears flooded the corners of his eyes. "I remember you taking me to church and to the park and to get ice cream."

"You do."

"Yea," he reached up to wipe his tears, "and I remember the look in your eyes when you left."

"Son, you have to believe me. I wanted to take you with me. I just couldn't fight your mama. She made me pay and then wouldn't allow me to see you. I tried not to give up hope, but every time I tried to come by and give you a gift, she said you were gone. Then when she started seeing that new boyfriend of hers, he wouldn't let her answer the phone anymore. They stole you from me, that's the truth."

"I know. But that doesn't change the fact that it was hard for me. Dirty Black used to..."

"You don't have to say it son. I can imagine the evil things he did, but you don't have to live like that. Not even in jail."

"I'm not afraid of jail. I've been before. But when I get out, I don't ever plan on going back."

"Mr. Johnson?" Both men answered, then laughed.

"Which one?" Elder asked.

"The hurt one."

"That would be my son." The EMT didn't waste any time with his message.

"We need to get your son to the hospital and into surgery. I know he feels better because of the fluids. But he has two bullets lodged in his chest and shoulder. We've already given him two pints of blood but he's still losing it too rapidly. So if you guys would like to continue this conversation another time. But right now, we have to go."

"Okay. Do that. And take good care of my son." Walter turned to walk away, but Jerard wasn't quite done.

"Dad?"

"Yes son?"

"I was thinking. I could leave the house and the money to you and my sister. That way, you guys can take care of me while I'm in jail and live a pretty good life. If you want to sell the house and buy another one, I understand. After today, I wouldn't want to stay here either. I just ask that you take care of my butler and maids and my drivers."

"If there's anything left after the feds run through your house and businesses, I think that could be an excellent idea."

"The feds won't touch anything. I put all of it into a trust years ago in your name."

"Well, that was smart."

"I'm not completely illiterate. Business is my major."

"I see. You're a very intelligent young man. You know that?"

"Yes, I do, but it's good to hear you say it."

"For what it's worth, I'm proud of you son."

"You are?"

"Yes, I am. You beat the odds. You made it out of a strange land. Now God has a promise for you, that is if you make the right choices and start living for Him. He will shorten your jail sentence."

"Really? God talks to you like that?"

"He speaks into my spirit so that I can pass on His message. It's nothing so great that I have done. It's all for His glory. God wants to use you son, to do some great things."

"He does?"

"Yes. I want you to think about it on your way to the hospital. And about the money situation, I guess we'll work out the details later."

"When?"

"I'll be at the hospital. I can come by your room in a couple of days with a lawyer and we'll take care of it."

"That's the best news I've heard all day." Walter smiled as the EMT's hoisted the gurney into the back of the ambulance and pulled away.

"Mr. Johnson?" *Now I know they're talking to me!*

"Yes sir."

"We're about to pull out. If you're riding, get on board."

"Oh, right." Once inside the ambulance, he watched his wife breathe, thankful that they all made it out alive. As if she knew he was there, she stirred on the gurney grimacing with pain.

"Sweetie, you've got to lie still."

"I know, but I just have to talk to you for a second and then I'm going to sleep."

"Okay, shoot. I mean... Uh..."

"I know what you mean. I'm not that sensitive. You think a bullet can kill my sense of humor?"

"I hope not," he smiled.

"Well, it hasn't. We need all the laughter we have the strength for in times like these."

"Absolutely dear."

"Um, Walter?"

"Yes Angel?"

"I'm so sorry for everything. It was never my intention for things to go this far."

"I know sweetheart. No one is to blame here. We all played our part in it and now it is over."

"Do you think our family is going to survive this?"

"I know so."

"How can you be so sure? Kindness and Jay seemed pretty upset."

"Yea, but I believe for the most part, everyone is relieved."

"Relieved? Did you see what just happened in there? We all could have very well died."

"But we didn't. God is still blessing and performing miracles. And you are going to be fine. No one is going to die."

"Do you think Kindness will ever forgive us?"

"Honestly, it may take some time. Despite living a sheltered life, she learned street fast."

"Yea, our little girl got a lot more buck in her than she used to have, but I think it'll be good for her in the long run."

"I think it will be good for both of our children to have experienced a taste of the streets. They're not as gullible. I feel safer knowing they know how evil the world can be. Maybe they won't allow the glitz to trick them into thinking that's the life to live."

"Amen to that!" She raised up off the bed, forgetting how much pain it would cost. "Ahhh!"

"Oh honey, calm down. You can't be getting too rowdy."

"I know. Oww, that hurt." The EMT was back there in a flash, administering a pain killer into her IV.

"That should help with the pain Mrs. Johnson."

"Thanks."

"So, you never told me how you can be sure that Kindness will forgive us."

"Oh right. It's a simple answer really. I can tell you in one word, truth."

"Truth?"

"Yes. Truth is freedom. It is the only thing that can free us all. Everyone needs truth in order to be liberated and grow."

"Truth makes you free, John 8:32."

"Exactly. If we had not all been here today to hear the whole truth, there would still be questions as to how well we could function as a family. But knowing the truth can heal old and new wounds, help us love each other better and move forward. Finally, we have nothing to hide. We are truly free Angel. Angel?"

"She's just sleeping, Mr. Johnson. We'll be at the hospital in 20 minutes."

"Okay great."

The EMT went back to the passenger seat and Walter buckled himself in for a quick nap. Drifting
off to sleep he smiled to himself muttering, "It's about time for a new beginning."

Despite all the blood, chaos, lights, sirens and police, optimism was in the air. And they had no one but God to thank for that.

# Chapter 25: The Ugly Truth

Standing outside the hospital door, Jay nervously held on to his sister's hand. The feeling of being a little boy and not a man rushed his heart, but this time he didn't care. He knew at some point he would have to answer for his part in this tragedy. The police labeled him a victim but the truth was he was an accomplice. God's grace once again had showed up in his life. Love really does cover a multitude of sin, especially the love of Jesus, but you still have to reap what you have sowed. The consequences were just about to begin.

"Are you okay?" Jay's head snapped up and he responded hurriedly.

"Yea, sure. I'm good." She rubbed his hand.

"You know you don't have to pretend for me. This has to be hard on you."

"Yea but it has to be done."

She really didn't know the half. The truth about how all of this started was going to shock both father and sister. Jealousy, envy, covetousness all played a part in the vengeful plan he, his mother, Money and Dorothy concocted. They all had gotten tired of the false pretense of perfect relationships and Walter's unfailing love for his princess. He sincerely didn't care how Walter would feel in the end. The nervousness came from knowing that the one person who seemed to love him the most would be hurt the most. The very person who had his back time and again, and she was holding his hand.

"Come on. Let's go in." She knocked on the door before he could protest.

"It's opened." The sound of Walter's voice made him second guess the decision to agree to meet. How in the world could he face his whole family with the ugly truth? No one had a clue but his mother and even she didn't know it all. Jay only looked at his father, and then he addressed Angela.

"Mom? How are you feeling?"

"Better son. Lot's better. Thanks for asking." She smiled.

"You're my mom. I love you, no matter what."

"It's good to see you."

She patted the bed for him to come to her. Their eyes met for a brief moment. She was still very weak. You could hear it in her voice and see it in her hand when she slowly raised it to reach for his. He rushed to her and fell on his knees beside the bed. If there was ever a time for him to feel like a little boy, this would be it.

"Mom. Mom I'm so sorry for all of this."

"It's okay," she lifted his chin with the crook of her finger. "I'm okay." He looked at her for a moment, then looked around the room, at his sister and finally eyes resting on Walter.

"It could have been way worse," he finally spoke to his father.

"Yea, it could have, but God's grace showed up like it always does. He's in control of this. The placement of the bullet wasn't fatal because..."

"No, no! Dad, please! Can you just stop preaching for one minute?"

Walter sat in angry silence, biting his tongue for the sake of his Angel. Obviously taken aback, he looked to her for support but she pleaded with her eyes that he not overreact and give the boy time to speak. He was calmed. Temporarily.

"Okay son. What else do you have to say?"

Standing face to face with his father for the first time since their fist fight, Jay's boldness suddenly failed him. He knew he had caught Walter off guard the first time but this time he was ready. Not that a fight was what he wanted, but he understood the body language now. His feet were planted, arms folded and eyes calculating. Jay took a few steps back before continuing.

"I have a lot more to say. I'm just not sure where to begin. So stop interrupting! Alright?"

Walter approached his son. When Jay turned away, he followed until they stood face to face again.

"Alright Jay. Stop running and start right here. Right here! Me and you!"

"Me and you, huh?"

"Yes, me and you!"

"You wanna know what I feel about me and you?"

"Yea, I do."

"Nothing! There is no me and you! There's only **you** and **her**." He turned his head to nod at Kindness and then back to his father.

"All my life, that's all there's ever been. My princess this, my puddin that! Never has there been me and you!" Walter was speechless. He expected anger not hurt. And definitely this was not the response he'd hoped for.

"Tell me, 'Pop'! Why hasn't there ever been a me and you?" Walter still remained silent, unsure of what to say or if he should say anything. While anger turned to rage inside of Jay, this time it was Walter who backed away.

"No! Stop running. Me and you, remember?! Is it because you already had a son? And looking at me reminded you of him? Huh?! Answer me!!!"

"I –uh... I don't know. To be honest, I thought we were doing okay until here recently."

"Okay? Okay?! You thought **our** relationship was okay? If you can even call it a relationship."

"Well, what would you call it Jay?"

"A pitiful excuse for a relationship! A mediocre existence! That's what I would call it! And you thought that it was okay?"

"Yea, I did," Walter spoke honestly.

"Let me guess why you'd think that was. You didn't have a good relationship with your *daddy*. He didn't protect you. He wasn't there for you. He left you to fend for yourself."

"Something like that."

"Something like that or just like that?" Jay asked arrogantly, trying to hurt Walter.

"You're right. It was all you said and a whole lot more."

"Really? Well go ahead, we're listening." Jay stood with his arms stretched wide towards Angela and Kindness. Then he folded them and waited.

Walter looked at Angela, who started to answer for him until Jay put up his hand to hush her.

"No mom. Let him speak. I'm sure it would sound better coming from you, watered down with compassion, but I'd love to hear what **he** has to say."

"Alright son. You want the ugly truth. Here goes." Now it was Walter who looked around the room. He took a deep breath and continued.

"When I was born my mother died. Giving birth to me was too much for her or maybe God showed her some grace and took her on home. Whatever the case, she died and my father never let me forget it. He used the story to torture my mind. I had no memory of her of course, I only had a picture. And he used that picture as a tool of abuse. He would hide it while I was at school, so when I got home, I'd have to search for it. If I found it, mostly it was in his room. And if he came home and caught me in his room, he would either beat me, have sex with me or both. Now one day he beat me so badly that I ran away."

"Walter, that's enough!" Angela firmly whispered.

"No Angie, the boy wanted the truth. I'm going to give him ALL of it. Then maybe, just maybe we can move on from this tragedy!" He took a deep breath, thankful for the short break.

"Anyway, when I ran away, I never planned on going back but I grew tired of trash can scraps. Plus, I missed seeing my mom's face."

"So, you went back to get the picture and he caught you?"

"Yes."

"What happened then?"

"I had packed a bag with a few changes of clothes, some food and utensils. But I couldn't find her anywhere. I was in his room looking for the picture when I heard him stumbling through the door. Somehow, he knew I was there, in his room. He was calling me his little sweet lips, talking about how much he missed me."

"Were you scared?"

"A little, but by that time I was mostly angry."

"Did you find the picture?"

"I found more than that. The .9mm that I'd been practicing with was in his closet. I dropped it at my feet when I lifted the mattress looking for the portrait. It was there. My mom smiled at me and I at her. But when I dropped the mattress, he was in the doorway. With a rush of adrenaline, I picked up the gun and pointed it at him. He thought it was a joke but I was tired of his games. I wasn't playing anymore. At that point, I was ready to kill for my life and all fear left. My hands stopped shaking. It was his life or mine."

"You killed him!" Jay finished the story.

"Yes, I did."

"Daddy, no." Kindness was shocked by the entire story. It was all she could muster to say. Jay on the other hand wanted to hear everything.

"Did you go to jail?"

"I was under aged. The state sent me to a Youth Detention Center for a year and a half. I got counseling and education. And because I was the model inmate, they let me out early. In their eyes I was rehabilitated."

"You weren't?"

"I wasn't what?"

"Rehabilitated."

"It seemed that way, but not really. The street life was in me and I had gained a lot of respect from the males in YDC. That reputation followed me to the streets and suddenly I had a name for myself."

"You didn't feel trapped in jail?"

"No. I was free. Otis couldn't torture me anymore."

"Money said jail is the worst form of torture."

"Maybe that's because even though he was abused, it wasn't so bad because his mom was there. He had someone to miss and come home to. I didn't."

"Why weren't you there?"

It was the question they all wanted and needed answered. The room was so quiet, you could hear a pin drop. This time it was Walter who felt like a little boy.

"I tried to be there for him, but she threatened me with Angela. She was gonna tell her everything, including some fabrications. I wasn't as strong in God then as I am now, so I cut them off. I didn't know how else not to lose my family. I'd just gotten them back."

"But why didn't you fight for him?"

"Your mom, my Angel, she didn't know I had another child..."

"I knew," Angela butted in. He turned to her.

"You did? How?"

"Gossip. Woman's intuition. Maybe it was a little bit of both. But I dispelled the rumors for as long as I could, then it became too much to bear. Some of the ladies in the church made accusations, so many in fact, that we all ended up in the Elder's office. First Lady had to be called in because I was ready to whoop a couple of those women. What she said to me that day is the foundation of my character as a woman and a wife." Jay was like a dry sponge, and her words of truth, living water.

"What did she say?" he asked.

"She said that everything the Lord reveals to us is not to be acted upon. Some things we should simply pray about and let God work them out."

"So why did you get involved with the evil plan that Dorothy and Money formed?" It was the question Walter desperately needed answered. He wanted to ask but recanted, thinking he would have to take it to the grave, but since God had opened the door he may as well walk in. But he never expected to hear his son's voice answer.

"Because it was not their plan."

"Then who's was it?" Walter again heard an unexpected voice answer his question.

"Jay's," Angela answered.

"You knew! How?" Jay was dumbfounded at the insight his mom had. He thought he was carrying the burden alone, but she had known all the time.

"Son, like we've always told you and your sister. And have even mentioned to some degree today. God reveals things and the more He does so the clearer a vision becomes. I started noticing your behavior long before anyone else did. You love your sister but you despised the closeness she and Walter shared. I hoped you guys would work it out, but as the relationship rapidly deteriorated, I started to lose heart. I got weary in well doing. That's why when Dorothy came to me, I felt the need to do something, if not only to chaperone this mess. She obviously had a plan she was sure to carry out without me. I know I acted foolishly, as if I could work things out better than God."

"Wait mom. You knew the **entire** plan was mine?"

"I knew you had befriended a bad seed whom I later found out was your big brother."

"No mom. I mean the **entire** plan to destroy this family was my idea."

"Excuse me!"

Angela gained enough strength from within to push herself up in the bed. Kindness promptly fluffed a couple of extra pillows to place behind her, though she was operating in semi-shock. It was hard to try and process all the information she had heard. After helping her mom, she sat again unresponsive and unquestioning. Angela continued.

"Did I hear you right? You didn't just get caught up in this evil plan. You are its author?"

"Yes. That's exactly what I've been trying to tell you. All of you!"

"And what about what happened to your sister? Did you know about that too?" Jay threw both hands in the air.

"Know about it?! I orchestrated it! All of it!! Everything from the kidnapping to her hearing my voice at Xavier's to her being drugged by Big Boi and Bossy, all the way to the Private Dance for dad at Money's mansion. It was ALL me!"

"No! I don't believe you! You wouldn't do that to me. Would you? Why would you do that to me?!" Kindness was crying uncontrollably.

"Sis please, please forgive me?! Remember, if God can forgive you, you can forgive me."

He knelt at her feet, grabbing her hands, needing to feel the warmth of her love. However, the look he got was hard and cold. Her hands lay limp in her lap. Jay desperately gripped them but her body remained unresponsive, tears still streaming from a frigid glare.

"I'm sorry! I'm sorry okay! I was blind with pride and jealousy. The relationship you and dad have, I wanted it. I needed to feel like he loved me too. But he seemed to only have love for you. Do you know how bad that feels?"

Finally, she looked away and he thought he'd peeled back a thin layer of her wrath. It was true. She was a witness to the numbness with which Walter interacted with Jay. Often, she tried to compensate by showing more love to him than anyone else.

"I guess the love of a sister is not enough to make amends for the lack thereof from a father." Her response was dry. It was very evident that she was hurt to the core.

"Sis, I'm thankful. I'm so thankful for your love. I was sinking into the darkness of a thug's life. My heart was growing cold. I was learning not to care about anything. But by the time I thought about what was really taking place, it was too late. Money and Dorothy took to the plan like sharks to fresh blood. I was in way over my head."

"So, the plan was yours, but the details of that plan were Money and Dorothy's?"

"Yes, for the most part."

"I guess the saying is true."

"What saying is that, Sis?"

"You better read the fine print because the devil is in the details."

She stood up and looked around the room with glossy eyes. It was hard to know how to feel. But for the first time, she was ashamed of her family. She felt that she had no life with them or the church any more. So she turned the doorknob, endeavoring to walk back into the life this tragedy shoved her into.

"Kindness, where are you going?" Angela had a pretty good idea but let her daughter answer for herself.

She shrugged, "Back to my life."

It was a definite statement void of clear meaning however it seemed everyone understood one thing. She wasn't coming home with them. They all watched as the door closed behind her. She walked down the hallway alone, in a daze. No one followed her and she was glad because when she reached her car, something inside of her broke. She barely had enough strength to turn the key. She felt empty and cried until her body was so tired, she couldn't move. Unsure of how long she'd been in the parking lot, Kindness shut off the car and laid her head on the steering wheel. *What do I do now?!*

"Tap, tap, tap."

Uuuggh! She groaned. This better not be my brother. And it sure enough better not be 'daddy dearest'. When she finally looked up, the sight before her was welcomed by her heart. She didn't realize how much she missed him until that very moment. Yet, she was slow turning the key to let down the window. He was patient. He waited. As soon as there was a crack, he didn't hesitate to speak.

"Are you okay?"

"Yea," she lied. She didn't know if she should expose the details of why she looked so wretched. "I just have a migraine."

"You look like you've been crying." That was the understatement of the day.

"Yea I have." At last, some truth.

"Do you wanna talk about it?"

"No not really." She couldn't even look into his face without getting teary eyed.

"Look Kindness. Your dad called me and asked me to check on you. He sounded really worried."

"Hmph, and here I was thinking you came looking for me because you miss me." He was temporarily stunned. It wasn't what he expected to hear. She mistook the brief silence as validation for doubt. "Guess I was wrong!"

She cranked the car and put it in drive so fast that if he'd taken one more second to move, he would have needed the ER more than the ER needed him.

"Kindness? Kindness, come back!" He jumped in his truck and followed her. "Oh no, you're not getting away that easy."

She needed a place to cool off and think. The mall had always been a resting place for her, and even more so since she started dancing. It was the one place Big Boi didn't follow her to and where she didn't fear anyone. That's where she was heading until she noticed his pursuit in the rearview. Instead of going straight down Chapel Hill, she turned onto I-20 East.

"I'll lose you on the freeway!"

She yelled as if he could hear her. But the faster she drove, the more persistent he became. She tried weaving in and out of lanes, but he was unrelenting. She was paying more attention to the chase than her speed. And, inevitably, it caught up to her.

"Whoop, whoop!"

The blue lights were blinding. She knew she was guilty and immediately pulled over. Samuel pulled over right behind them. The officer noticed the truck and called for backup. It was only about 30 seconds before another squad car pulled up. Both cops got out of their vehicles, one approaching Kindness and the other Samuel. By the time the officer retrieved Kindness's license, insurance and registration, the other cop called him. Sam was out of the car, shaking hands with the both of them.

"Really!" She was disgusted with the fact that the one person holding her up was the same person she was running from. Well, at least he was one of them.

"This is not happening!" She screamed at the top of her lungs, then grabbed her head, remembering the splitting headache which could no longer be ignored. She leaned forward to search the glove compartment, in hopes of an ibuprofen. She had never been one prone to taking medicine, but in the days of decreasing faith and increasing hangovers, ibuprofen was a part of her daily regimen.

"Ah, found them."

She looked up to see the policemen were gone and only Samuel remained. He was standing outside her window again. This time there was no need to roll down the window. He put the personal documents in her hand asking the same question as before.

"Are you okay?"

"Yea."

"Are you sure? Cause if not give me a minute to move. I don't have much room to back up here on the side of the highway." He teased.

She took a deep breath. "Yea, I'm sure."

"I don't think you're being completely honest with me," he pointed to the two pills in her hand.

"Right. Well, I did tell you I had a migraine."

"Yes, you did. And I'm glad to see you in a much calmer state."

"Yea, about that. I'm sorry for being so presumptuous."

"I understand you've been through a lot these past few weeks."

"More than you know," she muttered.

"Yea, more than I know," he echoed.

"You heard me?"

"Yep. I'm a very good listener. I have to be. Most of the people I talk to on a regular basis are weak in mind and body. And those people tend to speak in a much lower tone."

Remembering who was in God and what he does so selflessly only added to the guilt. She had no cause to treat him so badly.

"Just because I'm in a vulnerable place doesn't give me the right to take advantage of your kindness."

"Kindness. You have a beautiful name and it fits you. You are a beautiful woman with a spirit to match."

"Amazing. You can still call me beautiful after how I acted. Let alone what I do for a living. There's nothing beautiful about that."

"You're a dancer Kindness, not a stripper. Even when you worked in the club, it was for a greater purpose."

"That doesn't make it right."

"No, it doesn't. But you don't have to continue in it just because you made a mistake."

She dropped her head, expecting sympathy or at least empathy. But Samuel gave neither.

"Kindness, I'm not here to join your pity party. I came to encourage you and lift you up. I'm here to call you back to the faith. Not help you wallow in guilt!"

"I know I need to come back. I know I do! It's just that... Oh you wouldn't understand anyway!"

"It's just what?! You're too ashamed to repent openly?"

"Yes! I am! No matter how I try to explain, I am a backslider. If I come back people are going to be looking and talking."

"Honey, they're going to do that anyway. People are always going to stare and gossip. Let God deal with them. You just come. Remember, if you are ashamed of God, He'll be ashamed of you. Remember?"

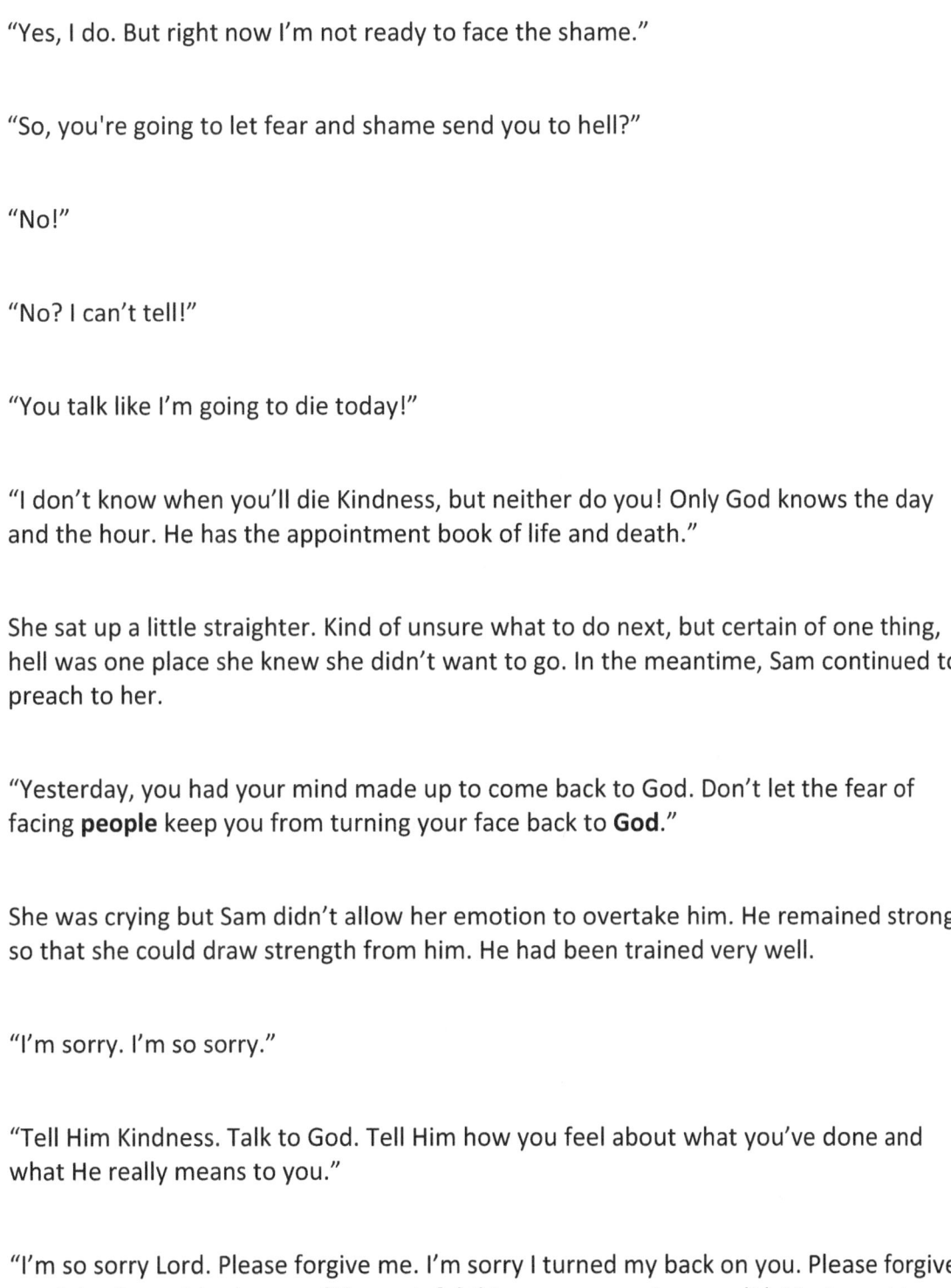

"Yes, I do. But right now I'm not ready to face the shame."

"So, you're going to let fear and shame send you to hell?"

"No!"

"No? I can't tell!"

"You talk like I'm going to die today!"

"I don't know when you'll die Kindness, but neither do you! Only God knows the day and the hour. He has the appointment book of life and death."

She sat up a little straighter. Kind of unsure what to do next, but certain of one thing, hell was one place she knew she didn't want to go. In the meantime, Sam continued to preach to her.

"Yesterday, you had your mind made up to come back to God. Don't let the fear of facing **people** keep you from turning your face back to **God**."

She was crying but Sam didn't allow her emotion to overtake him. He remained strong so that she could draw strength from him. He had been trained very well.

"I'm sorry. I'm so sorry."

"Tell Him Kindness. Talk to God. Tell Him how you feel about what you've done and what He really means to you."

"I'm so sorry Lord. Please forgive me. I'm sorry I turned my back on you. Please forgive me. I don't want to do any of these sinful things anymore. I never did. I just want to please you. Please forgive me for being fearful and allowing evil to overtake me. I miss your presence and your love. I need your protection and your power. I love you Lord

Jesus. You are my everything and without you I am nothing. I am your daughter and my purpose is to dance for your glory not money. I will not do it anymore!"

She was still crying out, but mentally she was getting stronger and stronger. Just that fast, the power of God had changed her because she let Him back in. When she was done she spoke aloud to God, herself, Minister Samuel and whoever else may have been there. In no particular direction, to no one in particular, she spoke openly.

"Wow! I forgot how simple it is to please Him."

"You've made the best decision you could make in your life! You feel better, huh?"

"Yes, I do. Thank you." She was wiping her face.

"Why are you thanking me?"

"For the tough love. You made me remember how easy it is to get caught in self and end up in hell. No one knows the day, nor the hour their name will be called. I've been preached to all my life but somehow I forgot that simple instruction."

"Well still, don't thank me. Thank God Kindness. **He** is love, tough or otherwise."

"I am very thankful."

He sighed. "It's good to hear you in better spirit."

"Yea. But now I got to figure out my living situation."

"Mhmm. But I know one thing, you have got to move away from that club."

"Temptation," she stated plainly.

"No man **or woman** is above it."

"I know that's right."

Their eyes met and the air between them was electric. He wanted to kiss her and she wanted to be kissed, but neither moved. They stood there for just a moment, before Samuel realized temptation was about to take them over. He broke the silence.

"Hey, I've got a great idea."

"What's that?" She asked nonchalantly, as if they both hadn't just dodged the bullet.

"Let's go pack up your things. I've got my truck for the big items. And we can call Jeff and Chance to help with the packing."

"Sounds good to me, but where will we take my stuff?

"We can get you a storage for your furniture and you and your clothes can go to your parent's house."

"My parents! And my brother! Oh I almost forgot about them. How selfish of me! They must be worried sick!"

"They were, but I told them you were fine."

"You talked to my parents? When?"

"As soon as the officer pulled you over."

"Oh yea, I meant to ask. What did you say to them?"

"Nothing really. I didn't have to. Your name has been in the news for months. They knew who you were from your license. And the officer who questioned me remembered me from the hospital."

"So, if they knew who I was and who you are, what took so long?"

"We got to talking about Jesus and the law, and before we knew it both were promising to come to church on Sunday. I don't know if they'll really come, but I'm hoping."

"Minister Samuel James, always working for the Lord."

"I have to. It's the work that we should do until the day we die."

"Absolutely right." She looked at him sincerely, "I am so glad you are in my life."

"The feeling is mutual."

"You make me want to go dance right now!"

"The right kind of dancing I hope."

"Yea, for now. But when you are mine. Oh baby, the time we will have."

"I can't wait." He smiled. "Come on, let's go get your stuff. I'm sure your parents can't wait to see you."

"I hope they're not too mad at me."

"I'm sure they are thinking the same about you."

"The only thing left to do is forgive each other so we can grow past this."

"Do you forgive them?"

"Yes. I have to. I can't afford not to be forgiven."

"Is that the only reason?"

"No. I forgive them because I love them. And everyone deserves a second chance, no matter how many they've had."

"That's right. But only if they have good intentions."

"True, I think they do. Even my brother, after he told me what he's done, his part in this whole fiasco, I believe his apology was sincere."

"Your brother was kidnapped and held hostage."

"You know what I've learned most from all of this?"

"What?"

"Nothing is ever what it seems to be. That's why it is so important to walk by faith and not sight. And I really lost sight of that because I was afraid. My God did not give me that spirit of fear. The origin came from a dark person with demon influence."

"And God took care of them, despite us all losing our way."

"You lost your way in all of this?"

"Yea, but that's a story for another day. Let's get back to how your brother played a part in the plan that nearly destroyed your family."

"We'll have story time later. First things first," she smiled. "Come on, follow me. I'll lead the way to my apartment. You can call your brother and Chance and they can meet us there."

"Sounds like a plan to me. We're already headed in that direction anyway. Let's go."

He got in his truck and she pulled off with him following. She felt blessed to have so many people who loved her, old and new. It was all because of Jesus. And she couldn't wait until Sunday morning to dance again for His glory. 'It may be from the audience for now, but it's a start,' she thought. While she was reflecting on her blessed life, suddenly she got a sharp pain in her head, right behind her eyes. This was more than a migraine. It seems everyone had forgotten she just had surgery, including her. Other issues took precedence over her health but it could no longer be ignored. Samuel noticed her car swerving and speeded up to get a closer look. He let his window down to yell to her.

"Kindness, what's going on? Are you okay?" She wasn't really responding. She looked at him holding her right temple and it looked like she was about to pass out. Sam struggled not to panic.

"Hit the brakes! Hit the brakes, Kindness!" He wasn't sure if she heard him. She was no longer looking at him but the car was slowing down. Then it happened. The car veered off the road and crashed into the median. Sam pulled right over grabbing his cell phone in stride.

"911, is this an emergency?"

"Yes!"

"Sir, I need you to calm down. And tell me what's going on?"

"Okay, Okay. She's in the car and she crashed."

"Sir, what is your name?

"What does my name matter?! Get an ambulance out here NOW!" Sam was freaking out. There was no sense of calm.

"Okay. I'll get someone right out. But Sir I'm going to need for you to stay calm and answer a few questions, Okay? Where are you?"

"On I-20 East near Six Flags."

"Before Six Flags or after?"

"Before."

"Okay. I have an ambulance on the way and the police will be there soon."

"Okay."

"Can you see the victim?"

"Yes, I'm right here with her but I can't open the door."

"Sir?"

"Sam." He was calming down, hearing the sirens approaching in the distance. A few passersby had stopped and were standing near. He didn't feel so anxious now.

"Okay Sam. If you get the door opened don't move her."

"I won't but what can I do?"

"Is she breathing?"

"Yes, she's breathing but she's not conscious."

"You're good at this. That was my next question. Now has the young lady suffered any sickness or illnesses in the past?"

"Well, she did have surgery on her eyes earlier this week."

"And she's out of the hospital? Was it an outpatient procedure?"

"No, she was in the hospital for a few weeks before the surgery. She had to heal from a nasty fall that caused a gash on her right temple. And she has been complaining about a headache all day."

"And you didn't think about the injury to her temple and the recent surgery?"

"Ma'am, it'll take me all day to explain the details of what has happened to this young lady and her family this week."

"What did you say the young lady's name is?"

"Kindness Johnson."

"Oh okay. Now I understand a little better. She has been the talk of the station. Police officers, EMT's, Dispatchers, we all have been talking about the Johnson family."

"Yea, they've been through a lot these past months." Sam moved out of the way as the officers and EMT's approached.

"The EMT's are pulling up."

"Yea, they just got on the scene. I moved out of the way so they could start working on the door and getting her out."

"Sam? I just want you to know you did great."

"Thank you." He said blankly, watching them pry the door open.

"The EMT's and the Police will take it from here okay."

"Okay."

"And, Sam?"

"Yes ma'am?"

"Good luck." Those two words snapped him back to reality.

"Ma'am, I don't believe in luck. It's temporary, unstable, and uncertain. But I do believe in divine intervention. God is in control no matter how much we want to panic and lose control. He is the calm in the middle of a storm. He's the only guarantee in life."

She laughed a little. "I'll be sure to remember that. You take care."

"Yes ma'am. You do the same."

Sam and the other bystanders watched as the emergency workers freed Kindness from the car. The EMT's took over, checking her vitals which Sam overheard them saying she was stable but still unconscious. They got her onto a gurney and into the ambulance. As they all were pulling off, the wrecker showed up to tow Kindness's car. He could get the information later for insurance purposes. In the meantime, Samuel decided to follow them back to Douglasville. He would wait to tell her parents until he got there. There had already been too many informal communications for such serious events. He was used to talking to people face to face, giving them natural reports and encouraging them to believe in the healing power of Jesus. Not giving challenging news over the phone was one of his pet peeves.

# Chapter 26: Healing

"Why didn't you call us first?!"

"Mr. Johnson, please stay calm and let me finish."

Walter was tired of everyone shushing him and making him calm down. This was the wrong time for manners as far as he was concerned. The "old man" had been awakened in him in the past few weeks and all that knew him were sure to see a different Elder Johnson, a realer and better version hopefully. And that transformation started right here with Minister Samuel.

"Now you look here boy! I don't know who you think you're talking to but I'm not one of your patients or a broken family member that needs help coping with death or the threat of loss. I am an angry man of God who is concerned for his only daughter. You should have called me **first**!"

"You're right! I'm sorry. I'm so used to being in charge and helping others handle their situations, I completely forgot you don't need to be encouraged."

He was sincere with a twinge of sarcasm. Everyone needed help at some point, and encouragement too. Elder ignored taking a shot back at him.

"I'm going to check on my daughter. You're welcome to tag along, or not!" He was halfway down the corridor before Sam joined him.

"I decided to stand by you no matter how pigheaded you are," he said hoping to conjure a laugh or a smile from the man. But Elder only smirked and hit the elevator button.

They rode to the main floor in silence having nothing else to say to one another, but having one common goal. They both truly loved Kindness and prayed for swift recovery. She put her life on the line for her family and no one acknowledged that fact until now. As the elevator door opened, they were met by Chance, Jeff and Jay.

"Dad! I'm so glad you're here. They won't tell us anything. It has to be a parent."

"Yea, and the nurse is being a real butthole!"

"Jeff, could you just watch your mouth for once in your life. Jesus."

"Uh-uh big bro. Don't you dare use the name of the Lord in vain."

"It wasn't in vain. I really need him to help me not to strangle you!"

"Ok. I'll shut up now."

"Good idea," Chance jeered, smiling at her new beau. He smiled back, secretly thankful for this dangerous situation, without which he would never have met her.

"As much as I am enjoying this volley of foolishness, I've got to go check on my baby." Elder patted Sam on the back simultaneously as Sam shot him a look that could kill.

"I'm coming with you, dad."

It was good to be getting back to family. Hearing Jay call him dad almost brought tears to his eyes, but now was not the time to be emotional, at least not for waterworks. It was time to get some answers.

"May I help you?"

The kids were right. The intake receptionist was very rude and disrespectful. Maybe she was having a bad day or maybe she doesn't like her job, but at any rate, Elder refused to allow her attitude to be his focus.

"Yes ma'am." He smiled. "My daughter was brought in about an hour ago, and I was wondering if I could get an update on her condition.

"Sir, I'm going to have to tell you, like I told your children. I'm guessing they're your children!" She rolled her eyes in their direction. "I **don't know** anything yet. When **I** know, **you'll** know."

"Well, **ma'am**," Elder emphasized, "I am asking **you** to find **out**. Then **you** will **know** and **you** can tell **us** and **we all** will **know**!"

The nurse rolled her eyes again. It was obvious she was lazy and really didn't want to move away from her desk. There were freshly opened snacks and a cup of juice, he noticed. But the look on Elder's face said he meant business. She could very well lose her job and she definitely couldn't afford for that to happen. She sighed deeply, loosing her grip on the cup.

"Hold on a second. I'll go check."

She took her sweet time, checking paper work and having short conversations with coworkers on her trip from the desk all the way to the double doors leading to the ER rooms. Once she was out of sight, Elder stopped gritting his teeth. He didn't have time to go off, but she was pushing it.

"If that lady don't hurry up and let me know what's going on with my Kindness, I'm going behind that desk, find the button to open those doors and I'll get answers for myself. And maybe I'll get a scare out of it for her. You know, teach her a lesson!"

Jay looked at his dad, and laughed. "You would do that, for real?"

"For my kids, I'll act a plum fool up in here!" He smiled.

"You pretty bold for an old man," he was joking but Elder shot him that don't test me look so he subsided.

"Any news yet?" Elder looked over his shoulder to answer Sam.

"No, not yet. I was wondering how long you could keep your nose out of other folks' business."

"No disrespect Elder Johnson, but Kindness **is** my business." Elder turned full circle.

"Okay. Now, you have my attention. I'm very interested in knowing how you can assume **my** baby is any business of yours?"

Jeff and Chance scooted closer, so the men now had an audience. He didn't want to make a scene, but it was too late for Sam to back down. He had to stand up to the man that he planned on being his father-in-law.

"Well, I've grown very fond of your daughter in a very short time."

"Very short time indeed! What makes you think my baby will reciprocate *those feelings*?"

"She will," he stated confidently.

"Oh. Arrogant, are we? I must warn you, don't think too highly of yourself. The fall can be detrimental to your life. Trust me boy, I know!"

"Again, no disrespect Mr. Johnson but your daughter and I have a close, strong bond not even your mockery can break."

"Oh yeah, how strong?"

"Stronger than a three-strand cord."

"Not easily broken. Hmmph, we'll see about that."

"Only time will tell, **sir**!"

"Indeed!"

They stood toe to toe, both standing up for the woman they loved, neither backing down. *This guy may fit into our family just fine Elder thought.* The intake receptionist returned right after the heated discussion began. She stood close, watching intently but it looked like the fire was dying.

"As much as I love manly displays of strength and arrogance, I really hate groups of people standing in front of my desk sooo..."

"What's the news on **my** baby?" Elder interrupted, completely ignoring the woman's snide comments.

"She's very weak but stable."

"Well can we see her?"

"Two of you can. And she's asking for you."

"Of course, she's asking for me, I'm her father."

She shot Elder a hard look and then smirked. "I meant him. She's asking for you Sam."

He tried to act nonchalant about the news, but inside he was shining like a boy who'd just won his first fist fight.

"Me? Okay. Um, I'm ready."

"Let's go."

Elder was unmistakably dismayed as both men followed the receptionist, who passed them off to Nurse Abbey. The youngsters watched until they went through the double doors, secretly hoping no one threw a jab or punch. Once they disappeared, Jeff, Chance and Jay only looked at one another. Neither had said much during the stand-off and none really knew what to say now. They all had seen enough fights, arguments and drama for a while. None of them cared for a fist fight in ER. The three of them gladly sat in peace, waiting on the next verdict. Time seemed to be ticking by with the speed of a sloth, and Chance was getting antsy. It had only been thirty minutes but it seemed like hours had passed before either of them uttered a word. Finally, she could take no more and broke the silence.

"Do you think your dad was able to keep his cool in there?"

"I sure hope so. But, why do you ask?"

"Because, he wasn't too happy that your sister asked for Minister Samuel. And they looked like they were about to come to blows!"

Jay laughed. "Well, I believe that no matter how much dad **wanted** to hit Minister Sam, he wouldn't dare. He's going to have a hard enough time as it is finding his way back into good graces with his Princess Kindness."

"If I didn't know any better, I'd say you were jealous." Jeff always managed to find the worst thing to say at the absolute worst time.

"And I'd say **that** is none of your business!"

"I beg to differ."

"Oh yea? Care to explain?!"

"Don't mind if I do!"

"Jeff, not here okay. Can we do this later?" Chance was trying to play peacemaker. It wasn't working.

"Naw babe, this is the perfect time for me to get the answers I need!" He turned back to Jay.

"You see, me and my brother risked our lives and we don't really even know what's going on here. I think somebody owes us an explanation. What started all of this? Why did Kindness have to be a… dancer? We need the down and dirty just as much as the Johnson's." He used quote fingers. "You see, me and Sam are all we got! So if something happened to him, somebody gone have hell to pay!"

"And?!"

"**And**, I got a good feeling you know more than you letting on."

"What makes you think you know me so well?"

"I don't. But I do have strong intuition, street smarts if you will. It's a gift. On the streets you can lose your life before quick get ready, so you got to be able to size a man up quick. And I did you!"

"So you think I have all the answers?"

"No. But I do believe they start with you."

"Well, you're wrong. They start with my dad."

"Maybe it starts with your dad concerning the Johnson family, but to the James's I'd bet my life that I'm right. So, tell me, am I right?"

Jay got up and walked to the window. He knew he had a choice. He could either act a fool right now and tell this idiot off, which would only lead to more headache, and from the looks of this guy in more than one sense. Or, he could level with them. At the end of the day, Jeff was right. They all risked their lives to help save someone they loved. And it was entirely his fault. He put everyone at risk and so he owed them all an explanation. He turned back towards Jeff.

"Look man. I don't expect for you to understand everything so I won't try to tell you everything. But I will say this. I'm sorry for dragging you guys into this. I never expected for my actions to affect so many people I don't even know. I just wanted my dad to be honest with us and tell the truth about his life and my brother. I never meant for any of this to happen."

"Guess what Einstein?! It did!"

"I know!"

"And your sister could've died! Your mother was shot and your dad was very near biting the bullet himself! Let alone, Chance, me and my brother. I ask you, was it WORTH IT!!"

"Yes." He spoke calmly. "Yes, it was."

"But how can you say that!" Chance joined in. "A man died the other day, and a few more seriously injured, because of the evil plan you obviously played a part in! How can you sit so smug and say it was worth it?!"

"Because, it was."

"REALLY!"

"Yes! REALLY!!"

"Oh, now **I'm** dying to hear this explanation!"

When Chance sat back down, she noticed that rude receptionist was standing nearby eavesdropping. She wanted to confront her but didn't want to give Jay an easy way out. Ignoring her, she crossed her arms and legs in anticipation. The nurse returned to her desk just as Jay was about to spell out everything. She had a message for them but it seemed what he had to say was juicier and she couldn't wait to hear. She and some others were following the story from the beginning and not too many people could say they had the inside scoop. Her bridge buddies would be so jealous. They all had their own little story line going on, but when her turn came to speculate, she'd actually be telling the truth. It would prove to be a much more compelling rendition than any of their imaginations. She sat with arms folded, anxiously waiting for him to speak again.

"You don't know what it's like. Having a dad in the house, wanting his attention and approval so badly, trying so hard to impress him with grades and accomplishments. But nothing ever seemed to be enough. And all **she** had to do was come into the room, that's it! He dropped everything and gave **her** his undivided attention. Do you know how much that weighs on a little boy's heart?"

"Let me get this straight. You're complaining because you had a dad and he didn't give you the attention you thought he should have?!"

Jeff didn't wait for an answer before folding over in laughter. Chance didn't join him; however, she did snicker a little, laughing more at Jeff's comics than at Jay.

"You think this is a joke, huh?!" Jay walked over to Jeff and stood him up straight, ready to plant a fist in his mouth but Jeff was still laughing. He didn't care if this guy hit him. It was worth the price to pay for amusement.

"Stop laughing! It's not funny!"

"Oh yes, it is!" He continued in pure delight. Jay let him go and sat on the other side of the room. "Awww, po pitiful J.J.! So, is this what you do? And used to do when you didn't get your way?!" Jay didn't respond.

"You get in a corner because your daddy wasn't perfect?!" Jeff was suddenly serious. "Shoot, I wish my dad had stuck around long enough to hear me breathe!"

"Did he die?" Chance asked, hoping to calm the rage, covered up with cheer. His head snapped towards her as if he'd forgotten she was there.

"I wish. At least, then I would have closure."

"Where is he then?"

"Hmph! Your guess is as good as mine. When my mom went into labor, he dropped my brother off at our aunt's house and then dropped mom off at the ER. No one has seen him since."

"What?"

"Yea. We lost the house and our car. Mom had to move us in with Aunt Ruth. Her husband didn't want us there though so we left when I was two. He said that was enough time for anyone to get on their feet. But I remember watching my mom try her best, waking us up at 5:30 am to go to daycare only to work a job that barely paid for the daycare and what Uncle Homer asked. She couldn't save any money. It wasn't until she started going with Brother Esau that our lives improved some. He really loved her but he didn't care too much for us."

"Did he treat y'all bad?"

"Nah, he didn't interact with us much. He gave mom money to buy us things though. But Sam! Sam couldn't stand him. He always said when he turned eighteen, he was going to leave and make his own way. But on his sixteenth birthday Esau gave him three weeks to find a job or get out."

"How did your mom react?"

"She was upset, but at the end of the day she wasn't going to leave that fool."

"What did Sam do?"

"He left. About a year before, he started running strong with some gang. It was better for him than a job. I can't remember a time after that where Sam was broke. He kept at least a stack on him and he had major juice on the streets. Esau hated his new lifestyle. The more E warned me about that life, the more I wanted to be just like Sam, cause I sho'll didn't want to be like him."

"And that's why you are the way you are?" Jay awakened from sulking. "You're still trying to live up to his reputation."

"Who's?"

"Big brudda, that's who's!"

"I wouldn't say that."

"I would. It's true. Your mom raised you to love God and live right but the glamour of the life your brother was leading pulled you to the streets. And you've been fighting God ever since." It was Jeff's turn to shut up.

"You really want to live for God, but not before you make it as big on the streets as Sam. I guess shooting Dirty Black gave you all the props you need to be a beast on the streets."

"You think you know me? You don't know me!"

"Oh, I think I pegged you just fine! Not bad for a "church boy" huh? Sized **you** up perfectly!"

They were walking towards each other. Many fights had been avoided today, but this one seemed certain. There was a time when Jay would have been afraid of a street thug like Jeff, but hanging with Money dispelled all those fears. He was ready.

"Okay, that's enough!" It was Sam. "Jeff, sit your stupid butt down before I jump in and end this fight for everybody!"

"Jay, what's going on? Have you lost your mind?" Elder agreed.

"No. For the first time in a long time I can say I'm acting totally in my right mind. This boy..."

"Boy!? I'll show you better than I can tell you churchy!"

"Oh, you want to be me so bad you can taste it!"

"And I could say the same bout you!"

"Enough! Both of you!" Elder spoke a little too loudly.

"Excuse me gentlemen! There are more pressing issues than vain male egos." *Why did she always have something negative to say? She could mess up a wet dream.* At the sight of Nurse Abbey, the receptionist scooted back to her post, pretending to work.

"Nurse *Crabby* is right!" Elder teased.

"And that includes you Mr. Johnson."

"Of course, it does." He rolled his eyes at her. "But she's right. Kindness is more important."

"How is she?" Jay gladly forgot about his argument with Jeff.

"She's better. And..."

"And what?"

"She's asking for you?"

"Me?"

"Yes, you."

"Alone?"

"Yes."

"Dad, will you come with me?"

"Aww, want daddy to hold your wittle hand?" Jeff mocked.

Sam grabbed his brother by the neck and dragged him down the hallway. Chance followed suit without delay. Elder waited until they were out of sight and ear shot.

"Son, I could go with you, but I don't think what needs to happen would happen with me in the room."

"So that's a no."

"More like, I wish I could but I can't."

"Why not? You'd do it for her."

"If the shoe was on the other foot I wouldn't do it for her either. You guys need to put all your cards on the table and hash this thing out. I will not walk around my own house on eggshells because we neglected to address every elephant in the room."

"She's coming home?"

"Yes. And I hope you will too."

"You want me to come home? Even after everything I put us through?"

"We all played a hand in what happened these past few months. As long as we are honest and fess up to our mistakes, we can move forward as a family."

"But our family will never be the same."

"No we won't. We will be better."

Jay was proud of his dad. It was the first time in a long time they talked without him preaching. He was real, and he spoke openly. No scriptures necessary, yet he gave the truth. He wasn't opposed to a little preaching and Lord knows he needed all the divine truth he could get. It was just good to hear his father keep it one hundred.

"Okay dad. If you believe me talking to Kindness alone is a step in the right direction, I will do it."

"I do. I think you will be surprised at what you find."

"What is that supposed to mean?"

"You'll see when you get in there."

"Alright. Here goes."

Jay waited for the nurse to buzz him back and proceeded to the nurses' station. Elder heard the head RN giving him the room number before the doors shut behind him. He was happy everyone was speaking and working towards better. Now it was time for him to go be with his Angel. He missed her smile and vibrancy. Even from the hospital bed, she lit up his world.

"Come on in chump!"

"Chump! Now wait a minute."

"What? You think you're ready to challenge me."

"Uh, no not really." Jay was stunned. He expected hurt and disappointment, not joyful banter.

"I know you're not."

"Are you okay?"

"Don't I look like I'm okay?"

She was sitting up in the bed with wrapping around the top of her head. Seeing her bald made him realize just how much she risked by coming to rescue him. It only made him feel more guilty.

"Kindness, I'm really sorry for..."

"Look, you've already apologized enough. And after replaying it over and over in my head during surgery, I'm tired of hearing it! Let's talk about something else."

"Like what?"

"How about our brother Money? What was he like?"

"Really? You really want to talk about him?"

"Yea. Now answer my question chump!"

"I aint gone be too many more of your chumps!"

"Oh yea? What you gone do?" He approached slowly with his hands in the form of claws, saying one word with each step.

"Nothing. I'm-going-to-let-thaaaaa... tickle monster get ya!"

They laughed like they were kids again. Nonetheless, Jay was on edge wondering when she would snap and go off about what he told her yesterday. She read his mind.

"Look, I'm over that. It's time to move on. I don't even want to remember it, let alone discuss it. So please try your best to do the same."

"But Kindness, that's what got us in this mess in the first place, curiosity about what was true and secrets."

"True. But there is no curiosity this time and no secrets. We all know the truth. Everyone has apologized. Everyone has forgiven. What else is there to talk about?"

"I-I don't know. I guess I figured we had a ways to go before we could get back to joking and laughing."

"Why? Because you haven't forgiven yourself?"

"Maybe."

"Not maybe, exactly!"

"Man, I must be really transparent."

"Why do you say that?"

"Because this is the second time, I've been read in the past three hours."

"So, I'm right?"

"Yea. I suppose you are."

"Look Jay, you have to be able to forgive yourself just as much as you have to forgive others. It's the only way you can experience true freedom. Do you think I had an easy time forgiving myself for leaving God and stripping?"

"I guess not."

"You guess right! It was humiliating to admit I'd gotten so far away from God. Drugs, alcohol, lying, backbiting, whoring, stripping... I did it all! And I'm not happy about it either. I'm just over it!"

"Just like that?"

"Yep, just like that. So, what's your list of things you need to let go of?"

"I lied, cheated, stole, drank, smoked, shot a couple of people, got into a few fights, risked the lives of my family and some people I didn't even know... And I'm not proud of any of it!"

"But can you forgive yourself?"

"I hope so. How did you do it?"

"I let God do what He does. I cast my burdens on him and let him carry them for me. After that, it was easy to let go and move on."

"That's it?"

"Yep! And if you need someone to minister to you, I know a great one!"

"You really like him, huh?"

"Oh brother, it's so much more than like. That man does for me what no other even tried. He loves my spirit and my mind, not just my body."

"Mhmm, but I'm sure your body is not at the bottom of his list either!"

"Huh, I hope not!"

"How does he feel about your hair?"

"He knows it will grow back, until then, I have this!" She pulled a bag of wigs from under the bed. I got short, long, bobs, braids and just about everything else you can think of. Chance and I used to take hair and make our own wigs and looks. The rest of the girls spent hundreds of dollars a week just on hair, nails and clothes. We saved money that way."

"Speaking of money..." He leaned up and took off his backpack. It was stuffed with money.

"I hope that's hundreds!" She teased.

"More like thousands in hundred-dollar bills."

"Woah, where did you get all of that cheddah?"

"From you."

"You mean, that's the $2000 a week I sent to your kidnapper."

"Yes."

"So what are you going to do with it?"

"Not what I'm going to do with it. It's yours. What are you going to do with it?"

"You're giving it to me?!"

"Yea, it's yours. You earned it!"

"Oh wow. How much is it? Have you counted it?"

"It's a little over $50,000."

"FIFTY THOUSAND DOLLARS!!!"

Jay laughed. "Yea! That used to seem like a lot of money to me. But after living with Money for six and a half months, this is chump change."

"Well, I'll gladly be the chump on this one!" He handed her the money.

"Will you give me my purse out of the closet over there?" She was so excited, thinking of what she would do with the money.

Jay walked over to the closet just as Chance entered the room.

"Knock, knock!" Kindness covered the money on her bed with the covers.

"How did you get back here?"

"Jeff distracted the nurse while I pressed the button that lets you in."

She was looking at Kindness who only reached her hand out to her friend. Chance walked over and grabbed it.

"How you feeling Lady K?"

"Weak," she said in a raspy voice. Jay was startled until he realized she was messing with the girl. She fell to her knees laying her head on the bed beside Kindness chest.

"Oh, I'm so sorry K! I never thought this would happen. I blame myself. I could've stopped this at any time but I was afraid. Big Boi and Money had me petrified. It's been a long time since my life was my own and it made me a slave to fear. I hope one day..."

"Ha, ha, ha, ha, ha!" Kindness laughed. Jay joined in once the joke was exposed.

"Wait, what's going on? Am I missing something?" Chance was confused, slowly lifting her head from the mattress.

"Girl, I'm fine. God is good." She reached out and grabbed her purse from Jay. "The doctors were able to remove all of the glass and I didn't lose one bit of my eyesight."

"I guess I deserve that." She sneered at them both.

"No, it was just a joke. No biggie."

"How can you be so forgiving after all you've been through?"

"I asked her the same thing!"

"And?"

"And she basically said she doesn't have time to hold grudges. The past is the past and she's ready to move on."

"Yep!"

"She learned a new word too!"

"Yep!"

"And that's it? You don't have any questions or comments?"

"Nope!"

"So where do we go from here?"

"Home!" She said definitely.

"Hey Sis, I'm going to go check on mom."

"Call me when you get up there. I'll be moving to a recovery room in a few hours but you should make it by then right? Or do you need an escort?" She nudged Chance.

He shot Chance a short but extensive look then shook his head defiantly. "I think I'll pass. Besides it looks like this beauty is already spoken for." Jay made a quick exit. He didn't want to hear any girl talk.

"Ooo, do tell!"

"Well, his name is Jeff..."

"I know. I saw you guys together. I could see he was feeling you but I didn't know you felt the same. Tell me, what's he like?"

"A lot like your guy. He tries to play tough but really he's just a gentleman chasing a street reputation long forgotten."

"Is he saved?"

"Girl, you know I don't even know what that means."

"Well, how about you guys come to church with me and Sam after I get out of here? That way you can find out for yourself."

"Nah."

"No. Why not? Aren't you tired of that life?"

"Because we already promised Sam we'd start going before you get out."

"Oh, the jokes on me this time huh?"

"Yep!"

"And you stealing my word!" They both laughed.

"My life is so different now K. I don't even recognize it."

"Are you still dancing?"

"No. Jeff says I'm better than that."

"He's right."

"But I've been doing it so long, I don't know anything else."

"Sounds like it's time for a new beginning."

"I suppose so."

"Of course so. There's no one holding nothing over your head. You don't have to look over your shoulder no more. No more running Chance. You're free. We both are. How does it feel?"

"Feels weird and…" she looked around, "pretty darn good."

"Yes it does. You are in control of your own future now."

"That's something I never had."

"Honestly, me neither. Think about it. You can do what you want. Have what you want. Be who you want. What do you want the most?"

"A family."

"You already got that. You've got us."

"Yea. And you guys are great so far, as long as you keep the drama to a minimum!"

"Hahaha, in our family we don't do minimum. We go all out! You should fit in just fine."

"Right." They laughed. But Chance was talking about something more than living vicariously through Kindness. When she thought of family, she thought of her mom and dad, and possibly a husband and kids of her own.

"Hey, tell me about Big Boi and Bossy and how they were taken down by the mighty hand of Chance."

"I can't take all the credit. Dr. Reid did his thang too. But let me tell you. Girl, it was sooo exciting. Big Boi and Bossy were in his office when it all went down. Darnell turned state evidence on them for a plea bargain. And…"

"And what?"

"You know they are the ones that drugged you Karisma."

"Kindness."

"Sorry. That's what I meant."

"It's cool. I know it may take some getting used to. You've been calling me Karisma for so long."

"Yea, Maybe I'll just stick with Lady K. It suits you."

"Whatever floats your boat."

"Now what were you saying about how I got drugged."

"They had roofies put in your drink that night you passed out."

"You mean, Darnell put the drug in my drink?"

"Honestly, I think Bossy did it. Darnell usually waited until after the girl's dance. But Bossy had other plans. You see, no matter how much she was holding over Big Boi's head, she couldn't beat your natural talent. She needed you out of the way."

"Since we're being so honest, I'm glad she did. Of course, I didn't enjoy being hurt and having amnesia, being away from my family and especially the pain of two surgeries." She winced at the lingering pain behind her eyes. But God is in control. Her plan ended up working out for all of our good!"

"Yep, I guess you're right!"

"Now, tell me everything and don't miss a detail. I might want to write a book about my life one day."

"Ooh, can I be the editor?"

"Sure, if you tell the story right."

"Okay. Here goes."

Chance began to tell Kindness all of the details and had her hanging on every word. It was good to have the freedom to live in peace and converse with a friend, without feeling rushed. New beginning is what Kindness said and that was the only description that fit the situation. *Thank God for new beginnings.*

# **Chapter 27: Kindness and Marcus**

"Excuse me ma'am. No one's allowed in this room except family."


"And from what I know this fella don't got none!"


Kindness contemplated whether or not to retaliate on the officer. Chance would've called them rednecks or racists. And Karisma may have said something even worse. Both of these strong influences were proving to be her toughest adversaries as she strived to get back on the right path. However, there was one influence stronger than her enemies. She heard the Word of God repeated back to her, always in her father's voice. *Vengeance is the Lord's. Let Him fight your battles. You take the high road and God will fix it. You won't ever have to touch them.* She knew she had a choice, as always. The gift of God. But when her brother's life was on the line, black and white turned to gray. Compromise. Behind the guarded door was the man who put her in that position. He also had a choice, and she wanted to hear his side of the story without everyone else around.


"Officer, the gentleman in that room does have a family. I'm his sister."


"I didn't know Money had a sister?"


"Me neither!"


"Officers, one thing I've learned in life is you'll find there's a lot you don't know."


"You gettin' smart girlie?"


"No sir. Simply stating a fact."


"I got a fact fer ya. We gone need to see some ID!"

"Now that's a fact girlie!"

"Look sir. My name and my family's name has been all over the news for months. I'm sure you've seen it."

"What y'all some superstars now? Everybody sposed to know ya?"

"Not hardly sir. I just thought that since you are a part of the police force that helped arrest my brother, you might remember us."

"Nope, sorry."

"ID please!"

"Is there a problem here officers?"

"Oh, Nurse Abbey. Nurse Abbey! Thank God!" She grasped the back of her neck.

"Kindness, what are you doing out of your room?"

"I came to see Marcus," she whispered.

"Sugar, you are not well. Come on. Let me help you back to your room."

"No. I have to see Marcus first!"

"Well, your brother is only allowed one visitor per day. I think we have your dad scheduled later on in the evening."

Kindness pleaded with her eyes. And the soft spot that God reserved specifically for this young lady was touched in that moment, just as it was from the first night she was wheeled into ER.

"Okay. But only for you," she whispered back. "There will be two other officers for the night shift. We'll just pretend that when your dad comes, he is the first."

"How are we going to get past these creeps?" They were still whispering and the officers paid them no mind.

"You leave that to me."

Nurse Abbey cleared her throat. "Gentlemen, have you eaten anything this morning."

"We had a biscuit and coffee around 6am, but come to think of it, I sho am hongry again."

"Me too. It's been bout five 'ars."

"Strapping young men such as yourself need nourishment. How about, I watch the door for thirty minutes and let you kind sirs go get some lunch, on me?"

"Free lurnch. I'm game."

"Me too!"

"Good. I'll call the lunch room and tell them to charge you to my account."

"Thanks Nurse."

"Yea, you aiight."

The men gladly gave up their post for a couple of hamburgers and fries. However, one man hesitated, figuring the nurse was playing them to let the girl in the room. But she didn't look like she would harm anything, so he joined his partner. Besides, he wasn't turning down a free meal. No way! Nurse Abbey waited until she heard the elevator door close before turning back to Kindness.

"You got twenty-five minutes. The kitchen manager is going to call me when they are on their way back. Whatever you need to find out in that room, you'd better make it quick."

"Yes ma'am. Thank you."

Kindness started to knock, but Nurse Abbey reached for the handle and opened the door. Money turned his head, immediately recognizing her.

"What's up Sis?" He said blandly.

Having heard his voice so many times as Money and as Marcus, she was quite unsure of how to respond. Who was she talking to today? But she didn't have time to waste.

"I was gonna ask you the same thing, Bro."

"Nothing. Trying to stay alive in these streets."

"You ain't in the streets no more."

"I'm headed to prison." He looked out the window again.

"And?"

"Same thang, but instead of streets and alleys they got cells and blocks. It's worse inside than out here."

Kindness remembered that Jay said Money told him prison was the worst form of torture. But she also remembered their dad saying it was a place of freedom. Even Sam testified that God used prison to save him from the streets and give him opportunity and time to change.

"Dad is trying to see if he can get you in a low security facility. He said somewhere they only send people with health issues."

"That aint gone work."

"Why you say that?"

"Girl, do you know how much dirt I done did out here? These cops been waiting on they opportunity to lock me up and throw away the key."

"You'd be surprised what God will do."

"Oh right. I forgot about y'alls faith. I never had any need for it. The name Dirty Black kept me safe on the streets. Even the police wouldn't touch me. But once they found out my mom was Dirty Black and the real man is dead, I knew that was it for me."

"Our faith goes way further than Dirty Black ever could. He saves completely."

"You really believe that?"

"I do."

"Then why you drop your faith to go strip at Queen City? Where was your faith then?"

Kindness forgot about all the things she promised she wouldn't do when he antagonized her faith in God. She wanted to be as kind to him as she had been to Jay. But they are two different people. Money liked to play mind games. Residue of his upbringing, but infuriating just the same. She jumped to her feet.

"You had my brother! And threatened to kill him!!"

"Ahh, there she go. Karisma! I've missed you." He spoke slyly.

"The name is Kindness, not Karisma!!"

"You not being too kind right now. You're acting irrational. Is that how a Christian is supposed to act?"

"How you know how a Christian is supposed to act anyway?"

"I used to go. I was young, but I remember."

"Whatever! You can't possibly remember much. Look at how you acting and what you've done!"

"Indeed."

"What's that supposed to mean?"

"Nothing."

She finally stopped to take some deep breaths, pacing the length of the bed. If it wasn't for salvation, she would choke him to death. And that is a fact! The thought made her calm down. He had rubbed off on her and not in a good way.

"I just have one question." Marcus said.

"And what is that?"

"If you was praying to your almighty god, then why he didn't tell you I was lying?"

"I don't think you was lying, because I was talking to Money then. Today, you are Marcus?"

"Hahahahaha, you think you know me don't you?"

"I know you got more than one personality."

"I am a cat that wears many hats."

"Right, cause when mommy spoke you was a scared little boy."

"The little boy that lost his father to a spoiled princess!"

"Why is everybody so jealous of me and daddy's relationship?! I don't get it!"

"Cause, you the only one he really loved the entire time."

"That's not true!!"

"Isn't it! Cause from what I remember, my dad was there until your mom got pregnant with you. Then he was there sometimes, but not like at first. But by the time you started walking he made up his mind that you needed a full time daddy. And I had to suffer for it!"

"That is not why he left!"

"How you know?!!"

"Because I know my dad. He wouldn't deliberately hurt no one. I believe he made the best decision for his relationship with God, which included honoring his marriage vows. He stopped coming to see you because of my mom, not me."

"I take that back. You right. Dirty used to tell me that all the time. She told me that one day we would get him back for leaving us to fend for ourselves. She said he had to pay for leaving me to be abused by her boyfriends. She blamed him for everything."

"Your mom had a problem. She couldn't see her wrong and what she did to push my, I mean our dad away from you. He wanted to come see you. I'm sure of it."

"Why did you come in here anyway?!"

"I came to get answers."

"Did you get em?"

"Yea, I did. I wanted to hear your side of the story. But the more you talk, the more I realize it's basically the same as everybody else's. Jealousy. And I still don't get it."

"How could you when you had everything you wanted. Dad loved you unconditionally and to the extreme. The love he didn't give to Jay and that he couldn't give to me, he poured it all out on you. You had it all and we had nothing."

"You? I understand your anger. But Jay is spoiled. Or maybe your influence over him kicked in and made him look at his life another way."

"So it's my fault."

"I'm not placing blame. But he never acted like it bothered him before."

"That's not what he told me. When your mom and my mom decided to introduce me to Jay, he confided in me. He said he needed a big brother, someone he could connect with, because his dad ignored him most of the time unless he was preaching. He wanted someone he could ask questions to and get answers from. Your dad made him feel uncomfortable, like he had to be perfect all the time. It was easy when he was younger and wasn't so curious about life. It was easy to do what he was told. But every time he asked a question, your dad pulled the Bible out and gave a sermon."

"What's wrong with that? We do everything according to the Word of God."

"Yea, maybe that is the problem."

"Wait a minute now."

"Hear me out. I believe I also remember there is a scripture that says you overcome by the word of your testimony."

"You're right."

"So why after dad had all of that testimony about growing up in the streets and being a thug, drug dealer, gang banger. Why didn't he ever share that with his beloved kids?"

"He didn't want us to know that life."

"You know it now. Eventually, you were going to have to face the real world. Real life. Your mom understood that. It's the reason she wanted Jay to meet me in the first place. She asked me to show him the ropes. And he was hongry. And I do mean hongry with an O!"

"That had to be when Jay first started showing signs of change."

"Mhmm."

"He wouldn't tell me, but I knew he'd been fighting and selling drugs or something. I mean, he didn't have a job but always had a pocket full of money."

"You right. He thought maybe you needed to see there were other ways to make money. Before I tell you this, do you know the whole story."

She sat at the foot of the bed, sighing hard.

"He told me. It was his idea."

"How did you take it?"

"Shock. I was stunned. He was never in any real danger."

"Nope. Not from me anyway. Treybo was the one who always tried to yoke him up. It's the reason I sent him on a long trip."

"Yea, well a lot of good that did. I couldn't believe after I did all of that for him, it was a setup. I was trying to save him from death and he was the devil in disguise."

"Yep. He came up with it all on his own. Of course, when I mentioned it to mom, she and Treybo took over and added the more graphic details."

"It seems the love you missed from dad; your mommy stepped in."

"Nah, not really. Dirty Black didn't know how to love. After dad left, she changed."

"How so?"

"Her heart turned cold. She was ruthless. When the real Dirty wanted to leave the street life and move us to a better place, she had him setup and killed. Once she took over, Dirty Black took on a deeper, darker meaning. You saw her."

"Yea, what I witnessed was gruesome. She didn't even seem to care about you anymore."

"All she could see was jealousy, hatred and revenge. That's why she's fighting for her life right now."

"I'm sorry Marcus."

"Me too. But I pray for her and asked dad to pray for her, that is while she is still alive, that her heart would be turned to God."

"You've been praying. I thought you didn't need faith?"

"After the other night, I realized that there are a lot of things I was raised to believe that are absolutely wrong. Prayer seemed like the right thing to do."

"You said you have been praying that your mom's heart be turned to God. What about your heart? Have you turned your heart to God?"

He pretended to not hear her questions and continued talking about his mother and her issues. Kindness didn't press. She knew he heard her loud and clear.

"Mom acted like Dirty Black couldn't be touched, but she killed the first and now she is about in the same boat. The only thing that will last is the name."

"I wonder with you gone, will someone else take over the name."

"Maybe Xavier will. He so soft, he need the juice."

"He is sweet."

"Too sweet!"

"That's just cause you all extra hard. To you everybody is weak."

"Naw to Dirty Black, everybody is weak."

"Dirty Black is no more." She patted his leg through the covers.

"Owwwch!"

"Sorry." She twinged. "Where were you hit?"

"In the thigh, but my whole leg is throbbing right now. If the bullet had hit a couple of inches to the left, I'd probably be dead."

"I'm glad that didn't happen."

"Why do you even care?"

"Because you're my brother."

"Why do you have to be so nice? So kind?"

"Blame it on the name. You are the definition of your name."

"Hmmm, I never thought of it like that. Money. As Money, that's all I could think about. But as Marcus, all I could think about was the betrayal of my dad. I was a nicer version of me, but revenge was in my heart no matter which one I was."

"And my brother followed the same path as our dad, only he didn't kill his father. He knocked him off of his feet though."

"Kill his father. Who killed their father?"

"Umm, that's not my story to tell." She rushed to change the subject. " So, if dad can pull some strings for you, your sentence will be 3 do 1 1/2 and the rest on paper. What will you do when you get out?"

"What you know about sentencing?"

"I do watch crime investigation shows and court tv. And Sam explained it to me." She confessed. "You act like I'm some naive little girl."

"And you're not!"

"No! I'm not that green."

"You could've fooled me."

"Maybe before, but not anymore. I have officially been broken in."

"Riiight." He looked at her, almost like he was embarrassed. "I want to apologize to you for making you do that."

"It's done. Water under the bridge."

"How can you do that?"

"Do what?"

"Act like nothing has happened."

"I'm not acting like nothing has happened. I have to forgive in order to be forgiven and I refuse to give the past any power over my future."

"Alright." He threw his hands up and gave a short laugh. "If you can forgive that fast, you should be back to dancing in the church in no time."

"I'm not rushing."

"You're good you know."

"Yea. Mom always told me it's a divine gift, passed down through her bloodline."

"Your mom was a dancer too?"

"Mhmm, at the Pink Kitten a loooong time ago."

"Wow, who would've known?"

"Your mom!"

"Right. I'm telling you, the idea came from Jay, but the details came from the devil herself."

"That's what I used to say about you. Now I know you were just the messenger."

"Make no mistake, I can be deadly too." He looked away for a second. "She taught me well."

The door opened, and both of their heads snapped towards it to see who was there.

"Kindness, are you about done? The officers are heading back up the elevator as we speak."

"Oh, Nurse Abbey. Thank God."

"I told you I'd take care of you," she winked at her. "Are you done?"

"I guess I have to be."

"Did you get what you came for?" Marcus asked.

"Yea, I think I did. At least it's a start in the right direction." She walked towards the door, "And don't tell dad I came by. If he tells you anything you've heard before, just act surprised and be thankful. He is trying desperately to make amends with everybody."

"I guess I can try to do that."

"I hope so." She was almost out of the door.

"And Sis?"

"What brother?" She put strong emphasis on the latter.

"Come visit me when they move me. I've always wanted a little sister."

She couldn't help but smile, tears stinging the back of her eyes, because she always wanted an older brother.

"I will."

"And Sis?"

"After dad comes to see me, I have a surprise for you and Chance. Tell Chance she has nothing to worry about. Her account with me is paid in full and I'm turning all the profit over to her."

"Oh wow. She will be so happy to hear that." She stood in the doorway smiling ecstatic, but the tears were still waiting to be released.

"And if Minister James gets to acting crazy, remember you got an even crazier brother to protect you."

"Haha, I'll keep that in mind."

"Goodbye Kindness."

"I'll see you later, big brother." He returned her smile as Nurse Abbey fastened the door tight.

Kindness could finally let the tears stinging her eyes roll freely.

"There, there child. I know that must have taken a lot out of you."

"Yea, it did." She said, wiping her eyes.

"Well, how did it go? Is everything alright?"

"No. But I believe we are on the right track."

"Good. I knew from the moment I saw you that you were an angel from God. I knew He was going to use you."

"You did?"

"Yes, I did. I didn't know what for, but now I do."

"What?"

"You don't know by now child?" She gave a hearty laugh. "God has used you to bring your whole family back together."

It was the truth. Though she went through some horrible situations, God still worked everything out for the good of everybody involved. Only God can do that. Kindness suddenly realized how blessed she was, and also tired. She leaned against the wall.

"Here, let me help you back to your room."

"Thanks Miss Abbey." Nurse Abbey gave a short laugh.

"What happened to nurse?"

"You're more than that to me now. You are my friend mother."

"Thank you Precious Angel."

Kindness was feeling very weak and was happy that Nurse Abbey carried more than her share of the load, all while talking her ear off about her kids and her grandkids and how much she loves her son-in-law. It was all very amusing, but Kindness couldn't wait to get in the bed to take a nap. Her conversation with Marcus was more stressful that she planned, but all in all, good results came from the meeting. She looked forward to getting to know more about the good side of him.

# **Chapter 28: Fresh Start**

"I'm here to see my son."

Marcus could hear the officers giving Elder Johnson a hard time. Normally, the thought would make him angry. He never liked police officers. Though there had to be some good ones somewhere, he had never met one. But right now, he welcomed the time to prepare to meet the man who betrayed him, having abandoned him over twenty-five years ago. It was okay talking to him when life seemed short, bullet hole in his side and blood oozing. However, after a successful surgery and with days looking brighter, the difficulty of facing him was unbearable. How could he stand before him, without a gun, without anger, and tell him how he really felt? He knew that was what Elder Johnson wanted, because it was what Kindness wanted. They were so much alike, the three of them. They all wanted the same thing, for in the end that is all Marcus ever wanted. The truth.

"Look, I don't have time to argue with the two of you. I have an appointment to see **my** son and I'm going in!"

Marcus heard the door crack and contemplated playing sleep, but that seemed to be the cowardly way out. As the door opened wider, he turned his head towards the window again and waited. The door shut and he knew his father was in the room, silently watching him. *I guess this is not going to be easy for either of us.*

"Um, how are you doing son?"

"I'm okay." He replied, without moving his head. The sun was bright and it felt good, warm to his skin, comforting.

"It's a beautiful day isn't it?"

"Yea."

Elder was uncomfortable and he knew his son was too. Neither of them wanted to have this talk, but it was necessary. Still to begin would be challenging. How do you talk to your grown son about the feelings of an abandoned boy? Thoughts weighed heavy on his heart all night, so much that he hardly slept a wink. Sleep more than likely wouldn't come easy until they took the first steps in building a bridge to cover the last twenty-five years.

"Listen, Jerard..."

"Marcus."

"What?"

"My name is Marcus. Jerard is an alias, just like Money." He was still looking into the sun.

"Oh. That's good to know." Elder scratched his head. "Um, Marcus. Son, this is not going to be an easy fix. I want you to know that I don't expect for you to forgive me and love me and jump into a relationship, like add water and instant family. Matter of fact, I expect quite the opposite. You have the right to be angry with me. But what I want from you today is the opportunity to introduce the truth. Is that alright with you?"

"Yea." He replied, so Elder continued.

"Do you have any questions before I begin my story?"

"No."

"Okay." Elder thought about sitting, but quickly denounced the notion. He paced instead.

"Marcus, the hardest thing I ever had to face, at least until your brother was kidnapped, was the day I left you and your mom."

"He wasn't kidnapped."

"Right, he wasn't. But, from my point of view as a father that is all I knew. He was gone. And I felt like I was reaping because of how I left you."

"You were."

"You're right. I guess you never know how the reaping is going to come." He came to stand at the foot of the bed. "I had lost two sons. And all I could think about was how bad of a father my dad had been to me. A lot of bad memories resurfaced. I had to reconsider things that had been buried long ago."

"Buried, but not dead."

"I guess so." He walked around to stand near the window and joined his son, gathering strength and warmth from the sun.

"Marcus, my dad was a terrible man. There were times where I wished he had left me and my mother. Maybe she would have lived longer."

"How old were you when she died?"

"She died giving birth to me."

"I'm confused. How did you wish he would leave you and your mom, when she was dead at your birth?"

"After I was old enough and realized how bad he had to have been to my mom, I found myself wishing he had left while she was pregnant with me."

"But without those things happening, you wouldn't be the man you are today."

"And neither would you." He said definitely.

Marcus understood, but added nothing in return. Silently, he was watching Walter from the back, but when he moved away from the window, he turned and looked him right in the face. Neither spoke nor moved for a moment. There was so much to be said. Today was a foundation. There would be many more opportunities, many bricks to lay before they could even think about reestablishing the relationship. Walter broke the silence and Marcus looked back at the sun.

"I wondered for a long time, every day, what became of you. Your mother," he stopped pacing, shaking his head at the vision, "Your mother, though in the beginning was a blessing to me, turned out to be more hellish than I ever was. As I grew in God, she became more than I could

bear. I pleaded with her to change, to come back to God, for her sake and for yours. But she refused."

"She always said you left because you loved Angela and Kindness more than you loved her and me."

"That is so far from the truth. Son, I loved your mother. She helped me through a very tough time. Had she not left God, the shoe would be on the other foot for Angie."

"What?!" Elder had Marcus' full attention.

"Yea. I loved her. I wanted to be with her, but she did not want God."

"And that's the real reason you left?"

"Yep. She knew it, she just didn't want to admit it. If she faced the truth, the only person she could have to be mad at was herself. So she made it about Kindness and Angela."

"All these years I hated you. Every tear she shed made me hate you more. And you mean to tell me she chose that pain?"

"Sounds crazy don't it."

"Yea, it does. But then again, my mom aint exactly the sanest person in the world!"

"I know that's right!" He chuckled a little.

"But there's more to the story, I am sure."

"There is."

"So tell me."

"What do you want to know?"

"Everything. Tell me how Angie took the news that you loved my mom."

"How did you know I told her?"

"I didn't, but if you love a person, you are not the only one who can tell. I'm sure she knew. She probably even brought it up."

"Very intuitive."

"I'm right, ain't I?"

"Yep."

"So tell me. What did she say?"

"Boy, I can't tell you all that woman said, but she scared me. I never saw her that angry before. Not even before she left me. We were divorced for two years before we remarried, and things were still shaky until the day she told me she was pregnant."

"That's when you left us."

"Yea. I'm not proud of it, but yes. When she told me, I knew I had to make a choice. I went into prayer because I didn't want you to think that I didn't love you. But for the sake of my marriage, I had to make a tough decision."

"You say you told Angela about my mom, but what about me? Did you tell her about me?"

"No."

"Why not?"

"Like I said before, she scared me. I knew if I told her, she would flip out."

"So you kept me a secret."

"Yep, and I lived a double life for as long as I could."

"What really stopped you from coming by to see me?"

"Marcus, I didn't just stop coming to see you."

"I was five."

"Yea, and I tried to come to an agreement with your mom, but you know how difficult she is..."

"My way or the highway!"
"Exactly. There was no reasoning with that woman. She tried to sap every bit of life, energy and money out of me that she could until I had had enough. But I couldn't quit cold turkey."

"Why not?"

"I still loved her." He finally sat at the foot of the bed. "I loved her so much that God gave me an ultimatum. I remember it like yesterday. Pastor was preaching from Matthew 6:24. He said you cannot serve two masters and referenced it to the Dr. Dolittle animal, Pushmi-Pullyu. I recall he said 'You want to move forward in both directions, but you can't, so you end up stagnant. And if you don't move, you will die right there. May not be physically, but nothing you set your hands

to do will turn out the way you desire because you have not chosen to be loyal. You can only be loyal to one god."

"The choice you made was sort of like choosing between Jesus and the devil?"

"No, it was exactly that. Jesus or the devil."

"And I guess my mom referenced the devil."

"What do you think?"

He said nothing. For in answering that question, he would also answer so many others. If his mom was a worker of evil, then so was he. All of his life, he strived not to be like his father, the betrayer. He chose his loyalty to his mom. And she was a liar. His entire life had been lived based off of lies. It was a hard pill to swallow. Suddenly, Marcus had no desire to continue.

"Son?"

"Yea?"

"It's okay."

"What's okay?"

"How you're feeling."

"You know me so well?"

"I don't proclaim to know much outside of what God teaches me and shows me on a daily basis. I talk to Him and listen to His Spirit speak back to me in meditation."

"And?"

"And, I know how you feel."

"Really?!"
"Yea, really." He paused, taking a moment to rub his waves, before continuing. "You feel like if you answer the question, you are condemning yourself. That's what the Word of God calls "pricking the heart". You feel guilty, maybe even a little disgusted at all the things you did."

"What you know about it?"

"You are **my** son. I'd like to think that some of what I taught you as a child still remains. Besides, I did some things in my time."

"Such as?"

"Robbed and beat up folk, ran a gambling ring and I've even killed."

"Killed!"

"Yea. Like I said before, there's a lot I'm not proud of."

"No, let's go back to 'killed'! How old were you when you murdered your first victim?"

"My only victim. And I was fifteen years old."

"What?! Oh, I got to hear this!!"

"Don't get so excited about it!"

"Why not?! It's rare that a Christian tells their "real" testimony."

"Now, that is not true. How many Christians have you been around lately?"

"Including you, and your family? Four."

"That's what I thought."

"Anyway, we ain't talking about that right now. Get back to the killin'!"

Elder shook his head. But the glint in his son's eye made him happy. They had missed so much time with each other. Memories they never made. Today was the beginning of a different Elder Johnson. He was ready to be honest with everyone.

"C'mon now Elder Johnson! Don't keep me waiting!" Marcus was on pins and needles.

"Alright, but it's not a pretty story."

"It never is, not the real ones."

"Okay." Elder stood up, pacing helped him stay focused on the story. "Well, like I told you before, my mother died when I was born. And my dad never let me forget it. He blamed me for her death, calling me a murderer more than he called me by my name. He was a mean drunk." He took a deep breath and walked over to the window, losing consciousness of his surroundings until there was nothing left except the story.

"I had to have been about five or six when he started beating me. Oh sure, he would parade me around to his girlfriends and make me act out scenes from movies for their entertainment of course. We didn't own a television and it was kind of fun. When they were around, he pretended to love me. And I didn't mind those times so much. It gave me something to do besides dream of a better life. After they found out who he really was and left, the beatings started again. I got used to it after a while." He shot a quick glance at Marcus, trying to read his reaction. Nothing. The boy was stoic and expressionless. He was waiting on something. The events leading up to the killing were just something he had to endure in order to get what he wanted. Elder stared out the window for another second before continuing. This would be the hardest part of telling his childhood story. It always was.

"But when I was older, I'd say around twelve, he started..."

Elder dropped his head, feeling like a little boy in trouble. Marcus didn't say a word. He wanted and needed to hear what he already felt like he knew. Waiting on the old man to drop the bomb was more tortuous than he ever imagined. But he waited. He heard Elder clear his throat and knew the story was about to commence.

"How could a man be so cruel? That's the question I asked myself every morning before heading out to school. He was cold. He didn't care if I ate, slept, or did my homework, just as long as when he needed me to perform, I was there. But how could a man... A real man do what he did to me? His own son! His only child!!"

He turned again to Marcus with tears in his eyes. It all the strength Marcus had not to shed tears with his father. He didn't have to say the words. Marcus knew the pain he spoke of without exactly speaking it. He wanted to hear the whole story, but he couldn't blame Elder for skipping the details.

"I hated him." He almost whispered the words, but then he yelled them. "I HATED HIM!!!"

"Dad, please. Settle down. You don't want the police to escort you out of here." His voice was calm and comforting.

Elder moved back towards the window, tears still flowing. He wondered why Marcus was being so quiet and understanding. There was no way he could know that his firstborn went through the same thing with Dirty Black. He secretly told himself his mother had the man killed to avenge him. It was the only love he knew and he had held on to it since he was a boy. He didn't know if his father would finish the story or not, but they did not have any time to waste.

"Dad?"
"Yea." He wiped his face.

"We don't have much time. If you want to finish telling me another time, I understand." He didn't want to rehash any old memories with Dirty Black no more than Elder wanted to with his dad.

"No. I'll finish now. I have to."

"Okay." He waited, but this time Elder spoke loud and sure.

"I hated him. I hated him for blaming my beautiful mother's death on me. I hated him for making a joke out of me. I hated him for beating me. But I never wanted to kill him, until he started molesting me. He would get drunk. That's how I knew when it would happen. Then he started getting drunk every day and it depended on how drunk he was. Sloppy drunk meant he wouldn't make it past the living room, and that was fine with me. But some days, no matter how drunk he was he came in with a different spirit. It was pure evil. The last time he made me perform oral sex on him, I ran away. I never would have come back but I missed my mom. I had a picture of her that I used to talk to all the time. I still have it. But anyway, when I left the house without her, I knew I had to go back and get it. When I returned, he was gone. I rushed into my room and packed a small bag of clothes, put some food items in the bag and searched for her picture. My dad had been in my room and moved it. I tried my best not to panic, but I had to go into his room. I hated that room almost as much as I hated him. But I loved her so I went in. I looked in the closet but her picture wasn't there. That's when it happened. I heard him unlock the door, but I forgot to lock it back. I should've put the chain on it. But I didn't. He knew I was there. 'Hey boy! My sweet lips done came home. Did you miss me boy?!' His voice taunted me. That is when I panicked. I couldn't find her and there was only one place I hadn't looked."

"Under the mattress."

"Yep. How did you know?"

"That's where I kept my picture of you."

"Oh, I'm sor-..."

"No, no. It's not about me right now. Finish the story."

"Right. Well, he was half way up the hall when I lifted the mattress. And there she was, beautiful as ever. I grabbed the picture and dropped the mattress. And there he was, standing in the doorway, smirking. 'What you doing boy?!' He said. I didn't answer. Helpless and scared. I felt trapped. The gun was at my feet, where I laid it before lifting the mattress. Why I grabbed it from the closet? I don't know. Maybe it was just my dad's time to die. He took me for a joke and I had to show him I was a man and I wasn't going to let him hurt me anymore. I remember the smell of hot metal and blood like it was yesterday. He took one step and I raised the gun, he took another and I pulled the trigger. It was over. I stood on the other side of the bed and watched him take his last breath. When he died, all fear in me died. I knew I would go to jail, but I felt freer there than I ever did when I was at home with him. I know that might sound harsh, but it's the truth. Shoot, the only time I have felt more free is when I gave my life to Jesus."

Silence filled the room again. *Wow! My dad, the Holy Roller is a killer. I wonder what else he's done. Probably was a pimp and a gangster too. I guess I get it from both sides.* Marcus didn't know what to say, so he said nothing. He knew Elder wouldn't let him remain silent.

"What are you thinking?" Marcus shrugged and turned to look back out of the window.

"I expected a bigger response than that."

"What? You wanted me to get excited and pat you on the back?"

"No. I just expected for you to express your opinion, like the rest of my family did."

"Oh. You'll have to excuse me. I haven't been a part of the family very long."

"You've always been a part of the family Marcus. We simply had to overcome some challenges."

"Challenges?! That's the understatement of the year!! From the time I was five years old..."

"Marcus, please..."

"No! I gave you time to speak, now it's my turn."

412

His voice was one of authority. He hadn't lost his sense of power, he only needed to learn to use it in a different way. That would take some time.

"Alright. You're right." Elder put his hands up in surrender. "Go ahead." Marcus didn't hesitate.

"From the time I was five years old, my life has been one challenge after another. I'm not talking about the challenges of a normal little boy or teenager. You know, learning to ride a bike and falling. Getting back up and trying it again, and again. Or being nervous the first time you kiss a girl or had sex. I welcomed those times because they were easy. They made me feel normal. But shoot, living with my mom..." His voice trailed off shortly as he thought of her mean spirit, "Man that was a challenge in itself. You talked about your dad and how he used to parade you in front of his girlfriends."

"Yea."

"My mom, she did the same thing to me."

"I remember telling her a little about how my dad treated me. But I never..."

"Be glad you didn't tell her about him molesting you or you killing him. She would have found a way to use it against you." He got quiet for a split second. "You know. I love my mom. She was the constant in my life. But she was evil, like your dad."

"Did you ever want to kill her?"

"I thought about it a couple of times when I was in my early teens. Especially when she started dating Dirty Black. My challenges went from difficult to unbearable. That man, if you can even call him a man. He intentionally created things to do to hurt me. He watched me. He knew what I liked and what I loved. He ran the only girl I ever loved away from me. Sherry... She was beautiful inside and out. Raised in the church. She even had me wanting to go, but mom forbid it. I snuck and went with her anyway, but I didn't go in. I waited for her outside. Humph, Dirty still found out. When he told mom, she was so mad, she told him to do with me what he wanted. That's when hell began. From that point on, he disciplined me and his discipline was torture. The last time I saw Sherry was in my bedroom. Dirty was in the middle of chastising me when she knocked on the door. He told her to have a seat and then he took me to my room. He tied me to a chair and forced me to watch him rape my girl. I can hear her screaming like it's happening right now." He swallowed hard. The pain of remembering her was too much, but there was no time for tears. "Yea. Him... I would've killed for free."

"I guess when the Feds picked him up, that was God's way of delivering you."

"I guess." He looked away, back out the window where the sun was shining, reminding him of happier times. Before the day Walter Demarcus Johnson abandoned him.

"Something tells me you have a lot more to say, and that he did more to you than you're willing to share."

"He did. Lots more. And I don't have a problem sharing, it's just that we have so much time to talk about the past. But only a few more minutes to handle some business. Let's talk about my estate."

"Right." Elder went to the door where he sat his briefcase, and pulled out a fat folder.

"Did you have a chance to get the lawyers to sign everything?"

"Yep, and all we need is your signature on these. I put an X and highlighted the lines to save time."

"Good thing too. The officers will be in here in less than ten minutes."

"Wow. It doesn't seem like we've been talking that long."

"I guess that will make visitation enjoyable. We have a lot to discuss."

"Yes we do."
Marcus continued to skim, read and sign documents but he couldn't let Elder leave without asking one last question.

"How's my family?" Elder smiled.

"Everyone is getting things in order. My wife, your stepmother, is recovering nicely. She'll be in here for another month or so, but her strength is increasing daily. Your brother misses you. He says he can't wait to come see you. I would have brought him but I knew we needed to lay down a firm foundation for our relationship first. There will be plenty of time to bond later."

"And Kindness."
found out. When he told mom, she was so mad, she told him to do with me what he wanted. That's when hell began. From that point on, he disciplined me and his discipline was torture. The last time I saw Sherry was in my bedroom. Dirty was in the middle of chastising me when she knocked on the door. He told her to have a seat and then he took me to my room. He tied me to a chair and forced me to watch him rape my girl. I can hear her screaming like it's happening right now." He swallowed hard. The pain of remembering her was too much, but there was no time for tears. "Yea. Him... I would've killed for free."

"I guess when the Feds picked him up, that was God's way of delivering you."

"I guess." He looked away, back out the window where the sun was shining, reminding him of happier times. Before the day Walter Demarcus Johnson abandoned him.

"Something tells me you have a lot more to say, and that he did more to you than you're willing to share."

"He did. Lots more. And I don't have a problem sharing, it's just that we have so much time to talk about the past. But only a few more minutes to handle some business. Let's talk about my estate."

"Right." Elder went to the door where he sat his briefcase, and pulled out a fat folder.

"Did you have a chance to get the lawyers to sign everything?"

"Yep, and all we need is your signature on these. I put an X and highlighted the lines to save time."

"Good thing too. The officers will be in here in less than ten minutes."

"Wow. It doesn't seem like we've been talking that long."

"I guess that will make visitation enjoyable. We have a lot to discuss."

"Yes we do."
Marcus continued to skim, read and sign documents but he couldn't let Elder leave without asking one last question.

"How's my family?" Elder smiled.

"Everyone is getting things in order. My wife, your stepmother, is recovering nicely. She'll be in here for another month or so, but her strength is increasing daily. Your brother misses you. He says he can't wait to come see you. I would have brought him but I knew we needed to lay down a firm foundation for our relationship first. There will be plenty of time to bond later."

"And Kindness."
found out. When he told mom, she was so mad, she told him to do with me what he wanted. That's when hell began. From that point on, he disciplined me and his

discipline was torture. The last time I saw Sherry was in my bedroom. Dirty was in the middle of chastising me when she knocked on the door. He told her to have a seat and then he took me to my room. He tied me to a chair and forced me to watch him rape my girl. I can hear her screaming like it's happening right now." He swallowed hard. The pain of remembering her was too much, but there was no time for tears. "Yea. Him... I would've killed for free."

"I guess when the Feds picked him up, that was God's way of delivering you."

"I guess." He looked away, back out the window where the sun was shining, reminding him of happier times. Before the day Walter Demarcus Johnson abandoned him.

"Something tells me you have a lot more to say, and that he did more to you than you're willing to share."

"He did. Lots more. And I don't have a problem sharing, it's just that we have so much time to talk about the past. But only a few more minutes to handle some business. Let's talk about my estate."

"Right." Elder went to the door where he sat his briefcase, and pulled out a fat folder.

"Did you have a chance to get the lawyers to sign everything?"

"Yep, and all we need is your signature on these. I put an X and highlighted the lines to save time."

"Good thing too. The officers will be in here in less than ten minutes."

"Wow. It doesn't seem like we've been talking that long."

"I guess that will make visitation enjoyable. We have a lot to discuss."

"Yes we do."
Marcus continued to skim, read and sign documents but he couldn't let Elder leave without asking one last question.

"How's my family?" Elder smiled.

"Everyone is getting things in order. My wife, your stepmother, is recovering nicely. She'll be in here for another month or so, but her strength is increasing daily. Your brother misses you. He says he can't wait to come see you. I would have brought him but I knew we needed to lay down a firm foundation for our relationship first. There will be plenty of time to bond later."

"And Kindness."
found out. When he told mom, she was so mad, she told him to do with me what he wanted. That's when hell began. From that point on, he disciplined me and his discipline was torture. The last time I saw Sherry was in my bedroom. Dirty was in the middle of chastising me when she knocked on the door. He told her to have a seat and then he took me to my room. He tied me to a chair and forced me to watch him rape my girl. I can hear her screaming like it's happening right now." He swallowed hard. The pain of remembering her was too much, but there was no time for tears. "Yea. Him... I would've killed for free."

"I guess when the Feds picked him up, that was God's way of delivering you."

"I guess." He looked away, back out the window where the sun was shining, reminding him of happier times. Before the day Walter Demarcus Johnson abandoned him.

"Something tells me you have a lot more to say, and that he did more to you than you're willing to share."

"He did. Lots more. And I don't have a problem sharing, it's just that we have so much time to talk about the past. But only a few more minutes to handle some business. Let's talk about my estate."

"Right." Elder went to the door where he sat his briefcase, and pulled out a fat folder.

"Did you have a chance to get the lawyers to sign everything?"

"Yep, and all we need is your signature on these. I put an X and highlighted the lines to save time."

"Good thing too. The officers will be in here in less than ten minutes."

"Wow. It doesn't seem like we've been talking that long."

"I guess that will make visitation enjoyable. We have a lot to discuss."

"Yes, we do."
Marcus continued to skim, read and sign documents but he couldn't let Elder leave without asking one last question.

"How's my family?" Elder smiled.

"Everyone is getting things in order. My wife, your stepmother, is recovering nicely. She'll be in here for another month or so, but her strength is increasing daily. Your brother misses you. He says he can't wait to come see you. I would have brought him but I knew we needed to lay down a firm foundation for our relationship first. There will be plenty of time to bond later."

"And Kindness."

"You don't know?"

"What you mean? How would I know?"

"Boy, stop playing with me. I know she came to see you today."

"How did you find that out?"

"I went to her room and she was gone. I knew there was only one reason she would be out of bed." Marcus smirked.

"She's a lot like you."

"And you too. Determined and unmovable. When she set her mind to do something, she gets it done. I know you are the same."

"Can't deny that."

"We gone be alright."

"It's hard to believe that after all that I put you all through, you still want me in your family."

"Son, we can't deny you as part of the family. You were here first. We got a lot of ground to cover but what we've always been is willing and obedient. If you can be those two things, God will move heaven and earth for you."

"And people thought you guys were the perfect family. When really, you had the perfect plan and you worked it like a team."

"The perfect plan. God's plan. If you follow it, He'll make you look good."

"I can see how that works."

"Yep."
"Alright. I'm all done."

"I'll take those." Elder flipped through the pages before placing them back in the folder.

"What did the judge say about prison?"

"Oh, yea. They are going to ship you to a halfway house in Atlanta for two years and you'll do ten on parole."

"Are you serious?!"

"Yep!"

"Man, that's good!"

"God is good son, and don't you ever forget it!"

"I won't!" They shared a firm handshake and a smile. Elder stood up.

"I told our lawyer I'd be in his office before 6 o'clock so I'd better get a move on."

"Yea you do that, and go ahead and surprise them cops. Don't let em come in and escort you out. Show em we black folk know how to do things on time." Elder laughed.

"No CP time here. We operate decently and in order."

They nodded at each other, still smiling then Elder walked out. There was no need to say goodbye or see you later because it would never be goodbye again and they both knew they would see each other soon. Now that they were in each other's lives, there was no turning back.

# Outro: Back Stories

## Who's Story would you like to hear next?
Chance
Jeff and Sam
Walter and Angela

## Social Media Platforms

Instagram -- IG: @strogetter_4lyf
Facebook -- ConzuelusZayin LoveStrozier

You can vote for your favorite backstory on any of my social media platforms. The winning story will be posted on each. Thank you for reading my book. There will be more to come.

# ABOUT THE AUTHOR

My name is Conzuelus "Zayin Love" Strozier. I am a 47 year old Christian devoting everything I am to the Glory of God. Growing up as a child, I was a loner because I didn't fit in with most crowds. But that gave me time to develop my imagination. While other girls were playing with dolls and seeking attention from boys, I was climbing trees and taking nature walks. I remember thinking myself to be good at very little except running, singing and English. I never imagined that my gift would emerge in this way. Today, I am thankful to be alive and saved despite all of the challenges I have had to face. My family pushed me, urging me to complete this book. Two of those family members have passed away, one being my son. However, I thank each and every one of them for believing in me enough to not allow me to give up. I dedicate this book to them. Mary F. Bonner, close friend who was more like a mother before her passing. Ali "Tailor Made" Strozier, my beloved son who has gone on to be with the Lord. Kendra Strozier, my daughter and friend, who never lets me settle for less than the best. Bishop Barry D. Walker, who encouraged me to keep writing no matter what. And Sherryl "The Pearl" Wilson, for being my rock and best friend. You guys believed in me. You planted seeds of hope into me, and this is the fruit. Thanks again.

www.ingramcontent.com/pod-product-compliance
Lightning Source LLC
Chambersburg PA
CBHW080742250626

47162CB00010B/2990

* 9 7 8 0 5 7 8 2 4 2 3 9 2 *